CW01501163

Early Mornings at
the Laksa Café

JANET TAY is a Tin House Winter Workshop alum, and her short stories and journalistic pieces on literature, food and parenting have appeared in various collections and magazines. The first act of her full-length play *Reunion* was longlisted for the Windsor Fringe Kenneth Branagh Award for New Drama Writing. She lives in Kuala Lumpur with her husband and son. *Early Mornings at the Laksa Café* is her debut novel.

Early Mornings at the Laksa Café

JANET TAY

HARVILL

1 3 5 7 9 10 8 6 4 2

Harvill is part of the Penguin Random House group of companies

Vintage, Penguin Random House UK, One Embassy
Gardens, 8 Viaduct Gardens, London SW11 7BW

penguin.co.uk/vintage
global.penguinrandomhouse.com

First published by Harvill in 2026

Typeset in 11.01/15.2pt Calluna by Six Red Marbles UK, Thetford, Norfolk
Printed and bound in Great Britain by Clays Ltd, Elcograf S.p.A.

The authorised representative in the EEA is Penguin Random House
Ireland, Morrison Chambers, 32 Nassau Street, Dublin D02 YH68

A CIP catalogue record for this book is available from the British Library

HB ISBN 9781787305298
TPB ISBN 9781787305304

Penguin Random House is committed to a sustainable future
for our business, our readers and our planet. This book is made
from Forest Stewardship Council® certified paper.

For Azrul and Liam, with all my love

Perpetual Broth

Ah Hock, Swatow, China, 1938

The gingko tree towered over their vast courtyard, its leaves carpeting the ground in a golden yellow brilliance. Slender branches stretched out their vibrant fan-shaped leaves over Lim Ah Hock, who looked up at the ancient tree. He turned four that day, a baby compared to the tree that must have been thousands of years old. His mother told him that her great-grandfather had chosen to build their ancestral home here because of this majestic tree.

He kicked up the fallen leaves and scattered them around the courtyard. Gusts of wind shook the tree's branches and more pretty yellow leaves rained down on him. His mother sat at a stone table nearby, drinking tea. Smiling, she called out to him, but he could hardly hear her.

He turned and saw her calling to him again, but he didn't go to her immediately. The cool breeze was gauzy on his face. A middle-aged maidservant came out of their house with a straw broom and told Ah Hock to go to his mother. He stuck out his tongue at her, then ran to his mother when the maidservant shook the broom at him.

His mother received him with open arms. She was wearing a knee-length white qipao dotted with tiny red flowers. She smelled like peonies. Her tiny feet were dressed in pink lotus shoes, smaller than his own. She stroked his head as she told him he was now a big boy and the cook would make red eggs and longevity noodles in sweet soup for his birthday lunch.

Ah Hock was sniffing his mother's cup of Tieguanyin tea when the front gates burst open. His father ran in, snatched Ah Hock and carried him into the house while rushing around the rooms, looking for something. There was crying and screaming, the maidservant and his mother's voices indistinguishable. Ah Hock wailed for his mother, smearing tears and mucus over his face with his hands. His father shushed him and told him to be quiet.

A few other servants around the house came out to see what the commotion was. When Ah Hock's father found what he needed in the kitchen, he dashed out of the house with Ah Hock's mother trailing behind them, pleading through her sobs. Outside the front gates, a black car was waiting with its engine running.

Ah Hock's father got in with him and slammed the door shut. Ah Hock wriggled free from his father's grasp and stood up in the back seat. Through the rear window, he could see his mother crying and waving, gradually getting smaller into the distance until he couldn't see her anymore.

'Papa, why are we leaving Mama?' Tears streamed down Ah Hock's cheeks. There was a pain in his chest, a heaviness he had never felt before.

'It's not safe here, I'm taking you to a place where it's safe,' his father replied in a stern voice. Ah Hock swallowed hard and wiped his face with the backs of his hands. He thought of the spankings his father had given him whenever he played too loudly or broke anything in the house, but he spoke anyway.

'But I want Mama safe too,' he said, his lips quivering. He opened his palm and saw the dried gingko leaf he had been holding.

'She will be. I just . . . I need to take you away. The Japanese devils are coming.'

'Japanese devils?'

'Yes. Don't ask so much, do as your papa tells you.'

'What's that, Papa?' Ah Hock pointed at a gourd bottle his father had taken from the kitchen.

'Our ancestral broth. We must take good care of it.'

'What's it for?' Ah Hock reached for it. His father smacked his hand away and Ah Hock yelped.

'Don't touch it! I'll let you have it when you're old enough. When you're ready. This is the most important thing in our family. You must never lose it!'

'But Mama is important too,' Ah Hock cried, crumpling the dried gingko leaf in his hand. The fan-shaped leaf fell to pieces in the car.

'This broth is the soul of our family. You must make sure it stays in the family. Pass it on to your sons. Otherwise, we will be cursed! Do you understand me? Cursed!'

Ah Hock shook his head. He didn't understand anything. The car was going too fast. He looked at his father and saw only a man with a face as fierce as Kwan Kung, the God of War, with beads of sweat on his forehead, fear and fury in his red-rimmed eyes.

PART ONE

I

The Best Laksa in Town

Ah Hock, Kuching, Malaysia, 1994

Ah Hock stood before the bubbling pot of grey, orange-tinged laksa soup, glaring at it as if it were a stubborn child.

He was five foot two, his belly straining against a white singlet and bulging over his knee-length black shorts, but a look from him or a stinging remark was enough to subdue a customer who had too many requests. He was convinced it was the fools asking for extra sambal or kuay teow in their laksa who had caused his close-shaven head to grey rapidly over the years.

Steam rose from the pot of soup as he stirred it, its spice-filled aroma the only scent in the kopitiam. He tasted the soup again.

Not right, not right at all. He couldn't understand it. He'd used fresh prawn shells and bones from chicken that had been newly slaughtered at the market. If he had his way, he would buy live chickens and slaughter them himself. But Kim Choo said it was too much work. Especially since it was just the two of them now.

He felt like throwing the laksa soup away and making a fresh batch, but there was no time. It was already six, and the kopitiam opened its rusted folding doors at six-thirty in the morning when Carpenter Street was still empty, before cars came to scramble for parking spaces for lunchtime at Lau Ya Keng, the Chamber of the Gods, a temple that doubled up as a food court. The food court was just across the road from the kopitiam and was the reason Carpenter Street was so busy at lunch and dinner time. There, the smells of food jostled for prominence. Rich, earthy broths boiling to make fishball noodle soup; stir-fried radish and glutinous rice-flour cakes combining to become heavenly soft squares of oily, savoury char kueh; spicy laksa soup and the sweet smoke of charcoal-grilled pork satay. Ah Hock's favourite was kuay chap – rice noodle sheets, pig innards and bean curd braised in a dark herbal broth.

He reached for the salt and sprinkled some carefully over the spicy soup, letting it simmer before tasting it again. Almost there, but not yet. More star anise or cumin? Impossible – it couldn't be the spices.

Kim Choo was breaking the tails off beansprouts and peeling prawns at the sink. She was his only constant now. It used to be the soup too, but he was beginning to wonder if he was losing his touch. His focus was off today, even after his usual kopi-o.

He sighed and closed the pot with a loud clang.

'What's wrong with it?' she asked.

'Needs more broth.' He shuffled to the brass pot of broth in a corner of the kitchen, its bottom blackened by the decades of use. The broth was rich with the essence of fish and meatiness of fowl, the smoky flavour of charcoal giving it the depth ordinary broths didn't have. Ah Hock's father had taught him how to ensure the broth never lost its depth, by adding chicken bones, dried flatfish, prawn heads, or a whole chicken if needed.

Ah Hock ladled some of the golden liquid into the laksa soup and tasted it.

'All right now?' Kim Choo asked.

'Better. But not there yet.'

'You don't need the broth. Maybe more salt.'

'You don't believe in it after all these years?'

'I didn't say that.'

'It's not the same without it.'

'You've never tried not using it,' she said. He didn't answer and Kim Choo didn't push further.

The broth had been simmering on a clay charcoal stove for almost sixty years, its fire never extinguished in the decades it had existed in the shophouse. The broth had been bestowed upon an ancestor by a deity, so the legend went, passed down from generation to generation of the Lim family. All of whom had used it for the base of the dishes they served in their restaurants in Swatow, until Ah Hock's father left China for Borneo, and for the first time, the broth found its place in a humble spicy noodle dish instead of a sour-savoury steamed grouper or a fish maw and sea cucumber treasure pot. Decades had passed, but Ah Hock still remembered the first time his father had told him about the importance of the broth and the dangers of its curse.

Ah Hock tasted the laksa soup again. It wasn't perfect, but it would have to do. He carried the soup pot to his stall at the front of the kopitiam then heaved it with a grunt into the opening in the counter. He winced and inhaled sharply. A sudden pain in his left arm. It used to be the boy's job. The pot was beginning to feel heavier with each passing day.

*

Towkay Lau was usually the first customer at the kopitiam. People called him Towkay, the Boss, because he was Lau Meng Tian, the local tycoon who ran a myriad of businesses from building airports to exporting timber. He was about the same age as Ah Hock, but had fewer lines on his face, less grey in his hair and smelled of Imperial Leather soap, of which Ah Hock caught a whiff every time Lau stepped into the kopitiam.

He strode in wearing his usual attire – T-shirt, shorts and slippers, his square face framed by rectangular gold-rimmed glasses, with a rolled-up newspaper under his arm and a silver Rolex gleaming on his wrist – and looked over the tables as if he were the proprietor instead of Ah Hock.

'Good morning, Ah Hock! My usual – one bowl, special. Make sure you give me the big prawns!' Towkay Lau pulled up a chair at his usual table.

'Have I ever given you small ones? Don't insult me!' Ah Hock arranged a few plump prawns into the nest of beehoon he had put in a bowl and scattered beansprouts, shredded omelette, and strips of chicken over the noodles. He smelled the bubbling soup and shook his head. Never mind, it wasn't like Towkay Lau could tell the difference. Ah Hock ladled the soup into the bowl and garnished the laksa with a few sprigs of coriander, then asked Kim Choo to bring it to Towkay Lau's table.

The businessman slurped a spoonful of the laksa soup. 'Soup's good! You never have an off day, Hock! That's why I love coming here. You're consistent!'

Just as he'd guessed. The man wasn't discerning at all. 'No, today the soup is not so good,' Ah Hock said.

'Nothing less than perfection is good enough for you, Old Hock.' Towkay Lau chuckled. 'I keep telling you, a master like you should open a nice restaurant. I provide the capital, we split the profits! Make big money! Have branches everywhere! Franchise it! Teck Boon's Laksa!'

'It's hard to maintain quality when you have branches,' grumbled Ah Hock. Every now and then, Towkay Lau would bring up this subject, which Ah Hock was loath to discuss. He was not about to sully his father's kopitiam by having branches and menial workers replicating a decades-old recipe. It had begun after Teck Boon died. The moment they reopened the kopitiam, not even three days had passed after Ah Hock had buried Teck Boon before Towkay started talking about future plans for the laksa. Swooping in like a vulture.

'How do you think branches work? Naturally, the master must go around to check on the quality at each branch! It's hard work, but big money! You've got to think bigger than this, Hock.'

As Towkay Lau expounded the benefits of expansion, two men and a woman walked into the kopitiam. They were in their twenties, in shorts and T-shirts, carrying backpacks. Tourists. Two of them sat down at a table and one of the men approached Ah Hock.

'Good morning, Uncle,' he said politely in Mandarin. Ah Hock didn't look up at him. The man scrutinised the stall, as if he were looking for something, then spoke to the woman in English before turning back to Ah Hock. 'Uncle, can we have three laksas? With yellow mee?'

'Laksa comes with beehoon,' Ah Hock said in Teochew through gritted teeth, not caring if the man understood or not. He could hear Towkay Lau chuckling. The woman walked over to Ah Hock.

'Sorry, Uncle, you really don't have yellow mee? Yesterday we tried a stall near the Sarawak Plaza, and we could ask for beehoon and mee mixed together,' she said in accented

Hokkien. She spoke well but Ah Hock knew she wasn't local. Her long straight hair was tied in a ponytail. A pretty girl, smiling cheerfully at him.

He felt like throwing a handful of beehoon at her earnest face. 'Then you go back and eat there,' he said.

Towkay Lau burst out laughing and called over to the two strangers who were taken aback by Ah Hock's words: 'Young people, you don't know who this is? This is Lim Ah Hock, Kuching's famous laksa master! Have you ever tasted laksa made with centuries-old broth? Take my advice, order three bowls of special. You won't regret it.'

'Sorry, Uncle.' The girl remained courteous. 'Can we have the laksa to take away then? Three laksa, normal. With beehoon.'

'No tapau,' Ah Hock said curtly. He couldn't understand these idiots. The laksa didn't taste the same if you took it home and reheated it.

The man who had been sitting at the table stood up and raised his voice. 'We don't have to eat here, there are many other stalls around, this guy is so rude. Let's go.' He stormed out of the kopitiam, the other two trailing behind him.

'Aiyah, Ah Hock, why did you have to chase them away?' Towkay Lau said, drinking the last of his laksa soup.

'Chase who away?' Kim Choo asked as she came out of the kitchen.

'The customers, as usual.'

'Did they ask for extra sambal?'

'No, they wanted yellow mee,' Ah Hock said. 'And they wanted to take away the laksa. Useless people!'

Kim Choo sighed. 'What's wrong with that? I hear some places offer three choices now – beehoon, mee or kuay teow.

We should let them take away. At least we'll have more tables available.'

'We have plenty of tables.' Ah Hock pointed to the empty tables around Towkay Lau.

'Don't scare your customers away-lah, Ah Hock. But kuay teow in laksa? Even I wouldn't eat that!' Towkay Lau laughed.

'They don't like it my way, they can eat somewhere else!' Ah Hock felt his chest tighten and tried to turn his attention back to the laksa soup.

'Eh, take it easy, Ah Hock, we aren't young anymore, you better watch your blood pressure.' Towkay Lau downed his tea and put down ten ringgit on the table. 'See you tomorrow!' he said in a sing-song voice as he walked out of the kopitiam.

Ah Hock grunted. He was glad whenever Towkay Lau left quickly instead of sitting around pestering him about opening branches. You couldn't trust someone who only looked at dollars and cents. On top of his general dislike of Towkay Lau, Ah Hock would never forget it was the wily businessman who had paved the way for Wei Ming to leave their family home for some Cantonese restaurant in Hong Kong he was a partner in. Although he couldn't blame Lau entirely, the boy had been itching to leave for some time.

He could not deny that the money sounded good. During those moments when he found himself tempted to accept Towkay Lau's offer, he would pray at his father's altar, asking him for guidance – a sign that Teck Boon kopitiam should expand. But his father's portrait merely stared ahead, and nothing ever happened to change Ah Hock's mind.

*

Third Uncle came into the kopitiam at eleven. He was an old Teochew signboard-maker who plied his trade a few shops away. Third Uncle made signs for most of the shops on the street, including Ah Hock's kopitiam. The black signboard above the kopitiam's entrance bore his father's name, Teck Boon, in capital letters, and Chinese characters below them, both in gold paint.

Third Uncle did the calligraphy himself, then traced the characters on the wooden board before carving them. Each carved character was so smooth it looked as if it had been painted on. *A good sign is an auspicious sign,* Third Uncle always said. *Brings the shop owner much fortune and good luck.*

Ah Hock had known Third Uncle since he was a small child, hence the nickname. Third Uncle was a family friend, not least because he was a fellow Teochew, a kakinang – what Teochews all around the world called 'our own people'.

'How are you?' Third Uncle gave Ah Hock a pat on the back as he limped to the table nearest to the stall. Hearing Teochew made Ah Hock feel at home while he was surrounded by other Chinese languages, Iban, Malay and English.

'Aiyah, not good, not good. Some idiots made me angry early in the morning. Tourists. Asked for yellow mee! Then wanted takeaway!'

Third Uncle laughed. 'They don't know you, Hock. As you said, they're tourists.' The old man was like a Buddha. Never a frown on his peaceful face.

'I'll get you your laksa first.' Ah Hock returned to his workstation. He glanced at Third Uncle from time to time as he prepared a bowl of laksa for him. From his thirties to his eighties, Third Uncle had changed little. A strong, lanky man with slender fingers and long limbs, none of these features had diminished in his twilight years. He seemed as alert as he had been in his younger days. The only thing that showed his age was his hair, which had thinned and gone completely white and wispy over the years.

Ah Hock took longer than usual to prepare Third Uncle's bowl, making sure everything was in place, adding extra-big prawns, smelling the omelette to make sure it was fresh, then a whiff of the soup, which was unsatisfactory to him. Trust Towkay Lau to say it was good! He had a feeling Third Uncle would not share that view. Ah Hock garnished the laksa with sprigs of coriander then called Kim Choo to bring the bowl of laksa to Third Uncle.

Ah Hock and Kim Choo stared at Third Uncle as the old man sipped the laksa soup and ate a mouthful of beehoon. They scrutinised his masticating jaws, momentarily ignoring new customers who were stepping into the kopitiam. Third Uncle sniffed the shredded chicken before he brought it to his lips, then ate it with relish.

'The beansprouts are crunchy?' Ah Hock whispered to Kim Choo. She nodded vigorously. Third Uncle finished everything in his bowl, down to the last drop of laksa. Ah Hock peered at the bowl, and his gaze lingered there for some time, to ensure there was really nothing left.

'How's the soup?' Ah Hock asked.

'Not bad, not bad. Not as good as last week's though,' Third Uncle said.

'I knew it!' Ah Hock slumped his shoulders.

'It's good, don't worry. Come, sit.' Third Uncle patted the stool next to him.

'Only you know what it's supposed to taste like. That Lau, he said it was fantastic! I could water it down and he'd never know the difference,' Ah Hock said as he sat at the table.

Third Uncle laughed. 'You can't expect everyone to be so particular about taste. As I said, it's good enough. Even your father wasn't as consistent as you think.'

Memories of Teck Boon throwing his ladle on the floor with a loud clatter came to Ah Hock's mind. And the shouting that followed whenever Ah Hock forgot to add salted flatfish to the broth.

'My father . . . I don't remember the soup being anything but good when he made it.'

'Don't worry. The soup is good enough today. Like the old times.'

'It will change someday.'

'Hopefully, by then, I'll be dead,' Third Uncle said, smiling.

'Don't say that. You're as healthy as a horse.'

'Aiyah, these old bones . . . even when I walk slowly over here, my legs feel like jelly. One of these days I'll collapse on the way over.'

'You're strong, Third Uncle. I'm turning sixty but I feel at least ten years older.'

'It's not an easy business. Look at you, morning till night, checking on your ingredients, on the soup . . .'

'If I don't do it, who will?' Ah Hock said with a sigh.

'What about Wei Ming?'

At the mention of his son, Ah Hock let out a long exhale. He folded his arms and stared at the dusty ceiling fan turning lazily above them.

'Where is he now?' Third Uncle asked. 'Still in Hong Kong?'

Ah Hock nodded glumly. 'I haven't spoken to the good-for-nothing boy in years.'

Wei Ming had left them eight years ago, to pursue his dreams of being 'a real chef', as he called it. Didn't want to be a laksa seller. Didn't want to just sell noodles. Ah Hock had

16

all but disowned him, but the boy and Kim Choo spoke on the phone.

'Does he intend to stay there forever?'

Ah Hock shrugged. 'Who knows? The boy found his wings, won't come back to this small town.'

'A tree can grow ten thousand feet tall, but its leaves will always fall back to the roots,' Third Uncle said. 'You are father and son after all. It's been so long since he left. Better make amends.'

Ah Hock scoffed. 'Me? I am the father! He should come back and kneel before me, begging for forgiveness.'

At this, Third Uncle laughed loudly. 'Even I know that's so old-fashioned. How will you get your son to understand you? We are all not getting any younger. You should persuade Ming to come home.'

'You think he'll want to come back here after living his high-class life in Hong Kong?'

'You won't know if you don't ask. It would be a pity if this kopitiam disappears after you're gone, Hock. Of course, I'll be gone before you, but I feel sorry for the new generation who won't get a chance to taste real laksa.'

'It's true, it's true, look at the rubbish they're serving in food courts these days. They call it laksa, but I wouldn't feed it to a dog!' Ah Hock said as Third Uncle nodded in agreement. 'But the boy, well, you know, he's a stubborn one.'

Third Uncle finished his kopi-o and sighed. 'He is your only son. You won't know the pain of losing one until it happens.'

'I don't feel like I have a son. What's the difference? Look at me now, breaking my back, carrying these heavy pots of soup myself.'

'There *is* a difference. When there's no more hope. When you can only speak to them in dreams.' Third Uncle spoke in a distant voice and his eyes had a faraway look, as if he were remembering something.

Ah Hock didn't know much about Third Uncle's past but there had been talk about a son who had died during the Communist Insurgency. Is that what he meant?

Third Uncle stood up and left three ringgit on the table. They always charged him less and the coffee was complimentary. Ah Hock would prefer not taking Third Uncle's money at all, but the old man would not hear of it. Normally, Third Uncle would wave at Ah Hock as he left, but today he plodded back to his shop looking preoccupied, not even looking up when the goldsmith's wife said hello as he passed her on the street.

2

Omakase

Wei Ming, Hong Kong

My left eye twitched as I stared at the display screen of the ATM. I blinked twice. Five thousand dollars. It couldn't be. Yet, there it was. My life savings after eight years working in Hong Kong.

I tried not to think of my landlord's face if he knew I was using rent money to gamble. Ah Weng had said it was a sure thing. He was planning to bet ten thousand dollars on the horse himself. That's what he'd said, that lousy bouncer from the Jade Pavilion. Good for racing tips when he wasn't busy pimping out the girls from the nightclub.

I took a deep breath, withdrew four thousand dollars and stuffed the notes in my pocket.

Hungry Ghost month had ended a few days ago. I wasn't proud of myself for having to close Haruto, the sushi restaurant where I worked, for an evening just to go to the racecourse, but I couldn't wait anymore. People said gambling during the seventh month of the lunar year was bad luck. There were so many taboos to be observed when the gates of hell opened and the souls of the dead roamed the earth. I wasn't the superstitious sort, but even I wouldn't break any taboos then. I already had all the bad luck I could ever need. Now the month was over it was time to start a lucky streak.

I hopped on a tram heading to the Happy Valley Racecourse. The doors opened at 5.15 p.m. and the first race was at 7.15 p.m. I hoped I wasn't going to be late. It was already almost five. As I sat down, I said a prayer in my head to Kuan Yin, the Goddess of Mercy, even though she probably wouldn't approve of gambling.

*

The next day I woke up late, and it was close to noon when I finally arrived at Haruto. Thanks to Ah Weng's lousy tips, I'd lost big at the racecourse. After that, I'd gone to the Jade Pavilion and downed god knows how many shots of Jack Daniel's until Ah Weng said I'd had enough.

Styrofoam boxes of fish that had arrived from Tsukiji Market were stacked in the kitchen. Takashi, our kitchen helper, must have received them and just left them there. If only the boy would make some effort. I wasn't in the mood for his careless attitude.

'Takashi!' I called. There was no answer. I opened the back door and found the boy leaning against the back-alley wall, cigarette in one hand, typing a message on his Nokia phone with the other. Ever since he'd bought it when it first came out earlier that year, he'd spent more time on that mobile phone than washing dishes or packing away seafood deliveries. I remembered when he'd showed it off to me and asked me to get one too. I thought now about my father still insisting on using the rotary telephone at our family kopitiam in

Kuching instead of a push-button one. Maybe Takashi was right. I should keep up with the times.

His hair was blue today. Last week it had been purple. The most he would do for me was tie his hair back in a ponytail and wear a bandana, but he refused to keep it black.

'Takashi, unpack the boxes please,' I said gruffly.

He looked up at me with a vacant expression, then put out his cigarette on the wall. He was twenty-one and lacked discipline, although when he decided to do something, he would do it brilliantly. In fact, he could probably slice abalone as well as me, but would rather text on his mobile. How many friends or girlfriends did he have to text, anyway? I barely knew anyone who had a mobile. Maybe I should buy myself one so I could send angry texts to Takashi instead of having to wait for his return to Haruto after an extended lunch break.

'Yes, Chef,' Takashi drawled, then shuffled to the kitchen.

'You shouldn't have left the fish there. Always unpack them immediately after delivery,' I said, shaking my head.

'I was on a cigarette break,' he said with a shrug. I gritted my teeth and imagined giving the boy a slap upside the head. I was already easy on him. He should try growing up in Ah Hock's kitchen. The old man was always on my case, yelling at me about one thing or another. It was impossible to do anything right for him.

'Check the maguro,' I said. Takashi opened the boxes and inspected their contents. Ah Hock was a real hard-ass but he was obsessed with the freshness of everything, so I had learned a thing or two about seafood. Good fish should smell like seaweed. Ah Hock never tolerated seafood that didn't smell like it had just come off the fishing boat. Thanks to him, all I needed was a whiff to tell me whether I could use or needed to bin a piece of fish.

'Maguro is good. Kohada, not so good.' Takashi wrinkled his nose.

I looked at the silvery fish. He was right. The gizzard shad's colour was lacklustre and smelled slightly fishy. We could pickle it, find a way to salvage it somehow. I took a sniff.

Nope. No way could we serve it at Haruto.

I'd have to call Ito. I hated having to give suppliers shit for not giving us quality fish. Ito seldom gave us bad fish, though. At least not before Sensei had returned to Japan for a year and left me in charge. Inamura Hiroki, the owner of Haruto, was my master and the boss. I called him Sensei, and would forever regard him as my teacher, the man who saved me from a brutal Chinese restaurant kitchen seven years ago.

I dialled the Tokyo number on the restaurant phone, and it rang for some time before Ito picked up.

'Hello, Ito-san, this is Lim Wei Ming, from Haruto sushiya, Hong Kong. Thank you for the fish, we have received it. The maguro is beautiful, but I am sorry, the kohada is not suitable.'

'Oh?' Ito sounded surprised. 'It's very fresh. I chose the best. Hard to find good kohada now. Maybe it is a transportation problem?'

'I cannot use the kohada, Ito-san.'

'Only the best, I chose them myself,' Ito insisted.

'Inamura-san would never allow me to use these,' I said, to cut the argument short. If I didn't mention my master's name, he would argue with me until the break of dawn. It didn't help that my Japanese was kind of rubbish so I probably

22

sounded uncouth to him. But I knew it was more than that. It was because I wasn't Sensei. I didn't know what Ito really thought of me, but I knew he wouldn't send a kohada like that to my master.

Ito backed down the moment I mentioned Sensei. Just as I'd predicted. He still tried to slip in a small charge, but I said no. He finally gave in, and about time too because my mouth was aching from speaking so much Japanese. I passed the phone to Takashi to work out the logistics. I knew I needed to improve my Japanese; I couldn't rely on the boy all the time.

I rubbed my jaw and noticed an envelope with Japanese stamps on the counter. Takashi must have put it there. I tore open the envelope and read the letter from Sensei.

Dear Wei Ming,

How are you? One year has passed quickly and it is autumn already. I miss the ajisai that were everywhere after the summer rain. I was lucky enough to see some rare blue ones one month ago, after one week of rain. I was happy for the flowers but the summer this year was too hot. Now the leaves have turned red and brown.

I have not heard from you in two weeks, you must be busy. Thank you for working hard at the restaurant. I am grateful you are taking care of Haruto while I am away. I hope Takashi is behaving himself with you.

I will return soon and bring back sake and koshihikari rice for Haruto.

Inamura Hiroki

My palms grew cold and clammy. I felt like throwing up. The restaurant's accounts reeked of two-day-old sushi. Then there was the inventory of the sake refrigerator, which I'd been treating like my own personal collection for a month now whenever I didn't have time to pop out to get liquor from the 7-Eleven.

The postmark on the envelope showed that the letter had been sent a week ago. Sensei could arrive at any time. As I contemplated the depth of my predicament, Takashi popped his head in from the kitchen.

'Is that from Taisho? What did he say?'

I put the letter back in the envelope. Takashi called Sensei the boss. A reminder that I wasn't the boss, even though Sensei had left me in charge, even if the customers ooh-ed and aah-ed whenever I made sushi for them. Even though any day now I was going to earn that second Global Restaurants Guild star for Haruto. It wasn't the Michelin, but it was still a prestigious award. Often it was the Cantonese restaurants in Hong Kong that won stars, but Sensei had managed to earn one for Haruto, which was no mean feat. I intended to surpass that with a second star.

Hadn't the *South China Morning Post* reviewer called me 'the up-and-coming sushi master' of Hong Kong? They'd even printed a photo of me slicing sashimi, right next to the article about Cantopop star Jacky Cheung's latest album. And to be the first Malaysian chef to earn a star! Then Sensei would forgive the accounts being in disarray and the missing sake, once I got that second star. Two stars! I couldn't help smiling as I thought about it.

'Something about ajisai,' I said, and Takashi raised an eyebrow. I laughed then slapped his back.

'What is the menu today, Chef?' Takashi asked. We were

an omakase restaurant, which meant the menu changed almost every day, according to the chef's choice. There were a few appetisers and side dishes like pickles, chawan mushi or suimono – clear soup – that we offered regularly, but otherwise the chef decided the menu of the day. Often, Sensei would plan his menu based on what was in season at the market, so I did as well.

'Let me look at what else we got. We're using the maguro for sure.' I needed to prepare for the dinner sitting. The kohada was out, but luckily there was that beautiful tuna, its colour a luscious maroon. There was also koika, small squid, and geso, its tentacles, as well as salmon roe, horse mackerel, saltwater eel and ark shell clams that had arrived a few days ago. Could throw in some uni, sea urchin roe – the expensive stuff – and mark up the menu price.

The ark shells were plump and red, their freshness dazzling. I shucked them, then removed the adductors attached to the shells. Stripped off the flesh and rinsed it in clean water. Strings and guts were sliced off before I cut open the flesh to remove the dark red innards. It was satisfying to clean the shellfish and scrub dirt off their flesh, eventually seeing neat, clean, impossibly fresh slices of gleaming seafood on beds of sushi rice.

Sensei had taught me that shari, the sushi rice, was more important than neta, its topping. Even if the neta was fault-less, inferior shari could ruin the sushi. We used filtered, purified water to cook the rice. Sensei often griped about the quality of tap water in Hong Kong. But his standards were incomparable – how could we possibly match the mountain water he was used to growing up in Niigata, the snow country?

*

Our first sitting was a group of office workers. They were easy to please, although that could be a bit boring at times. I wasn't bothered today though, since the second sitting provided the real challenge for me. Sensei's yearly clients from Tokyo. It would be the first time I'd be making sushi for them instead of Sensei, and I wasn't sure how they would feel about it.

The Japanese couple were in their sixties, well dressed – the lady in a black shift dress and pearls, the man in a dark grey suit and a navy silk tie. As they walked in, Takashi and I bowed deeply. When they asked about Sensei, I explained that he had been away for a year. The man gave his wife a sidelong glance, and she shook her head. They remained standing, as if contemplating whether to leave. My shoulders stiffened. It would be such a great shame if Sensei found out I couldn't convince his regulars to stay.

'Please, don't worry, I will be using Inamura-san's autumn menu today.' I gave another deep bow. The man nodded at his wife and took his seat at the counter. The wife followed suit and gave me an apologetic smile. I exhaled, then began preparing the seafood. They ordered some octopus and mackerel sashimi as appetisers. Everything was going well until the man requested the Kenbishi Kuromatsu sake.

Shit. My heart pounded as I opened the sake refrigerator. It was that bottle I'd brought back to the flat a few days ago. And finished. I smacked my forehead with my palm. Idiot! Of all the sakes I could've taken!

I went back out to the sushi counter and suggested another sake, Hakkaisan Tokubetsu Junmai. 'From Niigata. Very good with the appetisers you have ordered.' I smiled till my face hurt.

The man's face darkened. He insisted on the sake he wanted. His wife tried to explain something in Japanese but I couldn't understand her. Breaking out in a cold sweat, I apologised and bowed many times before going to the kitchen to ask Takashi to translate.

'She says her husband always has this sake in this restaurant,' Takashi said. 'Taisho always has it ready for him.' Takashi then spoke to the man rapidly, bowing several times. The man said something angrily to Takashi, who replied with something that pacified the man.

'Okay, I said the sake you recommended instead is complimentary.' Takashi winked before disappearing into the kitchen. The cheek of that boy! It was an expensive sake, but it was better than offending the customer.

The man looked mildly appeased, but it wasn't going to be easy to make sushi under his watchful glare. It brought me back to the first time I made sushi for customers. The first time Sensei had asked me to lead the performance. My hands had trembled then, and it had taken all my willpower to focus and ignore the pairs of eyes on me, especially the most important pair of all, staring at my hands from the kitchen doorway.

I took a sip of hot matcha and asked Takashi to lower the volume of the music I'd been playing to centre myself, the melancholic 'Goodbye Pork Pie Hat'. Making nigiri to Mingus usually eased me into the flow of things, but I was worried it would bother the couple.

I let my yanagiba slide through the flesh of the abalone. The knife did most of the work, gliding along smoothly even as I struggled to wield it properly. Every time I wrapped my fingers around the hilt of the yanagiba, I was reminded of the joy the dependable instrument brought. The slice was thin enough, by general standards. But I knew Sensei would ask me to slice it again if he saw it.

I shaped the nigiri in the palm of my hand, pressing it with the gentlest touch, like handling a baby bird. The abalone clung to the sushi rice like a child to its mother. A brush of sweet nitsume sauce, and it was ready. I placed the sushi on the tsuke-dai, my favourite hinoki serving board.

Next was the nodoguro sushi. I gave the sliced sea perch a delicate brush, leaving a sheen of nikiri on it. It had taken me two years to get the nikiri sauce just right – a mixture of rich dashi, shoyu, mirin, and sake from Niigata.

The order in which each sushi was presented was carefully planned, so its flavours were not overwhelmed by the sushi before it. Kanpachi, a lighter-flavoured amberjack, came before buttery rich tuna belly.

When the last sushi was served, the husband asked for okan, warm sake. I chose the Chotokusen Daiginjo and mentioned Sensei himself enjoyed it after a hard day's work. The man relaxed his frown. I warmed the sake gently and served it to the guest in an indigo-blue sake cup. The man removed his wedding ring before taking the cup. A considerate gesture, to avoid scratching it. The man took a sip and said, 'Umami,' and I bowed in response.

They declined the complimentary mochi I offered and left soon after the husband had had his fill of okan. Outside, Takashi hailed a red taxi for them and we bowed deeply as the car sped off.

I exhaled as if I were resurfacing from underwater. The nervousness I'd been holding back now gushed out like a waterfall. It was a good kind of exhaustion, an honest day's work, a job well done. I lived for days like this.

'A good sitting,' I said to Takashi. 'Thanks for translating for me.'

'I don't think they will come back,' he said. 'The husband is fussy. Racist.'

'What do you mean?' I'd used Sensei's menu, the rice was fragrant, the right temperature, and the texture of the neta wasn't too bad. The sitting had been like a well-conducted orchestra, not a sushi out of place. What had I missed? Surely the omission of one sake hadn't ruined the whole experience?

'Don't worry about it, Chef.'

'What did they say, Takashi? Tell me.'

'Only the man. He was disappointed Taisho wasn't here. He said next time they will try a real sushiya, with a real Japanese master. Forget it, Chef. You cannot make everybody happy. I'll go clean up,' Takashi said, then went back into Haruto.

What did they know, those Tokyo snobs? Takashi was right, the guy was probably racist. Saw I was Chinese and assumed I wouldn't be up to par. To hell with him. I stayed outside, letting the cold air clear my head. It was a quiet Wednesday night. The empty road was coloured by the crimson glow of the street lights.

I was about to go back inside when a familiar figure walked towards the restaurant. I groaned. He was the last person I wanted to see. Mr Tan, my landlord, looking less cheerful than usual. My stomach tightened. Mr Tan knew where I worked, but this was the first time he had come to the restaurant.

'Mr Tan, surprising to see you here,' I said, trying not to stammer. We usually spoke in English, something I was more comfortable doing since Mr Tan's mother tongue was Cantonese and he didn't speak a word of Mandarin. He was from Kuala Lumpur, where most people spoke Cantonese. Easier for him to assimilate in Hong Kong city, unlike me.

'You never at home, so what choice I got? You know why I'm here, right?' he said, brow furrowed. He lit a cigarette and took a puff, exhaling in my direction. I waved the smoke away.

'Yeah, I know I'm a few days late. Sorry, man.'

'Few days? More like few weeks! I gotta cari makan too, you know,' Mr Tan said. 'I tell you first-ah, I got this Malaysian family looking for a place. Willing to pay double what you're paying.'

I swallowed hard. No one else would be willing to charge the same rent for such close proximity to the MTR station and to Haruto. I knew Mr Tan charged a lot less than the other landlords in Wan Chai.

'I know, I'm sorry,' I said. 'Wait here, let me pay half now.' I went back into the restaurant. Takashi was in the kitchen, washing dishes. I opened the till and took a handful of cash. It was the first time I'd ever done this. Never mind, I'd replace the money, one way or another. Then it'd be like it never happened.

I stepped outside and slid the shoji door closed behind me. 'Take this first. I'll have the rest later.' I pressed the money into my landlord's hand. Mr Tan counted the money then stuffed it into his pocket.

'Next week you give me the rest. Or you're out.'

'I'll have the money, I promise,' I said, looking at my feet.

'That's what you've been saying for a few months now. I need to survive, you know? I'm not a charity-lah, you got to understand my position too.' Mr Tan took a long puff on his cigarette. 'I know we know each other long time already, but I also need to survive, what.'

'Next week, no more delays.' I tried not to sound like a loser. It didn't make sense that I was about to earn a Guild star and here I was begging my landlord. Couldn't he just wait a while more? When the restaurant had two Guild stars, we'd be booked up for the next two years. Rolling in money, for sure. Everyone was so bloody impatient.

'Why don't you go back home, Ming? Your parents have a kopitiam right? I know it's not glamorous like here-lah, your fancy Japanese restaurant, but at least you have family there. Better than here, working all the time, for what, seven, eight years now? And nothing to show for it.'

His words hit me like a sucker punch. I guess he was pretty angry. It had never occurred to me to go home, to the never-ending rain in Kuching hammering the zinc roof of our shophouse. Not before I made something of myself. I often fantasised that the day I went back, I'd have something to brag about to my old man. Like owning a restaurant. Telling my father that going to Hong Kong was the best decision I'd ever made, instead of staying and cooking laksa for the rest of my life, like him. *That* was the real family curse.

Mr Tan dropped his cigarette on the ground and stubbed it out with his shoe. 'See you next week,' he said, then walked towards Pottinger Street. I picked up the disgusting cigarette end and went back inside Haruto to dispose of it.

I didn't have the money for next week. Or the week after. Then there was what I owed the moneylenders, but I didn't want to think about that right now.

I picked up the telephone and dialled the number in Kuching. It rang three times before I came to my senses and hung up. I wanted to slap myself for thinking about it. All these years my parents had thought I was a great success in Hong Kong, and I was going to borrow money from them? It would break Ma's heart. And the old man, well, I could just imagine the I-told-you-so's coming out of his mouth.

The sake refrigerator beckoned. Screw it all, I needed something extra-special. I scanned the fridge and spotted the Juyondai. One of our most expensive bottles. Sensei waxed lyrical about its multilayered flavours. I grabbed it then sat down at the counter and took a swig. The sake cost a whole month's wages. I buried my face in my hands.

Eight years with nothing to show for it. Exactly what Ah Hock would say if I went back to that old kopitiam now, my tail between my legs.

3

Chicken Rice Memories

Ah Hock was jolted awake from a dream by the ringing phone downstairs. The bedside clock showed 10.30 p.m. Who could it be at that hour? He threw off his blanket, already prepared to yell at the caller, but the ringing stopped. Probably some idiot had dialled the wrong number.

He went back to sleep but ended up drifting in and out of bad dreams until three in the morning. Normally, he woke up at four every day. A habit instilled in him when he was a boy by his father. Kim Choo snored softly next to him. He reached over and lightly touched her arm, to make sure she was real. The back of his neck was covered in sweat. Over and over, he'd dreamed of his father warning him about passing down the broth.

He groaned as he eased himself out of bed. Another reminder of mortality. His father had been this age when he died but Ah Hock tried not to think about it. He walked to the window and opened the wooden shutters. The twilight sky was lit by a waning moon and a couple of street lamps.

Ah Hock brushed his teeth and washed his face. When he looked in the mirror, he could scarcely recognise his own reflection. Was that really him, an old man, with close-cropped hair completely grey-white, a stubby nose, and saggy jowls? He patted the pot belly that bulged against his white singlet. Who had time for exercise? All that rich laksa soup didn't help.

He went downstairs and switched on the dim fluorescent lights in the kitchen. He always began his mornings by offering joss sticks at his father's altar, and whispering an apology, even though he didn't know what it was for. For a while, the smell of incense would replace the broth's savoury aroma in the shophouse.

The altar had a black-and-white photograph of his father taken when he was in his forties. The portrait showed only his top half, but from the collar and the buttons you could see he was wearing a magua, a traditional formal Chinese jacket. It was the only time Ah Hock had ever seen him in something other than a tattered white singlet and knee-length black shorts.

His father had an oval face, a stern expression, the same close-cropped hair, and a high nose. His eyes were dark and severe, and every time Ah Hock offered the joss sticks, he felt his father's disapproving eyes boring into him. Maybe he resembled his mother more, with his rounder face, bigger eyes, flatter nose. If only he could remember her face.

He hadn't thought about his mother for a while now. Had she died in the Second World War? His father had always said they left because the Japanese army was advancing in Swatow. But whenever he overheard the old folk talking about the war, it seemed the army had only invaded Swatow in 1939, while Ah Hock would try to work it out over and over again, with his age as a guide. But the numbers never quite added up for Ah Hock. They must have left at least a year before that. And why had they left his mother behind? He had never dared to question his father about any of it. He didn't want to be a pest. There were times, especially when his father yelled at him for the slightest mistake, when he had felt like the unluckiest boy in the world, a boy without his mother. Then, he would imagine her alive and well, still missing him, still waiting for his return. The other thought, which he preferred not to have, was her with a new baby, a new husband. She was a blurry montage of memories, but he still felt a twinge from time to time, even at his age, when he considered that she might have forgotten he ever existed.

Ah Hock looked at the altar, wishing he had a space for her next to his father's photo, wondering who was offering incense to her.

*

Ah Hock checked the broth every morning, to make sure the fire hadn't gone out and to reset his palate for the day. He drank a small bowl of the broth, its deep flavours warming him. Still, when he mixed it into the laksa soup this morning, something was missing. His dreams had unsettled him.

It was a story his father had told over and over, so Ah Hock would never forget it. Ah Hock's ancestor had been a cook for the royal kitchen during the Qing dynasty, or so his father said. Young and inexperienced, but talented. This ancestor was proud of his Teochew origins and wanted to showcase the food of his childhood. But naturally, the head chef only prepared food the emperor liked. It was unheard of to prepare anything the emperor had not specifically requested.

35

The young cook let his arrogance get the better of him, little realising the gravity of disobedience at the palace. He had been tasked to prepare the emperor's favourite dish, a rich seafood soup made with the freshest oysters, fish, prawns and squid from the fishing boats arriving in the morning. The head chef had given him specific instructions on the ingredients and the method – exactly what the emperor wanted.

The young cook was ambitious and coveted the position of the head chef, who was bland and boring. A corpse could cook better than him, Ah Hock's ancestor would mutter to himself as he grumpily gutted fish or carved a turnip into a decorative swan for a platter of roast duck. Cooking was his heart and soul and it pained him to see the lack of creativity in the royal cuisine.

So he replaced oysters with abalone, which he felt was a much richer, sweeter substitute. He even added some salted fish, a humble ingredient used to prepare the servants' meals. The emperor would notice him now, the young cook thought happily as the head chef gave the dish a cursory glance and took it to the emperor, not bothering to taste it – for if he had, he might have noticed the difference in flavour.

Not only did the emperor notice the change in ingredients, he was also in a terrible mood after receiving bad news of an advancing army. He summoned the head chef to have his head cut off, as was the punishment in those days for anyone who offended the emperor even in the smallest way. The head chef blamed the young cook and begged the emperor for mercy.

When the heavens smile on a mortal, no harm will come to him or her. The young cook got wind of the emperor's rage, and only had time to pack food before sneaking out of the palace to embark on a long road to anonymity. After days of walking, he decided to rest under a tree and unpacked whatever food he had left. One stale bun. As he was about to take a bite, someone spoke to him.

'Hello, boy. Will you spare some food for an old man? I'm starving.'

The young cook turned around and saw an old beggar in tattered clothing, covered in boils and scabs. He recoiled. At first, he didn't want to have anything to do with the beggar, but he relented at the sight of the old man's pitiful state and gave him half of his bun. The beggar thanked him, and they ate together.

The young cook told the beggar about offending the emperor. After the beggar finished his bun, there was a flash of light, and he was transformed into a handsome man dressed in fine clothing. The young cook jumped to his feet and stumbled backwards, almost losing his balance.

'Do not be afraid, my child. You have a good heart, and you will be rewarded. Here is a special broth you can use to cook any dishes you like, and you will be famous. Never again will you cook a dish that is imperfect. But you must never waste this broth. Pass it on to your children. Or your family will suffer misfortune for generations.'

The young cook rubbed his eyes, thinking he was in a dream or was hallucinating from hunger or thirst. He blinked, and the deity was gone, leaving a gourd of broth in his place.

It had been embedded in Ah Hock's mind, the importance of the deity's broth – as important as the blood coursing through the veins of generations of Lim chefs. *The chain must not be broken*, his father had warned him. *Pass it on.*

The sacrifices his father had made to keep the broth boiling. The sacrifices Ah Hock himself had made. He couldn't imagine Wei Ming doing the same, and yet he had to do everything in his power to convince the boy to keep the broth going. 'Bad luck will befall the Lim family if the deity is offended!' These words had accompanied the cane that struck Ah Hock's legs whenever he forgot to tend to the broth.

*

'Why didn't you wake me up? It's already five-thirty.' Kim Choo yawned and stretched as she walked into the kitchen.

'I wanted you to sleep more. I can manage. Do we have any more chicken bones?' Ah Hock asked.

'In the blue plastic bag. I bought them from the market.' She took the bones from the back of the freezer then soaked them in water. She stared at him. Kim Choo always knew when something was bothering him. 'You're worried about something.'

He shook his head. No sense in telling her he had been dreaming about his father for the past few weeks. Kim Choo always warned him not to follow a deceased parent in dreams, no matter how inviting it looked. Ah Hock took the dreams as an omen, messages from his father from the afterlife, reminding him of the ancestral promise to pass the broth on to the next generation. Would Ming know what it needed to keep its depth? He was a chef now, he must know all about taste.

The truth was, Ah Hock had no idea what his son knew. The boy had never been a good student. Too impatient, too impulsive. No focus. The boy had listened to his mother, but not to him. Kim Choo had consulted a fortune teller, who said the father and son's bazi clashed. Too much fire in their elements, both of them. Ah Hock wondered if the difference in their zodiac signs – Ah Hock, the hardworking Dog, and Wei Ming, the Pig who enjoyed life but not the slog – had anything to do with their inability to get along.

'I'm getting too old for this work,' Ah Hock said, although he didn't really mean it. He expected to be able to cook and manage the kopitiam for at least another twenty years. Hadn't the chicken rice uncle over at Belview Road run his famous stall until he had a heart attack at eighty? The chicken rice uncle was an old Hainanese man who would not sell you chicken rice if you rushed him. If anyone got impatient and tried to jump the queue, they would be denied service and their money returned. There was even a quota. No one was allowed to buy more than one whole chicken.

The chicken was sweet and fresh, steamed just right, its glistening corn-yellow skin brushed with nutty sesame oil. The rice was fluffy and cooked with chicken fat, complementing the chicken in perfect harmony. The finishing touch was the home-made garlic chilli sauce, the right balance of sweet, sour and heat. Ah Hock's heart warmed, thinking of the flavours that mingled in a mouthful of Belview Road chicken rice.

The chicken rice was never the same after the Hainanese man's sons took over. The legend faded and, ten years later, the younger generation in Kuching did not know the famous chicken rice had ever existed.

The idea that something his father, the kopitiam's namesake, had painstakingly built could disappear with time, frightened Ah Hock.

'How old was the chicken rice uncle over at Belview Road when he died?' Ah Hock asked his wife as he stirred the laksa soup.

'I think he was seventy?'

Seventy! Even younger than he'd thought. Only another ten years before Ah Hock would be the same age.

'Why?'

'Nothing. Just recalled him.'

'That reminds me. Your birthday is coming up! Turning sixty is auspicious. Bad luck not to celebrate it! Let's have a party! I can ask Ming to come back for it.'

The boy coming back? Ah Hock's heart lifted but he kept his lips pursed.

'He won't come back. You don't need to beg him,' he said with an air of indifference.

'He's our only son. If you can't think of yourself, then think of me. All these years not seeing him,' Kim Choo said, her voice breaking. He didn't look at her, not wanting to see her eyes brimming with tears, the same look she'd had when Wei Ming left for Hong Kong.

'If that rascal says no, tell him no need to come home ever again, since he loves Hong Kong so much.'

'You see, you see, this stubbornness is why both of you cannot be in the same room. He's our only child. Let me talk to him.' She took out prawns and eggs from the refrigerator and began preparing the toppings for the laksa. Ah Hock heated up the wok and started to fry the laksa paste.

The smell of spices filled the kopitiam as Ah Hock turned the paste over and over in the wok, making sure it didn't burn. The chilli powder made him cough, and he wiped the sweat from his temple with the back of his hand.

'I think you should start doing this the night before. It's too much for you in the morning,' Kim Choo said.

'It's fresher this way.'

'I know it's fresher this way,' she said gently, and touched his back. She sighed, then picked up some beansprouts to be rinsed.

*

They closed the kopitiam early that day. It was raining, the only time Carpenter Street slowed down and had fewer customers.

Ah Hock stood outside on the five-foot way, nodding at the bookstore owner who walked past. Carpenter Street's shops had been there for decades, owned by hard-working, honest, down-to-earth people. People who cared about the things they made and sold, not just about turning a profit. Some of the artisans, carpenters, tinsmiths, joss paper makers – even the coffin makers – took pride in their work, ensuring each product they made for their customers matched the money paid for it.

He looked up at their signboard, glad it was still there. The name that had remained unchanged even after his father's passing. Ah Hock hadn't bothered to change it to his own name, because everyone in Kuching already knew the famous Teck Boon kopitiam on Carpenter Street. During those sleepless nights, he wondered if it was because he didn't want to tamper with the legacy left to him, one he felt he had never really deserved.

He went back inside the kopitiam and sat down at one of the tables. He sipped his kopi-o as Kim Choo mopped the greasy floor and upended the chairs on the marble-top wooden tables. At fifty-five, her brown eyes were as bright as ever, sparkling even in the early hours. Her curly bob was already greying rapidly, a contrast to her youthful looks, her smooth skin which she slathered in cream every night, her swanlike neck, her delicate lips.

He wondered if she ever regretted leaving the opera troupe. It was strange in a way that the theatre of Yang Choon was so near their kopitiam, yet such a vastly different world. She had only had to cross the street to build a new life, one he hoped was better than a lifetime of singing a dying art.

Her eyes were what had drawn him to her during her performance as Su Liu Niang, the tragic heroine of a well-known Teochew opera, during the mid-autumn festival more than thirty years ago. Lee Kim Choo, plucked from the theatre troupe before she got truly famous, her fans grumbled. They had never let him forget it. What did it matter that a life in an opera troupe could have been one filled with poverty? Besides, he had given her a better life, hadn't he? They owned the best laksa shop in town – who didn't know them? They would never starve. It was a better life. He was sure of it.

He stared at her, and for a moment he could see Su Liu Niang again, grand opera robes and porcelain-white make-up, smoky red around her eyes and bright rouge on her lips, pining for her lover.

'Have you finished your coffee?' Kim Choo said. Ah Hock passed her the coffee cup then got up from his chair, hearing a creak in his bones. He only felt the strain of standing for hours when the customers had gone, leaving the kopitiam dark and quiet.

He went to check on his flatfish drying at the back of the shophouse. The cat from the bookstore had been coming around lately to sniff at the dried fish. He used to find the stray cats in the area pesky until he realised they were keeping the shops free of rats. Since then, he had always kept some fish for them and fed them whenever they came around.

The bookstore ginger tabby was there, walking near the flatfish but not touching them. He looked up expectantly at Ah Hock, who chuckled, then went to the fridge to take out some cheap mackerel Ah Lek, his seafood supplier, had given him. He put it in a small dish for the tabby and watched the cat carefully chew the raw fish.

'Eat up, so you'll have energy to catch rats,' he said, stroking the tabby's head. While the cat ate, Ah Hock collected a few pieces of flatfish that were ready. He went back into the kitchen and added them to the broth. He put more charcoal in the stove and the broth started to bubble. When enough time had passed, he tasted it and nodded. The dried flounder never let him down.

The tabby mewed at him from outside. 'What? More fish? I don't have any more, come back tomorrow.' The tabby scurried away as rain continued to patter on the street, the earthy scent of wet asphalt lingering in the air.

4

Braised Pork in Soy Sauce

One thing I had never got tired of after eight years in Hong Kong was taking the Star Ferry between Hong Kong island and Kowloon. I would sit on the lower deck to look at the rippling water, enjoying a brief respite from the city that never slowed down. I even looked forward to saying hello to the weathered middle-aged sailor who lowered the gangplank for passengers and barely nodded as I walked past.

That night, after closing up Haruto, I didn't feel like going home. I got on the Star Ferry from Central to Tsim Sha Tsui. The journey helped me unwind as I gazed at the city skyline of Tsim Sha Tsui, its magical neon lights twinkling in the distance. From far away, Kowloon was beauty, opportunity, chance and movement. Everything but calm. People said it was faster to take the MTR, but to me the ferry ride always ended too soon.

From the pier, I walked briskly towards Nathan Road. I didn't mind the thirty-minute walk, the autumn night breeze gently cooling my face and clearing my mind. As I was passing Austin Road, I noticed a large poster for *Chungking Express* – the new Wong Kar Wai film that had been released a few months ago – splashed over the London Classics Cinema. The fact that *Chungking Express* had been filmed in Chungking

Mansions – a building near Jiayi's restaurant on Nathan Road filled with low-budget guesthouses, curry restaurants and various shops – intrigued her and she wanted to watch it. I'd daydreamed about us going to the cinema together, like a real couple, when she probably went with her boyfriend instead.

When I arrived at Malaysian Kitchen, I went round the back and knocked on the door.

Jiayi opened it and her eyes lit up when she saw me. She was in her chef's whites. The white double-breasted jacket looked too big for her petite frame. By now, it was wrinkled and stained with oil and sauce. Her long black hair was tied up in a loose bun, with strands of flyaway hair around her forehead and slender neck. I wanted to brush them back with my fingers. The memory of her supple body, my lips on her smooth skin and her long legs entwined around me, gave me goosebumps. The softness of her hair against my palm, a hint of the apple-scented shampoo she used.

'Hey, come in,' she said in Mandarin, ushering me into the kitchen. Hearing the familiar Malaysian Mandarin accent always lifted my spirits. I took her hand, but she pulled away and shook her head. There were a couple of kitchen assistants washing dishes.

'Not now,' she said in a low voice.

I nodded. 'How's business today?' There was a strong smell of pork broth in the air.

'Good, good. Times aren't great, but my food, you know, it's cheap,' Jiayi said. 'I made tau yew bak today. New dish on the menu.' Soy sauce pork with hard-boiled eggs was my childhood favourite. 'Almost sold out, just a tiny bit left. Want some?'

'Sure.' Nothing could beat a bowl of hot, steamed rice, drowned in dark sauce and generous morsels of pork belly.

Growing up, having this dinner waiting for me at home would make me forget I'd had a bad day in school. Even being sick with a fever wouldn't stop me from having an appetite for this dish.

'You're lucky I have leftovers. There was a big crowd today.' Jiayi ladled the pork stew into a bowl. She took another small bowl and filled it with rice, then put both bowls on the kitchen counter and pulled out a chair.

I took the chopsticks she held out to me and popped a morsel of pork belly into my mouth. It was tender and had fully absorbed the essence of the sauce. I tore into the hard-boiled eggs browned by the sweet soy sauce, even though I wasn't hungry.

'So? Good or not?'

'As good as my mother's,' I said, and Jiayi laughed. The way my mother laughed when she served me my third bowl of rice with the pork stew, asking me not to eat so fast.

'Wow, then it must be spectacular.'

'It is. Marry me.'

She laughed again and shushed me.

'It's been too long since I last ate here. The pork's so fresh. No gamey smell. Where did you get it?'

'Ah, I was lucky. I saw fresh pork at the market, that's why I snapped it up and decided to add tau yew bak to the daily specials at the last minute. So tender, right? And juicy. Want a Tiger?'

I nodded. She opened the fridge, took out two cans of beer and gave one to me. 'How's business?' she asked.

'So-so. Got our regulars, they think the food's great even without my master around. Hope the Guild critics thought so too. Did you see Haruto's review in the *South China Morning Post* last week?'

'What review? I'm too busy to read the papers regularly.'

'Oh, nothing much, some food reviewer saying I'm the next up-and-coming sushi master, that sort of thing. Good for business,' I said, trying to downplay my excitement. She clapped.

'Fantastic! You should be so proud. Wow, the newspapers, huh? So you have nothing to worry about!'

'I still want to get a Guild star.'

'Oh, the Guild. What, one star isn't enough for you?' she said, slapping my arm playfully.

'My master earned it, not me. Besides, imagine how Haruto would look with two stars! I don't think any Japanese restaurant here has earned two stars yet. We'd be the first. It would blow Inamura's mind,' I said, hoping it would blow hers too.

'How is he?'

'Okay, I guess. Still in Japan.'

'Coming back soon?'

I nodded. 'He sent me a letter saying so, but I don't know when. Maybe when he's back I can take a break. Right after they announce the second star.'

'Imagine, two Guild stars.' I could hear a tinge of envy in her voice. 'Guess you won't need to moonlight here anytime soon,' she said with a chuckle. I liked to hear her laugh. I missed our days of banter in the alley outside Kowloon Palace's kitchen, where we were colleagues eight years ago, smoking, talking trash about the boss and the fussy customers. Jiayi was something special. Not least because she had the finest palate I'd ever known. Even better than Sensei's, but of course I would never tell him that.

'I wish I could. I need the extra cash.' I downed the rest of my beer.

Jiayi tilted her head at me. 'You're not still gambling, are you?' When I looked down at the counter, she groaned. 'I've told you it's a terrible habit. That's what destroyed my useless father. If you need money, I can help.'

I shook my head. 'I'm fine.'

'You're not fine if you're still gambling.'

'It's one bet. I got a good tip.'

'You always say that,' she said, frowning as she stacked the empty bowls. 'Isn't Inamura paying you enough?'

'It's not that. I . . . don't have enough for my own restaurant.'

'You practically have your own place now, with Inamura away.'

'It's not the same. And all I'm doing is realising his vision. I want my own creations too. You should understand – you can make whatever you want here, it's all yours. Anyway,' I said, trying to change the subject, 'how are things here?'

She smiled. 'Business is good. I never imagined Malaysian food would do so well here. Can you imagine, competing with all that glorious Cantonese food?'

'And yet you do. Don't undersell yourself. I can see why business is good. Guess he must be happy.'

She shrugged. 'I don't cook to make him happy.'

I tried not to talk about her boyfriend, but it was hard to pretend she didn't have one either. Lam Cheng Man was the former sous chef at Kowloon Palace. Man had links with the underworld and behaved like a gangster in the kitchen. He made everyone call him Man Kor, Brother Man. He was your typical bad boy: cocky, wouldn't take no for an answer. Whatever Jiayi wanted, he could give it to her. He had bought Malaysian Kitchen and let her run it. He was no longer the sous chef at Kowloon Palace; he had bigger businesses now, being an errand boy for the Triad.

He was handsome too, like that Hong Kong actor and singer Leslie Cheung. His hair looked good even in a steam-filled kitchen. Well built, strong jawline. Turning forty had given his face more character, made him more rugged-looking. But looks couldn't have been the only reason for her to be with him.

I wasn't too shabby-looking myself at thirty-five – in the prime of my life, good skin. Sure, I was no Andy Lau, but people said I took after my mother, who had been quite the beauty in her day, apparently. I had her oval face, high-bridged nose and cheekbones, and long, graceful neck. Our large eyes were the same shade of hazel brown; both of us had graceful hands, slender fingers suited for the piano but relegated to peeling prawns and cleaning beansprouts.

My hair was wavy like my mother's and often dishevelled. There'd been women who said they loved my messy schoolboy look. So what if they were from the Jade Pavilion? It wasn't as if I had as much money to spend as the drunken businessmen there, but they still fawned on me as if I were a millionaire.

'You want to catch a film?' I asked, even though I knew what her answer would be. After she'd started dating Man Kor, we never hung out in public anymore. 'I see *Chungking Express* is still showing.'

'Nah. Been a long day. Just want to go home, take a hot shower and collapse into bed.'

'You're not meeting him?'

'He said he was busy. I'm tired anyway. You're not tired-ah?'

'We could get a quick drink somewhere.'

'You know I can't.'

'We were careful the other night.'

'I never know who's watching.'

'I know. I'll head over to the Jade Pavilion then.'

'I can never understand why you like that club. The stench of stale beer and cigarette smoke. It's the women, isn't it? All men are the same.' She took out a pack of gum from her pocket, then offered me one. 'Chiclet?'

I shook my head. 'Don't want to lose the superb taste of tau yew bak in my mouth.'

She laughed. 'Exaggerating-lah, you.' She popped one into her mouth.

'Quit smoking?'

She nodded. 'I read that it kills your taste buds.'

'You're a super-taster, your taste buds could never be killed. If you continue to smoke, maybe your taste buds would simply become normal.'

'I can't taste good food if my taste buds are just normal, can I?'

I pointed at the empty bowls. 'This . . . this is the sort of food I want to cook.'

'Then why don't you?'

'Obviously not in a sushiya. That's why I want my own place. To cook whatever I want.'

'It's so different from what you've learned from Inamura, though. Sushi and Malaysian stews?'

'I've learned important things from my training as a sushi chef. Freshness is everything. That's the foundation of Teochew cooking – the clean, pure taste of food. The subtlety of taste. A light touch that accentuates the natural freshness of the ingredients. Learning to work with raw seafood has helped me a lot to understand the importance of freshness. This tau yew bak deserves a star.'

'Too bad you're not a Guild critic then,' she said with a chuckle and cleared the table. The kitchen assistants had changed into their street clothes and were ready to leave so she opened the back door for them. As soon as they left, I reached for her and kissed her neck. She pushed me away gently.

'Hey, we . . . I can't do this anymore.' She smelled of broth, sweat, and floral perfume. A mixture of savoury and sweet I badly wanted to taste again. 'It's too dangerous.'

'What about that night?'

'It was a mistake. We're playing with fire here.' She hugged me and I touched the small of her back gently, summoning all my willpower not to kiss her lips.

She let go, then opened the back door for me. I stepped out of the warm kitchen into the cool night. After she closed the door, I stood there, waiting for it to open again. When it didn't, I made my way back to the neon lights of the busy Nathan Road, letting the sea of people and their loud chatter drown out the thoughts in my head.

5

A New Neighbour

'Beautiful morning, Ah Hock! Cool and crisp air. You should take a walk sometime around here. It helps to clear your head,' Towkay Lau boomed as he walked into the kopitiam, folded newspaper under his arm.

'I don't have time to waste like you do,' Ah Hock said under his breath as he assembled a bowl of laksa. Kim Choo was busy preparing milk tea in the kitchen so Ah Hock brought the laksa to Towkay Lau, who was absorbed reading the business pages. When he saw Ah Hock, he put down his paper and asked Ah Hock to sit with him. The businessman was insistent. Ah Hock sat down reluctantly as Towkay Lau ate a spoonful of prawn and beehoon. Ah Hock noticed the tycoon's smooth hands, the enormous jade ring on his finger. The hands of a person unused to manual labour.

Kim Choo came out from the kitchen and set down a cup of milk tea in front of Towkay Lau. He nodded at her. 'Your husband, he's a master at what he does. He has expertise. Talent. Pride in his work.'

'He's just a laksa seller, not a big towkay like you,' Kim Choo said, then went back to the kitchen. Ah Hock stared after her. *Just a laksa seller?* He looked at his own calloused hands, a testament to years of handling hot pots and boiling broths. So what if he wasn't a big boss? He was a man who knew the value of an honest day's work, unlike the sweet talker in front of him.

'Your wife is a flatterer indeed! What big towkay? I'm a poor orphan who got lucky. Make a bit of money here, make a bit of money there. I must say, I've always envied you, Hock. Your father passed down this shop to you – you never had to slog and beg for favours like I did.'

Ah Hock was barely listening to him. He had no interest in Towkay Lau's ramblings.

'I don't care what the doctors say. If I can't start my day with a bowl of this laksa, I can't start my day at all.' Towkay Lau rubbed his belly.

'I've got to prepare more bowls.' Ah Hock stood up to leave but Lau pulled him back down.

'Wait, Hock, I've got some news. Listen, I've bought the shop next door.'

'You mean the tinsmith shop?' It used to be noisy growing up with the familiar sounds of tin hammering next door, but Ah Hock had got used to it, and when they'd closed their business, he found himself missing the steady clang of hammer against tin.

'What used to be the tinsmith shop. It's been empty for some time now, as you know.'

'So why are you telling me this?'

'Because I'm opening a shop next to yours. We're old friends, aren't we, Hock?'

Towkay Lau had been his regular customer for decades, and told people Teck Boon kopitiam had the best laksa in town, but Ah Hock hardly regarded him as a friend. 'What shop?'

'That's what I wanted to talk to you about. I bought it cheap, it's a great location.'

He just had to brag about his money, didn't he? *Cheap!* More like he would cheapen the place. And what was he doing, buying up humble shophouses on Carpenter Street when he could be investing in Hong Kong, Singapore or anywhere else in the world?

'What kind of business do you think I should open, Hock? A bookstore? A grocery store?' Towkay Lau laughed.

'It's up to you, why ask me?'

'What about a laksa shop?'

Ah Hock stared at Towkay Lau. Surely, he had heard wrongly. 'What did you say?'

'A laksa shop.' Towkay Lau looked as pleased as a cat who had stolen a fish.

'What?'

'All this time I've asked you to partner with me, and you've refused. Well, don't say I didn't warn you.'

'What is the meaning of this?' Ah Hock raised his voice. Hearing him, Kim Choo came out from the kitchen.

'What's going on?' she asked, her eyes flitting between Towkay Lau and Ah Hock.

'This . . . he . . . he's opening a laksa shop next to ours,' Ah Hock said, glaring at Towkay Lau.

'It's just friendly competition. Your laksa is the best, don't worry, Hock. Unless . . . you want to expand? Let's make this kopitiam bigger, renovate it, make it brighter, modern. What do you think?' Towkay Lau smiled and rubbed his jade ring. Ah Hock wanted to wipe that smirk off the businessman's face.

'What is this, a threat? This is my kopitiam and I'm not letting you do anything with it!' Ah Hock banged his fist on the table, spilling Towkay Lau's milk tea. Kim Choo held Ah Hock's arm and told him to calm down. Towkay Lau downed whatever was left of his tea, put down his ten ringgit and stood up.

'Think it over, you might change your mind later. I'm planning on opening in a week's time, Hock. I can postpone it if you want to discuss things further. Plenty of time for you to decide. If not for yourself, do this for your son. Don't you want him back in Kuching?'

How dare he bring up Wei Ming! It was his fault the boy had gone to Hong Kong in the first place. 'My family is none of your business!'

'You think he wants to come back to this old kopitiam after living it up in a big city? You know, young people these days, they want modern, clean – something fancy. Think about his future. See you tomorrow!' Towkay Lau waved as he walked out of the kopitiam.

'Don't bother coming back, I won't serve you!' Ah Hock called after him.

'Aiyoh, keep your voice down, you don't want to scare away the customers!' Kim Choo said, shushing him. A lone young man in work attire looked up from one of the tables at the back of the shop, then resumed slurping the last of his noodles.

'I can't believe the cheek of that man! Opening a rubbish place next to mine!' Ah Hock snatched a bowl from the stack next to him and scattered beehoon and beansprouts into it without looking.

'He's been asking you for years to join him.'

'Are you saying it's my fault he's doing this?'

'Maybe it's good to expand, I don't know.'

'That's right, you don't know!' He waved her away. She

shrugged, then went to the kitchen. She knew better than to bother him when he was in a mood like this.

He didn't speak for the rest of the morning, assembling laksa bowls mechanically, not bothering with customised orders of extra prawns or more beehoon. Kim Choo had to take over, because he was getting the orders wrong and customers were complaining. Ah Hock ignored them. All he could think about was Towkay Lau's laksa shop next door. It was all a game to him, wasn't it. A man who didn't know the intricacies of a good dish! The freshness of meat and produce; the fresher, the better. Combined with depth, the resulting clean taste was called xian wei. Flavours that were intense but subtle. Like the ancestral broth, flavours in perfect balance.

Towkay Lau understood nothing of this. A man who only wanted to make money would ruin the dish. All that talk over the years about modernising the kopitiam! Ah Hock imagined a soulless, plastic joint next door to Teck Boon kopitiam, serving laksa like fast food. He thought with horror of the quality of laksa they would be serving – or worse, if people confused his shop with theirs. No, that would never happen. He couldn't let it happen.

6

Awabi No Kataomoi

'Chef! Are you okay?'

Takashi's voice was a mallet to my head. I opened my eyes to the boy standing over me: blond today, mouth open. 'Did you sleep here last night?'

It took a few seconds to register that I was lying on the floor behind the counter in Haruto. At first, I had no memory of how I'd got here from the Jade Pavilion last night. After the fifth glass of Jack Daniel's, the women had become a mirage of blurry images melding into one another. The stench of cigarette smoke and stale beer mingled with cloying jasmine musk on my clothes. I could taste the traces of vomit in my mouth. Then I remembered Ah Weng, cigarette dangling from the corner of his mouth, hauling me up by the collar of my shirt and bundling me into a taxi. He must have told the taxi driver where to send me. Probably paid my fare too. He was rough when customers misbehaved, but still had a soft spot for me, it seemed.

Since I last saw Jiayi almost a week ago, I'd been going to the Jade Pavilion every night. I had to stop. I did it to make her jealous, but all I'd accomplished was bad hangovers and making a fool of myself in front of Ah Weng.

I got up and massaged my temples. The morning sun streamed in through the shopfront windows. The wall clock showed eight o'clock. At least I was on time today.

'No, I . . . got in too early this morning.' If Takashi could smell the baijiu on my sour breath, he didn't say anything. 'Can you go check on the awabi? I want that on the menu today.'

Takashi nodded then went into the kitchen. I dragged myself to the toilet sink to splash my face with cold water, cringed at the sight of my bloodshot eyes, then ran my wet fingers through my unruly hair.

I took the navy-blue noren curtains outside and hung them above the shoji doors with unsteady hands. Inside, Haruto was a minimalist but cosy space with two tables with chairs, and a sushi counter that seated ten. The counter was divided from the kitchen by a pair of white door-curtains.

Sensei's handmade ceramic tea bowls were displayed on a hinoki wall shelf. Wooden andon lamps with intricate kumiko panels adorned both ends of the counter. Latticework was difficult and tedious, and something I hadn't tried yet, not until I mastered making half-decent masu cups.

I picked up the tea bowls from the display shelf and wiped them. The ceramic bowls were cool to the touch and I loved the varying textures of glaze on my fingers. There was something alive about them, each one having its own character. The sky-blue one. The green-seafoam one. The white and pink one, sakura blooms of spring. I wished I could make the bowls too, but I didn't have the focus for pottery. Tsugite – joinery carpentry – was hard enough. Sensei was a still lake while my head was full of waves crashing all the time. I could only ride the waves and hope I wouldn't drown.

My head was throbbing. Arturo Sandoval's 'Here's That Rainy Day' played over the restaurant speakers. The soothing trumpet and the steady tempo grounded me, each lingering verse kept me focused and relaxed as I sliced the awabi.

It felt like a slippery eel in my graceless hands. I tried to summon the same focus I had when making the square wooden masu cups, where every chisel had to be so precise or the pieces wouldn't fit together. It would be a shame to ruin the beautiful awabi I had fought so hard for, cajoling Ito, dropping Sensei's name. All the way from Tsukiji, shipped over from Tokyo to Hong Kong in a day, almost as fresh as if it had just come off the fishing boat.

Sensei used to say that awabi was to be treated with great respect and care. In Japan, it was the women who did the dangerous diving for it, grandmothers in their sixties or seventies.

I tasted a thin slice of awabi. Even while hungover I could taste the sweet kombu it fed on. I would simmer the awabi with sake from Niigata, the way Sensei made it.

*

It was a slow day, with only two bookings that night. As I cleared the tsuke-dai, the telephone rang. It was late; nobody would be calling at that hour to make a booking.

'Haruto restaurant. Sorry, we are closed. Please call back tomorrow.'

'Hello, I'm Raymond Cheng from the Global Restaurants Guild. May I speak to Chef Inamura please?'

I inhaled sharply. This was it. The news I'd been waiting for. I cleared my throat and tried to keep my voice even.

'I'm sorry, Chef Inamura has gone to Japan for a break. I am Chef Lim.' I felt weird introducing myself, but I wanted the Guild to know who had earned the second star.

'Ah, I see, I did hope to speak with Chef Inamura.'

'I've been the chef in charge for one year now. Anything you wish to inform Chef Inamura of I will relay to him.'

'Very well. I'm sorry to inform you that Haruto has lost its star. Please convey the unfortunate news to him. Do you have Chef Inamura's number in Japan? We wish to tell him personally, as a matter of courtesy.'

I had to hold on to the counter's edge to steady myself. 'I don't understand,' I stammered. 'Lost? Wait, I—'

'I'm very sorry about this. Haruto restaurant has been excluded this year. We hope to see it back in the running next year.'

I just about squeezed Sensei's number out of my mouth before dropping the phone receiver. It hit the floor with a clatter. Takashi parted the door-curtains and peered in from the kitchen.

'What happened, Chef?'

'Nothing. That was . . . the Guild. Said we lost our star.' Everything felt unreal, like I was in a nightmare. Takashi's voice was an echo.

'What do you mean?'

'I was so sure I'd get the second star, but . . . now not even one . . .'

No second star. No star at all. Maybe it didn't matter. Or, at least, had never mattered to Sensei. Our guests enjoyed their food.

I covered my face with my hands. Who was I kidding? It mattered. Sensei had earned that star and now I had lost it. It was my fault. The Japanese couple knew it, even if the others didn't. That Lim Wei Ming was a fraud, pretending to be sushi master when I was just a stand-in for Inamura Hiroki. How could I have been so wrong about everything?

'Are you okay?'

'Yes.' I cleared my throat, not looking at Takashi. 'I'm sure it's a mistake. I will call somebody to check tomorrow.'

'Wow, the star is gone. Taisho will be surprised! But, if it is a mistake, what can they do? Do they ever make mistakes?'

I wanted to scream at his questions. Haruto was a quiet place. When Sensei was angry at someone, he would merely not speak to that person for the whole day. Voices were never raised in Haruto even in the worst of moments, unlike Kowloon Palace, where expletives were thrown around as greetings and shouting was the only way to speak to one another.

What could I have done to offend the anonymous Guild critic so much that he or she had recommended stripping Haruto of its star? I had the urge to smash my fist into the counter. Tears welled up in my eyes at the thought of Sensei receiving the bad news through a late-night phone call. I tried to gather myself, so I took my favourite sky-blue tea bowl from the shelf and stared at it. Instead of making me feel better, its perfect imperfection made me angry. The bowl's beauty mocked me, told me I would never be good enough to make something as breathtaking.

Before I realised what I was doing, I'd smashed the tea bowl on the floor. Shards of ceramic scattered everywhere. Takashi gasped behind me. The silence in Haruto was broken. My face was burning hot and I hung my head in shame. I knelt down and picked up the pieces carefully.

'Please throw these away for me.' I tried to sound normal, but how could I sound whole when everything was shattered inside me as well? Takashi sprinted to the kitchen and returned with a box. He held it out to me and I put the fragments gently into it.

'Don't worry, Chef, we can put it back together. I know a master here, he can repair it. It will look even better than before.' Takashi's tone was unusually kind. He took the box with him to the kitchen.

I sank down onto the floor behind the counter and closed my eyes.

A sudden loud knocking on the shoji door startled me. We served customers who booked tables, never walk-ins. I dragged myself up and looked out the window. Two Chinese men, one tall and thin, the other short and burly. The tall one was in sunglasses and a long black coat. The other was in a black leather jacket, staring at me like a tiger at its prey. The tall man took off his sunglasses and smiled. I'd never seen them before. They were the type the Triad sent to collect money.

The shoji door slid open. The two men walked in, looking around the restaurant.

'Sorry, we are closed,' I said. I shook my head at Takashi, who was about to come in from the kitchen. The short man's stare made the hairs on the back of my neck stand on end. He was wearing a bright green jade ring on his right hand.

'Nice place,' the tall man said in Cantonese.

When I arrived in Hong Kong eight years ago, it had been an unfamiliar world. I was surrounded by brisk Cantonese chatter and surly, impatient people. Being Chinese, I should have felt right at home, but I didn't. I was Teochew, and a Malaysian Chinese at that. To the Hong Kongers, I was no different from a foreigner, being neither fluent in Cantonese nor a native. I had this constant feeling of being watched, sized up, judged all the time. Like they were checking to see if I belonged, whether I was one of them.

The tall man was sizing me up now, and decided that I wasn't.

'Fancy place like this, but you can't pay your debts?' he continued. I swallowed. A bad mistake, borrowing money a few months ago. A couple of thousand dollars, but by now it must have ballooned with interest.

'Sorry, Big Brother, I . . . I need a bit more time.'

'You need time, then what do we live on? Eat the northwest wind?' The tall man nodded at the short man, who then punched me hard in the gut. I doubled over, gasping. The short man threw me a right uppercut to the jaw, his jade ring bashing into my face.

I fell to the ground, the metallic taste of blood in my mouth. As I lay there, the two men kicked me over and over. I closed my eyes, letting the pain of each blow numb the shock I felt. They continued kicking me for a few more minutes before the tall man raised his hand and the short man stopped.

'Kicking a sack of potatoes is more fun than this. Don't say we weren't nice to you. Hey, check out the sushi knives. They're very sharp, aren't they?' The tall man took my yanagiba while the other pulled me up by the collar. The tall man rested the edge of the blade on my face. The cold steel was starting to draw blood. 'We're not leaving here without a single penny, you understand? At least pay your interest.'

'There's some cash in the till, let me get it for you,' I stammered. The short man let go. I wiped the blood off my face with the back of my hand, trying to ignore the sting of the small cut. Holding my stomach, I hobbled to the till and opened it.

'No funny business.' The tall man opened his coat to reveal a gun. 'I don't want to waste a bullet on you.'

I grabbed the night's takings and passed them to the short man, who counted the cash and nodded. The tall man gestured to him.

'Let's go.' Then he turned to me and added, 'You're lucky we're kind people. Brother Loke here has just become a Buddhist. You have one week to pay up the rest. Oh, and Man Kor sends his regards. He's got a message for you. If you set foot in Malaysian Kitchen again, this beautiful restaurant is going to burn. All your raw fish will be cooked.'

The men slid the shoji open roughly, not bothering to close it behind them. Takashi scurried over and helped me to one of the tables. 'Who are those men? Why did they hurt you?' he asked while I fought back my tears.

'Stop asking so many questions.' I wrenched my arm from Takashi's hold. It was the first time they had come to Haruto. Now Takashi would know about them as well.

'We need to tell the police.'

'No police!' I snapped. When I saw Takashi's hurt expression, I said, 'Please, Takashi, no police. Not now.' I felt guilty thinking of how he was just trying to be kind, but I didn't want him to know more than he already did.

Takashi nodded. 'Okay. What about an ambulance?'

'No need, I'm okay.' I took a paper napkin from the table and spat blood and saliva into it. 'I need to go home. Take some Panadol.'

'Will they come back, Chef?'

'I hope not,' I said, averting Takashi's gaze.

'Those men were like yakuza. Bad guys.'

'They were, yes. Listen, if they come again and I'm not at the restaurant, tell them I'm gone and you don't know where I am. If they refuse, call the police.'

'Are you planning to leave, Chef?'

'I don't know. Promise me, if it happens.'

Takashi nodded. 'Go home, Chef. I'll close up today.' He went back to the kitchen, and soon water sloshed in the sink and dishes clattered. I grabbed my wallet and keys from my locker. Outside the restaurant, I winced as I slid the shoji shut behind me.

I looked around for the men, but they were nowhere to be seen. A red taxi sped past me, leaving behind its musty exhaust fumes. I had spent eight years in Hong Kong, only to end up unknown, broke and broken.

7

The Original Taste of Ingredients

Ah Hock was checking on his flatfish drying at the back of the shophouse when the phone rang. It was Ah Lek, his seafood supplier.

'Ah Hock! I've got two boxes of fresh prawns, caught this morning, and of course you're the only customer worthy of them!'

Ah Hock laughed. It was the kind of news he loved to receive. 'Why didn't you call me in the morning, you rascal?'

'Hey old man, I know you're busy with customers in the mornings! It must have been non-stop over there!'

'Next time, tell me the moment the prawns come in. I can send Kim Choo to pick them up.'

'You work your wife too hard, Ah Hock! Come pick up your treasures!'

Ah Hock wasted no time in going to Pending, the seafood market where Ah Lek's shop was. Ah Lek always gave him the freshest prawns; no one dared to pull a fast one on Ah Hock. As he walked towards Ah Lek's shop, the fishmonger saw him from a distance and waved.

'Ah Hock! It's your lucky day, the fishing boats came in with a catch of big ones. Take my word for it, all plump and juicy. I'll give you a big discount, because I know no one else will appreciate these.' Ah Hock inspected the crustaceans, even though he knew he didn't have to. His father had bought seafood from Ah Lek's father; the family connection had lasted decades. Ah Lek packed two kilos of prawns into plastic bags filled with ice and helped put them in the boot of Ah Hock's car.

He drove back with a light heart, pleased with his bargain. This was the sort of relationship he wanted to pass down to Wei Ming – the right people in Kuching who would make sure the ingredients were of the highest quality and wouldn't cheat him. He would introduce them when the boy came back. *If* he came back. He sighed. Perhaps he should trust Kim Choo to convince Wei Ming to return. The boy might do that for her sake.

There was a time when he and the boy had got along, when the boy was a small child. What a joy he had been then! The first time Ah Hock had seen the beautiful baby, held him, smelled his sweet, milk scent. His son. Ah Hock's heart had soared the day Wei Ming was born, then broken when the boy grew up and wanted to tread his own path.

He smiled at the memory of Wei Ming as a toddler, smelling pepper for the first time then sneezing into the laksa spice mixture. Ah Hock had picked up the boy, dusted the pepper powder from his nose, then stirred the broth with Wei Ming in his arms.

'You see, Ming, this is our ancestral broth. Your grandfather brought it over from China. I take good care of it and someday you will too. Smell it! Doesn't it make you hungry?' Wei Ming had peered into the brass pot and tried to grab the ladle from Ah Hock, who'd swiftly moved his hand away and laughed.

When Wei Ming turned eleven, Ah Hock had considered

letting him look after the broth, like he had taken over from Teck Boon when he was ten. But after seeing Wei Ming engrossed in reading comics and forgetting to do his chores, it didn't seem like a good idea. As a child, Wei Ming could be lazy, although at least Ah Hock could still push the boy to watch him while he chose the spices they needed, making him smell them one by one so he could tell the difference between each unique spice.

When he turned fifteen, things had changed. All that nonsense about being a chef, like Teck Boon had been in Swatow. Ah Hock blamed Kim Choo for telling the boy too many stories about his grandfather, filling his head with all those fairy dreams of being a culinary genius.

The boy had dreamed big even before learning the basics! Ah Hock had refused to teach Wei Ming until the boy learned some humility. But he had underestimated how stubborn Wei Ming could be. Kim Choo had warned him he was pushing their son away. And she had been right.

8

Masu

Jiayi was standing outside the door to my flat. Her chef's uniform was stained with sauces, her backpack slung over a shoulder, and she was holding a bottle of champagne.

I'd come home to be alone, and the last thing I wanted was to talk. On any other day, I would have been thrilled if she'd shown up at my door like an early Christmas gift. Her smile turned into a frown as I walked towards her.

'Your cheek . . . it's a little swollen. Were you in a fight?' She touched my face with her forefinger.

I shook my head. 'I'm fine. It's nothing.'

'Oh no. Man Kor's boys? You've been borrowing money from them? I told you not to, oh god. Are you okay?' She held my hand, her face creased with worry.

'Yeah.' I looked around the corridor. 'Is it safe for you to be here?'

'I don't know,' she said. 'I was so excited I rushed here without thinking.'

I pulled her into the flat and locked the door behind us. It was dimly lit, with old, frayed carpeting, and the only natural light filtered in during the day from dirt-streaked windows that looked like they hadn't been cleaned in years. I hoped she wouldn't notice my unmade bed or the dirty cups in the sink.

69

'What's the champagne for?' I asked.

'Oh, I feel so silly now, with what's happened. But guess what, Malaysian Kitchen got a star! I can't believe it, it's like a dream! They told me I'm the first Malaysian chef to have won a Guild star. I didn't even know a Guild critic came. It's so amazing, I'm in heaven! The ceremony is next week and I don't have a dress. Or do you wear chef's whites? No, that would be weird, right?'

I felt the blood drain from my face while she tittered like an excited schoolgirl. I should've been happy for her, shared her joy and encouraged her. She deserved it. I knew her food deserved a Guild star. I'd said it and meant it.

But it wasn't fair. I'd worked hard all these years to prove myself, and nothing had come of it. She could call herself a Guild-starred chef now while I had nothing.

'We lost our star,' I croaked.

She tilted her head at me. 'What're you talking about?'

'Haruto is not starred anymore.' Hearing her news had crushed me. What an absolute fool I'd been! All this time, thinking I was going to earn that second star, when I couldn't even keep the star Sensei had earned. That felt worse than taking money from the till.

'There must be some mistake.'

'They don't make these kinds of mistakes. I'm sorry, I forgot to congratulate you.'

'Thanks. But I can't feel happy, knowing you're not.'

'I'm happy for you.' She could probably hear how insincere I sounded.

'I wish today was a happy day for you too.' She hugged me and I buried my face in her hair, smelling traces of citrus and sesame oil.

I tried my best to smile. 'Ignore me, I'm stupid. It's just

70

stars, like you said. I'm happy for you. Here, sit at the table. I don't get many visitors. Actually, I don't get any visitors.' I pulled out a chair for her. I didn't have a sofa, only a small table, two chairs and the bed.

We sat down, and I pushed the pieces of masu joinery and my tools away from her side of the table. She looked at my face again.

'You wanna ice that? I'll go get some—'

'No, it's fine, really. It's nothing.' My face and stomach hurt and I needed some Panadol, but I didn't want her to fuss. She picked up the half-finished masu and looked at it.

'Nice. Did you make this?' she asked. I nodded. 'What is it?'

'It's supposed to be a cup for sake. Masu.'

'Oh.' She put it back down on the table. 'This is cool. No nails?'

'No. That's the beauty of it. Inamura said I needed to have a hobby to teach me focus. This is the most basic. There are carpenters who do so much more with joinery. They make furniture, doors, build temples. This is nothing.'

'It's not nothing. It's beautiful. It's in pieces now, but after you make them all fit together, it's going to be a perfect sake cup. Wanna drink the champagne with this?'

'Not in the mood, sorry. The cups aren't finished anyway.'

She pursed her lips and put the champagne bottle into her backpack, then looked around the flat. 'It's emptier than I remember. Did you take something away?'

'Nope. It's always been like this.'

We sat in silence for a while, until I spoke again. 'I'm happy for you. Getting the star is a big thing. I think Malaysian Kitchen's going to have lots of new customers.'

She smiled widely. 'I'm happy too, but sad about Haruto. I don't understand it at all.'

71

'I don't either. I didn't expect it. I mean . . . I didn't realise my food was so bad it got Haruto kicked out altogether.'

'You are an excellent chef. I've seen you work. I know how good you are. Maybe it's because Inamura left for Japan. I've heard of this – sometimes they just take away stars if a different chef takes over the restaurant. You know, like you've got to earn your own stars or something. It's silly. Who knows what they're thinking.' She squeezed my hand.

Despite her efforts, I didn't feel better. I needed to lie down. As I was walking to my bed, I saw a half-empty bottle of Jack Daniel's next to it and nudged it under the bed with my foot. She followed and sat on the edge of the mattress. 'I'm sorry, I didn't mean to make you feel worse.'

'No, not worse. Just tired.'

'Do you want me to go?' She was about to stand up when I pulled her down to me. The buttons on her chef's jacket were tricky so she helped me undo them. I couldn't get enough of her scent, her warmth and her softness. For a moment, everything disappeared except for us, together, intoxicated with pleasure. If there was a memory I was allowed to preserve forever in the afterlife, it would be this. It was the only time I could truly know her feelings for me. The same kind of high I felt when walking home alone after a tiring but good day at the restaurant, a short-lived contentment as I revelled in the sights and odours of the big city – neon lights, exhaust fumes, white-noise chatter, people brushing past me. But when I arrived at my dark, squalid flat, the energy of the city would leave me, and I'd be plunged into emptiness once more. Like the melancholy I felt when we had finished.

'Do you want to go back?' I asked. She was stroking my face. Her fingers smelled of ginger and garlic. I kissed them, tasting salt, then moved my lips further up her wrist, onto her kitchen burn scars.

'Back? Where?'

'To Malaysia. Let's go back. Start a restaurant together. Away from here, from all the craziness.'

She sat up, pulling the duvet to cover herself. 'I don't know. The restaurant's doing so well, and it's got one star now, I. . .' She trailed off guiltily.

'We'll be together there. No more secrets,' I said, kissing her shoulders. She moved away from me, then rummaged around the bed. 'It could work.'

She didn't respond. Holding her chef's whites and trousers, she got up, then walked to the table where she had left her backpack. I loved watching her naked form, recalling her moans of pleasure from just a few moments ago. There was a tattoo of a Chinese character, 胜, on her lower back.

'What does that tattoo say?'

'You can't read Chinese?'

'I studied at a government school, not a Chinese school like you did, remember?'

She shrugged. 'The word *sheng*.'

'You mean "life"?'

'No, *sheng* as in "to succeed",' she said, emphasising a different intonation. 'Like the idiom "*Zhan wu bu sheng*". To triumph in every battle.' She took out a pair of jeans and a grey blouse from the bag and started changing.

'Come with me to Kuching. My mother would love you.'

'I can't.'

'Why not?'

'The star changes everything—'

'You could reopen Malaysian Kitchen in Malaysia and earn another one.'

'You talk about it as if it's so easy to earn a star. Even this one, who knows what it was that did it? I can't lose it just like that,' she said, then added hastily when she saw my face cloud over, 'Sorry.'

'As long as I have my regulars, who cares, right?' I didn't mean to sound snide, but her change in tone had annoyed me.

'Yeah, so why can't you stay on and continue what you're doing? Maybe next year things'll be different. It's so unpredictable how they decide when to give or take away stars.'

'That's easy for you to say, since you just got one. I lost the only star we had and it wasn't even mine to begin with.'

She tied her hair up into a bun and exhaled hard. 'You know what? I've always been hungrier than you. Hungrier for success, to strike out on my own,' she said, buttoning her jeans. 'Instead of whining, why don't you figure out how you can get the star back?'

I sat up abruptly. I couldn't believe she was saying these things. Had winning a star changed her so quickly? Or had I been blinded by my infatuation with her, failing to see who she really was – an ambitious chef who was willing to sacrifice anything to be the best?

'I'm not hungry for success? Is that why I've been busting my ass here for the last eight years? Put up with abuse at Kowloon Palace?' I said, my voice raised.

She turned and looked me in the eye. 'You have a family business you can inherit. I have nothing back in Malaysia.'

'I don't want the laksa shop. You know I want my own restaurant. I just don't have someone I'm sleeping with to buy it for me,' I said, immediately regretting the words as soon as they'd left my mouth.

She stared at me, her eyes brimming with tears, then she grabbed her bag and stormed out of the flat, slamming the door behind her. I should have gone after her and apologised, but I just sat there on my sagging mattress, feeling like the unluckiest man in the world.

9

The Promise

Ah Hock sat in bed, watching Kim Choo set her hair in curlers in front of the belian dressing table he had ordered from a talented carpenter when she moved into the shophouse all those years ago. It had been a wedding gift for her, the only feminine thing to grace the bedroom he had slept in as a child. The Bornean ironwood table had lived up to its name – stable and sturdy, without so much as a chip, after all these years of them being together.

He tried to relax, but soon he found himself thinking about Towkay Lau's plans again. 'He knows next to nothing about flavour and now he's opening a laksa shop. Which idiot is he going to get to cook for him?' he muttered to himself angrily.

'What are you grumbling about now?' Kim Choo said as she put in the last curler.

'That Lau. How dare he open a laksa shop right next to mine?'

'Your laksa is good, people will still come to you.'

'I'm not worried about that. I'm . . . I'm worried his bad laksa will give my place a bad name,' he said lamely. He was afraid, but he couldn't let it show. There had been fewer customers lately. He didn't know why. It was true the laksa soup hadn't been as stellar as it used to be, but that would hardly make a difference to the average customer. If Third Uncle enjoyed it, then he didn't have anything to worry about. Still, something nagged at him. What was missing? He hadn't been doing anything different for the past forty years.

'Don't worry, let's see what happens when the day comes,' Kim Choo said. Ah Hock was glad he had her. She was the anchor his life needed. Even when things had been bad, when Wei Ming left, she was the salve for the wound their son had inflicted on Ah Hock.

'Have you heard from the boy lately?' He tried to sound as nonchalant as possible.

'Ming? He called last month.'

'Oh.'

She turned to him and smiled. 'Why? You miss him? I'll call him soon, ask him to come back for your birthday party.'

'Don't talk nonsense. This unfilial son, running off, bringing shame upon me. I'll see if he dares to come crawling back here.'

'He says he's doing very well over there. Their restaurant has won prizes. He's a famous chef there now.'

Ah Hock scoffed. 'Famous? Who's heard of him?'

'It's an expensive restaurant. They've won prizes for their, what you call it, *su-see*?'

'What's that?'

'Raw fish on rice, or something. Japanese cuisine.'

'Japanese. . . His grandfather would turn in his grave if he knew. Says he wants to be like his grandfather and ends up cooking Japanese cuisine. We ran away from them and now he goes running back to one. Oh, wait, it's not cooking. It's raw fish, isn't it? He's just cutting fish. Could learn to do that right here. Ah Lek could teach him how to cut fish if he wants to be a fishmonger. Young people these days, no respect for their ancestors.'

Kim Choo said nothing. Her silence made him feel guilty. She was an orphan who had grown up in an opera troupe; she didn't even know who her parents were, let alone her ancestors. Still, he continued. 'That's why we pray to our ancestors, for guidance and wisdom. They leave their mark, the way the tea leaves leave their fragrance on the teapot. Without our past, we are nothing. Yet it is so easy for the boy to forget where he came from. Japanese food! What a joke!'

'He's still a chef. There's an art to it, you know.'

'What do you know about their food? They don't even know how to cook, they have to eat it raw! He wants to be pretentious, let him.'

'Why are you asking about him?'

'I was talking to Third Uncle. It's time to prepare the boy to take over the kopitiam.' If the boy refused, maybe even partnering with Towkay Lau, as annoying as he was, would at least ensure its future. It was better than closing the kopitiam eventually and fading into oblivion. Ah Hock couldn't stand the thought of future generations never knowing Teck Boon kopitiam had once existed. A few regulars might reminisce about the laksa, talking about it as if it were an urban legend. But when they were gone, the stories would be too.

He wished he knew what Teck Boon would have wanted. No, it was the easy way out, going into business with Towkay Lau, making the deal with the devil. He had to persevere. He would have to find a way to convince the boy to take over. Kim Choo could talk some sense into him.

'You haven't taught him how to cook the laksa. How will he . . .' Her words trailed off as she gave Ah Hock a knowing look. Even she did not know the recipe.

Ah Hock bought the spices himself every week from an old spice shop at the Main Bazaar. He would come back with big plastic bags of shallots, garlic, dried chillies, candlenut, and ground spices like cumin, cardamom, clove, nutmeg. There were thirty ingredients altogether, whereas most laksa stalls used prepackaged commercial pastes that had far fewer – half of what theirs contained. Ah Hock would blend the ingredients together and pound them into a paste, a daily ritual for the past forty years. An electric blender would have made his work a lot easier, but he refused to use one, convinced the taste would be different against plastic and metal, compared to his trusty old stone mortar and pestle.

'If you want to pass the kopitiam down to him, he has to learn,' Kim Choo said, applying Nivea Milk to her arms. She walked over to her side of the bed and got under her blanket, yawning. Ah Hock smelled the familiar fragrance of her moisturiser, but it didn't soothe him as it usually did.

'You know what he's like. It's impossible.'

'When did you learn to make laksa? When you were ten, twelve? Your father let you in his kitchen when you were five.'

'The boy grew up in this kopitiam. Saw everything. But refused to learn!'

'You never let him even stir the laksa soup.'

'Even stirring it wrongly can ruin it! It's not like you don't know this!'

'I know, I know. But I also know not everything has to be perfect before things can be completed—'

'And that is why you don't know the recipe. You don't understand.'

'If I knew the recipe, it would taste just as good.'

'You better not talk nonsense. I'm not in the mood.'

'I'm being practical. You write down the recipe, exactly

how much of everything we need, the weight, the amount. I'll help you to blend it all, then you can show me how much water we need, how much coconut milk. If you are so precise and everything is so exact, won't it turn out the same every time?'

'You and your simple head! If it turned out the same every time, why don't we use a machine? It's not as easy as you say. If it was, we wouldn't be the most famous laksa stall on Carpenter Street!'

'Ah, you stubborn old man, I should've known better than to bring this up. Your father would've wanted Ming to learn his recipe—'

'My father was a famous chef back in Swatow. He could cook thirty different dishes with one type of fish.'

'But he didn't open his own restaurant here. Only a kopitiam. He was happy with cooking laksa. Your father passed down this legacy to us, and if not for him, we would not be so well known in Kuching.'

'I never even tried to open a restaurant. Maybe I could have learned his recipes.'

'You learned the most important one.'

'He would have wanted me to open a restaurant here, like his place back in China.'

'He would have said so. I don't think he wanted that. Look at how he adapted to life here, coming up with his own recipe for laksa, catering to local tastes. I think he wanted to make a fresh start.'

That was true. A fresh start with just the two of them, in a foreign country with foreign tongues, foreign palates. Almost as if he'd wanted to forget his life – and his wife – back in China. And yet, Ah Hock remembered his father sleep-talking about the restaurant. He was maybe five or six years old, when they still shared a bedroom, and he'd heard his father mumbling about some five-flavour fish dish and lotus root and fish maw soup. Mentioning Ah Joo, the name of his sous chef. His right-hand man. They had never seen each other again, and Ah Hock had no idea whether Ah Joo was still in China.

'Maybe. It's just that sometimes he let it slip that he missed his restaurant there. Did he ever mention Ah Joo to you? Eh, are you listening?'

There was soft snoring next to him. Ah Hock turned and saw his wife sleeping soundly. 'That was fast. Poor woman must be tired.' He stroked her hair gently, careful not to rouse her. 'You should've married a big towkay, then you could go shopping or to the hair salon, or stay home and watch drama serials, like Towkay Lau's wife.' Ah Hock switched off their bedside lamp and turned onto his side. The mattress felt lumpy that night.

*

Ah Hock was ten years old the first time he was allowed to stir the ancestral broth. Teck Boon was in a good mood, and business was brisk. Third Uncle came by, as usual, then sat at his table and chatted with Ah Hock's father. They were both in their prime then – good-looking, robust men. Third Uncle would help Teck Boon by carrying sacks of supplies over his shoulder as if they were light as a feather, and hot, heavy pots of soup while the latter protested.

They were like brothers, the two men who spoke to each other happily in Teochew. Ah Hock was glad for their friendship, which filled the void of his mother. That day, in the middle of a conversation with Third Uncle, Teck Boon asked Ah Hock to join them. Ah Hock had been clearing a dirty table, but obediently put down the bowls and glasses, then went over to their table.

'You think he's ready?' Teck Boon looked Ah Hock over as if he were sizing up chickens to buy.

'He's been watching you all this time. Let him try,' Third Uncle said, smiling. 'Ah Hock, you want to learn to cook like your father?'

Ah Hock nodded eagerly and looked at his father.

'I was only allowed to touch the broth after my leaving-the-garden ceremony,' Teck Boon said. For Teochews, the coming-of-age ceremony was celebrated at the age of fifteen. In ancient times, a fifteen-year-old was either ready to get married or sit the imperial exams.

'That was back in Teo-Swa. You are not bound by the old rules here. It is up to you, Boon.'

'I'm ready, Pa. Let me learn,' Ah Hock said earnestly.

'You see, the boy is keen. Not everybody wants to learn their father's trade.'

'All right.' Teck Boon got up from his stool. 'Follow me. Walk carefully and don't do anything stupid.' Ah Hock followed his father to the corner of the kitchen where the precious brass pot was waiting, bubbling away on the charcoal stove. Ah Hock held his breath as his father took a ladle and lifted the lid. Ah Hock tried to peer into it carefully, avoiding the rising steam. It was the first time he had been allowed to be so close to the broth. Its aroma was far stronger now and seeped into his nostrils, the meaty flavours infusing his being.

'Never let the fire die, do you understand, Hock?' Teck Boon stirred the broth slowly with the ladle. 'You stir. Carefully.' He passed the ladle to Ah Hock, who took it, trembling.

He couldn't believe it. 'Now you need to add something to it. What do you think we should put in?'

'You decide, Pa,' Ah Hock said in a timid voice.

'No, it is also yours now, you will have to decide.'

'Maybe some dried flatfish?' He was sure Teck Boon would disparage him. But his father smiled a rare smile and nodded his approval. Teck Boon went to get the flatfish he had been drying outside the kitchen, at the back of the shophouse.

'Dried flatfish is good.' Teck Boon broke a few pieces into the simmering broth. 'Now wait for half an hour, then taste it and tell me what else it needs.'

This went on for a few hours as Ah Hock and Teck Boon took turns tasting it, while Teck Boon explained what it lacked and when it was just right. That night, young Ah Hock had a deep, dreamless sleep, and when he woke up the next day, he felt like he had grown a few inches taller. He was practically an adult, now that he had taken over his father's responsibility of making sure the ancestral broth never lost its depth.

That was fifty years ago, and it was a duty he had been performing ever since. Throughout his childhood and his youth, his father had never failed to admonish him about the broth needing to be passed down to the next generation. Ah Hock's children would have to take over the broth, or calamity would befall the family. Keeping the broth safe was sacrosanct, even when Teck Boon had crossed the seas to new lands. Would Wei Ming be able to keep this divine promise?

10

Ittekimasu

I got up from bed and tripped over the bottle of Jack Daniel's I'd finished after Jiayi left the previous night. I threw it into the kitchen bin then stood by my telephone, wondering whether to call Ma.

The old man would be busy preparing laksa, so there was a high chance she would pick up the phone if I called. I practised saying hello a few times before I dialled the kopitiam's number, hoping I sounded sober.

'Hello?' It was Ma. I hadn't realised how much I missed my mother until I heard her voice.

'It's me, Ma.'

'Ming!' Her exclamation was a mixture of surprise and panic. 'I was going to call you! Is everything okay?'

'Yeah, everything is fine.'

'Why are you calling?'

'It's been a while.'

'I know. You must be so busy. I'm so glad you called, I have something to ask you.'

'What is it?'

'Your Pa's sixtieth birthday is coming up. You know we must celebrate it. He doesn't want to but I'm insisting. Bad luck not to, you know. So, do you want to come home?'

'Okay.' The word rolled off my tongue before I had time to think. I just wanted to be away from here. What was left in Hong Kong for me anyway? The prospect of being kicked out by my landlord, chased by people I owed money to and drinking myself to death wasn't appealing. Not to mention Sensei returning to see how I'd managed to bungle up everything, including Haruto. I felt guilty for making Ma think I was returning home solely for my father's birthday. But all I knew was, I had to reset somewhere, go someplace I could think. At least it would make Ma happy.

There was a pause before my mother spoke again. 'Really?'

I laughed. 'You thought I'd put up a fight, didn't you?'

'I did. I had all these reasons prepared to convince you. Is everything all right?'

'Yeah, fine. I need a break I guess.'

'Only after eight years you need a break?' She sighed. 'But I'm happy.' I could hear the lightness and surprise in her voice, the way she sounded whenever I did something to please her, like helping out with chores without being asked. I hadn't heard that in a while. 'I'll cook all your favourite dishes. Come home. You don't have to stay long, even a week is enough.' She hung up before I could say goodbye. Maybe she didn't want to give me a chance to change my mind.

Was going home the solution? Not that I had many options. I was haunted by the image of the red-faced Ah Hock at his stall, boiling with rage, and the devastation on my mother's face when I decided to leave for Hong Kong eight years ago. The fight I'd had with Ah Hock before I left the family home.

I was already twenty-seven when I'd asked to use the broth back then. I'd been making a dish of chilled grey mullet as a treat for my father. Ma had told me it was one of my grandfather's special dishes, and I couldn't wait to try it out. I marinated the mullet with salt, then added softened dried scallop on and inside the fish. My grandfather's recipe required a few tablespoons of the broth to be steamed with the fish, but Ah Hock said I wasn't ready to use it.

'When will I be ready? I'll be turning thirty in a few years!' I couldn't believe it. All I had asked for was a few tablespoons, and he couldn't even oblige.

'That's the question I ask myself every day,' he replied.

Ma protested with tears in her eyes when I threw away the raw mullet, and I spent the rest of the evening lying down in bed, hating Ah Hock. A few days later, Towkay Lau appeared with the offer of a job and lodgings in Hong Kong. Of course, I'd snatched up the opportunity without asking my parents.

Once I left Hong Kong, I knew I would lose the flat, and my job. Mentor or not, Sensei had a business to run, and I wasn't sure how he'd feel about what I'd done. I didn't want to think about what the gangsters would do to the restaurant if I stayed and didn't cough up the money I owed.

And leaving Jiayi with the way things were? I could go home for a week, like Ma said. But who was I kidding? One week wasn't enough. It wasn't a holiday. How would I break the news to Sensei? The idea of leaving Hong Kong brought back the nostalgia of when we first met.

*

I had gone to the fish market with Man Kor to buy seafood for the Chinese New Year festive menu at Kowloon Palace. As I was picking out live prawns and scallops, a stranger spoke to me in English.

'You have chosen good shops to buy from.'

I was surprised to see a Japanese man in his late forties, with crew-cut hair and a goatee, carrying a plastic bag.

'You are a chef?' he asked.

'No,' I had managed to reply as Man Kor walked over. 'He is the chef.'

'I am Inamura Hiroki from Haruto restaurant.' Sensei bowed. He held out his hand, which Man Kor shook.

'I am Ah Man, from Kowloon Palace. You don't get good fish?' Man Kor pointed at the plastic bag Sensei was holding.

'One seabass. It is not the best. Maybe better another day.'

Man Kor nodded, his eyes darting elsewhere. I could tell he wasn't interested in a conversation about fish. But I found Sensei fascinating. Maybe it was his calm disposition, or his kindness towards me. He was the opposite of Man Kor, who treated everyone in the Kowloon Palace kitchen with contempt.

'What kind of fish are you looking for?' I asked Sensei.

'Anything that is fresh. I plan my menu that way. I prefer actually to catch fish with a line. But day-boats, they catch fast and bring back to the port in one day. That's very fresh.'

'For Japanese restaurants, fish is raw. So you need fresh,' Man Kor said to Sensei, then turned to me and added in Cantonese, 'We don't need to spend that kind of money. We can use heavy sauces to cover the frozen fish taste.' He laughed while I remained silent and Sensei smiled politely.

'You know ikejime?' Sensei asked us. Man Kor shook his head. 'Ikejime is a way of killing fish so it is fresh longer. I want to teach the fishermen here to do this.'

'Could you take me along next time?' I asked Sensei.

'Ming is not a chef. He is one of our kitchen helpers,' Man Kor said, scowling at me.

'I want to be a chef one day,' I persisted, and Sensei smiled.

'I want to teach ikejime to as many people as I can. Please come to Haruto when you have time.' He took out a card from his pocket and gave it to me, then bowed as he moved on to other stalls.

'You so friendly, huh?' Man Kor said with a snide smile.

'He was nice to us.'

'Maybe he's trying to steal restaurant secrets.'

I shrugged. Whatever secrets Kowloon Palace had, I could see nothing worth stealing from watching Man Kor in the kitchen.

Our first meeting had been seven years ago. A lifetime. I would be forever grateful to Sensei for saving me from Kowloon Palace.

11

The Wager

Ah Hock was at his stall preparing bowls of laksa when lorries arrived in front of the kopitiam. Wooden tables and chairs, refrigerators, freezers and stoves were unloaded, and moved to the shop next door. The clattering of furniture and pots on the pavement, and the never-ending shouts of 'Put it here!' and 'Be careful with that!' distracted Ah Hock. He looked up occasionally to see what the movers were bringing into the shop, but pretended he didn't notice them while Kim Choo stood at the kopitiam doorway and gawked.

'Wow, they have so many things! And the furniture, it looks so modern. Must be expensive,' she said, looking longingly at the chairs being unloaded.

Ah Hock snorted. 'Expensive? All I see is cheap plastic and laminated wood. None of it is solid wood. Don't be nosy, go send this bowl of laksa to the customer over there,' he said gruffly, and handed her a bowl of laksa. She rolled her eyes, then took the bowl from him and served it to the customer before returning to the doorway.

'Of course we have to be nosy. Don't you want to check out the competition?' She stared at the workers bringing in kitchenware. 'Wow, those pots look so shiny! How many do they need?'

'Competition? Don't make me laugh. You think that lousy businessman knows anything about food?' As Ah Hock spoke, Towkay Lau walked over to the kopitiam.

'Good morning, Master Lim! Sorry about the inconvenience, we are moving in today! An auspicious day! Let me introduce you to my cook.'

Before Ah Hock could protest, Towkay Lau called out to someone outside and soon a young man walked over. He couldn't have been more than twenty-five. Even younger than Wei Ming. He was tall, with a well-chiselled face, handsome as a film star. What a joke! The boy looked too pretty for this kind of work.

'So, this is the famous Master Lim!' The young man spoke in Hokkien and extended his hand. Ah Hock glanced at him and grunted, continuing to put skeins of beehoon into bowls and scattering beansprouts and strips of omelette on them. The men's presence annoyed him and he almost forgot to add shredded chicken into one of the bowls.

The young man grinned and put his hands in his pockets. 'My parents used to bring me here for breakfast. It really is good. But you know, these days, young people, they prefer a more modern setting. Cleaner, too.' The young cook wrinkled his nose at the old mosaic-tiled floor and the yellowed walls.

'Are you saying my kopitiam is dirty?' Ah Hock glared at him. The impudence of the boy! Such snobbery when he was barely out of diapers! Who the hell did he think he was, coming over here and looking down on the kopitiam? So what if the kopitiam was old, or worn? That was the beauty of Carpenter Street, with its old shophouses that transported people back in time. Did the young people appreciate it? Would a new coat of paint make the laksa taste better? All they wanted was shiny fake things. This moron wouldn't know authenticity if it hit him in the face with a ladle.

The young man shook his head and laughed. 'Sorry, sorry, Uncle, that is not what I meant. Oh, and I forgot to introduce myself, my name is Tan Chee Seng. Call me Billy.' What an idiot, with a dumb English name he expected people to remember.

'Billy may be young, but he's a hard worker and has a great recipe. Come by sometime, Hock, your first laksa will be on the house! Of course, after that you'll have to pay. We need profits too!' Towkay Lau said, laughing loudly. Billy laughed with him, then said he had to get back to work.

After Billy had left, Towkay Lau leaned over to Ah Hock. 'There's time to think about this. We can have branches. Billy can do the cooking and you do the tasting. We'll keep hiring cooks like him – all you have to do is make sure to teach them your magic. Then sit back and wait for the money to roll in! We can do takeaways, food deliveries! Think big!'

'You know nothing about good food! Nothing!' Ah Hock slammed his hands down on the stall counter. Towkay Lau was unfazed, smiling coldly at Ah Hock, who was bristling, red in the face. The customers in the shop looked up from their laksa bowls and stared at them. 'Your shop is going to close down! You think people are stupid? You think they don't know how to taste food? You put your shop next to mine, you're just asking for trouble. I'll be here waiting – waiting to see you close shop!'

Towkay Lau folded his arms and laughed loudly as if Ah Hock had made a joke. 'Are you willing to bet on this?'

'What nonsense are you talking about now?'

'It so happens that a celebrity chef will be coming from

New York to Kuching in a few weeks. Alan Boucher. Really famous. They're shooting a food programme here. Oh, but you don't watch TV, do you?'

Ah Hock huffed. 'I don't fill my head with rubbish.'

'You know, these chefs make a lot of money making these programmes. Maybe even more than running their restaurants. My people are bringing him around Kuching. Of course, I told them about your laksa shop. That was before I decided to open my own. Now, I can choose to ignore your kopitiam and have them focus on mine. But I want to be transparent about this. Let him taste both our laksas and judge which one is better.'

Ah Hock couldn't believe his ears. Towkay Lau had surpassed himself with his absurdity.

'You want me to let some angmoh decide which laksa is better? Are you drunk? How on earth would an angmoh know anything about laksa?' Ah Hock took his ladle and stirred the laksa soup so roughly some of it splashed onto the floor.

'He's a chef. He's eaten all types of cuisines all around the world. Including laksa.'

'This is the stupidest idea I've ever heard.'

'Put your money where your mouth is. You say I'll close shop but I'm sure I'll win this contest.' Towkay Lau's eyes were gleaming, like he was a tiger about to pounce on a gazelle. Grinning as if he had already won.

'I don't want to play your stupid games,' Ah Hock said, putting too much beehoon in one bowl and too little soup in another.

'It's not a game, Ah Hock. I know you're a master at what you do. And I'm willing to help but you've snubbed me so many times. And now you say I'll fail. Well, I bet you I won't.

But if I lose the bet, I'll close shop. I'll never set foot in your kopitiam and bother you again. How's that sound?'

To lose to a young fool who looked like he should be on a variety show instead of sweating at a noodle stall! Was this a joke? It was insulting, that's what it was.

'Wait. Let me understand this. If I win, you'll close shop? And stop bugging me about branches and all that nonsense?' Ah Hock said, looking Towkay Lau in the eye.

Towkay Lau nodded. 'You have my word. And if you lose—'

At this, Ah Hock snorted.

'Oh, don't you want to know what happens if you lose?'

'Sure. What do I lose?'

'If you lose, you give me your kopitiam. Signboard and all. We'll take over and sell your father's laksa. You'll have to tell us all your secrets, the recipe, everything. We'll be marketing Teck Boon kopitiam everywhere, even outside Malaysia.'

The audacity of the man! The heat from the broth and his anger intermingled in a fireball in his heart. That sneak! He just wouldn't stop, would he? Why was he so obsessed with cheapening Teck Boon's laksa? Was it just about money? It was obvious Towkay Lau would continue to badger Ah Hock about the kopitiam. Towkay Lau taking over the family business? How degrading! Ah Hock felt like punching the man in the face, but instead he remained stoic. He wasn't going to let this worthless person enjoy the satisfaction of a reaction.

'You sure know how to daydream,' Ah Hock said.

'All businessmen daydream. But if you're so confident, Ah Hock, you shouldn't be worried.'

'I'm not worried. This is stupid and I want you to close shop. You want a bet, you've got it. Now get out of my sight. You're not welcome here anymore.'

'Be careful, Ah Hock. I don't make decisions when I'm emotional. If I offended as many people as you did, I wouldn't be where I am today. You are always welcome at our café.' He smiled at Ah Hock, then walked next door. Ah Hock could hear him shouting at the workers, instructing them where to put the furniture and the stoves, then laughing with the young cook.

'Oh, there aren't many customers now. I'll peel more prawns. Where are the fresh ones you got from Ah Lek?' Kim Choo asked as she took an empty mug from one of the tables.

'Who knows!' Ah Hock snapped. She looked at him quizzically.

'Aiyoh, what is it now? Did you have another fight with Towkay Lau? What did he say?'

'Nothing. Just rubbish, as usual. Nothing good comes out of his mouth.' Ah Hock tried to look unperturbed. He wasn't going to tell Kim Choo, at least not yet. His hand shook as he stirred the laksa soup, and he hoped Kim Choo didn't notice. What else could he have done? The bet would settle things once and for all, and the thought of never seeing Towkay Lau in the kopitiam brightened him. Branches outside Malaysia, indeed! What did the man think Teck Boon kopitiam was? A fast-food chain?

'I know you don't like him, but don't offend him. He's a powerful man in Kuching.'

'So what?'

'So don't fight him. You won't win,' she said with a big sigh. 'I'll go get the prawns.'

'Who says I won't win?' Ah Hock said to himself as he poured laksa soup into an empty bowl – glistening, rich and aromatic – and tasted it. Had he forgotten the cumin? No, he'd

94

definitely used that. More salt? Or was there too much star anise. He scratched his head so hard it hurt his scalp. He was driving himself crazy trying to figure it out. It didn't have to be perfect to win. Even on a bad day, it would be better than what that baby cook had to offer. There was no way he would lose that stupid bet to Towkay Lau.

12

Kazunoko

After calling Ma, I went to the fish market and bought bags of scallops, king prawns, oysters, lemon sole, cod and turbot with the urgency of a fisherman who was worried there would be no seafood left in the ocean. I followed my nose at the market and found some fresh iwashi. The insides of the small sardines were bright red, the flesh firm, and their bright eyes stared back at me. There was monkfish liver, cod roe – which I would salt later – and octopus tentacles. For the sushi, there was turbot, flatfish, halibut fin, bream and a fatty yellowtail.

Back at Haruto, Takashi groaned when he saw kazunoko. I laughed. Takashi found it tedious to remove the membrane of the herring roe, but I made him do it anyway. According to Sensei, kazunoko sushi was Japanese New Year food, but I loved the texture and deep taste of the yellow caviar and wouldn't pass up a chance to make it, even when it wasn't for the New Year. To lessen Takashi's suffering, I let him play Nirvana's 'Smells Like Teen Spirit' on repeat at full blast while we worked.

I had bought the freshest seafood I could find without a menu planned. I wanted to experiment with different options. What was the use of playing it safe? I'd lost the star regardless.

As we were prepping, a familiar voice called out 'Tadaima!' to us. I washed my hands and went to the sushi counter, Takashi trailing behind me.

It was Sensei in jeans, a white T-shirt and a black blazer. As usual, he looked younger than his fifty-five years; you wouldn't believe he was a day older than forty. He wore a Yankees baseball cap and his face looked ruddier than before. It looked like a year in Niigata had refreshed him. He had a large trolley bag and hand luggage. Must have just got off his flight. I swallowed and felt my hands turn clammy. I hadn't figured out how to break the bad news to him.

'Okaerinasai, Taisho!' Takashi said, bowing briefly then hovering around him like an excited puppy.

'Sensei.' I gave a deep bow. He bowed back.

'You look tired, Wei Ming.' Sensei looked concerned. He had always been intuitive but I didn't want him to know any of my problems right now.

'I'm okay. Why didn't you tell me when you were coming back?'

'It was a sudden decision. But it was time. My father was starting to find me annoying, I think,' he said with a chuckle. He unzipped his hand luggage and took out two plastic bags, which he held out to Takashi. 'Please unpack these for me, Takashi-kun. Be careful, there is sake and rice.'

When Takashi went to the kitchen, I gave Sensei another deep bow. His sudden return must have been due to the loss of the Guild star.

'I am sorry to cause you trouble, Sensei.' I blushed and kept my head down, not wanting to see his expression.

'What do you mean?'

'You're back because of the star, right?'

'What happened?' Sensei sounded puzzled.

So, he didn't know. 'Didn't you get a call last night? Someone from the Global Restaurants Guild?'

'I was already on the plane. What did they say?'

'We lost the star. You've come back to . . . nothing. I'm sorry.'

'I see. No star?'

I shook my head. I was glad to have finally told him, but I wanted this moment to end quickly.

'Moushiwake arimasen.' I was bowing as low as I could, but I still could not shake off my remorse.

There was a pause before he spoke again. 'I see. It cannot be helped. We will earn it back, that is all. Life has its ups and downs. We must not let this setback stop us from moving forward.'

'You have earned the star and now it's gone because of me.' I couldn't keep the quiver from my voice. Sensei touched my shoulder, and I looked up at him. He looked solemn, but at least he was still speaking to me.

'Think of it as a good thing. We can start with a clean slate. You will earn the next star for Haruto.'

'But, Sensei, this is your restaurant.'

'I never think of it as my own. Whoever works with me owns it as much as I do. It is a child with many parents. I want you to love it as much as I would love my own child. What I think is, you do not feel the same love for it.' This time, there was melancholy in his eyes.

'I am grateful for your teaching, Sensei. Everything I know as a chef, you have taught me.'

'But I sense something is missing. I can teach you all the techniques and methods, Wei Ming, but I cannot force you to love it. I know very well love cannot be forced,' he said. 'Your emotions are your own.'

98

I didn't want to discuss my feelings when Takashi could reappear at any moment, so I changed the subject. 'How is your oto-san, Sensei?'

'Thank you for asking. He has some good days. I enjoyed my time with him, reliving many childhood memories. Ah, before I forget, I have something for you.' Sensei took out an elegant, gift-wrapped box and a white A4-sized card from his trolley bag. 'These are yokan, a kind of sweet, hard jelly wagashi. Very popular in Japan. I bought the best one from a master I know well in my home town.'

I took the gift box and the card, which had pressed flowers on it. Blue hydrangeas. 'I took my father out for walks so he could look for the summer ajisai. They are not easy to find. My father was weak, but when he saw them, he forgot his pain. The fresh smell of flowers in the air and the rain, it made him feel alive.' Sensei smiled at the recollection. 'He made me laugh when he said he could taste the air because it was so sweet.'

'This is beautiful, Sensei.' I gazed at the pressed hydrangeas. Ajisai were Sensei's favourite flowers. A lot of work and patience must have gone into pressing those blue hydrangeas onto the card.

'This is oshibana. I'm glad I managed to press ajisai. Usually, they disappear fast. Sometimes you see them for two weeks. So brief you almost forget they ever bloomed.'

'It must have taken time to make.'

'I learned oshibana from my mother. She passed away when I was ten years old. Ajisai make me think of her.'

I didn't know what to say. The fragile beauty of the pressed flowers frightened me, as if they were entrusting me with their lives. I took the flowers, even though I felt like I was making a promise I couldn't keep.

'I'm glad your trip was pleasant. It's good to have you back, Sensei,' I said, not really sure if I meant it.

'I'm going back to my apartment to rest. Why don't we go fishing tomorrow morning? Take a taxi to Sai Kung. I'll meet you at the pier at seven?'

I nodded. After Sensei left, I remembered the money I'd taken from the till and slapped my forehead. There was no doubt about it. I was being punished by the heavens. For leaving the family home, for not being a good son and obedient to my father's instructions. For not readily accepting my destiny of inheriting the kopitiam and honouring the deity's broth. There were days when I figured my father was right about the curse. All my life, that was all that had mattered to him.

No matter how hard I worked, I didn't feel any closer to being skilled or capable enough to run my own restaurant. As if I was always working against the odds. Maybe the gods were preventing me from escaping my fate.

I went to my locker and opened it. My brown leather knife bag, frayed at the seams, that contained my only valuable possessions. The chef's knives had been a gift from Sensei on my first day at Haruto. 'A different tool in different hands yields different results. A chef's knife is very important. You must master knife skills. I have bought you this set of knives. Keep them with you. Always use your own knives. Do not use another chef's knives unless they give you permission,' Sensei had said as he presented me with them. Every time I cleaned them at the end of the day, I felt as if I'd received the gift for the first time.

My favourites were my yanagiba, which I used with surgical precision on sashimi, and the hardy gyuto, my multipurpose dependable companion. Having such excellent knives made slicing or cutting anything a joy, and every day I looked forward to using them. Whenever no one was looking or within earshot, I talked to them, thanking them for never letting me down.

I took good care of them, washing them and drying them carefully. Every week, I would apply tsubaki oil to my knives to prevent rust, and every six months I would sharpen them on a whetstone then polish them till they shone.

I was the last person Jiayi would want to see now, but I had no choice. I grabbed a cap and took my knife bag, then slipped out unnoticed as Takashi wiped the tables with Metallica's 'Nothing Else Matters' blasting at full volume.

13

Gyuto

When I arrived at Malaysian Kitchen, there was a line at the entrance at three in the afternoon. Was it because of the Guild star? I tried to stifle the green-eyed monster raising its ugly head. I wasn't sure if Jiayi wanted to see my face again but I had no one else to ask.

I pulled my cap over my eyebrows, glanced over my shoulder, and knocked on the back door. It swung open, and one of the kitchen staff came out with a bag of rubbish and nearly bumped into me. I entered the kitchen and Jiayi was there barking out orders as she tasted a spoonful of sauce.

'What the hell are you doing here?' she snapped when she saw me, then pulled me into her office. 'I don't have time for your shit today.'

'I'm sorry. Really. I would give anything to take back what I said.'

'Whatever. I'm not in the mood for your apologies.'

'I need your help.'

'Are you kidding?'

'I wouldn't ask if I wasn't desperate. I need a thousand dollars.'

'You want to borrow money from me?'

'Not borrow. I'll . . . I'll sell you one of my knives.' I opened the knife bag. The yanagiba was the most expensive of all, but there was no way I could sell that. It was a Sakai Takayuki. I could get at least two thousand dollars for it. The knife I used every day, with its slender blade that danced as it made the finest of cuts on an ink squid.

She didn't need a sashimi knife. She would probably find a multi-purpose knife more useful though. I used the gyuto every day too. The way it slid down daikon or ginger with the slightest pressure from my hand; it never failed me, whether it was tofu or an onion I was cutting.

'You'll love the gyuto knife. You can use it for everything. I'll let you have it for a thousand. It's a bargain. You can sell it for more, but I think you'd want to use it. It's a real treasure.' My hand trembled as I took out the gyuto. It was like trying to decide which of my children to sell. My consolation was knowing the knife would be safe with Jiayi. I liked the idea of leaving a part of myself with her too.

'You're selling your knife to me? Does Inamura know this?'

'He doesn't. I wouldn't be doing this if I didn't have to.'

'I'm not going to take your knife. I'll lend you the money.'

'No, in that case, I can't take your money.' I wanted to leave. Pretend it was temporary insanity. Yet I stayed, on the verge of begging her, salvaging my pride the best I could by pretending we were doing a business transaction.

'I told you not to gamble so much.'

'You don't have to worry about me,' I said, swallowing the lump in my throat.

'How much did you lose? Tell me.'

'Three . . . three thousand dollars.'

She closed her eyes for a while, as if thinking about what a failure I was before she opened a drawer at her office desk and took out an envelope. 'Take this,' she said. I opened it to find a Malaysia Airlines ticket. Hong Kong to Kuching, with a transit in Kuala Lumpur, booked for tomorrow night. 'I was going to give this to you today. I talked to Man Kor. I'll sort out your debts. Go home.'

'What do you mean, "sort out"? I'll pay his thugs myself. I'll . . . I'll find a way.'

'I already found a way. Take the ticket and go. You'll be safer in Kuching.'

I took her hand. 'Come with me. Please. It's not too late. I promise things in Kuching will be different. You'll have a family with us.'

She shook her hand free and looked away. 'I can't. Even if I wanted to. Man Kor says he'll forgive your debts if you leave and I stay.'

'Don't do this for me. He won't know if you leave today.'

'I gave him my word. Don't make it harder for me.'

'Harder for you? You want to stay, don't you? Now that you've got your star.' I felt like she was chasing me away. She sighed and pinched the bridge of her nose.

'I thought I was helping you. Look at what his boys did to you. You want to stay and get killed?'

'Stop saying you're helping me!' I shouted, and slammed my hands on the table. She glared at me then took my gyuto. 'I'll take this in exchange for the ticket since your manly pride is hurt. I've got to go, it's been non-stop since noon,' she said before going back to the kitchen.

The kitchen was noisy like Haruto had never been. It brought back memories of Kowloon Palace, where cooks had shouted instructions like 'Throw the peelings', 'Wash knives!', 'Dry chopping board!', accompanied by 'Too slow!' or 'Faster! Faster!' Now Jiayi was calling out, 'Wash this! Clean the floor!

Where are my knives? Wipe off the stains!' The instructions were in a mixture of English and Cantonese. A barrage of orders came in, with the waiters calling them out to the cooks in the kitchen, who in turn yelled at the dishwashers to wash pots and pans.

As I opened the back door to leave, Jiayi called out for someone to slice pork and another to send the order to table fifteen, never once turning to look at me.

*

I opened the till at Haruto and exhaled hard. I didn't have enough money to replenish the till.

A coward. That's who I was. That's why Jiayi had bought the ticket for me. I should forget about going back. Tell Ma it was impossible, I was too busy.

But I'd promised. I didn't know which was worse, breaking my mother's heart or disappointing Sensei. I imagined his crestfallen face when he found out about the money from the till. The sake inventory. The mess I'd made of the restaurant accounts. And if I stayed, I could never see Jiayi again without endangering her or myself.

I went to the office and sat down at the desk in front of my Toshiba laptop. Sensei seldom used computers, preferring to write everything down by hand. I had printed out all Sensei's menus and put them in a file. Today, I didn't reach for it as usual. I took a pen and paper and started scribbling furiously, letting my imagination run wild. If the customers hated it, Sensei would be there the next day to placate them with the usual celestial selections that had earned him the star.

'I prepped the neta, Chef. Which menu are you using today?' Takashi popped his head around the office door.

'A new one,' I said, writing the last of my notes. I looked up at him and said, 'Takashi?'

'Yes, Chef?'

I wanted to tell Takashi I was leaving. That I was sorry I hadn't set a good example for him. To thank him for all the times he'd said nothing to Sensei about my visits to Happy Valley, and for pretending not to notice the missing sake or my hangover after a night at the Jade Pavilion.

'Don't smoke so much now that Sensei is back. It's a bad habit.'

'We all have bad habits,' he replied with a cheeky smile.

In the kitchen, I lifted the bamboo cover of the rice steamer, and the fragrance of the rice and vinegar hit me. Takashi had cooked it. The rice tasted good. Takashi was nearly as good as me now. If Sensei had met Takashi first, maybe the boy would be heading Haruto instead of me.

We only had one sitting that evening – one of our regulars, John Chan, a barrister who came once a fortnight. The middle-aged bachelor was a seasoned guest and knew how to appreciate food properly. Takashi said two other parties had cancelled their bookings at the last minute and I was sure it was because of the news that Haruto had lost its star. It hurt, but I steered my focus towards making my menu instead. John was sure to like the ankimo – monkfish liver – which was the foie gras of the sea. We salted cod roe and marinated monkfish liver in one of the premium sakes, boiled octopus tentacles and sliced them.

Everything was completed minutes before John walked in at eight p.m.

'It's a pleasure to welcome you, John,' I said, then added awkwardly, 'I'm sure you've heard about our star.' I wasn't going to bring it up at first, but seeing John's familiar face had made me blurt it out.

'I haven't actually, what do you mean?' John took his seat at the counter.

'We lost our Guild star.'

'Oh. Well, is the food still good?' John said with a chuckle.

I laughed. 'I think so. Why don't you tell me after this?'

'I can't wait!'

'We have a different menu today. Something I created myself, not Inamura-san's menus. I hope it's okay for you.'

'Wei Ming, anything you make with your hands is okay for me. Bring it on! After how my trial went today, I need your best sake!'

I served him a customer favourite, Hakkaisan Junmai Daiginjo, to accompany the salted roe and the octopus tentacles. I left the ankimo for last so the taste would be allowed to linger before I prepared the sushi. My yanagiba danced like a ballerina on the yellowtail I sliced. I didn't worry about perfection or making mistakes, and let my intuition guide me as I shaped sushi in my palms. I hadn't felt this free in a long time.

I served the kazunoko sushi to John, who ate it with his eyes closed then raved about the buttery herring roe. Each time I served a new sushi, John would praise me, saying it was exquisite and a delight to savour. It was hard not to let it all go to my head. At the end of it, John looked up and said, 'Is that all? No encore?'

'Would you like tamagoyaki? On the house. Always a good finish.'

'Ah, that heavenly omelette.'

Something so deceptively simple – an omelette that had taken me five years to learn and two years to perfect. The omelette pan needed to be heated just right. Excess heat would ruin the omelette. I'd had to practise countless times the way the egg mixture had to be shaken and flattened to avoid air bubbles. Flipping the omelette properly had taken thousands of attempts. The hardest part of all was knowing when it was ready without prodding it too much. After a while, it became instinctive, but the tamagoyaki at Haruto never tasted as good as when Sensei made it.

I put two pieces of tamagoyaki on the tsuke-dai for John. He popped one into his mouth, his eyes widening as he chewed. 'Chef! This is the best tamagoyaki I've ever tasted . . . maybe, even better than the master's?' John exclaimed with a wink. 'I could have this every night if my meal didn't cost five thousand dollars.'

I bowed. John was my favourite customer, but I knew it wasn't flattery alone. He was a man who enjoyed his food and wasn't shy about expressing his enjoyment of it. I was glad I was able to prepare a final meal for him, but I couldn't tell him that.

'Thanks, John. I appreciate your words. If only the Guild critics felt the same.'

'Ah, who cares about them!'

I do.

'My master is back.'

'Ah, Big Boss is back. Does this mean he will be here tomorrow?'

'Yes, I think many customers will be happy for that.'

'Nonsense! Don't sell yourself short, young man. This is something special. It's different, but it tasted right. You have good instincts.'

I thanked him. Deep down I wished I didn't feel like I had been filling in a temporary position. It seemed the customers, even John, regarded Sensei as the boss, the soul of the place.

I poured John one of our best sakes, the Eikun Junmai Daiginjo Ichigin, into a masu cup.

'Pour yourself one too, Wei Ming. My treat.'

'Oh, I shouldn't—'

'Nonsense, you're done for the night. Come on, join me.'

I relented and poured myself a cup of sake.

'To Inamura!' John said. 'Kanpai!'

We raised our cups and I drank deeply. The sweet, fiery liquid rushed down my throat, and I exhaled in satisfaction.

'I'll miss the music too. Who knew Chet Baker paired well with otoro?' John sipped his sake contemplatively. 'It's so quiet when Inamura is behind the counter, isn't it? Like nothing should distract me from enjoying his food.'

I went to my CD player, put on 'Round About Midnight' and savoured the deep, sweet flavours of the rich melody, Monk's pain infused into every note, while my favourite customer basked in the afterglow of the perfect meal.

14

A Thousand Mountains and Ten Thousand Waters

The ship was rocking so hard Ah Hock wondered if a sea monster was flinging them from side to side. The other people around them were all huddled together in that cramped, dingy space at the bottom of the ship – mostly young and middle-aged men, and a few women. Two of the middle-aged men were wearing silk maguas, like Ah Hock's father. They looked out of place at the bottom of the ship, sitting on a grimy floor that stained their once-pristine white trousers. The other men and women were in plain cotton shirts and trousers that looked as worn as their solemn faces. Ah Hock heard faint weeping from one of the women, and another muttered a prayer to Mazu, the Goddess of the Sea, to keep them safe.

Ah Hock was the only child there. The stench of urine and vomit was an unwelcome companion to the ship's violent movements. His stomach churned and bile was hovering at the back of his throat. He didn't dare tell his father, who had been in a foul mood ever since their journey began.

They sat in a corner of the ship, his father holding their gourd of broth while Ah Hock held his stomach. His mother knew what to do whenever he had tummy troubles. But she wasn't there. His eyes welled up with tears. He wiped them away with the back of his hand and tried to think of happy things. The smell of mandarin oranges and peonies in summer. Piles of gingko leaves he jumped into in autumn. Hot bowls of noodles in the winter, warming his belly. Biting into the first peaches of spring, crisp sweetness bursting in his mouth.

A woman about his mother's age who sat opposite him saw his discomfort and smiled at him. She wore a plain grey top and black trousers that were faded from too many washes. Her short hair was half covered with a pink kerchief with white flowers, and her face looked a bit smudged with dirt. So different from his mother's porcelain skin, her cherry-red rouge and her white and pink qipaos.

'Little boy, are you feeling well?' Her gentle voice was a balm for Ah Hock. She was motherly but there was no child with her. Had she left someone behind, too? He nodded. His father stared at her but said nothing. 'If you want, I have some nutmeg oil here. You can sniff it, it might make you feel better.'

'Thank you, we don't need anything,' his father said to the woman coldly. She shrugged and rummaged in the worn jute bag strapped across her chest, fishing out a biscuit which she held out to Ah Hock. He looked at his father, and his father nodded. As Ah Hock walked towards the woman, the ship suddenly lurched sideways. Ah Hock fell and knocked his head on the floor. The pain made him burst out crying. The woman rushed to him, stumbling as the ship continued to sway violently. Ah Hock's father remained huddled in the corner, hugging the gourd. Ah Hock touched the sore part of his head and saw his fingers were bloody. The woman saw the blood and gave a cry.

'Your son is bleeding!' she said to Ah Hock's father. He glanced at them both, continuing to hold his gourd tightly.

'I'll check it later when the seas have calmed a bit. I can't leave this here, it'll spill,' he said, caressing the gourd. The woman scowled and shook her head at him, then sat down next to Ah Hock and held him in her arms.

*

Ah Hock woke up with a gasp. Another bad dream. He felt like something was sitting on his chest. The back of his singlet was drenched with sweat.

He turned onto his right side and stayed still for a few minutes. The pain was beginning to subside. It was probably nothing, but it worried him. He wiped the tears from his cheeks and turned to look at the sleeping Kim Choo, glad he hadn't woken her up.

All those years ago. That journey to Borneo to build a new life with his father. He hadn't thought about it in decades. Why had he dreamed about that now? Was it a sign? He wasn't sure, but he didn't like it at all. Dreaming of dead parents could be ominous. *Never follow them*, as Kim Choo said. *Even if they plead or try and coax you to go with them.*

Three o'clock again. Might as well get ready for the day.

*

He had already finished preparing everything in the kitchen when Kim Choo came downstairs at five.

'Aiyoh, I thought I was late. How long have you been up?'

'Don't worry, I've finished. Why don't you rest if you're tired?'

'I'm not. Woke up a bit later, that's all. You've been up early these past few weeks. Can't sleep?'

'It's nothing.'

'You never tell me anything,' she grumbled. 'I don't know who I should invite to your party.'

'Easy. Don't have the party.' The party sounded like such a chore. So what if he was turning sixty? Kim Choo was overly superstitious. Probaby because Ah Hock's father hadn't celebrated his sixtieth. Teck Boon had never liked celebrating anything apart from the New Year. Then he'd had a heart attack shortly after he turned sixty. Kim Choo thought it was because he had offended the gods by not having a party.

'Don't be stubborn, old man! I think you behave like this to vex me on purpose. We're going to invite Third Uncle. What about Towkay Lau?'

The mere mention of that man was enough to set Ah Hock on edge. 'Are you joking? The man set up a laksa shop next to ours! Why would I want to invite my enemy?'

'Enemy? Just because he opened a business? Then all the hawkers in Lau Ya Keng must be our enemies too,' she said with a laugh before she noticed his sombre expression. 'What is it, old man? There's something you're not telling me.'

He knew he should have told her earlier. 'I . . . we made a bet,' he mumbled.

'A bet? With who?'

'That scoundrel Towkay Lau. He said his laksa will be better, what a joke! And he's getting some angmoh chef to judge us! An even bigger joke!'

'What did you bet?' Kim Choo asked, her face creased with worry.

'If I win, he'll close shop and never bother us again. I'll look forward to the day that moron stops badgering me with opening branches.'

'And if you lose?'

'I won't lose,' he said with a shrug.

'Tell me!' Kim Choo seldom raised her voice, so he knew she was truly upset. She looked like she was about to cry, and a sudden feeling of guilt overwhelmed him. He washed his hands then dried them.

'He'll take the kopitiam. And have branches using the same name.'

She gasped and grabbed his arms. 'Don't be crazy, what will we live on?'

'I told you, I won't lose.'

'If your father were here—'

'He's not here! I am here and I'm telling you, I won't lose to that degenerate!'

'You're not a gambling man, Hock. Tell him we will work something else out.'

'You don't understand!' Ah Hock stormed out of the kitchen. He felt like a slab of stone was pressing on his chest. He stopped at the bottom of the stairs, wheezing.

Kim Choo followed him and tried to rub his back, but he waved her away. 'I can't believe you're betting the kopitiam,' she said. 'Let me talk to Towkay Lau. We can't do this, Hock. The kopitiam is all we have.'

As he was about to protest, Third Uncle arrived. He was early that morning, it wasn't even seven yet. Ah Hock regained his composure and showed Third Uncle to his usual table.

'So early today, Third Uncle, what a nice surprise. Ah Choo, prepare a bowl for Third Uncle.' Ah Hock took a seat at Third Uncle's table and spoke to him in a low voice. 'Third

Uncle, I need to ask you, do you have regular check-ups at the hospital?'

Third Uncle shook his head. 'No. I should, I know, but I feel all right. Why?'

'I've been having these . . . chest pains . . . They come and go. Should I see a doctor?'

'Chest pains? You better see someone. Ask Kim Choo to go with you.'

'Nah, I don't want to worry her. She's gone through enough hardship with me, and with Wei Ming. She's already worried about the boy all the time. I don't want to be another burden to her. Could I ask a favour, Third Uncle?'

'Sure, what is it?'

'Could you come with me to the hospital?'

Third Uncle laughed. 'All right. As long as the doctor doesn't ask to check me too!'

Ah Hock thanked him as Kim Choo put a bowl of steaming hot laksa in front of Third Uncle.

'Thank you for what?' she asked.

'Ah, for . . . for the other day, he gave me some dried flatfish,' Ah Hock stammered.

'Dried flatfish? Where did you put it?'

'I'll show you later. Don't take his money today, Choo.' Kim Choo nodded, then went back to the stall.

'You shouldn't lie to her,' Third Uncle said, slurping his laksa.

'I don't want to worry her. How's the soup today?'

The old man nodded. 'It's all right. But not like your usual.'

Ah Hock sighed. 'This is driving me crazy.'

'Don't worry too much, my taste buds are old. I'm living in the past, that's all. It's still good.'

'Not good enough.' Ah Hock watched Third Uncle chew

the prawns attentively, as if he were reflecting on their quality. 'Those are fresh and springy. Ah Lek specially reserved them for me.'

'Yes, all the ingredients are fresh. It's only the soup that doesn't taste like usual. Don't think about it, Hock.'

'I can't help it. You know that.'

Third Uncle smiled and shook his head. 'Like your father and his high standards.'

As Third Uncle finished his laksa, Ah Hock told Kim Choo he was going out on an errand with Third Uncle. He drove slowly and more carefully than usual, feeling like he could not rely on his reflexes that day.

*

The hospital waiting room felt like a freezer. Ah Hock had on a short-sleeved shirt over his singlet. He wished he had worn long sleeves and trousers instead, although that would have aroused Kim Choo's suspicions. He didn't speak much to Third Uncle, trying to settle the butterflies in his stomach as his eyes constantly checked the wall clock. The minutes felt like hours.

When they called his name, he got up too quickly and almost tripped on the way to the examination room. The doctor was a kind young lady in her thirties. She asked about his family medical history, and chuckled when he complained about running on the treadmill. After all the tests had been completed, she sat down and read the results.

'Uncle, I see something of concern in your stress test,' she said. 'We won't know if it's serious unless we do an angiogram. We inject dye into your arteries and watch how it moves around in your body. That way we can see if your arteries are blocked. If they are blocked, we can either do an angioplasty to widen your arteries, or a bypass surgery. You don't have to worry about all this until we do the angiogram, but you need to do it to be sure.'

Ah Hock gripped the edge of the plastic seat on which he was sitting. 'So there is something wrong with my heart? Am I going to die?'

She smiled and shook her head. 'Nowadays, there are great medical advancements for cardiac health. We have many ways to look after your heart. I will refer you to a cardiologist, you can do your angiogram with her, and she will advise you on the next steps for treatment after that. Please do it fast, Uncle. It's better to check early.'

Ah Hock nodded glumly. As they left the clinic, Third Uncle looked at his downcast face and laughed. 'Anyone would think you've been given a death sentence!'

'I might as well have.'

'It's normal to have health issues at this age.'

'You're one to talk. You don't even have check-ups.'

'I haven't had any chest pains. For all you know, the cardiologist may say you have nothing to worry about at all. Let me know again when you want to go,' Third Uncle said as he got into the car.

*

They closed the kopitiam early that day. Ah Hock was too distracted to serve anyone properly, ignoring a customer who had complained there were no beansprouts in his laksa.

'What's with you today?' Kim Choo asked as she washed the laksa bowls.

'Nothing. Just tired.' He sipped his kopi-o as he sat and reflected on his hospital visit. Third Uncle was right, it was probably nothing. A follow-up appointment would confirm that. Another doctor! What a waste of time. It was stress, probably. Damn that Towkay Lau. But what if the bad dreams lately were a sign of something? A bad omen? He was getting to be as superstitious as Kim Choo.

'You should see a doctor.'

'Don't be stupid.' He almost spilled his coffee, wondering if Kim Choo had guessed where he and Third Uncle had gone earlier.

'Are you too tired to slaughter chickens? I got some live ones. Mrs Lee from Lau Ya Keng let me have a couple; she went to the market early this morning. You're always saying you like fresh chickens.'

It was true, they hadn't had freshly slaughtered chickens in a long time. This would spruce up the laksa soup and improve the taste. His mood brightened. He went to the back of the kitchen where the chickens were, their feet tied up with raffia string. They were quiet, as if they already knew what was coming to them. But every chicken was different. Some fought to the very end, squawking furiously even as they were tied up and helpless. Ah Hock had been slaughtering chickens for decades. It wasn't something he enjoyed doing, but fresh ingredients were vital to him.

These two chickens looked easy; they seemed so restful he wondered if they were sick. He sharpened the cleaver for good measure, then took one of them. He was about to cut its throat when it turned to him with imploring eyes. Almost human.

He dropped the chicken in shock as it squawked, its body flapping on the floor helplessly. He looked at it sadly, then said aloud, 'Poor you, this isn't a fair fight, is it? You're tied up and I have this sharp knife. Not fair at all.' He picked it up again and tried not to look closely at its face. *Yuan zhi yuan wei*, the original taste of ingredients. *A good cook must know where his food comes from.* His father's words echoed in his head. It wasn't because he found solace in them, it was more because he was used to his father's commands.

He swallowed, then gave the chicken's neck a quick slice. It was not deep enough. The chicken struggled violently and escaped from Ah Hock's hands. Flapping around the floor, squawking, its lopsided head turned to him accusingly. It left trails of blood wherever it flapped. Ah Hock put a hand over his mouth and gagged.

'What's all that noise? Hock! What's the matter with you?' Kim Choo caught the chicken then took the cleaver from Ah Hock's hands. He stood there, frozen, watching the chicken flapping around trailing blood. She slit its throat in one quick action and collected its blood in a bowl. 'Are you all right?'

He nodded wordlessly and went back inside the kopitiam. He needed a shower.

15

Ikejime

I paid the taxi driver then got out and ran towards the Sai Kung Pier. Sensei was already waiting there, looking out to the vast horizon of the sea. He was in a waterproof hoodie and trousers with a satchel over his shoulder, wearing a bucket hat and carrying a cooler box. Anyone who saw him would never have guessed he was a great sushi master. But Sensei had a stately air about him that ensured no one took him lightly.

I apologised for being late and took the cooler box from him. Around us, people were jogging and buying seafood snacks from the stalls at the pier. I loved the sea air, the space. It felt easier to breathe than when I was in the city.

Jiayi and I used to come here one winter, a long time ago. When we were just friends, and she was not yet with Man Kor. We'd come on a whim on our day off, jump into a taxi and take long walks in Sai Kung town and along the beach. We'd have oyster omelette, steamed scallops and crabs stir-fried in onion and chives, sitting outdoors at a café and drinking freshly brewed coffee.

'I've been thinking a lot since I went back to Japan,' Sensei said. 'About home. My father being ill has given me a different perspective on life. Maybe I am tired of the city. I would like a big space with plenty of natural light. With kumiko doors.

Like my family home in Niigata.' He had a look in his eyes that I knew well. The longing for home, but not wanting to return. 'Maybe I will sell Haruto, set up a smaller place here. Or even Cheung Chau island. I will name it Furusato. I can make food from my home town, not just sushi. Can you imagine it, Wei Ming, we could cook simple food, heart- and stomach-warming food, with seafood we catch ourselves?'

I could imagine serving fresh seafood to appreciative customers and enjoying the salty sea air. Sitting on deckchairs with the blue-green horizon before us, the sound of waves crashing against the shore, nursing cold Tsingtao beers, discussing where to find fresh anago. It was a nice fantasy. But why would Sensei want to have anything to do with me once he found out what I'd done at Haruto?

'What does Furusato mean, Sensei?'

'It means "home",' he said, and I smiled.

Rough waves crashed against the pier and seagulls circled above us, cawing. I looked at the horizon and felt a stirring that I hadn't felt in a long time.

'Is there something bothering you, Wei Ming?' Few things escaped Sensei's attention. He would have known about my discontent sooner, had he not been in Japan. It had been a while since we'd had a heart-to-heart talk. There were so many things I wanted to tell him. How I felt out of my depth helming Haruto even if I told myself I was doing a great job. How I felt pride in my work at Haruto but it was love I wanted to feel, love for whatever I cooked. How eventually I had felt like I was drowning, spiralling into the gambling, taking sake and money from the till, borrowing money from people I shouldn't have, getting involved with Jiayi.

'I feel I have disappointed you by losing the star.' It was the only thing that wasn't too appalling to mention.

'A star can be earned back. We have customers who appreciate that we do our best. And we learn new things, every day. The old itamae who have been around for forty, fifty years, they do not say "I am the best" or "there is nothing else for me to learn". So, after thirty years, I am still a baby.' He looked at me intently and said, 'Be honest, what is it that you want?'

The nearness of the sea grounded me. I felt more able to distil the chaotic chatter in my head. 'I want to own my own restaurant one day. My grandfather was a famous chef in China, a long time ago. But all my father wants to do is cook laksa noodles. He wants me to take over his noodle shop one day.'

'There is no shame in owning a noodle shop. In Japan, good ramen chefs are respected like good sushi chefs. You can choose one thing you love to do, and work hard at it. If you make good food and you respect your customers, that is enough. And try to make it better every day.

'You know, before I came to Hong Kong, I was working in Tokyo,' Sensei continued. 'And before that I worked for my father in my home town in Niigata. I realised something. In both restaurants, I could not find my true self. I learned many skills. I am grateful for those lessons. But I could not fit into their – how do you say it – mould?'

'I'm not sure what you mean, Sensei.'

'It was like learning to sing, but I was not using my own voice, you know? It did not matter how well I sang, I was not myself. It is important for a shokunin to find his own style. You keep practising singing or playing the instrument until you get it right, until the song reaches its full potential. Imagine how you feel when you have done it, when one day something you made turns out exactly the way you wanted. It's not just about hitting the right notes. I can teach you the formula, the right way of doing things. But you must find your own way to make it better. Make it yours.

'In a way, you and I are similar. I also did not want to take over my father's restaurant. He and I have different ideas of making food. My father inspired me, yes, but we do not walk the same road. If I live in Japan, all I will do is try to please him. I don't want to do that. I mean, of course I want him to be proud of me, but I do not want to be him. I want to be better.'

'I . . . I do want to be better, Sensei,' I said softly.

Sensei gave a weary sigh. 'I know you try your best, Wei Ming. I think I have made a mistake. I tried to choose your path for you. Like your father. Like my father for me. I did the same thing they did and forgot you have your own dreams too.'

I kept silent, letting it all sink in. All I had wanted eight years ago was to get away from my father, the person who stood in my way of wanting to learn more than just making laksa, to be a real chef like my grandfather. All Ah Hock ever did was criticise, making sure I knew I wasn't good enough. I would never be good enough.

When Sensei handed over the reins of Haruto to me a year ago, I'd felt a surge of happiness and anxiety. I'd taken the reins like an actor takes a role, performed as best as I could, never missing a line. I was sure I was doing well, until I lost the star. The Guild critics knew after all – that I wasn't a real chef, just someone pretending to be one.

*

The speedboat Sensei had chartered was a medium-sized boat that could seat up to eight passengers. They didn't have anything smaller, he said.

When we were on the water, Sensei steered the boat like an expert. I could taste the salt in the air while seagulls cawed above us in the cloudless sky. We didn't go very far before Sensei turned off the engine. My stomach was growling and I took out a paper bag. I'd grabbed a butter bun from a bakery near my flat since I hadn't had time for breakfast. I took a bite and chewed. It was a little plain. Sensei looked at me.

'Put away the bun. I have something better.' He opened the cooler box and took out two round, wooden bento boxes that looked like dim sum baskets.

'It's still warm, try it. I made it this morning.' He passed one of the bento boxes to me.

'What is it, Sensei?' I lifted the lid. The aroma of the cedar-scented rice hit me before I saw the dish. An array of colours decorated the bento. Coral-pink salmon, light brown anago, glistening oyster and morsels of chicken, with shiny orange orbs of salmon roe scattered all over the lightly steamed seafood resting on a bed of koshihikari rice.

'This is wappa meshi, rice cooked in magewappa. This is a container made of sugi – cedar wood, the same wood used to make sake barrels. It is food from my home town, a flavour I have brought back with me. In Niigata, I can get the freshest wild salmon. It would taste better. When I miss home, I make this.' He gave me a wistful smile as he passed me a pair of wooden chopsticks.

I ate a spoonful of rice and bit into the salmon roe, its salty creaminess bursting in my mouth. The chicken and anago, like the rice, were scented with cedar, their fragrance complementing the harmony of oyster and salmon.

'How is it?' Sensei asked. I nodded and gave him a thumbs up. My mouth was busy trying to comprehend the orchestral mix of flavours. I must have looked like a hungry animal as I shoved rice and ikura into my mouth with barely a pause in between.

'What do you think of selling wappa meshi? Will people like it?'

'They will love it,' I said. 'This is comfort food. Like something a mother would make.'

He nodded. 'Exactly, that is why I love it. I think going back to Niigata has reminded me of how much I miss the food of my home town. Finish it, there's more. Better than your bun, I am sure.'

'I'd bought it to fill my stomach,' I said. 'I didn't look, just grabbed something and paid for it.'

'Fill stomachs,' Sensei said, nodding. 'What a pity if that's all food is for.'

*

After we ate, Sensei took the fishing rods and baited them. He passed one to me then cast his own rod into the sea. The line floated gracefully and soared until it landed with a gentle drop in the water, making the slightest of ripples. There were no instructions from Sensei. Fishing was a skill I had never picked up from him. I tried to imitate his cast but ended up with clumsy movements and was lucky I didn't get my line tangled up in his.

We stood there for at least half an hour, not speaking, although Sensei occasionally threw an encouraging glance my way. Standing there motionless for so long reminded me of Ah Hock when he was salting the broth, standing there until it was ready.

A sharp jerk on Sensei's fishing line pulled him to his feet. The rod flexed as he calmly raised and relaxed it intermittently, gradually reeling the fish in. Soon, a medium-sized mackerel appeared, twisting and turning its iridescent green-blue body, its silvery tail glinting in the sun.

Sensei unhooked the fish in one swift movement and passed it to me. Ikejime was something I wasn't keen on doing, even after all these years. It improved the taste, because of the slowing down of rigor mortis after the death of the fish. The flesh would not then harden so quickly and would have a better texture. Best of all, the fish suffered less this way.

I stabbed the middle of the fish's head above its eyes with a T-shaped tool with a sharp point, twisting it in its brain. After draining the fish of blood, I rested it on a bed of ice in Sensei's cooler.

'Nice mackerel,' I said. 'Good size.'

'Yes, we will make good sushi later. But I hope we catch suzuki too. Or marbled sole, or flounder.'

I looked at my unmoving line. 'Nothing's biting on mine.'

'Something will,' Sensei said. 'Patience. This is what it's about. Waiting.'

'Maybe that's why I don't like fishing.'

Sensei gazed into the horizon. 'It's not a question of whether you like it or not. It teaches patience. And for a shokunin, patience is the essence of your soul. But I do enjoy it now. Even the waiting. The quiet.'

It wasn't long before my line had a sudden jerk as well. I called out for Sensei to help, not wanting to lose the fish. He took the rod and, as before, gradually and persistently reeled in the fish. If I had struggled and tussled, it might have broken free. But not Sensei. In mid-air, the silver scales of the fish gleamed, the sunlight reflecting off them.

'Suzuki!' Sensei couldn't contain his excitement, laughing as he landed the fish before stabbing it in the brain. 'A bit small, but I'm happy. You bring luck to the boat,' he said. 'I tried to catch suzuki in my last few fishing trips, but no success. Thank you.'

'You're the one who caught the fish,' I said. 'If I had tried, the fish would have escaped.'

'The waiting, the patience to hold the fishing rod, that is part of the process. Do not underestimate preparation. It is the same in cooking. And in life.' Sensei looked at the two fish on the ice, grinning broadly. 'I am excited thinking about the delicious sushi we can make with them.'

We stayed on the boat for two more hours, during which Sensei caught another mackerel and I managed, with his help, to land a turbot. The diamond-shaped flatfish, black-brown with speckles, pleased him greatly. At the end of the trip, we had six fish in our haul, enough for the two sittings that evening.

After we left the boat at the pier, I tried to hail a taxi but Sensei beckoned me to a diner nearby. It was a little dingy, but the roast goose and hunks of barbecued pork hanging on hooks in the window looked inviting. Inside, we sat in one of the available booths.

When Sensei disappeared to the toilet at the back of the diner, I slipped open the note I'd written earlier.

Dear Sensei,

I have failed you. I am not the person you thought I was. Thank you for being the best teacher a student could have. I do not deserve your kindness and your wisdom. I will be going back to my home town and I do not know when I will return. Nothing I say here will make up for everything I have done wrong, but I hope one day you will forgive the mistakes of your foolish student.

Lim Wei Ming

The least I could do was to give him a heads-up before the first sitting tomorrow. We had four sittings. News must have spread that Sensei was back. I couldn't think about that now – leaving him to do so much work without my help – but I was sure Takashi would be able to manage. It was too late to worry about them hating me.

I folded the letter and put it back into its envelope with the pressed ajisai Sensei had given me. I didn't deserve something Sensei had made with so much care and attention.

I deftly slipped the envelope into his satchel before he came back and ordered roast goose with rice for the both of us. Our order arrived barely two minutes later. The skin was slightly crispy and glistening with oil, the flesh tender and firm. It was full of flavour, moist, and went so well with the fluffy white rice. Even the blanched kai lan, though plain, complemented our meal perfectly, providing a balance for the heavy red meat. It brought me back to those long days at Kowloon Palace, when I'd finally sit down to my dinner at eleven p.m., and see that the staff meal was Jiayi's roast goose and rice. The sheer joy of chewing on the fat, juicy meat and wolfing down bowls of hot steaming rice was a memory I would cherish forever.

'There is an excellent balance of flavours in the meat. You can taste it? So many spices, yet not too much burden on the taste buds,' Sensei said as he ate.

I had learned so much from this man. The prospect of him

not forgiving me when he found out what I'd done made it hard to swallow the succulent meat.

'I am truly grateful to you, Sensei,' I said, my eyes misting over as I spoke.

He laughed and patted my shoulder. 'The roast goose is that good? I agree. Manzoku.' He wiped his mouth with a serviette, looking like a man who had found the love of his life.

PART TWO

16

Kopitiam Blues

It was noon when I arrived at Carpenter Street. Customers were fighting for parking spaces, the queue of vehicles inched forward on the narrow street. Memories of all the good food there came flooding back. The old shophouses, the earthy smells of spice and herbs. Smoky pork satay grilling on charcoal, fish ball noodle soup simmering in tin pots. It was nice to see the old shops hadn't changed much, apart from the tinsmith next to Teck Boon kopitiam which seemed to be a place called 'The Good Luck Café' now.

The taxi dropped me right in front of the kopitiam. Ah Hock was at the stall, as if he hadn't moved from where I'd left him eight years ago. Everything looked the same, except Ah Hock's hair was mostly white now.

I paid the taxi driver and got out to take my luggage from the car boot. My heart raced as I walked to the stall, pulling my trolley bag behind me. As I stood in front of my father, he didn't look up. 'What you want?' Ah Hock said impatiently in Teochew.

He really didn't see anything else besides the broth and the laksa, did he. Not even his only son. I felt a twinge when I saw how much my father had aged. We could start over. I was older, not wiser, but Sensei had taught me how to exercise restraint. I could try to ignore Ah Hock's snide remarks or shouting.

'I'm back, Pa,' I said in Mandarin. Ma had been the one to encourage me to speak in Mandarin at home instead of Teochew or Hokkien, the lingua franca in Kuching. Even though I could understand them both, I'd never learned to speak any Chinese language apart from Mandarin, due to Ma's insistence. To her, Mandarin was the language of the educated, even if Ah Hock disagreed. '*Teochewnang buay hiau ta teochew uay*, what a shame!' he said time and time again. A Teochew who could not speak the language was an embarrassment.

My father looked up at me and dropped the bowl he was holding. It shattered on the floor, beehoon, egg and chicken now strewn all over the already grimy mosaic tiles. Ma rushed out of the kitchen when she heard the bowl break, then gasped when she saw me. She ran up and hugged me, tears rolling down her cheeks.

'You silly child! Why didn't you tell us what day your flight was?' Her voice was high-pitched and ecstatic.

'I wanted to surprise you.' I blinked back my tears. I was grateful Ma hadn't changed a bit. Seeing her considerably aged would have saddened me, thinking it was because I'd left for Hong Kong. When Ma let go of me, I told her I would clean up the mess on the floor. I stood there awkwardly while Ah Hock regained his composure and continued to fill empty bowls with beehoon.

'Why are you back? Lost your job?' Ah Hock said.

Ah, the old man was back. I'd expected the stinging remarks. There wouldn't be a red carpet rolled out for me after how I had left them. Though Ah Hock would say abandoned. Eight years. Eight years of words unsaid.

'Old man! I asked your son to come back for your sixtieth birthday. You see how filial he is?' Ma ruffled my hair.

'I'm taking a break. It's been a long time,' I mumbled, trying to downplay what she'd said. The last thing I needed was Ah Hock thinking I was such a good son, when I wasn't.

Ah Hock snorted. 'A break. I haven't taken a break in forty years.'

New customers were entering the kopitiam. I moved my trolley bag out of their way. 'I'm getting a mop.'

'No, no, before that, come and offer your respects to Grandfather. Come.' Ma pushed me towards the altar. She lit joss sticks and passed them to me. I bowed before my grandfather, and put the joss sticks in the brass urn. I looked at my grandfather's framed photo at the altar and whispered, 'I'm back, Ah Kong.'

The great Lim Teck Boon, the kopitiam's namesake. His shadow loomed over the kopitiam, reminding me, and even Ah Hock, that we weren't worthy of his legacy. My grandfather's expression was stern in the photo, as if admonishing me. The man I'd wanted to emulate, the famous chef in Swatow. I whispered a prayer, asking Ah Kong to help me realise my dream.

'What did you say?' Ma asked.

'I asked him to make sure his son behaves himself,' I said, and Ma slapped me on the arm playfully.

'Don't be cheeky! I don't think it'll work though. Even the gods don't know what to do with your father.' Ma sighed. I patted her back, then went to the kitchen to get a mop. The white tiles on the wall where the stove was had browned, but the floor was the same light green tile I remembered. The most unchanging of all was the sacred ancestral broth simmering on the charcoal stove in a corner of the kitchen. My inheritance. *Carry it on, do not break the chain, do not break this family* – the mantra Teck Boon had passed down to Ah Hock, drummed into my head as I endured Ah Hock's scolding in the kopitiam. It was not a broth made with love. Only duty and filial piety and responsibility.

I went back to the stall to clean up the spilled laksa on the floor and took orders from the customers who had just sat down at tables. Ah Hock was about to say something, but Ma squeezed his arm and shook her head.

I gave the customers' orders to my father, who nodded without a word and began preparing the bowls. Customers kept coming in but there were always tables available. I guess business had slowed. Lunchtimes in the past would have had customers forming a queue outside the kopitiam.

As I gave Ma the drink orders, I quietly asked her how business was.

She shook her head. 'Not as good as before. Even before Towkay Lau decided to open a laksa shop, and you know how people like new places.'

So that's who the café belonged to. 'What happened to the tinsmith?'

'The tinsmith closed. I guess they must have sold or rented their shop to Towkay Lau. There's a young cook there, Billy. Towkay Lau has been pestering your father to open branches, but he keeps saying no. Says it'll cheapen the laksa.'

'It'd be hard to manage branches, for sure. The problem is quality control.'

'I don't know why Towkay Lau is so persistent. And now he's opening his own shop. And with such a young cook too! I don't know why people eat there. But Towkay Lau could be right. Do young people these days prefer modern kopitiams?'

'Maybe.' I wasn't sure what to make of the competition. Towkay Lau had a reputation for making sound financial decisions. His wealth was evidence of his business acumen. It was odd to open a laksa shop right next door, unless it was to pressure Ah Hock into giving in and becoming his business partner.

But Ah Hock was as stubborn as they came. I couldn't imagine him buckling under pressure. He would live and die in this shop, unchanging. The sooner people realised that, the better. Why else would I have left for Hong Kong all those years ago? Things moved around or away from Ah Hock, who stayed rooted in the same spot even if it was bad for him.

'Pass these prawns to your father.' Ma handed me a bowl of freshly peeled prawns. I took them and walked back to the laksa stall, where I reached for the almost-empty container of shelled prawns and promptly refilled it. Ah Hock assembled two bowls of laksa, putting in all the ingredients except for beansprouts. The request from the two ladies sitting at table five. I was surprised Ah Hock hadn't said much about the customisation. Usually he wouldn't allow changes or would at least kick up a big fuss before Ma convinced him to comply.

'Table five.' Ah Hock shoved the two bowls into my hands. I served the laksa, then went back to him.

'Pa, I can help you assemble the bowls,' I said.

Ah Hock didn't look up. 'Are you sure? It's been eight years. You've probably forgotten how.'

Be cool, be cool. Don't take the bait. The old man sure was good at dangling it though. 'Of course I remember,' I said in the calmest voice I could muster. Without waiting for his answer, I took an empty bowl and filled it with beehoon. I wouldn't have dreamed of making a move at the stall without Ah Hock's permission eight years ago. I half expected to be shouted at, but Ah Hock said nothing and continued to prepare the other orders. I couldn't help smiling to myself. Things could be different after all.

I relaxed and made small talk with customers. I handled all the requests for variations, giving Ah Hock the orders that required no changes. The mood in the kopitiam became lighter, and people looked like they were staying longer, some even ordering a second bowl from me.

During a short lull, Ma asked me to sit down and have lunch. She took a bowl of laksa from Ah Hock, who muttered something as he gave it to her.

'Come and have laksa, it's been eight years!' She placed the bowl in front of me with a side of calamansi lime and sambal. I took a soup spoon and a pair of chopsticks from the cutlery stand on the table, and mixed a dollop of sambal into my soup. I drank a spoonful of the laksa.

The medley of spices and the depth of flavour consumed me. The taste that told me I was home. I ate a spoonful of beehoon and prawns hungrily. I hadn't realised how ravenous I was. The crunchy, fresh beansprouts – white, plump and pristine. The omelette was moist and neatly julienned, the shredded chicken aromatic and juicy. For a moment, I forgot my anxiety and simply enjoyed my meal. I didn't notice Ah Hock staring at me until I finished the last drop of the soup and wiped my mouth with the tissue paper provided on the table.

'You ate like you just came out of prison,' Ah Hock said, but I knew the old man was happy.

'Still good, Pa.' I gave him a thumbs up. He shrugged and went back to preparing more bowls of laksa. Still the same old Ah Hock. For me, the eight years had been spent in a world that might as well have been a different planet, but for Ah Hock, the only thing that had changed was the colour of his hair.

*

It was two in the afternoon when we sold out of laksa. I took my bag upstairs to my old room. A musty smell greeted me when I opened the wooden door. Everything looked the same as when I'd left it eight years ago. My mini compo was on my desk, a stack of cassettes next to it. Deep Purple, Queen, Led Zeppelin. The bands Dennis, my best friend in school, recommended. I hadn't spoken to Dennis in years. When I'd first gone to Hong Kong, I sent him a few postcards, but we lost touch after the second year. I wondered if he was still working at his parents' kolo mee stall.

My old music magazines had been tidied away in a stack under the desk. The bed was made. Ma probably washed the sheets when they got dusty. The single bed had always been too short for me, but Ah Hock had never been the type to spend money unnecessarily. 'Who asked you to be so tall,' he would say.

I opened the wooden shutter windows, letting the sunlight stream into the room. I looked out the window, down onto Carpenter Street. Now that lunchtime had passed, there were fewer vehicles on the road. The scent of laksa was in the air, as were the delicious smells of broth and satay wafting in from the food court at Lau Ya Keng.

The street felt both foreign and familiar. I was home but I felt empty, and that emptiness was beginning to fill me with alarm. My future was darkness. What was I supposed to do here? I was back where I'd started.

I unpacked my bag and laid out my clothes on the bed. I opened the wardrobe and saw some of my old clothes, worn when I was a teenager, in a neat pile. The bag of masu joinery parts took its place on the desk next to the mini compo. I put the yokan next to the cassettes and reminded myself to give it to Ma later.

I lay on my bed and stared at the ceiling. The familiarity of the bed I'd slept in for twenty-seven years comforted me. I was both glad and scared that the kopitiam had remained the same. What if I couldn't afford to leave? The rest of the world felt closed off to me, at least for now. The feeling I'd had growing up in Kuching, like I was trapped and could only resign myself to living out the rest of my life here, was coming back to me now.

Dennis had always been comfortable in Kuching. He had never yearned to be elsewhere like I had. I never understood how he could fit in with the other kids who came from rich and well-connected families. I had found a kind of solidarity with Dennis because we were both sons of noodle hawkers, but only I was teased for it in school.

Those obnoxious children had nauseated me. How I'd hated going to school with those spoilt brats. They would call me the laksa seller's son, ask me if I knew the recipe for my father's magic broth. Whether I liked to sweat over boiling pots and wash dirty bowls. They knew how grumpy Ah Hock was and teased me about my father's temper. 'You're going to cook laksa for the rest of your life in that old kopitiam, so why bother coming to school?' they'd jeer. They didn't tease Dennis as much, even though he too was the son of a hawker. Perhaps it was because he was so good-natured. He didn't see it as teasing at all, when they said he would be cooking kolo mee forever at his father's stall. It was a reality he accepted – even enjoyed. 'So what if my family sells noodles,' Dennis would say. 'It's the best kolo mee in town!'

Every year the class was made to pick their top three career choices and I would always put 'chef' as my first choice. 'My grandfather was a famous chef in China,' I would say proudly to the class teacher. 'I want to follow in his footsteps someday.' Even though my teacher nodded her approval, a few of the boys would laugh and mutter among themselves. 'Yeah right, selling noodles more like it.' 'Chef? You mean dishwasher!'

One of those brats had come to the kopitiam when I was ten years old. His name was Jason and he was picked up from school in a chauffeured black Mercedes-Benz with tinted windows. Whenever we had Jog-A-Thon cards to fill up with donations, Jason would ask his parents to donate two hundred ringgit so he wouldn't have to ask anyone else. He was the one who kept wearing expensive Nike sneakers until the school set a policy that only white canvas shoes were to be worn. One Sunday morning, Jason came to the kopitiam with his mother, a tall, thin woman with voluminous black curly hair, blood-red lips, and sunglasses she never took off during their meal.

I was helping Ah Hock to serve bowls of laksa to customers. It had been a busy morning and I didn't notice Jason until he yelled my name.

'Look who it is! Lim Wei Ming working hard serving customers! Hey, give me ten bowls of laksa and I want you to carry all of them at once!' Jason said with a loud guffaw.

'Is that your friend?' Jason's mother lowered her sunglasses to peer at me.

'He's from my class. Hey, Wei Ming, how about giving us free laksa? We're friends, right?' Jason said.

'We don't do that,' I stammered, then kicked myself inwardly for dignifying Jason's remark with a response.

'Come on, you can ask daddy. Hey!' Jason called out to Ah Hock while I gesticulated wildly for him to stop. As I hurried over to him, I dropped the two laksa bowls I was carrying, and they fell to the floor with a loud crash, hot soup scalding my legs.

I touched my legs instinctively now, recollecting the searing pain on my skin. I'd screamed while Jason laughed. Ah Hock came to see what the commotion was about and saw the broken bowls and beehoon scattered all over the floor.

'You stupid boy! I can't even trust you to carry two bowls of laksa! What a waste! The soup was good today too!' he shouted, then called for Ma to clean up the mess, not noticing the burns on my skin.

As I writhed in pain on the floor, comforted by Ma, who put a cold towel on my burns and picked up the broken pieces of pottery, I could hear Jason saying to his mother, 'Let's go to an air-conditioned restaurant, Mummy. It's so hot and dirty here.'

I didn't look up as Jason and his mother were leaving. All I saw were the boy's brand-new trainers and his mother's shiny red leather stiletto heels walking away from the kopitiam.

I closed my eyes at the memory. I hadn't seen Jason since we left school. I hoped he was abroad. His laughter still rang in my head after all these years. Maybe he'd been right all along.

17

The Spring Breeze that Nurtures Rain

Ah Hock woke up to the smell of laksa soup wafting into the bedroom. He had never been woken up that way before. Was he in yet another dream?

He looked at Kim Choo, sleeping soundly next to him. It couldn't be an intruder cooking laksa in the kitchen. A ghost? For a moment he thought Teck Boon had returned to the kopitiam to chastise him for the quality of the laksa soup.

Oh, the boy! He laughed quietly, thinking what a foolish old man he was. He had forgotten Wei Ming was back. But up before him? Unheard of. Perhaps the boy had grown up after all.

Ah Hock brushed his teeth and washed his face, then changed into his usual white singlet and shorts before going down the stairs. How would Wei Ming have known what spices to use?

Ah Hock entered the kitchen. As he peered over Wei Ming's shoulder at the bubbling pot, the boy dropped his spoon into the soup.

'You startled me.' Wei Ming blushed as he tried to fish the spoon out with a pair of chopsticks.

'What are you doing in here?' Ah Hock asked. The laksa soup was a lighter shade of orange and lacked something. He took a whiff. Likely the boy had used ginger instead of galangal. Not enough dried chilli. Probably hadn't used cumin seeds. And definitely not enough tamarind.

'Trying to help,' Wei Ming said, not looking at him. 'I prepared all the toppings already. Now trying to make the soup.'

'You don't know how to make the paste. How to help?'

'I'm figuring it out.' Wei Ming added salt to the laksa soup, then tasted it.

'It is important to use good salt, or the taste will be different. Back in Swatow, your Ah Kong used sea salt that people had been harvesting for a thousand years. But here, he used mountain salt instead.' Ah Hock rubbed grains of bario salt between his fingers. 'Someday, I hope to go back to Swatow, see how different the salt is.'

'Why haven't you gone back?'

Good question. Ah Hock didn't know why. Teck Boon himself had never mentioned going back for a visit. Perhaps he'd had less of reason to do so, compared to Ah Hock, who sometimes wondered where their village was and whether they still had any relatives there he could meet, especially on his mother's side. 'And who would look after the shop and the broth when I go? You?'

'I can. If I stay,' Wei Ming said non-committally. Ah Hock looked at him. Was the boy serious? He was always spouting nonsense.

'What do you mean, if you stay? Don't you have your fancy chef job in Hong Kong? Did you get fired?'

'No,' Wei Ming said. 'I . . . I can take time off. If you really

144

want to go. You've never left Kuching. Take Ma with you. You can have a holiday.'

Ah Hock laughed. A holiday! Kim Choo would be ecstatic. Why hadn't he thought of this before? But how would he be able to leave Wei Ming in charge without worrying? A pipe dream. The boy was full of them, and now he was infecting Ah Hock too.

'We use sea salt at the restaurant,' Wei Ming said.

'You use salt there? Don't you just slice raw fish?'

'I've learned a lot more than that.' Wei Ming rolled his eyes.

Ah Hock grunted. *Works in some Japanese restaurant and thinks he's a master chef.* How could he teach the boy when he wasn't humble enough to learn?

'What kind of salt do you use?'

'Moshio. It's seaweed salt – salt that also has the taste of seaweed.'

Seaweed-infused salt. It did sound intriguing. Imagine salting the flatfish with it! It would add another layer of flavour to the broth for sure.

'You didn't bring any of it back, did you?' Ah Hock asked.

Wei Ming shook his head. 'I can, next time.'

The boy really had grown. Ah Hock had never imagined he would be in conversation with Wei Ming about the differences in salt. More likely the boy would say, salt is salt, it's all the same. But Ah Hock knew it was not all the same. It seemed that now Wei Ming did too.

The boy was ready to learn. Whether he would retain the knowledge Ah Hock imparted to him was another matter.

Ah Hock bent over to gather the ingredients he needed from the sacks of spices near the kitchen cabinet. 'My laksa paste has the usual ingredients, write it down if you cannot remember. But to be masterful, you must remember it as well as you remember to eat, shit and sleep.'

The holy trinity of aromatics – shallots, garlic and ginger. Then a cousin of the ginger, galangal with its sweet, peppery flavour. Seeds – fennel, cumin, coriander, sesame, cardamom. Cloves, nutmeg and star anise, the spices that infused laksa with fragrance. Candlenuts and peanuts gave it a vital earthiness. Dried red chillies and tamarind for heat and tanginess. All these were vital for the many-layered taste of their laksa.

It didn't take long for Ah Hock to lay out all the spices on the kitchen counter before cutting, pounding and mixing them for the paste.

'Things may look the same, but they taste very different. Like these two,' Ah Hock said, holding the galangal and ginger for Wei Ming to see. 'Both look like ginger, but the taste, it's like comparing heaven and earth. The galangal is more complex in flavour, more citrusy, peppery, whereas ginger is lighter, mildly sweet, and spicy. But both are essential to making the laksa paste.'

Wei Ming took the galangal from Ah Hock and smelled it. 'Yeah, I haven't worked much with galangal. More familiar with ginger. We use that a lot to make gari. Pickled ginger you eat with sushi to cleanse the palate. It's easy to make, but we must use the right salt, the right rice vinegar. My master is particular about his ingredients too.'

As Wei Ming explained how to make the vinegared ginger, Ah Hock listened, intrigued. The boy sounded like he knew what he was doing. He was already thirty-five, after all. No longer a boy. It looked like he had found the right teacher.

Ah Hock put the paste he had pounded in a bowl, then asked Wei Ming to smell it. 'The secret to good laksa is not merely its ingredients, but how much you put in. I cannot tell you how. I don't measure them, it is something my senses tell me. So you need to watch me and taste it yourself, feel each ingredient yourself, know each ingredient so well that you'll know how much is needed to make good laksa soup. Develop an instinct from practising. I watched my father. I learned. I did not complain. I did the same thing every day. That is how you make good laksa.'

The boy was lucky Ah Hock was willing to explain the obvious. His own father had said very little and questions asked would be answered harshly or with a cane. One was expected to know through observation. He hoped Wei Ming would be appreciative of the concessions made for him.

'There is no short cut, there is no magic trick,' Ah Hock continued. 'Consistency is the key. Improve the laksa, and you'll look forward to waking up and being better at it each day. But there's no use talking so much. All there is to learn, you have seen. Or perhaps you haven't looked properly.'

'How could I have learned anything when you didn't even let me touch the ladle?' Wei Ming said. Ah Hock was about to retort, then stopped himself. It was true, after all. Kim Choo was right. He had been too protective of the broth, hadn't trusted Wei Ming with it. People did learn from mistakes. Ah Hock himself had made a few, and Teck Boon never let him forget them.

'Do you want to taste this?' Wei Ming asked, ladling the laksa soup he had been cooking into a bowl. Ah Hock was apprehensive, but he took the bowl from Wei Ming. He sipped from it, then spat it out on the floor. He didn't know what it was, but it wasn't laksa soup. It was like a fruit with its insides hollowed out, none of its sweetness remaining.

Wei Ming frowned as he wiped the floor with a dishcloth.

'It can't be that bad,' he said. 'I didn't use the broth. Is that why? What does it lack?'

'Everything.' Ah Hock took the wok, oiled it, and began to roast the laksa paste he had just made. 'Throw yours away.'

'Don't be crazy. I don't want to waste it,' Wei Ming tutted.

This was why Ah Hock found it hard to teach the boy. If Ah Hock had spoken like that to Teck Boon, his father would have responded with a backhander.

'If you didn't use the broth, you haven't wasted anything. Here, continue turning the paste, make sure it doesn't burn,' Ah Hock said. Wei Ming took the ladle from him and turned the paste over and over. It was tedious and delicate work. Too quick, and the paste would not be ready. Too long, and the paste would be burnt and binned.

Ah Hock took another soup pot and added fresh chicken bones and ladlefuls of the broth. The smell of the paste permeated the kopitiam, its spiciness overpowering Ah Hock's nostrils. He coughed. Now it smelled like all the spices were in harmony. Everything in its place, the galangal and cumin in a warm embrace, the candlenuts tempering the fierceness of the chilli.

'It's done. Add it into this pot,' Ah Hock instructed. Wei Ming coughed, then took it off the charcoal fire and scraped the freshly made laksa paste into the pot of boiling soup. They watched it simmer for thirty minutes, with Ah Hock tasting it, nodding and shaking his head until he declared: 'It's ready.'

Wei Ming tasted a spoonful of the laksa soup. 'Wow,' he said with a soft gasp. He tasted another spoon and nodded vigorously. 'There's so much depth. Everything's there, the cumin, the cardamom, star anise, ginger—'

'You see now why I spat yours out.'

'You didn't have to exaggerate how bad it was, but this

is definitely what the soup's supposed to taste like. Maybe I didn't put in enough ginger. Or galangal.'

'Doesn't matter. Don't overthink. Taste it and you'll know. Practise. Nothing else works except practice. Now we need coconut milk.' Ah Hock gestured to the hairy brown fruit on the floor in the kitchen corner.

Wei Ming took a few coconuts and cracked them in half with the back of a cleaver. With a grater, he had all the coconut milk they needed in ten minutes. Ah Hock took the bowl of white, rich liquid from Wei Ming and added it to the stockpot. Traces of white swirled around the grey soup tinged with chilli red. After a few minutes, Ah Hock turned off the stove and looked at Wei Ming.

'You see the colour? Now it's ready. Take it out,' Ah Hock said. Wei Ming carried the heavy soup pot to the laksa stall and inserted it into the opening in the counter. Then he stood at the stall and assembled bowls of laksa while Ah Hock sat and observed him. A few of the regulars came and were happy to see Wei Ming. With the customers, Wei Ming was cheerful, chatting with them, tossing the beehoon in the air and making them laugh.

Ah Hock almost laughed himself. He had thought the boy had grown up but there he was, clowning around. The customers liked it. Ah Hock preferred them to focus on enjoying the food though. Watching the boy doing silly tricks, wouldn't the customers be too distracted? They were here for good laksa, not a show. If that was what they wanted, they could walk across the street to Lau Ya Keng.

18

The Best Kolo Mee in Town

I drove my father's white Kancil to 3rd Mile, where Dennis's parents had their stall. It was another area with trade and food, with rows of shophouses selling everything from noodles to fresh fish, spare car parts to household sundries. It had been another world for me as a teenager, but a neighbourhood in which I was comfortable because it was Dennis's world. I smiled when I reminisced about my happy moments there, when on hot days we would walk over to get sundae cones at the nearby ice cream parlour, the perennial Sunny Hill, which had been a fixture in 3rd Mile since I was a child.

We had been inseparable in school, even though Dennis was the popular one. Dennis had a way with people, a charisma that made him instantly likeable. I never knew why he chose to be best friends with me. He had his pick of the cooler, richer, more popular boys whose chauffeurs picked them up in BMW and Mercedes-Benz cars while I took the bus home.

Dennis had looked like any other of my classmates, he wasn't particularly handsome or anything, but his sister Alice's friends had showered attention on him every time the siblings waited to be picked up after school. He had short, straight hair he kept well combed, small eyes and a flat nose, and a smile so friendly that he looked happy all the time, even when he wasn't. He had a good sense of humour, and among the chatter that surrounded him there would often be someone breaking into uproarious laughter.

It was Alice who'd had the good looks, with her long eye-lashes, full lips, and thick black hair in a neat ponytail. Her faraway dark brown eyes lent her an air of mystery. An ethereal beauty, like one of the seven fairy maidens, a daughter of the Jade Emperor, instead of a Form Five student with back-to-back tuition classes.

She floated from school to tuition then upstairs to her room, the only place she found rest from weary school life – a brief respite from the burden of being the beauty and the brains in the family. She had always been top of her class, from primary school to secondary school. Her parents had high hopes for her; with her academic prowess she could be a doctor, a lawyer, an engineer, anything she wanted. She was an all-rounder, representing the school in tennis and playing the piano during the annual school concert. In short, she was every parent's perfect child.

I seldom spoke to Alice, despite the amount of time I spent at Dennis's house. A raised eyebrow and one second of eye contact were all we exchanged if she was at home when I visited. Though there was one night when there was a storm and Mrs Tan asked me to stay until the rains subsided. Alice came downstairs to the living room to join Dennis and me watching a late-night comedy. She was in her nightgown, sleeveless and white with blue flowers. She sat so close to me I could smell peaches and baby powder, and whenever she laughed she would turn to me.

That night when I got home, I'd made a mixtape for her. I was relieved I'd never given it to her. She would've thought

I was gross, her older brother's friend hitting on her. Either way, nothing would have come of it. She was focused on her studies and had gone on to study abroad. Probably stayed on to work too. Must be married with kids by now. Someone like her wouldn't stay single for long. I felt a pang of envy for the man who was lucky enough to have her.

*

The kopitiam where Dennis's parents had their kolo mee stall was bigger than Teck Boon kopitiam. It housed five stalls, all selling different types of food. There was Dennis's parents' kolo mee, and four other stalls, selling laksa, fresh popiah, char kueh and belachan beehoon. It was two in the afternoon but the bustle at the kopitiam showed no signs of slowing down. Dennis was engrossed in taking orders from customers, his mother carrying a big container of soft-skinned pork dumplings over to his father, who was busy assembling bowls of kolo mee. My old friend had gained weight around his middle and a double chin, but he was the same old Dennis.

I found an empty table after a couple had left. I sat and ordered a glass of iced milk tea. It could not compare to Ma's signature tea – no other shops made such a comforting drink. But it was a hot day, so I gulped it down. It took Dennis a few minutes to spot me from the stall. He rubbed his eyes and blinked a few times before hurrying over to me. I stood up awkwardly and smiled.

'Man! Are you a ghost or what?' Dennis said. I laughed and held out my hand. 'What is this? I haven't seen you for, what, eight years? Give me a hug!' Dennis hugged me hard. 'I can't believe you're back!'

We spoke in English, although Dennis was more comfortable in Hokkien and spoke to his parents and other friends in it. 'Bugger! Should've called me at least. I haven't spoken to you in a long time. Thought you forgot about Kuching already. Man, I can't believe it. Let me pinch you to see if you're real.'

I laughed and pushed him away. 'How are you, man? Married already? Got a bunch of kids at home or something?'

'No-lah. So busy, where got time for girls. You?'

'Not married,' I said wryly.

'No wife and kids back in Hong Kong, ah? You back for a holiday?'

'Something like that.'

'Eh, we're standing here talking, let me get you a bowl of kolo mee. You haven't tasted kolo mee in years, you might die from happiness after eating it.' Dennis went back to the stall to get a bowl of noodles.

Like laksa, kolo mee was a dish that required a delicate balance of flavours. It was a simple dish – dry, curly egg noodles tossed in a seasoned lard sauce, and garnished with minced pork and slices of red roast pork, and a few stalks of leafy choy sum. If a bowl of laksa was as good as its soup, then a good bowl of kolo mee needed the right sauce. Not every kolo mee stall had pork dumplings, or kiau, and I loved the ones Aunty Tan made.

Dennis walked over with Uncle Tan, who was holding a bowl of kolo mee with a sprinkle of minced pork and a bowl of steaming hot clear soup with dumplings to my table. I helped to remove the bowls from the tray Uncle Tan was carrying and greeted him.

Uncle Tan patted my back. 'It's good to see you back, Wei Ming! How are your parents?' he asked in Mandarin. He was grinning, like he usually was, even if there were customers lining up and rattling off all types of preferences for their noodles. They were happy to wait, appeased by his joviality and tendency to chat at length as he prepared their noodles. He wore a clean, white apron over a light blue T-shirt and khaki Bermuda shorts, and never looked messy or dirty despite the greasiness of the food he was preparing.

'They're okay, thank you for asking, Uncle.'

'Your father all right?' he asked with a knowing chuckle as he walked back to his stall. Our parents had never exchanged more than a few words on the rare occasions they met. Ma would make a small effort with Aunty and Uncle Tan, asking them how business was and discussing the rising prices of fresh produce at the wet market.

Dennis pulled up a chair next to mine and nudged me. 'Eh, eat it before it's cold.'

I picked up a dumpling from the steaming hot soup and blew on it before putting it into my mouth. No one else made dumplings with skin so soft it melted on my tongue. The minced pork did not have a hint of gaminess, only a well-seasoned sweetness, the perfect marriage of salt and Sarawak black pepper. There was so much flavour in one small dumpling. I put a few more dumplings on my kolo mee to cool them down before shoving the tasty noodles into my mouth with chopsticks.

'I love the kiau your mother makes. Feels like I'm in heaven.'

'Oh yeah, the kiau, that's true – that's the crowd-pleaser. I tell my father, you better appreciate this woman, not only does she put up with your snoring and smelly feet, if not for her kiau, your kolo mee would be nothing special, like any other kolo mee stall.'

I envied the easy relationship Dennis had with his father. Uncle Tan never scowled when he was overwhelmed by orders or rude customers. He was the opposite of the Belview Road chicken rice uncle and my father. Uncle Tan let people buy as much food as they wanted, and tried to accommodate the customisation they preferred. Some wanted extra fried pork mince, some did not want any. Some wanted roast pork and extra kiau. Others wanted their kolo mee kosong – with nothing at all – or only with dumplings.

'Aren't you eating? I don't want to eat alone.'

'I think I'll order char kueh. Want to share or not?'

'Sure. Order both sweet and salty.'

There were two types of the wok-fried radish cake, made with grated white radish mixed with rice flour. The sweet one was fried with dark, caramel soy sauce and the salty one was fried with chai poh, salty preserved radish, and eggs, and I loved them both.

Dennis came back with two plates of char kueh, steam rising from them. A young woman I'd never seen before was frying the char kueh that day, expertly tossing pieces of radish cake while sprinkling soy sauce and fish sauce over them.

'Where's the aunty?' I asked. The familiar plump middle-aged woman who sold the char kueh was not there.

'Aunty Joy is not well these days. That's her daughter.' Dennis used his chopsticks to pick up cubes of char kueh from both plates. 'Not like Aunty's, but okay-lah. Pass.'

I reached over with my chopsticks and sampled the two different types of char kueh. 'So different! Hers has no taste! You probably like it because you like her, eh?' I nudged Dennis, who coughed as he nearly choked on the char kueh.

'Don't be crazy,' he said. 'It's not that bad.'

'Luckily you're the one who paid for this. I might have asked for my money back.'

'You're starting to sound like your father,' he said with a snigger.

'My father doesn't even come to this kopitiam. At least I'm willing to give it a try.'

'So you're back to take over your father's kopitiam or what?'

'I don't know. Things are complicated. Lots of stuff happened in Hong Kong. I'm taking a break.'

'What did you do there, man? Police looking for you or what?'

'No.' I wanted to tell Dennis everything that had happened, but I didn't know where to begin.

'If not police, then who? Gangsters?'

'Forget it, I don't want to talk about it.'

'Then what are your plans here?'

'I'm not sure yet. Help my parents out for a while, I guess.'

'Didn't you always say you wanted your own restaurant? Stay here-lah. Can buy one here, cheap cheap. By now you must've saved up enough, right?'

I thought of my near-empty bank account and gave Dennis a weak smile. I finished the last of my noodles, leaving nothing but the vestiges of oil in the bowl. I changed the subject and asked him if he kept in touch with former schoolmates. We reminisced about our teenage years, experimenting with cooking in his kitchen during the school holidays, until Aunty Tan came over to say hello. I tried to pay her for the noodles, and when she refused to take my money, I stuffed the notes into Dennis's shirt pocket. He grinned. 'Speaking of experimenting,' he said, 'wanna come over to my house? Let's cook up a storm, like the old times.'

The old times. That sounded good to me.

19

Ayam Pansoh

Dennis's family home was a suburban neighbourhood at 3rd Mile, one of the many terrace houses there. It was a small house but had a garden where they grew their own pandan leaves, lemongrass, onions, chillies and brinjals, alongside purple petunias and white and pink orchids. Large pots of purple paper-petalled bougainvillea and red ixora lined the fence around the house.

Inside, the furniture was simple and neat – rattan-framed sofas with comfortable, flowery cushions, a low, wooden coffee table on a colourful red Persian-design rug. Dennis's family had a television in the living room, where we used to watch *America's Top 10* on Saturday nights and episodes of *Knight Rider*, *Magnum P.I.*, *Remington Steele* and *The A-Team*. We loved Hong Kong comedies like *Aces Go Places* and learned some Cantonese from them. But TV was only a distraction for Dennis, whose main interest was experimenting with all sorts of recipes in his kitchen.

The kitchen in Dennis's house was big enough for a small Formica folding table. They had a proper dining room with a large, rectangular marble-topped dining set but I preferred to be in the kitchen, sitting with Dennis at the plastic table while Aunty Tan fried banana fritters or made soft-skinned popiah overflowing with julienned sweet turnip and sliced bean curd mixed in sweet sauce for our after-school snacks.

Whenever I went over to Dennis's house, we would end up making dishes that promised the inclusion of some exotic ingredients or food I'd never heard of before. I didn't know how Dennis could cook only kolo mee at the stall when he had such great ideas at home. These were the times when Dennis would choose the more outrageous recipes to try, dishes I'd never heard of, smells that would offend and excite at the same time.

'What're we making today?' I was excited to explore his culinary brain after eight years.

'You ever had pansoh? Chicken cooked in bamboo?' he asked. I shook my head. 'My parents have a family friend who's Iban, Uncle Danny, and this guy, he has these parties at his bungalow. It's a big place, sure, but he has around twenty relatives staying with him at one time, some permanent, some visiting. That's when I would see things I had never seen before, like bamboo chicken, grilled chicken butts, fried sago worms. Ever had ulat or not?'

I laughed.

'I'm not kidding!' Dennis said. 'Damn good, I tell you. Fat, juicy sago worms fried with chilli and onion.'

'So, we're frying worms today?'

'Nah. My mother would freak out. She didn't like it, but Pa and I ate so much of it at Uncle Danny's house. I managed to get a couple of bamboos from Uncle Danny without Ma knowing. I know she would make a fuss. And, believe it or not, I got daun bungkang. I'm going to make the ultimate bamboo chicken, boy.'

'Never heard of daun bungkang before.'

'It's some leaf that's supposed to flavour the bamboo chicken-lah. Without it, we make normal bamboo chicken, but with it, it's going to be super bamboo chicken. Come help me. You pound some ingredients for me while I cut up the chicken.'

Dennis went to the fridge and took out a whole chicken and a bunch of tapioca leaves. He rummaged through the pantry for shallots, garlic, lemongrass, ginger, and turmeric leaves. The last ingredient was the daun bungkang, from a small plastic bag hidden behind a big Milo tin.

'I didn't want Ma to accidentally use it or throw it away.' Dennis shook the leaves out of the plastic bag. He worked fast, chopping the garlic, shallots and ginger, and smashing stalks of lemongrass with the back of the cleaver before slicing them. He mixed everything in a big mortar and pestle, added a few turmeric leaves, then passed it to me. I helped him pound the ingredients, enjoying the heady smell of the spice bouquet. Dennis had the chicken chopped up into bite-sized pieces in no time and marinated them with salt. After that, he added a bunch of daun bungkang, mixing the chicken and leaves with his hands.

'Put your stuff in here, I want to mix it all up,' Dennis said. I emptied the contents of the pounded ingredients into his mixing bowl and scraped the stone mortar clean. While Dennis continued mixing, I washed the tapioca leaves, plucked them, and put them aside. Dennis went to the backyard and came back with two tubes of bamboo. He rinsed them, then stuffed them with the chicken mixture. He put the chicken into the bamboo piece by piece, then made sure there was enough room to add tapioca leaves at the end. He poured water into the bamboo tubes then put them aside.

I scrutinised his methods, fascinated. Soon there were two tubes of bamboo leaning on the kitchen wall. Dennis did not have formal training as a chef, but he had good instincts.

'Let's cook this!' Dennis's face was flushed with excitement. We went to the backyard, where Dennis started a charcoal fire. 'Ma's going to kill me, so this bamboo chicken better be good,' he said, stoking the fire. He put the two bamboos in the charcoal, tilted, then continued to stoke the fire, making sure it was precisely at medium heat.

I couldn't take my eyes off Dennis, watching how adept he was at manipulating heat without a stove. It was tricky, for sure. Heat makes or breaks a dish. Using charcoal was a skill both Sensei and Ah Hock had insisted I learn. Without charcoal, the ancestral broth would not have its depth of flavour. What made Haruto's tamagoyaki special was its hint of smokiness that could only come with cooking it on charcoal. Dennis seemed at home with charcoal, fanning the fire whenever it got too high and moving the bamboos around so the chicken would not be overcooked.

The heavy meaty aroma of chicken mingled with the fragrant bamboo and tapioca leaves, as well as the pounded garlic, shallot, ginger and turmeric, made me hungry. Dennis took it off the fire after an hour, then put out the flames before we brought the bamboos back into the kitchen. We wrapped them with dishwashing cloths so it would not be too hot to shake out their contents. The chicken pieces and the tapioca leaves came tumbling out with the fragrant soup, into our ready bowls. We left one bowl for Dennis's family, then shared the other.

The soup was laced with a tinge of golden essence from its sweet fat, mixed with greenish hues from the mixture of leaves. The still-firm texture of the tapioca leaves was a good contrast to the chicken that was falling off the bone.

'How? Nice ah?' Dennis slurped his bowl of soup and picked out bones from the chicken he was eating. I nodded and finished the rest of our bowl.

'I've never tasted anything like this before.'

'It's the daun bungkang. It brings out the flavours of the chicken, you know? Uncle Danny said bamboo chicken doesn't taste the same without it. All I know is, it's damn delicious! Can sell or not?'

'Sure! I would buy a bowl.' I couldn't believe all those years growing up in Kuching I'd never tried pansoh before. Such distinct yet delicate flavours, so many layers that required a pause between each one to truly savour them.

'Bring back some.' He ladled the soup, chicken, and tapioca leaves into a small Tupperware, discarding the daun bungkang and pieces of lemongrass. 'I almost forgot!' He rummaged in the fridge and took out a container of dried fish. 'I salted my own terubuk. Better than those you buy at the market.'

I smelled the dried, salty pieces. Terubuk is a herring with many bones, but its flesh is succulent and sweet – rewarding for those who care to pick out its numerous thorns patiently. Salted fish was perfect for kai wei, the process of opening the appetite, teasing the palate. It would go well with Teochew porridge, which was plain and watery, unlike the thicker Cantonese congee.

As Dennis handed the containers of food to me, we heard a car horn outside the house.

'Oh, Alice is back.' Dennis peered out the kitchen window.

I hadn't heard that name in eight years. My heart was pounding and I nearly dropped the containers of food Dennis had given me. I barely had enough time to compose myself before I heard the chirpy voice of a child.

'Mummy! It smells so good!' Then Alice herself, her voice low and alluring. 'Must be Uncle Dennis cooking. Lucky us! Let's go see what the delicious food is.'

Alice entered the kitchen, looking even more captivating than I remembered. Her long black hair cascaded in curls down her shoulders. As a girl, she had been somewhat ethereal, almost fairy-like, but now she looked like a goddess, in her white floral, flowy long dress, red lips and dark brown-lined eyes.

'Wei Ming? Oh my god. You're back!' Alice exclaimed. Her daughter looked up at her.

'Who's this, Mummy?' The little girl was pretty with dark curly hair, pink ribbon clips keeping it neat. Her dark eyes were curious and mischievous. She tugged at Alice's dress.

'Oh, your Uncle Dennis's old friend. Misha, say hello to Uncle Ming.'

I went over and shook her hand. 'Nice to meet you, Misha.' I ruffled her hair. Misha looked annoyed when I did that.

'He messed up my ribbons,' she whined, and Alice laughed.

'Don't be rude, Misha, please say hello.'

'Hello,' Misha said, looking at me shyly. Dennis picked her up and swung her in the air.

'How's my favourite niece? Hungry or not?' he said in Hokkien.

'I don't understand you, Uncle Dennis!' Misha replied in English with a laugh. There was so much happiness in the room. I hadn't pined for Alice in years, although when I'd first arrived in Hong Kong, her face had popped up in my mind whenever I felt lonely.

To see her now with a child made me forlorn, thinking of missed chances.

Dennis switched back to English and said, 'This angmoh kid, ah, Alice, you must teach her some Hokkien-leh. How to be Hokkien-lang if she can't speak Hokkien?'

'She's only half Hokkien,' Alice said, then turned to me. 'It's such a surprise to see you here! Why didn't you tell Dennis you were coming back? Or did you know all along and didn't tell me?' She smacked Dennis's arm.

'Ow! See, always accusing me of something I didn't do. I just saw him for the first time today-lah. He turned up at the stall like a ghost, right Ming?' Dennis rubbed his arm.

'Yes, I'm sorry, I wanted to surprise my parents.'

'You're in Hong Kong now, right?' she said, with what felt like a tinge of envy. 'So great. I wish I could go. I've been trying to get a job there, but it's not easy. So are you working in a restaurant?'

'He's a famous chef, my dear sister!' Dennis slapped me on the back.

I blushed. 'Don't talk nonsense, man.'

'Wow, is it a Chinese restaurant?' she asked.

'I make sushi actually.'

'But didn't Dennis say you went to work in a Chinese restaurant when you left Kuching?'

'Yes, but the work conditions were terrible. I'm so glad I found my master. I owe my life there to him.' I felt dejected again as I contemplated Sensei's reaction to the situation at Haruto.

'Ah, okay. Wow. A sushi chef. I would love to try your sushi one day.' Alice smiled. I could see myself making uni sushi for her. The rich creamy roe – salty and sweet with a hint of seaweed – that melted in the mouth.

'His restaurant is very expensive-lah. Better make sure you can afford it,' Dennis said.

'If I get a job in Hong Kong, I'll definitely treat myself there,' Alice said.

'You should get your husband to pay for a meal there,' I said. I had to be realistic. It wasn't going to be a romantic event.

Alice's expression turned grave, as if I had offended her. 'Let's get you in the bath, eh?' she said to Misha, then hurried her out of the kitchen.

'Did I say something wrong?' I asked Dennis. He shifted uncomfortably.

'Uh, it's a very difficult situation. Her husband died.'

'Oh, I'm sorry, I . . . I didn't know.'

'Nah, man, my fault, I should've mentioned it earlier, but you know, so much to catch up on after eight years!'

'Was he sick?'

'The husband? Worse. He killed himself.'

'What?' I was mortified. There was no way I could have known. Damn it. I should've kept my big mouth shut.

'Yeah. Bloody sad, man. I mean, especially for Misha. She's a great kid. She didn't deserve that.'

'But what happened?'

'They were living in KL. The husband was a successful lawyer, and so was she. My parents complained they worked too hard. I mean it's not like here, so lepak, all laid-back. People here have a work-life balance, they can go home at five-thirty, then go for a run at Reservoir Park. I used to hear about Alice working till midnight in KL. Longer if the clients wanted the contract the next morning. I think Misha spent most of her time with the maid. My mother was so upset. The husband was the same, stressed like hell also. Not sure what happened. They lived in a condo, then one day, you know, he jumped. I don't want to imagine what Alice went through. I know the dude had problems, but I get mad thinking of what he put Alice and Misha through. Anyway—'

'Is that why she's here?'

He nodded. 'Yep. Good place to take a break. She quit her job. I mean, they probably have enough savings for a while. My mother's happy they're here but obviously not about the husband.'

'I feel like such an idiot mentioning him,' I said remorsefully. I had been testing the waters, hoping she would say there wasn't a husband in the picture, but I hadn't expected such devastating news.

'Forget about it.' Dennis tasted the soup from the bamboo chicken again. 'Wow. This is good stuff. This is the kind of food we should be selling in Kuching.'

'You mean you want to open a stall to sell pansoh?'

'I don't know. We could open a restaurant, but I don't have a clear idea of what I want to do. You're the one who's been dreaming of your own place for years. I'll let you steal my recipe.'

I laughed. 'It's okay, I won't. But this is really good. You should sell it at the stall.'

'See how it goes-lah. Kinda funny to sell bamboo chicken and kolo mee together, but you never know, it might work.'

'What smells good in here?' Uncle Tan called from the living room. Aunty Tan came into the kitchen.

'Dennis cooked? Aiyah, the kitchen must be so dirty!'

'Ma, don't worry, I'll clean up and help you fry the vegetables and cook the rice. You rest!' Dennis said.

'You want to have dinner here, Ming?' Aunty Tan asked.

'My mother cooked already. I better go now.' I headed for

the front gate. Dennis and his mother stood by the gate and waved goodbye as I got into the car with the culinary treasures Dennis had given me. I placed the containers carefully on the front seat, making sure the soup wouldn't spill. Seeing Dennis had ignited a spark, and my mind was brimming with possibilities. I couldn't wait to impress Ah Hock with the bamboo chicken. I would show him there was a world of possibilities beyond the kopitiam. I felt a weight lift from my chest as I started the car and drove back to Carpenter Street.

20

Heart of the Home

The kopitiam was filled with the aroma of Chinese five spices used for lor ark, the Teochew braised duck I loved. Ma usually cooked three dishes for dinner – a meat dish, a vegetable dish, and soup. I had fond memories of her cooking a different soup every day: pork ribs with winter melon and goji berries, chicken ginseng soup, seaweed and egg soup, salted mustard with fish or duck, watercress or old cucumber with stock made from boiling pork bones.

I went upstairs to my room to get the yokan box. As I took it, I browsed through my pile of cassettes, searching for the one with the title *Mixtape for A*. It was filled with '70s love ballads by Chicago, Hall & Oates, Fleetwood Mac, Rod Stewart. My favourite was 'I'd Really Love To See You Tonight' by England Dan and John Ford Coley. Dennis would have cringed at the selection. I'd never worked up the courage to give it to Alice. Maybe if I played my cards right this time.

I went downstairs to the kitchen to see Ma. She was checking on her duck braising in the wok, poking it with chopsticks. A plate of washed midin, my favourite jungle fiddlehead fern, sat next to a plate of cut garlic and shallots on the counter. A pot of soup was simmering next to the wok.

I left the containers of food Dennis had given me on the kitchen counter, then held out the yokan box to her. 'For you, Ma,' I said. 'Sorry I didn't have time to buy anything else.'

'What's this? It's beautiful!' She unwrapped the box, which was wooden and had a faint, sweet scent. She opened it to four pieces of yokan, each in a different coloured paper with Japanese writing.

'It's called yokan, a Japanese sweet jelly dessert. You like red bean, right? Try it.'

Ma unwrapped one of the shiny, maroon-coloured jelly bars and took a bite. 'Oh, it's delicious! A bit sweet, I can't eat more than one. Thank you, Ming. And the box is pretty. I'll keep it on my dressing table.'

I knew she hadn't expected anything, but I felt bad I hadn't brought her something more substantial. 'Want me to help you cook?' I lifted the pot lid. The comforting smell of pork rib soup teased my nostrils.

Ma passed me the plate of midin. 'Go ahead and fry this.'

'That's the easy one. I could have helped you with the duck.'

'It's okay, no need to show off to your mother. I already know you can cook well,' she said with a chuckle.

'Where's Pa?'

'He's resting upstairs.' She switched off the stove fire and removed the braised duck from the wok. She put it on a plate and poured the duck gravy into a pot. 'Are you still angry at him?'

'I was never angry at him.' I washed the wok with a sponge with the soap wrung out, then put it back on the stove. 'I'll cook the midin now.'

'Go ahead. Don't fry it too long.'

A long time ago, I'd left spinach too long in the wok. Ah Hock had refused to eat it. Mistakes like these had made my

168

father distrust me more and delayed his imparting of culinary knowledge to his only son. It seemed Ma hadn't forgotten.

I poured in the oil, then stir-fried garlic and shallots for a minute before adding the midin. Ma watched the movements of my spatula, then looked at me.

'I know, I know,' I said, before she could say anything. 'Now.' I added a dash of red Shaoxing wine to the wok, then flambéed the vegetables. It was muscle memory for me, the rhythmic tossing of the wild ferns now glistening in oil and wine. I could do it with my eyes closed.

I switched off the fire then poured the contents of the wok into a dish. Ma used her chopsticks to pick up a sliver of midin and ate it. 'Better. Crisp and flavoured by the aromatic wine. Your father will like it.'

I put the midin on the table designated for our family meals, the one closest to the kitchen. Ma set down a big plate of braised duck next to the vegetables and patted my back.

'Don't worry, I will talk to him. It takes time. You can't suddenly come home and expect him to forget everything,' she said. 'Are you staying long?'

'I'm not sure yet. My boss came back from Japan so it's my turn now for a holiday,' I said, my eyes not meeting hers. She rubbed my arm.

'I'm glad. Kuan Yin heard my prayers.'

'Really? What did you pray for?'

'I prayed for you to come back for your pa's sixtieth birthday.'

'I don't want any fuss.' Ah Hock's voice boomed in Teochew, followed by his heavy steps down the stairs.

'Today the duck is very fresh. Eat more,' Ma said in Mandarin, then she went back into the kitchen to take the soup. Ah Hock pulled out a chair and sat at the table, scrutinising the dishes. Ma put a large bowl of pork rib soup down and ladled it into three small bowls. 'Drink more soup, Ming. You look like you need some nourishment. I bet you didn't eat properly over there. All that raw fish can't be good for your health.'

I laughed. 'I ate more than raw fish, Ma. You can find all types of cuisines in Hong Kong.' I put the containers of food from Dennis and three bowls of rice on the table. My father took a piece of duck breast and ate it. He never complained about Ma's cooking. The duck wasn't a difficult dish to make, although it took experience and finesse to cook it well. Sometimes people used lu shui, a braising brine that could be kept for years, to enhance the flavours of the duck.

We never spoke much during dinner time, unless we were eating out, and even then it was to critique the food. At home, Ah Hock eating silently meant he was tasting carefully and savouring each bite. If cooking was his religion, then eating was his meditation.

I stole a glance at Ah Hock, who was chewing the midin like a cow chewing grass.

'What's this?' Ah Hock pointed at Dennis's containers with his chopsticks. I sat down and took one of the rice bowls.

'Dennis and I made bamboo chicken. He also made some salted terubuk. I brought the food back for you to try.'

'Salted terubuk? Your friend knows how to salt terubuk?' Ah Hock said with a sceptical tone I decided to ignore.

'He knows how to cook all sorts of food.' I gave Ma a piece of the salted fish. Ah Hock nodded as he drank a spoonful of bamboo chicken soup while Ma complimented the salted fish.

'Your friend is so talented, Ming. Isn't he, Hock?' Ma took another small piece of salted fish and wolfed it down with rice. 'Everything is so full of flavour. You should start salting

170

terubuk as well, together with your flatfish. Isn't the bamboo chicken delicious?'

Ah Hock narrowed his eyes as he chewed. 'What did your friend use for the chicken? I don't know this herb. It smells interesting.'

I smiled. Ah Hock's curiosity could only mean he liked the dish.

'He put tapioca leaves in there. Lemongrass?'

'No, something else. Something I've never smelled before. It amplifies the taste of the chicken.'

'Ah, I think it's the daun bungkang. Some leaf Dennis said would make the bamboo chicken really special. We could try and add it to the broth one day? He says it brings out the flavour of meats.'

'It tastes interesting, but its personality is too strong. It would upset the balance of the broth,' Ah Hock said. 'Ideal for this bamboo chicken though. Thank your friend for letting us try his dish.'

'Ask him for the recipe, Ming. I would love to try and cook it too,' Ma said. 'I'm eating too much! Look, I'm finishing this soup all by myself! Take some, Ming.'

'It's okay, Ma, I already had a lot at Dennis's house. You and Pa enjoy.' It was rare to see Ah Hock enjoy something without criticism. They finished the bamboo chicken and the salted fish with genuine expressions of pure pleasure, as ephemeral as the blooming of blue hydrangeas after the rain.

*

'Do you want tea?' Ma asked when Ah Hock had finished his last spoon of rice. He nodded, putting down his chopsticks.

She made Tieguanyin using an old zisha clay teapot that had belonged to my grandfather. The dark oolong teas Ah Hock liked brewed well in this pot, which absorbed the smells of the brewed tea leaves. It was these lingering scents of the past that made the teapot special, and the present tea more fragrant, strengthened by its predecessors.

The teapot came with three cups. Ma poured boiling water into the pot and swirled the dried leaves, then drained the liquid into the three cups and emptied those as well. We never drank the first round of tea, which was to wash the leaves and warm the cups. She filled the teapot again, waited a few minutes, then poured half a cup for Ah Hock. After he had drunk the first cup, she refilled it to the brim. Only at the fourth round did she sit at the table and fill two more cups for herself and me.

'Where did you get this tea? From Old Wong?'

Ma nodded. 'His wife bought it from Anxi. They went there for a holiday,' she said, with a look of envy, I thought, but of course my father never noticed.

'It's fragrant. Good-quality tea. It's sweet but not cloying. Tea is good practice for your taste buds. If you can taste the different types of tea and note their individual characteristics, you can heighten your senses. You need to savour its fragrance before it goes down your throat.' My father was giving his usual lecture. 'Ask the boy what he thinks of the tea.'

Great, another test. I already knew all my answers would be wrong, even if they were right. I rolled my eyes, but Ma looked at me and shook her head.

'It's good tea,' I mumbled.

'Of course it's good tea. But why?' Ah Hock demanded.

The tea had a rose-like, gentle bouquet. I took a small sip and let it stay on my tongue for a few seconds before swallowing it. It was a good pairing with the duck. Although subtle, the tea was strong and astringent enough to balance the heaviness of the oily duck. It was fragrant but not too flowery. It matched our meal, which had been neither too meaty nor light.

I didn't want to give the old man the satisfaction of shooting down every opinion I had. 'I don't know,' I said, looking at Ma instead of Ah Hock. I knew I was acting childish. Could anyone blame me? Only just home and already interrogated like a prisoner of war. It was hard to be patient when Ah Hock's tone was condescending all the time.

Ah Hock pushed away from the table roughly, the legs of the chair screeching on the tiled floor. 'And he claims to be a chef. What a joke!' He stood up and went upstairs. I wished I had a bottle of sake or whisky. How was I going to survive my father's moods sober? Not a drop in the house. Ah Hock was a teetotaller and was against any kind of alcoholic drink being in the house.

Ma sighed. 'You and your father, both stubborn as mules.'

'He's the stubborn one.'

'He's older, so you should give in.'

'Who says so? He's always had things his way.'

'What makes you think he's doing what he wants? Your Ah Kong never gave him a choice. It was never in his head that he could be doing anything different from what he's doing now – what his father did before him. You left the house, Ming. You've proven to him you can do whatever you want. What else do you want from this old man?'

'Nothing. I just want him to stop being angry at me.'

'He's not angry at you, my dear boy. He's angry at himself.'
She got up and cleared the dishes from the table. 'Finish up
the midin and drink your soup. I'll keep the rest of the duck
for tomorrow's lunch.'

I ate the last grain of bario rice from my bowl, then stacked
the plates and bowls and carried them to the sink. I had forgotten how good the fine grains of highlands rice tasted. I
started washing the dishes, but Ma waved me away.

'You go sit down. I want to tell you a story.'

'What story?'

'About Ah Kong.'

'But I know his story. He was a famous chef, everybody
admired him. He's the reason I wanted to be a chef.'

'You know why your father wanted you to remain here and
cook laksa, right?'

I turned to the pot of broth simmering in the kitchen, as
if it were quietly listening to every word of our conversation.
'Was I ever allowed to forget it?'

Ma finished at the sink, then picked up a mop. As she
mopped the kitchen floor vigorously, the kopitiam was filled
with the odour of Dettol and the sickly sweet fragrance of
floor cleaning solution, but that would fade eventually, and the
warm aroma of the broth would once again fill the shophouse.

'The things old people say, you shouldn't take lightly.
Whether you believe in the legend or not, you have to at least
respect it.'

'I can respect it but I can't let it dictate my life, Ma. Like Pa
let it dictate his.'

'It wasn't his fault. He was raised by your Ah Kong. Who
else was he supposed to listen to?'

'I guess,' I said, imagining the canings Ah Hock would have
received if he didn't comply.

'Your Ah Kong was a stern man, but he was kind to me. He was harsh with your father, but that's what fathers and sons are like,' she said as she mopped the floor. 'So afraid of spoiling him, like your father was of spoiling you. And in the process, they forget how to love their sons.'

'Did you learn to cook from Ah Kong?'

'In a way.' Ma smiled as if she were recalling a fond memory. 'He cooked most of the meals for your father, and when we got married, he cooked for me as well. Always with the broth.'

'Sure, the magic broth.'

'Hush,' she said sternly. 'Your father would say that's blasphemy. That broth has been passed down from generation to generation. Your Ah Kong's Ah Kong passed it down to a son, and so on. Even if you don't believe in the deity like your father does, respect it because it came from your ancestors.'

'So what were your favourite dishes Ah Kong made?'

'He cooked every Chinese New Year. Just the three of us but he would cook an eight-course banquet. He called it the Emperor's Feast. Like the legend of the broth, you know. Imagine having an ancestor who cooked for the emperor!' Ma said, her voice rising in excitement. She was a young woman again, unencumbered by the toil of the kopitiam and the drudgery of domestic life. 'We would eat that food for days. I don't know why he didn't want to teach your father. He let me watch and learn his everyday dishes. But I never cooked the entire Emperor's Feast.'

'What were the dishes in it?'

'Oh, let me think. It's been so long. There was fish maw soup, braised duck of course, cold terubuk, fried prawns with dried flatfish, how many is that? Four? Braised sea cucumber with abalone and scallops, pork trotters. For dessert, orh nee was a must. Talking about these dishes is making my mouth water!'

The dishes sounded like a challenge I wanted to take on. 'Why don't we try and make these dishes, Ma? For Pa's birthday party?'

'I never thought about it! Your father has never asked me to. What if they taste terrible? We would be insulting the memory of your grandfather.' Ma was pensive, trying to remember how my grandfather had cooked those dishes. 'It was such a long time ago, and I can't recall exactly the ingredients he used. But the taste . . . I will never forget the taste. We'll have to recreate the recipes from my memory of the taste.'

I nodded vigorously. Ma was so lucky she had learned from the legend himself. If Ma's cooking skill was a mere fraction of my grandfather's, the Chinese New Year dinners they'd had must have been like banquets fit for emperors.

'They won't. We'll cook together and buy the freshest ingredients. It'll be unforgettable. Then Pa will be convinced I should have my own restaurant like Ah Kong did.' I imagined the guests at the party sighing with contentment, complimenting Ma and me. My father's look of scepticism turning to surprise, then approval, even admiration.

'I hope so,' Ma said. 'I'm going to shower. Offer new joss sticks to your grandfather before you sleep, okay?'

Ma plodded up the stairs. The wooden steps creaked under her slippered feet. The kopitiam had aged and so had Ma, after all. If only they could retire and let me take care of them.

But I didn't want the laksa business. How could I settle for that when my ancestors had cooked such celestial creations?

I would never be happy with the monotony of cooking the same thing every day, even if everyone loved it. My father may have been content being the laksa master of Kuching, but not me.

I went to the altar and lit three joss sticks for my grandfather. 'Teach me your heavenly dishes, Ah Kong,' I said aloud. I put the joss sticks in the brass urn and clasped my hands in prayer. 'I'm ready.'

21

Building Windmills in the Winds of Change

There was only one table left for Third Uncle when he came by. The kopitiam had been filled with customers since it opened that morning, but they were managing well. Wei Ming had been a great help since he had come home more than a week ago. With him at the stall, Ah Hock barely had to lift a finger.

As Third Uncle sat down, Wei Ming took a new bowl and filled it with beehoon, but Ah Hock nudged him aside and insisted he would personally prepare Third Uncle's laksa.

'Ming, it's been good having you around. I hope you're staying here permanently!' Third Uncle patted Wei Ming's back. The boy smiled at Third Uncle, who was like the grandfather he'd never had. Ah Hock doubted Teck Boon would have been as amiable with his grandson. If the boy had grown up with his grandfather, the same cane used to strike Ah Hock would have been used on Wei Ming as well.

'I haven't decided yet, Third Uncle.'

Hadn't decided yet? Ah Hock glanced at Wei Ming. Wasn't he here just for the birthday party? Ah Hock tried not to get his hopes up. The boy had always been whimsical, changing his mind whenever he liked without regard for others.

'Stay. Kuching is a good place to settle down in. You'll see.' Third Uncle sat at his table.

'Ah, why would he want to stay, he's at some fancy Japanese restaurant in Hong Kong,' Ah Hock said as he chose plump prawns and moist strips of omelette for Third Uncle's bowl.

'Japanese food? What would Teck Boon have said?' Third Uncle chuckled. Ah Hock had been too young himself to truly understand the effects of the Japanese occupation. Teck Boon had managed somehow to shield him from the worst of it. He recalled they'd had to keep the kopitiam closed most of the time, but were strangely left unharmed. He had a sudden memory of his father serving a Japanese soldier food in the kopitiam one time.

Ah Hock had been around nine or ten years old, peering at them from behind a wall. He could only see the back of the soldier, who ate in silence while Teck Boon stood behind him. The soldier had taken off his hat and placed it on the table, its neck flaps making it look like a bird with its wings spread out. The soldier's rifle was leaned on a chair next to him. The shiny bayonet sword attached to the rifle, the glint of its blade, aroused Ah Hock's curiosity. He wanted to go nearer to look at it, but Teck Boon saw him, shook his head and glared a warning. When the soldier was done, he put his hat back on, picked up his rifle, then stood up and bowed slightly to Teck Boon, who returned a deep bow.

That was the closest interaction Ah Hock had with soldiers during the war. Most of it was spent hiding, and with Teck Boon worrying about food supplies. But there had always been enough for them. Unlike most people, they didn't starve.

Ah Hock supposed his father and Third Uncle must have seen much worse.

'His Japanese master sounds like a good teacher. Anyone who can teach this boy is no ordinary person,' Ah Hock said, and Third Uncle laughed. Ah Hock gave the bowl of laksa to Wei Ming, who served it to Third Uncle.

'Don't mind your father, it's his way of complimenting you. You really have grown, Wei Ming. Now you look like you're ready to be a husband and father!' Third Uncle sipped a spoonful of the laksa soup. 'Soup's great today, Hock! See, I told you not to worry!'

'Worry about what?' Wei Ming asked.

'Your father worries about the soup. Says it's not consistent. I agree there are some days when it's really good, like now, but it's not so bad the other days. Have you tried next door's laksa yet?' Third Uncle said.

'Of course not! Have you, Third Uncle?' Ah Hock said. It had never occurred to him to step into Towkay Lau's café. What for? To confirm what he already knew, that they used frozen prawns, chicken stock cubes, store-bought laksa paste and substandard noodles?

'No, no,' Third Uncle said. 'But you should. See what's special about their laksa.'

'Hah! Nothing. Nothing could be special about their laksa unless they put in opium or something. Do you think a young punk could outdo me, Third Uncle? They've got a snotty-faced toddler there, pretending to cook laksa,' Ah Hock said.

'Oh? I don't know who the cook is. All I know is, Towkay Lau opened this shop next to you so you should see what they're doing.'

'What's the point? After I win the bet, they'll close down the shop and I won't have to see that bastard's face again.'

'What bet?' Wei Ming said, turning to Ah Hock. The boy had his brow furrowed. What a worry wart! Just like his mother. After all those years serving customers in the kopitiam, didn't he know their laksa was incomparable? The boy lacked faith, that had always been the problem.

'It's nothing! Just a stupid bet that I'll win, and that idiot promises to close his shop and stop bugging me about mine! I'll never hear his nonsense about branches and franchising or whatever nonsense he talks about! What a relief!' Ah Hock looked over at Third Uncle's table. The bowl was empty. Another good day for the laksa soup! There was no way he'd lose the bet.

'I'd better go. Got to finish up this signboard for a new place,' Third Uncle said.

'What new place?' Ah Hock asked.

'There's a coffee place opening, a few blocks down the road.'

'Coffee place? You mean a kopitiam?'

'No, I mean one of those fancy coffee places. With air conditioning. They only sell coffee, I think. You know, those western types. Not our local coffee.'

'Huh? Only coffee? And they expect to make money?'

'I think they might have cakes or pastries too. But a cup of coffee costs ten ringgit!'

Ah Hock laughed. 'Ten ringgit? Good luck to them! What fool would pay that much for coffee?'

'In Hong Kong, people like these cafés. And the coffee's good too,' Wei Ming chimed in.

'So if fools in Hong Kong waste money on expensive coffee, you think Kuching people would too?' Ah Hock scoffed. 'I'm tired of these new places sprouting up here. Carpenter Street should remain as it is, with shops centuries old, the quality that remains high. All these new, meaningless places sicken me.'

'You've got to adapt to changing times, Hock. New places make Carpenter Street more interesting and diverse. A mix of the old and the new!' Third Uncle said, reaching into his pocket.

'No charge today, Third Uncle,' Ah Hock said.

'Eh? What? No, no, there's no occasion for this.'

'The occasion is my son coming home, Third Uncle.' Ah Hock felt awkward saying it, but he wanted a reason to insist on Third Uncle not paying. The empty bowl reassured him that he hadn't lost the gift. That the deity had not stopped giving. That he wasn't yet punished for his shortcomings.

He wondered if it was Wei Ming's presence that had improved the soup. Had the boy added something extra? Would he have dared, without asking?

Third Uncle laughed. 'All right, all right, thank you. Wei Ming, you see, you've made your parents so happy being home. Think about staying, all right?' Third Uncle waved at them as he left the kopitiam. Ah Hock ladled some laksa soup into a bowl and drank. It did taste better today.

'What happens if we lose the bet, Pa? What does Towkay Lau want?' Wei Ming said after Third Uncle had left.

'We won't! You think some young punk can make better laksa than me?' The boy looked worried. Why would they lose to some inexperienced cook who knew nothing? People weren't going to eat their fancy chairs and tables, they were there for the food!

'I know Towkay Lau wouldn't make a bet he'd lose.'

The audacity of the boy! So the scoundrel had taken him to Hong Kong all those years ago and now Wei Ming had to kiss his backside? Ah Hock balled his hands into fists.

'I knew you would take the side of that devil man!'

'It's not that I want to support him, but some of what he says is right.'

'Right? When he tells you to throw away your inheritance and insult the memory of your grandfather? And our ancestors before him?'

'It's not like that. Times are different now.'

'Different? Different how? People like to eat bad food now?'

'No, but how many people are like Third Uncle, who can appreciate the nuances of your talent?'

'Talent? You think I was born with talent? This is hard work, years of struggle, of learning, understanding flavour and understanding life!'

'Yes, I know.'

'If you know, you wouldn't be considering whatever that devil has to offer. Why can't he leave us alone! There are plenty of other stalls, other kopitiams to bother!'

'Because he knows you're the best, Pa. The other stalls are not worth his time.'

Ah Hock snorted. 'So now you think we're the best. But you think we will lose the bet.'

'That's not what I'm saying, Pa. Why did you choose to bet with Towkay Lau? He's not someone to trifle with.'

'I'm not scared of that idiot. If this bet can stop him from hassling me, it's worth it. All these years, bugging me to have branches. If I listen to him, this laksa will no longer be the best. Branches, what a joke! His suggestion is to cheapen the laksa! Make it like fast food!'

'Maybe he knows something we don't. We live here on Carpenter Street, and you hardly go anywhere else, Pa. There must be food courts, big kopitiams, in different areas of Kuching, and they have many more customers than us.'

'So they are better?'

'I know our food is better, but what's the use if people don't come?'

'What do you call those people who come every day? Sometimes I don't have enough bowls to serve them.'

'We have regulars and people who work nearby. Nobody comes all the way to Carpenter Street just for laksa anymore. People want convenience these days, especially busy people. I think Towkay Lau wants branches because he thinks you'll have workers trained to cook for you at each branch, without sweating over boiling soup yourself. Take it easy and wait for the money to come in.'

Ah Hock looked Wei Ming straight in the eye. Wait for the money to come in? They had to make a living, sure, but what was more important was the laksa they served. What was the point of the money coming in if the laksa tasted bad? He didn't want customers swallowing food he'd made without tasting it properly, without appreciating the depth of the broth's flavour. Didn't the boy work in some fancy Japanese restaurant with a master who was particular even about the type of salt they used? And yet he still didn't understand.

'Young people these days, don't know what it's like to sweat blood for money. When your grandfather and I came to Kuching, all we did was work. Nobody waited around for anything. You use your hands to make food – good, delicious food you can be proud of – then you sell it at a fair price. Don't compromise on quality, don't embarrass yourself and taint your family honour.'

'I'm trying to see things from Towkay Lau's point of view. He's a businessman. A business is about money. You wouldn't give away your laksa for free, right? Towkay Lau's set up a laksa shop that looks new and modern, and young customers might be drawn there. They might not be too picky about the quality of the food.'

'Let the idiots go, then. It's not like the young ones know the difference between real food and rubbish.'

'But Pa, we cannot afford to lose customers. That's my point. You can't pick and choose anymore. The next generation might not care if you're the best or not, they just want a pleasant dining experience. Your customers can't all be gourmets. We have to give everyone options. The goal is to fill the tables. I'm not saying you must have branches. I'm just explaining Towkay Lau's rationale. There are other ways to modernise, to keep up with changing times.'

'I've been running the same business since before you were born and you think you know better, eh? I've eaten more salt than you've eaten rice! And what's wrong with old? People do business for generations. Your Ah Kong passed this down to me. And I am supposed to pass it down to you, and you to your children. You want me to die soon?'

Ah Hock felt his chest tighten as he said this. Imagine if he were to drop dead now! Then the boy would agree to the deal with the devil and have branches! Better to be dead when that happened. But how would he answer to Teck Boon in the afterlife? Or the gods? Did deities punish the dead too, or just the living?

'Of course I don't.' Wei Ming sighed. Two office workers walked in, and Wei Ming ushered them to their table.

'It was so simple between me and my father. I always knew I had to take over. And keep this place the way it was. Then you come along, try and disrupt everything, offending the gods,' Ah Hock said loudly. Kim Choo came out from the kitchen and served milk tea to the customers.

'Aiyoh, you two. What is this about now?'

'I was telling Pa about what businesses do these days to attract customers. It's not just about the food anymore,' Wei Ming said, shaking his head.

'Hock, why don't you see what Ming means instead of shouting down his ideas all the time? Let him bring you to see other kopitiams, try the food, see what the surroundings are like. I'll take care of the stall,' Kim Choo said.

'Look at other places?' Ah Hock said. What other places? The only decent laksa place he knew was the stall at Lau Ya Keng. Of course, it couldn't hold a candle to his, but it was far better than any of the others, for sure. What was this obsession with everything new? His laksa recipe was decades old. People still loved it. Why did he have to see what other people were making? Even if they were skilled, which he doubted, they didn't have the deity's broth, did they?

'Like Third Uncle said, you haven't even checked out next door. They're directly competing with us. And now you've entered into a bet with Towkay Lau. At least see what you're up against, don't leave anything to chance,' Wei Ming said.

'Chance? You think it's luck that'll win me the bet?' No way was Ah Hock stepping into that shop! The boy could, if he could stomach the experience.

'I'll go if you won't. See why the customers have been flocking there.'

Ah Hock grunted in reply, then turned his attention to a customer who came in and ordered one bowl special, extra prawns, extra beansprouts. It didn't hurt to see the mistakes others made as cautionary tales. It would be an opportunity for Wei Ming to see what not to do, and to convince him that popularity didn't mean the food was good. There was so much he could show the boy, if only he was open to learn.

22

More than Just Good Luck

We closed early, managing to sell out of laksa at one o'clock. When Ah Hock was taking his nap, I left the kopitiam and went next door. Black-framed glass doors marked the entrance. A red neon sign that said 'Good Luck Café' was mounted against a white-bricked wall. What a name, I chuckled to myself. I opened the glass door to a gust of cold air. The inside of the laksa shop was air-conditioned. It was two in the afternoon, and they were still serving people. There were at least six tables filled with customers, and a young man in a short-sleeved blue shirt and khakis with a white apron was busy chatting with another customer as he ladled soup into a bowl at the laksa stall.

Natural light flowed into the place through its many windows. It was a far cry from the usual hawker centres and traditional kopitiams with their dusty ceiling fans and stained, greasy mosaic-tiled floors. The seamless grey industrial floor gave it a modern feel, and there was a decorative walkway with concrete slabs on a bed of gravel. There were booths, counters where people could sit alone, and round tables that sat five or six people. The furniture was a mix of wooden and rattan tables and chairs. It could rival a trendy café in

Causeway Bay with its minimalist modern design. Apart from the neon sign, that is.

On the walls, there were pictures of Towkay Lau with various celebrities and politicians, and there was even one of him shaking hands with a former prime minister. Tacky, but bound to impress some people. When the cook spotted me, he waved me over to the stall.

'You must be Wei Ming! I'm Billy. I've seen you next door. Welcome! Towkay Lau already said, for you, everything free!' Billy enthusiastically poured laksa soup into an already assembled bowl. I looked at the toppings and noticed their prawns were considerably smaller, the omelette strips looked pale, and the beansprouts didn't have their browned tails removed. Apart from the usual toppings, there were crayfish, fish balls and fried tofu. Was that lobster or a tiger prawn? Who would order those toppings? Ah Hock would be enraged if he saw. But there was no telling customer taste these days. Maybe they had requested those toppings and Billy had catered to their requests. Crayfish was expensive. I wouldn't be surprised if they charged twenty ringgit for the expensive toppings.

'How much do you charge for lobster laksa?'

'Oh, please, no charge for you, Towkay Lau already gave me instructions!'

'No, no, I'll pay for this.'

'No way! Towkay Lau would be angry if he knew I took money from you. Have a seat! Try the counter!' Billy gestured towards the wooden counter, where a solitary woman sat drinking her iced coffee. I took my seat there and touched the counter, expecting real wood, but it was laminated.

The chairs and tables at Teck Boon kopitiam were made of solid wood carved by the carpenters on Carpenter Street. This counter hadn't been wiped properly, or at least not with a clean cloth. I could detect a faint odour of mildew and wondered how people could stand it. Billy came and set a bowl of steaming laksa in front of me. He had given me a generous portion of lobster and crayfish. It was strange to see it, as if I had ordered another kind of noodle dish and not laksa.

'Boss! Enjoy! Feel free to give me tips on how to make it better, yeah? We didn't use a magical broth but the customers like it!' Billy said with an annoying chortle before going back to his workstation. I blushed. Towkay Lau must have told him about the broth. I wished that damned broth didn't exist. Ah Hock refused to believe it was his own discipline and strong work ethic that contributed to the success of the laksa, not Teck Boon's recipe or the broth.

I took a sip of the laksa soup and tasted it carefully. It lacked something. The basic taste was there, but something was missing, and I wasn't sure what it was. And there was something else I couldn't quite put my finger on, so I kept drinking the soup. Likely they used Aijinomoto or Knorr chicken cubes. Some Maggi seasoning giving it some semblance of umami.

I ate a spoonful of beehoon and lobster. The lobster was springy enough but lacked taste. They must have used frozen lobster, otherwise it would be impossible to make any kind of profit. The crayfish had a slight fishy odour. I looked around and realised mine wasn't the only bowl with lobster.

I finished the whole bowl as I kept tasting the soup to analyse its flavours. It wasn't great but not inedible either. Billy walked over and smiled when he saw my empty bowl.

'Wow! You must have liked it! What a compliment, Wei Ming! Towkay Lau will be so happy when I tell him! I gave him a call and told him you came over.' As Billy said those words, Towkay Lau entered the shop. His eyes lit up when he saw me.

'Wei Ming! What an honour for you to grace our shop with your presence! I guess your father isn't here?' he said, laughing.

'I'm just being neighbourly,' I said, feeling like I'd betrayed my father.

'Yes, that's what your father doesn't understand. Come, come, let's take the booth over there. Billy! Bring the man a cup of coffee! We brew a good kopi-o here, but if there's one thing we can't replicate, it's your mother's milk tea.' Towkay Lau ushered me to one of the booths.

I sat down reluctantly on the dark green seat, upholstered with PVC instead of real leather. It looked good but it wasn't comfortable. Designed not to let people stay too long, probably. A high turnover was better. You didn't want people sitting and chatting for hours after ordering drinks.

'So what do you think of the laksa? You can be honest, Ming, I can take it! I didn't get to where I am by listening to sweet words all the time.'

'It was all right.'

'Are you sure Billy can't improve it in some way?'

'You're already taking our customers. There's no need to improve it.' Did Towkay Lau honestly think I was there to help them improve their laksa?

'Ah, shrewd, careful, like your father! But we all know these days it isn't only the quality of food that attracts customers. You need the whole package! Especially for the younger people. They want good ambience, good service, good vibes. Ah Hock doesn't understand it. The only people who would continue going to his place are the old regulars, but those old folk aren't hanging around forever.'

'Good job then, having this place, Mr Lau.'

'I didn't want to, you know. Your father pushed me to this.'

'I don't think you can say that—'

'Now that this place is open, I want everything of the highest quality.'

I held back a snort, thinking of the laminated wood and the PVC we were sitting on. Billy served us two cups of black coffee, and I had a sip. Too bitter. I coughed.

'So, you know about the bet?' Towkay Lau said.

'He told me.'

'How do you think your father will feel, losing the kopitiam?'

My eyes widened and I sat upright. What was he talking about? Did my father know what he'd got himself into? 'What do you mean, losing the kopitiam?'

'That's what he bet. The kopitiam. I'm hosting a chef from New York here in a couple of weeks. I'll let him taste your father's laksa, and the laksa we serve here. See which he prefers.'

I couldn't believe Ah Hock had been so impulsive. The kopitiam was his whole life. He would rather die than lose it to Towkay Lau. What was he thinking?

'Why don't you reconsider, Mr Lau? My father is an old man. Why bother with him? You have so many businesses. This shop isn't just his work, it's his life. Losing the kopitiam would kill him.' I tried not to sound like I was begging. I couldn't let this happen to Ah Hock, even if I didn't want my inheritance.

'Oh, don't be so dramatic.' Towkay Lau laughed. 'Speaking of drama, I heard about your little fiasco in Hong Kong.'

I shifted in my seat uneasily. 'What have you heard?'

'I have eyes and ears everywhere,' Towkay Lau said. 'I know of your days at the Happy Valley Racecourse. The women at the Jade Pavilion speak highly of you.' He smirked. 'Your gambling debts. You think you can set foot in Kowloon now? And Ah Man's girl? You've got some balls, playing dangerous games.' He leaned over and spoke in a low voice. 'I'm guessing your parents don't know about your complicated life in Hong Kong. You don't need to tell them. I don't need to tell them, but I think it would be fair for an exchange of something.'

I swallowed. I had underestimated the kind of clout Towkay Lau had outside Kuching. 'You're blackmailing me?' I said, keeping my voice steady. No wonder Ah Hock hated Towkay Lau. Pretending he had been a family friend all those years. An opportunist, Ah Hock called him. But if not for Towkay Lau, I wouldn't have gone to Hong Kong. I didn't know what to think.

'Eh, don't use that word, it's beneath me. I like making bargains. Like the bet I've got going on with your father,' Towkay Lau said. 'But don't say I'm not generous or fair. I've got a big offer for you. If you want, you can have your own fancy restaurant in Kuching.'

'Thank you, but I already have a boss. My master, Inamura-san. I wouldn't leave him to work for a new boss,' I said, feeling like a fake. He didn't need to know what I'd done to Sensei.

'But you wouldn't be. You'd be your own boss. I could give you a restaurant, young man. Imagine, being the king of your domain. Your own place to do as you wish.'

I couldn't believe my ears. My own place, courtesy of a deal with the devil.

Was it that bad, opening branches? Didn't it solve my problem too? If I didn't want to take over the kopitiam, Ah Hock could rest easy having other people work for him. The only thing he had to do was put up with some deterioration in quality. Besides, he could supervise the cooks and continue his favourite habit of shouting at people if they didn't meet his standards. It would be remiss not to at least think about it.

'But I need you to cooperate. Tell your father, join forces with me. He'll lose this bet, and lose the kopitiam. It's not too late for him to come to his senses and be my partner instead of my rival,' Towkay Lau said.

It made sense, except for Ah Hock having to work with Towkay Lau. Perhaps I could convince Ah Hock to take a back seat, let me and Towkay Lau run the business? And this restaurant offer, I'd have to iron out the details. It was too good to be true, but maybe that's how desperately Towkay Lau wanted a piece of Teck Boon's laksa. You never knew with rich people. They prided themselves on being able to buy everything, so they became obsessed with things you couldn't put a price on.

'Why don't you call off the bet, Mr Lau. My father is not easy to work with, but you and I can work something out?'

'No. The prize is Teck Boon's laksa. I'm sure you're a talented chef, Wei Ming. But to sweeten the deal with your restaurant, I need the kopitiam. I'll get it through the bet or through your cooperation. You think about it, Wei Ming! Not many would pass up this golden opportunity,' Towkay Lau said as he stood up. 'Ah, before I forget, I'm having a party at the Heritage Club. Come as my guest of honour. Imagine when I show you off to the luminaries there! It would be a great opportunity for you to rub shoulders with some big shots!'

The man was smiling as if we were great friends, and yet a moment ago he had been dangling a threat over my head. I didn't know what to think, except that I had to be careful.

'There's nothing to show off, Mr Lau.'

'Don't sell yourself short, young man! Ah Hock may not see the potential in you, but I know what you're capable of.'

I knew Ah Hock would hate for me to go to the party. But I was curious about the upper echelons of Kuching society. If I planned on having my own restaurant here, these people would be my customers. Dennis would probably jump at the chance of free food, and free expensive food, at that. Not to mention a reason to invite Alice to a formal event.

'Thank you, Mr Lau. I'll be there. Is it okay if I bring my friend and his sister?'

'But of course! Bring whoever you want! Sister . . . your girlfriend?' Towkay Lau winked.

'No, Dennis is my best friend, and he'll probably want to bring his sister.'

'Sure, bring anyone you like! Looking forward to seeing you and your friends there. I'm glad you're different from Ah Hock, Wei Ming. I knew I didn't waste my effort, helping you to go to Hong Kong.' He shook my hand. Towkay Lau certainly knew how to keep score.

Was I so different from my father? It didn't feel like a compliment. This was a man who was offering a carrot or a stick, trying to get me to convince Ah Hock to do something he didn't want to do. But I was drawn to this world, or at least curious about it. What if the way to my dream was through Towkay Lau? Money did open doors. I had to make my father understand that.

I thanked Towkay Lau and Billy, and tried to pay but was refused again. I went back to our kopitiam and was surprised to see Ah Hock already awake from his nap, sitting at one of the tables. He asked me where I'd gone and I told him.

Ah Hock looked at me enquiringly. 'And what did you think?'

'They serve lobster or crayfish with their laksa. There's fish balls or tofu if anyone wants.'

He laughed. 'What are they selling, curry mee? Is it KL people who are asking for fish balls or tofu?'

'The point is, they are customer-friendly. No one will get scolded if they ask for different toppings.'

'I can't serve lobster or crayfish. It would be the star of the show. Laksa is about balance. If someone eats lobster, they'll forget about the omelette, or the chicken. Imagine, who would care about taugeh if the lobster covered the laksa? People are easily distracted. This is why you must give each topping its place in the bowl,' Ah Hock said.

'I know, but think about it. When that chef judges both bowls, he might get swayed by the lobster. Lobster's always impressive.'

'If he's a chef worth his salt, he'll be able to differentiate substance from showiness.'

'Pa, you didn't say that if you lose, you'll lose the kopitiam too. It's not too late to back out of the bet. Let's sit down with Towkay Lau and discuss possibilities.'

'I want to settle this once and for all! When we win, he'll be out of our lives! I'll have peace forever, not having him hover over me like a vulture, waiting for me to sell the laksa like a prostitute hawking her wares!' Ah Hock was starting to sound antagonistic. There was no changing his stance on this. I'd have to try and talk to Towkay Lau again.

'Towkay Lau invited me to a party at the Heritage Club. Why not come with me? You can try different dishes. I hear the chef there is good.' Fat chance Ah Hock would say yes, but there was no harm trying my luck anyway.

'Not for me. I would feel out of place with all the rich towkays there. Us simple people, best to know our place,' Ah Hock said, his voice thick with sarcasm.

It was just like Ah Hock to be snide when it was completely

unnecessary. 'Where did that come from?' I said, although a part of me knew it had something to do with me leaving him for Hong Kong all those years ago.

'I'm not the one who thinks selling laksa is low-class. Better to mix with people like Towkay Lau. Doesn't matter whether they know anything about food. Money is more important!'

'I never said that, Pa. Is this all because I accepted his invitation? I want to try a variety of food in different places in Kuching so I can learn. You should come too, you'll enjoy the food.'

'No, no, as I said, all those rich, high-class people. Better not shame Towkay Lau with our presence.'

'What on earth are you talking about?' I sighed. 'It's just a dinner. We go there, eat, enjoy the food, then go home! You don't have to talk to anybody.'

'Count me out. You go. You want to be with rich people so much, go ahead,' Ah Hock said, then went to the back of the kopitiam. I didn't want Ah Hock in a bad mood. Convincing him to accept Towkay Lau's plans was going to be an uphill battle. I went to the kitchen and stood in the doorway, watching Ah Hock muse on his flatfish drying in the backyard while he murmured, 'Not ready yet. Tomorrow maybe.'

23

Dinner at the Chamber of the Gods

'The boy doesn't know what he's missing,' Ah Hock said as he sat down with Kim Choo at the kuay chap stall in Lau Ya Keng. It was six-thirty in the evening and the skies were already darkening. Kim Choo smiled and looked around at people ordering home-style dishes from a Teochew family's stall – fried salted vegetables with duck, kernels of crispy sweetcorn flash-fried with large, succulent chunks of fresh crab meat seasoned with Sarawak black pepper. These were Ah Hock's favourite dishes, but tonight he felt like having kuay chap.

He took a deep breath. The savoury smells that mingled in the air made him nostalgic. He and Kim Choo didn't eat out often these days, he wasn't sure why. Being here reminded him of the days before they got married, when they would have dinner, or even lunch during busy days at the kopitiam if Kim Choo was free then. He would tell Teck Boon he had to go to the haberdashery on China Street to buy thread and buttons, the joss paper shop for joss sticks, or the medicinal herbalist to get a packet of chrysanthemum and goji berries. Sometimes they would take longer than usual, especially when it rained, and he would tell Teck Boon he was late because he was waiting for the rain to stop. He would look forward to the smell of humidity hanging heavily in the air that warned him of impending rain, long before the skies darkened and the eventual downpour arrived.

'I hope Ming will have a great time! I can't wait to see him looking smart and handsome in the shirt and tie Dennis lent him,' Kim Choo said. Her eyes shone with excitement as if she were at the party herself. 'We should go too, Hock. I can still fit into that red and gold cheongsam made by the tailor auntie down the road, do you remember it? Before Ming was born.'

Of course Ah Hock remembered it. Seeing her in it had taken his breath away, not that Kim Choo needed a fancy dress to enhance her beauty. Even now, when she had on light lipstick and black trousers and a simple short-sleeved blue blouse with white flowers, she looked every bit the elegant soul she was.

'Waste of a night. These fancy restaurants don't serve good food. Can't beat a hot bowl of kuay chap for sure.' Ah Hock loved the broad rice noodles cooked in a braising sauce broth, served with pig innards. He ordered extra pig's ear, his favourite.

'Let him be. It's good for him to be out with people his age. Especially Alice, that lovely girl, I remember she was such a good student,' Kim Choo said. She was probably already imagining grandchildren. All that should come later, only when the boy had more definite plans, although Ah Hock himself couldn't help feeling a little pleased at the thought of Wei Ming settling in Kuching for good, with a wife and children. Maybe Kim Choo was on to something.

Their orders came – two bowls of square noodles and broth and two plates of pig treasures. The texture of pig's ear was unique. The rubbery skin of the pig formed the outermost layer, then there was the fat and meat in between the innermost cartilage, and the white soft bone that was firm yet yielding. After braising for hours, the pig's ear absorbed the flavour of the broth, which had a similar flavour to the spices used for lor ark. Sometimes there would also be pig's tail and trotters in kuay chap. To Ah Hock, the best part of the pig was not its meat, but its innards, skin, trotters and tail.

Kim Choo's favourite was the dao gua, blocks of firm tofu cut into big cubes, already browned from being braised for hours in delicious soy sauce broth. Ah Hock finished his noodles and picked out a pig's ear to chew on.

'Very fresh pork today. And cooked just right. This is flavour,' he said. 'The boy should be here trying this, then he'll learn something about how quality dishes should taste. Simple food is the best. He always likes to complicate things.'

'I'm sure there's plenty to learn over at the Heritage Club too. Mrs Wong says they have good seafood. Towkay Lau wouldn't serve anything frozen!'

'That idiot wouldn't know frozen from fresh. Frozen seafood looks fresh and does not have the odour of fish long dead, but neither does it have any sort of aroma. Never trawled the seabed for food or sped away from predators or swam against currents in the sea. Frozen seafood tastes almost as bad as chickens born and bred in cages, never feeling the sunlight on their bodies, never scratching for worms or just running free on the dirt, pecking at this or that, flapping their flightless wings,' Ah Hock said. He could always tell the difference with wild prawns. They had firm, springier flesh.

Kim Choo nodded. 'That's what your father used to tell me. *Yuan zhi yuan wei*.'

Ah Hock said nothing. He didn't like to talk to Kim Choo about his father. Maybe it was because he felt a little jealous of how his father used to speak to her without getting impatient, without making her feel like she was never good enough.

And he'd taught her his recipes instead of Ah Hock! He never understood why, and he'd never asked. At least he could use the deity's broth. That was still his. Even Kim Choo wasn't allowed to touch it because she wasn't Teck Boon's son.

Ah Hock drank a spoonful of kuay chap soup and sighed audibly.

Kim Choo laughed. 'This is how I put you in a good mood, feeding you kuay chap.'

'You feed me good food every day, anyway.'

'This one is different. You don't make that same "aaah" sound for my cooking.'

'It's still good, don't worry. But this soup, sometimes I do wonder what they use. Mine has help from the broth, but theirs, I don't know. Maybe they have their own ancestral broth.'

'Don't eat too much of this, it's bad for your heart. Look at your big stomach. It's time to exercise, old man. Think of your health!'

For a moment, he was afraid she had found out about his visit to the hospital with Third Uncle, but she did not say anything more. He still hadn't gone to see a heart doctor yet. Ah, what the hell, he would go later, maybe after the birthday party. While the boy was still around to distract her. He drank the rest of the soup, making sure there was not a drop left.

'Health? This is why we must make our soup so good that people forget about health. They will forget their fears, their reservations. They will remember their happy days, the last time they had good food, and shared jokes with good friends, how they felt when they were a child playing outdoors, being carried by their mother, hearing her heart beat against theirs, their father throwing them up in the air, and them feeling terrified and happy at the same time.'

Kim Choo stared at him with a puzzled expression. Ah Hock was surprised himself. Teck Boon had taught him rules and honed his skills, but he had never once expressed the beauty of the food they made. At least, not to Ah Hock. He chided himself for the temporary lapse into sentimentality. When he looked at Kim Choo, he noticed she had tears in her eyes. 'What's wrong? Are you upset?'

'It's nothing,' she said with a laugh, wiping her eyes with tissue. 'I'm just happy our son is home. And being back here, it reminds me of all those years ago, when I was in the opera troupe. It's silly, I don't want to talk about it. Too many feelings at the same time.'

Ah Hock wanted to hold her hand, tell her everything would be all right. That he would teach Ming, finally, and make him ready. Then the boy would stop wandering, stop searching for that elusive dream he imagined would make his life complete. What had Kim Choo said about that kolo mee seller's daughter again? Did Wei Ming like her? Maybe that would anchor the boy, tame his restless spirit, just like Kim Choo had tamed Ah Hock's all those years ago. It was as good a reason as any, as long as the boy stayed.

24

The Unforgettable Fish

'You should dress like this more often,' Ma said as she looked at me adjusting my tie. I'd borrowed a white long-sleeved shirt, black trousers and a navy-blue tie from Dennis. A suit would have been better, but Dennis didn't have one. 'Is this how you dress in Hong Kong?'

'I wore my chef's whites there, Ma,' I said, laughing. It's funny how Ma thought I'd be wearing a shirt and tie like an office worker. 'I was in the restaurant all the time.'

'I know. I thought your life there must be so glamorous and that's why you didn't want to come back,' Ma said. Glamorous? Maybe those moments at Haruto when I made sushi for customers. She wouldn't think my Wan Chai flat was so glamorous, or the seedy alleys I walked through late at night, hoping I wouldn't get mugged.

'Ma, it's not that I didn't want to come back. At first it was because of Pa, but later, so many things happened. And I got so busy. I just never found the right time . . .'

'And is everything all right now?'

'Yes. Everything is fine,' I said and changed the subject. 'Can you imagine Pa at one of these events?'

'Your grandfather would not have been out of place at these events. I heard he used to host fancy dinners and parties for all those rich Swatow people in his restaurant. How he must have felt when the guests asked him to come out so they could applaud him!'

I wondered if Ah Hock desired that kind of life at all, despite what he said. It sounded like a good life, living among the rich and powerful, impressing people who would look at him in awe. Not just a cook, but a chef, a magician who could move people to tears or ecstasy with the power of preparing food. Even if he didn't want it, Ah Hock deserved to be celebrated that way.

Dennis arrived early in his silver Proton Wira. Alice was sitting in the back seat. I got into the front and turned around to say hi to her. The car was scented with her perfume, sweet and refreshing like the white-fleshed Hakuto peaches Sensei brought back from Japan. I would never forget the honeyed sweetness of that soft fruit as I took my first bite, my nostrils deluged with its flowery fragrance.

'You look better in Dennis's clothes than he does,' Alice said, to loud protests from Dennis. We laughed. I loved seeing her smile, especially when she gave me a sidelong glance, as if she understood something about me I didn't. She looked as elegant as a queen, her face lightly made up with faint pink lipstick and some eyeliner. Her hair was held up in a loose bun with gold pins dotted with small diamonds, and she had on large, teardrop-shaped earrings. I could hear my own heartbeat, feeling as I had years ago when I saw her in her school uniform, a light blue pinafore, and a ponytail with yellow ribbons.

'Where's Misha?' I asked.

'With my parents. They're great babysitters,' Alice said. I tried to think of less mundane things to say. I couldn't believe I was in a car with her, going to a formal event together for the first time. We'd never had prom night or anything like that. Suddenly I was a teenager again, worrying about the spots on my face, whether I would say something stupid. I straightened my tie and brushed my hair back with my fingers. I looked in the rear-view mirror and caught a glimpse of her looking out the window, her earrings reflecting the street lights back at me.

It was a short drive from Carpenter Street to the Heritage Club. As we drove up a hill, a white colonial building with neatly landscaped lawns loomed. There were tennis courts near the car park and Olympic-sized swimming pools. Some kids from our school had parents who were members there and used the facilities after school, but Dennis and I had never seen the inside of the Heritage Club before.

A valet parked the car for us as soon as I informed him we were there for the party. An usher led us to the banquet hall, where Towkay Lau was greeting people in his tuxedo. The party was filled with the wealthy and renowned of Kuching. It looked like there were at least thirty or forty guests. Some of the guests were our former schoolmates, whose parents were doctors, lawyers, and high-ranking government officials and ministers.

No doubt they were in reputable professions themselves now. Money opened so many doors. Seeing them dredged up memories of being teased and bullied during my schooldays. A few of them knew Alice and Dennis and came over for small talk while nodding at me in acknowledgement. I had a feeling some of them were surprised to see me there.

I looked around restlessly. Maybe I shouldn't have come after all. Maybe Ah Hock was right. We didn't belong in this exclusive club. It wasn't like I didn't know how to conduct myself around wealthy people. I'd been working for the past seven years in a sushiya that charged three thousand Hong Kong dollars a head. But out of my chef's whites, I didn't know who I was at the Heritage Club.

'Hey! Laksa seller!'

I would have recognised that loud obnoxious voice anywhere. A feeling of dread slithered over me. I turned around to see Jason in a black, expensive-looking suit, holding a full glass of whisky. Could it be Armani? It looked a lot like what John Chan usually wore. Jason was prematurely greying at the temples and his huge beer belly pressed against the seams of his expensive light blue shirt, the buttons looking like they were ready to pop at any time. He had gained a lot of weight, and his eye bags aged him. I wouldn't have recognised him with his puffy cheeks if not for his grating voice.

I nodded at him. 'Hello,' I said, pretending I didn't know who he was.

'It's me, Jason! From school!' Jason slapped me so hard on the back I staggered forward. 'Don't tell me your memory is so bad! So, how are things? Still selling laksa at your father's stall?'

Before I could speak, Alice replied, 'Wei Ming's a renowned sushi chef in Hong Kong. In an award-winning restaurant!' I blushed. I didn't know she had heard him. I almost flinched when she held on to my arm as if she were my date. Her hands felt warm and I hoped she didn't notice I had goosebumps. As she leaned close to me, the smell of peaches consumed my senses. I looked at her and she gave me a knowing glance. Jason looked at us, downed his whisky and coughed. I smiled at his discomfort.

'Oh yeah, that's what you said you wanted to be, a chef! Amazing, I'll come by your restaurant sometime! I think I have a business trip lined up for next month. Make sure you're there, okay! What's your restaurant called?'

'It's nothing, a small place.' The last thing I wanted was for Jason to meet Sensei and find out I had left Haruto. 'I won't be there next month. I'm visiting my parents and I haven't got a return ticket booked yet.'

'Really? I can postpone my trip. I want to see this restaurant of yours,' he said with a glint in his eye.

'It's not mine, it's my boss's place.'

'You're the chef there,' Alice insisted. 'Wei Ming is so humble. I don't know anyone else who's a chef at an award-winning Japanese restaurant, do you?' she asked Jason.

'No! That's why I want to go! Where is it?'

'Somewhere in Central.'

'Fantastic, let me know when you're going back. Hey, we can take the same flight!' Jason said. Then he spotted someone and called out to her before walking off. Alice let go of me and crossed her arms, glaring after Jason.

'Such a disgusting buffoon. Your friend?' Alice asked. I shook my head vigorously.

'Definitely not. I hated him in school,' I said, only just realising I'd been clenching my jaw.

'I can see why.' She gave me an encouraging smile. My insides warmed. I was grateful for how she had spoken up for me. Pretending we were together was a nice touch. I felt like a country bumpkin next to her, and admired her finesse in handling people like Jason. 'You mustn't let these idiots get you down. I know the type. Plenty of them in law school.'

'Thanks, Alice.' I wished I could hold her hand. I fiddled with my tie and tried to loosen my collar. The men were dressed in expensive suits and the women in dresses fit for the Oscars. Everyone was happily engrossed in conversation, some seated at tables eating peanuts and drinking tea while others stood around Towkay Lau with wine glasses in their hands, their faces already red from pre-dinner drinks. Towkay Lau was busy with his friends but he hurried over as soon as he spotted me.

'Wei Ming! So glad you could make it. Ah, this must be your friend and his sister. I'm Lau,' he said, taking Alice's hand, his gaze resting a bit too long on her neckline. I didn't realise he spoke such good English.

'Pleased to meet you,' Alice said, then shook her hand free, which I was glad to see.

'Thank you for inviting us, Mr Lau,' I said.

'My pleasure. I wish your parents were here too, then they could try the good food! I brought my own fish today. You won't believe this, a thirty-kilo empurau! What do you boys think? Gigantic! I was lucky a fisherman caught this monster of a fish.'

'Thirty kilos? That's almost half my body weight! And wild-caught!' Dennis said.

Towkay Lau chuckled. 'Your friend knows about fish? You like fresh fish?'

'Who doesn't? You must've spent tens of thousands of ringgit on it! Wild-caught is double the price of pond empurau.' Dennis turned to me. 'They call it the "wang pu liao" fish. Because once you eat it, you can't forget it.'

Towkay Lau roared with laughter at this. 'It's good to see a young man who knows his food. No wonder you two are friends.'

'He's the real expert,' I said. 'You should see him, he's a wizard in the kitchen.'

'Ah, don't be so modest. A sushi chef like you pretending to be humble. Like your father, huh? He is a master, but he

207

pretends he only knows laksa. If a simple dish like laksa can be cooked so well by your father, imagine what he could do with an empurau! Or fresh lobster and crab! We have that tonight also, what do you boys think?'

'I think I'm going to undo a button on my trousers,' Dennis said, and Alice smacked his arm. 'What?'

Towkay Lau showed us to our table and introduced us to the other guests there. Mr and Mrs Ling and their children, Jonathan and Megan. They were a distinguished-looking family. Mr Ling was a lawyer and Jonathan was one as well, working at his father's firm. Megan was an architect, and she didn't give me a second look after the introductions.

There was another couple, in their sixties. Mr Ganding was a member of parliament but I wasn't knowledgeable about politics. The MP talked as if I was supposed to know him. I was beginning to feel bored as he droned on about himself, never once asking what I did for work. His wife spoke to Mrs Ling, carping about maids and drivers and how hard it was to find good help these days.

Then there was Mr and Mrs Tong, a couple about the same age as Mr and Mrs Ganding. Mr Tong was from Hong Kong and spoke halting English in a heavy Cantonese accent while Mrs Tong's accent was something I hadn't heard before.

'I'm originally from Shanghai,' Mrs Tong said in her sing-song Mandarin. She was a plump woman squeezed into a sapphire-blue silk qipao embroidered with two intertwined golden dragons. Mr Tong was a petite, mousy-looking man who wore glasses and didn't speak much. His small face was framed by thinning grey hair. He was well dressed in an elegant grey suit and dark blue tie, but he wasn't comfortable in them, as if his clothes had been picked out for him.

'You must be the young chef Mr Lau was talking about,'

Mrs Tong said. Towkay Lau had been talking about me? I didn't know whether to feel suspicious or flattered.

'Yes, I'm Lim Wei Ming.'

'Lau tells us your father is a great laksa master,' Mrs Tong said.

'He's just a noodle seller, Mrs Tong,' I said. Modesty was a trait that had been drummed into my head since I was a child. It was as if boasting about talent was a sin we could not commit, for fear of offending the deity.

'Lau says he's been asking your father to go into business with him, but your father is not keen.' She took a sip of her tea while chewing a pickled cucumber.

'It's a family business. We want to keep it that way.'

Mrs Tong nodded. 'I like generational shops. Nothing like a family business that gets passed down generation to generation. This tradition is dying out. We try to rescue businesses like these, buy them, then try to keep them going. But it's not easy without the master continuing. Their children don't want to take over the business, and if the master doesn't train anyone else, the cuisine is lost.'

'How many restaurants do you own?'

'About fifteen, including cafés. All around the world, but mostly in Hong Kong. Lau says you're thinking of setting up your own restaurant?' Mrs Tong said. I cleared my throat uneasily. I didn't know if Towkay Lau had told them about his offer. I didn't want anyone to know yet, and certainly not people I was meeting for the first time.

'Most chefs do. But it costs a lot of money, I have to be realistic.'

'Lau said he would talk to you about your business plan. It would be a first time for us to invest in a restaurant in Kuching. We have one in KL, a steakhouse. It's doing well.'

'Wow,' I said, trying to contain my excitement. Was this how Towkay Lau was planning to give me a restaurant? Through them? 'Are you looking around restaurants in Kuching now?'

'We see a lot of potential in Kuching. Property prices are affordable here, we could invest in a space as well. And anyone Mr Lau recommends will take priority in our decision, of course.'

Investors and restaurant spaces! I could pick a place near the Holiday Inn. That was a prime location. Or the Main Bazaar. I imagined tourists making advance bookings to have dinner at my restaurant.

Alice, who had been quietly listening to our conversation, whispered, 'Think carefully about any business you start, okay? Don't rush into anything. I can help you vet contracts.' I thanked her. She really was something. Beauty and brains. All this looking out for me made me yearn for her more.

But I had to get a hold of myself. I didn't know if she was in the right frame of mind to think about romance. We weren't in secondary school anymore. It wasn't puppy love or a crush. If I wanted to get involved with Alice, I had to think of Misha too. Not to mention Dennis. I didn't know how he'd feel about me being interested in his sister. And what about Jiayi? It was too soon, I hadn't even sorted out the mess I'd left in Hong Kong.

I listened to Alice talk to Mr Ling and Jonathan about some legal issue, correcting the cocksure Jonathan at one point. I wanted to laugh aloud. She was so cool. Most of the people there needed to be taken down a peg or two. If only I knew how to do it, but I was nowhere near as articulate as Alice.

'When's the food coming, man, I'm starving,' Dennis whined. My stomach had been growling for a while. At ten minutes past eight, we heard microphone feedback and Towkay Lau started to speak.

'Thank you, ladies and gentlemen, for gracing us with your presence. Today we will have a feast with old and new friends, all of you who love food as much as I do. The highlight of tonight's dinner will be my prized empurau. For now, please enjoy the other equally delicious dishes while waiting for the beauty to be prepared,' he said, ending his speech to applause.

The banquet hall's lights dimmed, and there was a sudden blast of trumpets and orchestral music, as if announcing the arrival of royalty. I chuckled quietly at the fanfare. As the music subsided and the lights came back on, waiters were standing near the tables, holding silver trays of food.

There were murmurs of delight as the dishes arrived. Dennis was the first person who reached over the table hungrily with his chopsticks, while Alice pulled him back and showed him the communal spoons available for use. First was the cold platter, also known as the Four Seasons. There was sliced century egg with pickled ginger, jellyfish salad dressed in soy sauce, vinegar and sesame oil, deep-fried prawns with sweetened mayonnaise, and steamed chicken served cold. The small bites were a great opener for the next dish, which was shark's fin soup. The broth was delicious, not too thick, and generously filled with small combs of shark's fin.

'I can't believe I'm eating so much shark's fin,' Dennis said, some soup trickling down the side of his mouth. I passed him a table napkin.

'You shouldn't,' said Alice with a heavy tone of disapproval. 'Did you know they cut off the fins then throw the sharks back into the sea? It's very cruel.'

'Aiyah, but it's so delicious.'

'There are many other delicious things that don't involve

cruelty to animals.' Alice pushed away her bowl of soup. Dennis took her bowl and finished that too, while she glared at him. Next was beggar's chicken, the Heritage Club's signature dish, baked in clay the traditional way.

'Clay! Very few restaurants serve it like that these days. It's so troublesome. Towkay Lau must have insisted.' Dennis looked at the dish in awe while a waiter in gloves broke the clay shell with a hammer and lifted the lotus-leaf-wrapped chicken onto another plate. As he cut open the lotus leaf, steam rose from the unwrapped dish and the smell of dang gui, goji berries and red dates perfumed the air. The waiter then cut the chicken in half, and pieces of dried scallop and Solomon's seal mixed with other Chinese herbs came tumbling out of its cavity. We were served small succulent portions of the meat, which was falling off the bone. I devoured mine like a hungry lion. The herbs had been infused in the meat and the dish was salted just right.

As I was about to get a second helping, Towkay Lau strode towards me. He leaned over and whispered in my ear. 'We need your help in the kitchen. The chef doesn't feel well and has gone home. He's prepared the other dishes except the empurau,' he said with urgency in his voice.

'But I haven't cooked empurau before, Mr Lau,' I said. Was this a joke, or a test? I unbuttoned my collar and loosened my tie. I didn't have much time, but fish recipes were already swirling around my head.

*

Towkay Lau led me to a glass aquarium in a storage room near the kitchen, where a large fish was swimming, unaware of its fate. It must have been at least a metre and a half in length. Its silvery scales glistened as it swam back and forth, its eyes dark and bright, with an almost regal bearing. I felt sorry such a majestic-looking creature had to be eaten, but curious how it would taste.

'Here it is, my treasure, all the way from the Rajang River! These days it's not often a fish this size comes along. I'll leave it in your capable hands! You have about forty minutes. There are two more dishes before the empurau,' Towkay Lau said before he returned to the banquet hall.

Why did I have to be the one to end this magnificent creature's life? At least it would feel no pain, thanks to the ikejime method. I was pretty sure no one else in the kitchen knew how to do it. The Heritage Club's main kitchen was fully staffed, with three sous chefs, various cooks, and kitchen helpers and dishwashers. I had the whole team at my disposal.

My mind conjured the images of my father frowning, ready to pounce on my every move, and Sensei standing in the doorway, watching my hands. One of the sous chefs cleared his throat. The kitchen staff looked at me expectantly, waiting for my instructions.

A fish this size needed more than one cutting board. The kitchen helpers cleared a counter and placed five wooden cutting boards on it. I rolled up my sleeves and asked for an ice pick. 'I need a sharp wire too,' I said, to confused looks all around, but one of the kitchen helpers managed to find one and gave it to me.

It took three sous chefs and two line cooks to lift the empurau out of the aquarium. The fish was wriggling and twisting its body so much that at one point I was sure it was going to slip from the clutches of the five men. They pinned down the writhing fish on the wooden cutting boards as I took the ice pick.

A swift stab between the eyes broke its skull and drove the ice pick into its brain. The fish shuddered and its jaw dropped open. I reflexively looked for my knife bag. I'd never cut fish without my trusty yanagiba before. I sighed when I realised it wasn't with me, but there was no time to think about that now. I had to settle for the sharpest slicing knife they had in the kitchen.

I cut its bright red gills and made an incision towards the tail, where I inserted the wire and ran it along the fish's spinal cord. When the fish stopped shivering, I removed the wire and let the blood drain.

'Try this method, next time you have live fish here,' I said to the sous chefs, who were agape. I felt proud to show them something new. Sensei would be happy to have the knowledge of ikejime passed on to more people. Would they remember me as the first chef who showed them ikejime? Word would spread, Kuching was a small place. 'It's ready. What was the original menu?'

'Chef was going to steam it with spring onion and light soy sauce,' one of the sous chefs said. That sounded sensible but conservative. I had to think fast. What about sashimi? But the empurau was a freshwater fish. Sensei didn't like making sashimi from freshwater fish, which had more parasites than sea fish. When the fish was this fresh, my work was cut out for me. But all I had to do was highlight the natural flavours of the fish and not hide its potential under thick sauces or seasonings.

'I'll make a cold fish dish,' I said to the bewildered sous chefs, and told them to prepare beds of ice on serving platters. It was a good compromise, cooked but cold, so its sweetness

214

could be amplified. Usually fish were steamed whole, but I would have to cut it into pieces so it wouldn't take forever to cook.

I sliced the belly open, exposing its massive entrails. As I was trying to gut the fish neatly, my knife slipped and punctured the intestines. There was blood everywhere, seeping into the cavity of the fish. I groaned. Just what I needed – more delay when I was already short of time.

I cleaned the insides with water, trying to make sure none of the bitterness of the entrails would affect the flavour of the fish. I scraped out the kidneys and bloodline running along the backbone of the fish and rinsed it. It was hard to be thorough with the ticking clock at the back of my mind.

I used a cleaver to cut the fish into large chunks, then rinsed them again under cold water to remove the rest of the blood. I hadn't used a cleaver in seven years. It felt different in my hand, heavy and secure. A knife made for chopping, dicing and speed. It was Ma's tool. She would balk at my knife bag, wondering why I needed so many knives for what her single cleaver could do.

We had ten chunks of fish to steam and needed four woks. The fish were steamed for ten minutes with just salt and a few slivers of ginger – scales on so they wouldn't dry out. Once they were out of the steamers, I asked one of the sous chefs to put the fish chunks in the freezer, and I checked on them every five minutes to see whether they were cold enough. Wasting no time, I instructed the platters to be ready to receive the fish. I had around five minutes to plate the fish once they were cold enough. Maybe less.

Meanwhile, I asked the sous chef to get the tau cheo sauce ready. It was made from salted fermented soybeans, which were commonly sold in jars in Malaysia. Most Chinese kitchens would have it, but the brand used in the Heritage Club kitchen wasn't the best one. I also instructed the serving staff to prepare a green lime, chilli and garlic dip for people who didn't like the taste of fermented soybeans.

I checked the fish in the freezer, crossing my fingers. They were cold, but not as cold as I'd wanted. I looked at my watch. About five minutes. It would have to do. I took the fish out of the freezer and laid them on a cutting board. I removed the scales. The flesh was moist. I breathed a sigh of relief. I removed the bones and plated the chunks of cold fish neatly on beds of ice on serving platters before slicing them into bite-sized morsels. Perfect.

I called out, 'Service up!' then left the kitchen as waiters scurried over to pick up the plates.

*

I went back to the table, adrenaline still pumping in my veins. I grinned at Alice and Dennis as I sank into my seat.

'Wei Ming! Your shirt . . .' Alice exclaimed. I looked down. My white shirt was splattered with blood. She called one of the club waiters, who brought me a black suit jacket to wear over my soiled shirt.

'It's like you just came back from surgery.' Dennis laughed. 'Dr Lim.'

He wasn't far off, considering the way I had to slice yellow-tail or awabi in Haruto with surgical precision. On our table were half-finished plates of lobster braised in scallop sauce, crab claws stir-fried with black pepper, and rice fried with dabai, a small purple fruit that looked like an olive but tasted like creamy avocado. I ate the last two spoonfuls left on the plate. Rich and buttery, it really hit the spot. All that excitement had made me hungry.

'They got you cooking fish back there?' Dennis asked. 'Didn't expect to be the guest chef here, eh? Tasty or not?'

'You tell me when you taste it.' Once again, trumpets announced the arrival of the next dish – the empurau. Each guest was served two morsels of the fish, which they dipped into the tau cheo sauce provided. Dennis ate his slowly, carefully, with his eyes closed as if enjoying some sensual delight. I looked over to Towkay Lau's table and caught his eye. The businessman gave a thumbs up. I exhaled in relief.

'This is the first time I've had cold fish,' Dennis said. 'It tastes better than it sounds!'

'I know. Like this you can taste its natural flavours without hiding anything,' I said. There were murmurs of approval around the table. After Megan tasted a piece of the fish, she stole a glance at me. Finally giving me a second look, huh? Mrs Tong was full of praise as she ate her second morsel of fish. When I had a taste of it myself, I sighed audibly. I imagined Sensei felt the same way when he tasted the suzuki caught with his own hands.

A fish so sweet and creamy it tasted like it had swum in delicate chicken broth its whole life. What had the fish eaten in all its years in the Rajang River to make its flesh so sweet? I hadn't added anything apart from a sprinkle of salt and some slices of ginger. It certainly was an unforgettable fish. And it was an unforgettable night. I couldn't believe I had done ikejime and prepared the cold dish at a moment's notice. If only Sensei were here to see me. Or my father. Would he think I was good enough for his broth now?

Dessert was orh nee, yam paste with gingko nuts, a Teochew specialty. Ah Hock would have loved the smooth, creamy texture of the dessert. As the guests were finishing dessert, Towkay Lau went on stage to make an announcement.

'Ladies and gentlemen, I hope you have enjoyed the feast, especially the highlight of this evening, the unforgettable fish! I must tell you that it was prepared by Lim Wei Ming, son of the laksa master Lim Ah Hock from Teck Boon kopitiam! I'm sure he didn't expect to find himself suddenly in the kitchen tonight, but as you all can see, he rose to the occasion and made a wonderful Teochew-style cold dish! The perfect recipe for a fish fit for royalty! Let's put our hands together for Wei Ming! Wei Ming, stand up and say hello to everyone!' Towkay Lau said to a round of applause. I blushed furiously while Dennis and Alice cheered. I stood up and waved at the guests awkwardly then sat back down.

'So that's where you disappeared to! I didn't know we had a chef at this table. How special!' Mrs Ling said. She hadn't said more than two words to me, and now she was smiling at me as if we were old friends.

After the last of the dessert was eaten, people were beginning to leave. 'Man, that was the best meal I ever had in my life,' Dennis said, patting his tummy as we walked out to the lobby.

'Better than your bamboo chicken?' I said.

'Surprisingly, yes,' he said, chuckling.

The guests filed out of the banquet hall to their chauffeur-driven luxury cars. People I didn't know came up to me and shook my hand, complimenting the fish. Jason swayed over, reeking of whisky, his shirt untucked and his jacket sleeve stained with chilli sauce.

'Excellent fish, Ming old boy. Who knew you could really cook?' he slurred. I turned away from his stale breath. 'Done well for yourself. No more laksa, eh?' He waved at me as a dark green Jaguar pulled up outside. I wondered what Jason did for work. He'd not mentioned it, but it looked like he still led the high life, without making much effort. I was glad I'd impressed him with my culinary skills but it didn't satisfy me as much as I'd thought it would.

*

The last to leave the Heritage Club were Towkay Lau and the Gandings as they walked to the lobby. Towkay Lau bid goodbye to them as their driver pulled up outside the lobby with their Mercedes.

'You kids need a ride?' Towkay Lau asked.

'No, thank you, Dennis drove,' I said. 'Thank you for inviting us tonight, Mr Lau. The food was out of this world. Your empurau was the freshest, sweetest fish I have ever tasted.'

Towkay Lau's eyes shone. 'And you did justice to it, my boy! Ah Hock would've appreciated the quality of the fish. Not everyone did, I believe. To some people, fish is fish. But this one melted in my mouth. It was so soft, and the flavours! Young man, I'm stealing your friend away for a short chat,' Towkay Lau said to Dennis, who nodded.

Once we were out of Dennis's earshot, he said, 'So, did you manage to convince your father to do business with me?'

I shook my head. 'I tried, but as expected, he won't budge.'

'You know, I'm not one to remind people of favours I've done for them, but if not for me, you wouldn't have become a chef in Hong Kong. Who else would arrange a restaurant for you to work in and a nice flat for you?' Towkay Lau said.

Kowloon Palace, where Man Kor had tormented me? Still, he was right. No one else could have opened the door to Hong Kong for me. 'And now it's time for me to fulfil your dreams again. Let me give you a restaurant, Wei Ming. Do something for yourself for once. It would be your own place, not assisting anyone. You'd be the boss, call the shots. Whatever you like, name it, it's yours.'

'But why would you . . . I mean, I don't understand—'

Towkay Lau leaned over and slipped a little sachet into my shirt pocket. 'All you have to do is put this in your father's laksa soup and disappear on the day of the bet. That's all.'

As I stared at him, he chuckled and said, 'Don't worry, it's not poison. Just something to make the laksa taste bad.'

'You're asking me to cheat for you? But why, don't you have faith you'll win anyway?'

'Why leave things to chance?' Towkay said, rubbing his jade ring.

'That's ridiculous, I can't do that to him, I'm—'

'But you'd be doing him a favour. Did you know he's ill?'

What was he talking about? Ah Hock seemed fine. He grumbled when he was tired but he was always grumbling anyway. Towkay Lau must be lying. This was the first I'd heard of it. If it was true, Ma would have told me.

'No. Did he say something?'

'I know people in this town. Including the staff at the hospital he went to. He had a test for his heart. If he continues working like this, I'm afraid your dear father may not last long. Don't want him to end up like your grandfather, do you?'

'What do you mean?'

'Lim Teck Boon had a heart attack at sixty. It's all that rich laksa soup and stress. All I know is, your father needs to retire. Or at least let me help. He should sit back, take it easy, let the young laksa cooks do the heavy work. But he refuses. You know how bull-headed your father is. You're not the same, I can tell. You know what you want. You know what this business needs. Kuching could do with a new chef in town. Mr and Mrs Tong are keen to invest, especially after your performance tonight. If they don't, I'll be your number one investor, so you focus on the artistry, not the money. You'd be set for life.'

'I can't, it would kill him to lose the kopitiam.' I was faltering. I wished Ah Hock would be more reasonable.

'It's killing him now, boy, don't you see? He's killing himself trying to make it work. They're barely making any money. My place is bustling with young people who don't care about quality, they just want a nice place to have laksa and not get shouted at by grumpy old uncles! With your father's recipe and our modern concept, our laksa shops would be unbeatable! I can foresee branches in Hong Kong!'

Ma had never said anything about money problems, even though I'd noticed the number of customers had dwindled compared to years ago. 'You're sure he's not well? My mother never mentioned this.'

'She doesn't know, Ming. Your father probably doesn't want to worry her. You'd be doing him a favour. Letting him relax, live longer. We can help him do all the heavy lifting, he only needs to oversee quality control. You can be the master chef your grandfather was. Fulfil your potential. Why do you want to play second fiddle to your boss and slice fish in Hong Kong, when you can cook whatever you like in your dream restaurant? You're a smart man, Ming. Make the right choice this time. And I don't just mean your career.' He winked. 'That friend of yours, his sister is a great beauty. I've seen the way you look at her. Build your career here. When you're a successful chef, the talk of the town, there's no way she will say no to you. Just like that, Wei Ming.' Towkay Lau snapped his fingers. 'You could have money, success, and the girl. It's not just a dream. It can easily become real. What do you say? Build your future with me, Ming. I didn't get to where I am by sitting still. You need change to succeed. I see it in you, you've got your grandfather's lucky star. You're destined for great things! This talent in cooking, it's in the blood. It would be a pity to see it go to waste.'

My grandfather's reputation as a formidable chef was well known, although the long family line of chefs had always attributed their success to the gift of the deity's broth. I felt no such connection. I owed nothing to the deity. Whatever talent I had, it was all from watching Ma, my own slaving in the hot kitchen at Kowloon Palace, and studying under Sensei over the years.

'So, if Mr and Mrs Tong don't invest, you will?' I asked. Towkay Lau's eyes lit up.

'Of course! It's nothing for me, Wei Ming. I spent much more on Kowloon Palace, as you know. Sold off my share now, for a tidy profit,' he said, grinning. 'This is more a favour for you, and well, it's worth it if I can franchise your family laksa.' Then he held out his hand to me. 'It's a deal, then?'

'Where would the restaurant be? Location is important.'

Towkay Lau laughed. 'Ah, already proving yourself so shrewd, eh? You don't worry about the details, I'll give you a prime location for sure.'

Maybe it was the high I was riding on after the banquet, the rush I'd got after everyone applauded. The magnificent empurau I had helped transform into a work of art. Ma would understand it was for the best, for our family. In time, even Ah Hock would see the wisdom behind my decision.

I swallowed the lump in my throat and shook Towkay Lau's hand. 'You've got a deal.'

'I knew you would do the right thing,' Towkay Lau said, smiling broadly, then he led me back to where Dennis and Alice were waiting. 'This old man has got to go home. You young people go enjoy yourselves!' he said, then he called out to his driver who was waiting nearby.

In the car, I didn't say much, thinking about the deal with Towkay Lau. Ah Hock looked older, but not sick. Towkay Lau was probably exaggerating my father's ill health, but my parents weren't getting any younger and there had to be some kind of preparation for the future. I couldn't imagine my father accepting this situation no matter what the reason. Maybe when he saw the final product, a five-star restaurant in the middle of Kuching city, a place VIPs frequented, he would realise I'd made the right decision all along. Imagine those snobbish kids from school coming to the restaurant, ordering the most expensive dishes on the menu to show off their wealth. Jason stumbling into the restaurant, drunk, asking to see his best friend the chef, only to be escorted out by burly bouncers. I chuckled at the thought.

'What's so funny?' Alice asked.

I shook my head. 'I was thinking about Dennis stuffing himself with shark's fin,' I said, turning to look at her. I could see what Towkay Lau saw: the three of us – me, Alice and Misha – in a bungalow in Kenny Hill, an affluent neighbourhood in Kuching. She could practise law while I ran my restaurant. When she was too busy, I could pick up Misha from school before the dinner sitting began. I knew I was getting ahead of myself, but it could all happen. I hadn't touched a drop of alcohol all night, even though there had been wine, beer and whisky. I felt drunk on the praise showered on me. Like I could conquer the world.

'You look beautiful tonight. We should dress up more,' I said, and Alice smiled.

'Eh, easy on the flirting. I'm here, man,' Dennis said as he turned into Carpenter Street. It was already eleven-thirty, and the street was quiet. It looked different, lonelier, with the empty parking spaces. 'Luckily we are near your place so I won't have to listen to more of this.'

Ma was sitting at one of the tables with a cup of tea, stifling a yawn, as I stepped into the kopitiam. 'How was the food?' she asked.

'Excellent. Towkay Lau was generous. Pa would've liked the fish. It was a big empurau.'

'Wah, yes, your father would've loved it. How was Alice? Did she look stunning?'

'She did.'

'You should get together with her. That's my dream. She's a lovely girl. Think about it, Ming. She's a great catch.'

'Go upstairs, Ma. You should be asleep.'

'All right,' she said with a laugh. 'I guess I'm too nosy. Don't forget to lock up and go to sleep soon.'

'I will.'

'Oh, why don't you light joss sticks for the altars? I forgot to do that earlier today.'

'You forgot? You do this every night.'

'Your mother is getting older, Ming.'

'You're not old, Ma.'

She squeezed my shoulder. 'You're thirty-five already, how can I not be old? Don't forget the joss sticks,' she said as she trudged upstairs.

I made some tea, skipping the kung fu tea rituals, and poured it into two cups. I sipped from the first cup, then looked at the clock. I picked up the kopitiam's rotary telephone and dialled Malaysian Kitchen's number, hanging up after three rings. A force of habit. I didn't know why I was calling when there was nothing left to say.

I lit eight joss sticks, three for Kuan Yin and five for my grandfather. I waved them to put out the flames. Holding them with both hands, I bowed three times to the Kuan Yin statuette and my grandfather's tablet before placing the joss sticks in the ash-filled urns. I felt my shirt pocket and took out the little sachet of white powder Towkay Lau had given me. I wondered what it was that would make the laksa taste bad. Ah Hock would be devastated. But it would just be the judging chef eating the spoiled laksa. It wasn't like the regulars would know.

No, I couldn't think about this now. More action, less thought, if I wanted things to change. After it was all over, I could comfort Ah Hock with my new restaurant. Maybe he could even help me plan the menu. Bring back the glory days of Ah Kong in his fine-dining kitchen in Swatow, cooking up a storm. We would be the owners of a restaurant, not just a laksa stall. Surely that would make up for the closure of the kopitiam.

I took a deep breath and put the sachet of powder under the Kuan Yin statuette. The smell of incense was starting to overpower the broth's aroma. I went to the simmering pot and ladled out a small bowl for Ah Kong's altar. Did I really have his lucky star? I would need it to face Ah Hock's wrath. I sighed and clasped my hands in prayer.

25

Children of the Pear Garden

'Ah Hock! Are you going for the tua hi tonight?' Third Uncle's voice made Ah Hock look up from the laksa bowl he was assembling. 'They're showing a comedy. I think you'll enjoy it.'

'Oh! I missed this one,' Ah Hock said. It was usually him who told Third Uncle about the performances lined up at Lau Ya Keng. Probably Wei Ming's return had distracted him. 'What are they showing?' he asked, pouring laksa soup into the bowl he had carefully assembled for Third Uncle.

'*The Tiger's Servant*. I've never heard of it. I was hoping they would stage something familiar, like *Lychee and the Mirror*, or *The Peony Pavilion*,' Third Uncle said.

'Love stories! Never knew you were the romantic kind, Third Uncle! No disrespect, but I thought only young people liked those kinds of stories.' The idea of watching Teochew opera brightened Ah Hock, improving his already good mood from the soup being satisfactory that day. He brought the bowl of laksa to Third Uncle's table and sat with him.

'Young people? Do you see any young people at the performances?'

Ah Hock nodded. 'True, true. Us old ones have to carry on supporting the theatre. Nowadays they don't know what culture is! In ten, twenty years' time, there might not be anyone watching these shows anymore.'

'You're younger than me, Ah Hock. Don't talk like you don't have more than twenty years left. As for me, I'm amazed I'm alive with each passing year.'

'You're healthy as a horse, Third Uncle. It's because you don't sit down all the time like those lazy youngsters.'

'I work because I don't have the good life to sit around, not because I want to be healthy. *Bo ho mia.*' Third Uncle chuckled. 'No good life for me.' He took a sip of the laksa soup and gave Ah Hock a thumbs up. 'It's good, don't worry, Hock. Why don't you ask Kim Choo to come along for the show too?'

'I can ask, but she always says no.'

'Maybe she doesn't want to see what she's missing,' Third Uncle said.

'But why should she? Look at the life she would have had. You can't make enough to eat as an opera actor. The young actors here don't do it for a living, I'm sure. It's a hobby for them. For Kim Choo, there was nothing else. Until she joined me in the kopitiam.'

'I've known Kim Choo since she was a little girl. Quiet, obedient girl. The troupe master then was a severe man. The kids were beaten during practice, but she never needed a lot of beating. She listened and obeyed, but you know, for the man, it was a habit, shouting at these children. They were orphans, they had no one to stand up for them. You gave her an opportunity to build a home, Ah Hock. I think she would have given up anything for that. Still, it's true, she was very talented. I thought she would become a big star, make films.'

Ah Hock laughed. 'Films? She wouldn't have gone into something as vulgar as that! Only loose women go into the films or TV!'

'Ah, I wouldn't generalise, Hock. There are many talented actors in films too, you should try watching some.'

'Do you think she knew what she was giving up when she married me, Third Uncle? If you're right, and she could have become a film star, it would be a very different life.' Ah Hock could see Kim Choo as a film star. She certainly was beautiful enough. A film star wouldn't marry a laksa seller, for sure.

'What I do know is Kim Choo chose you. She might have had dreams of her own, I don't know. But when Wei Ming left for Hong Kong, I saw what that did to her. Breaking up the family like that. She has patience but she's not Kuan Yin. Think of her, Hock, instead of the broth or laksa.'

Ah Hock nodded guiltily. He knew he had a good woman, and he didn't tell her often enough. She wasn't the type who needed flowers or diamonds. Right now, he knew the only way to make her happy was to make peace with the boy.

After finishing his laksa, Third Uncle said, 'I'll see you tonight at the show,' then left the kopitiam. Kim Choo came in from the kitchen, carrying a basin of beehoon to the stall.

'You want to go to the show tonight?' Ah Hock asked, even though he knew what she would say.

She shook her head. 'No, I can hear the music from upstairs. You go and enjoy yourself with Third Uncle.'

'It's a new show. I've never seen it before.'

'Even more reason you should go,' she said with a smile.

'The performances haven't been the same without you.'

'It's been such a long time.' She laughed. 'I'm sure they've managed without me.'

'There aren't many young actors left. Soon they'll be left with old men playing Su Liu Niang. I wouldn't go see that!'

'With all that face paint on, you wouldn't be able to tell

who's an old man! It's about the actor and the music, right? What does it matter what they look like, as long as you know the story and the songs? Who knows, these actors might surprise you with new costumes or skills.'

'Don't you want to say hello to the old gang? Is it because you miss them too much?' Ah Hock didn't want to push, for fear she would say he was right, that she missed her old life in the theatre. That he hadn't delivered on his promise of a better one.

'Nonsense, I'm too busy to think about them. I know, why don't you take Ming?' Kim Choo suggested.

Ah Hock laughed. 'Are you joking? He'll find it a torture.'

'At least ask. He can say no.'

It wasn't a bad idea. 'You ask,' Ah Hock said grumpily. It would be surprising if Wei Ming said yes. He had no clue what the boy liked apart from fancy dinners and strange Western music, those erratic beats and chaotic melodies Ah Hock found distracting. How he could prepare food with that noise, Ah Hock didn't know.

It was different from the gentle silk strings of the pipa, a four-stringed lute with clear, crisp sounds that accompanied the lament of a wronged concubine, or the sharpness of the guzheng's notes amplifying the intensity of a fighting scene. There was so much complexity in the music, Ah Hock himself didn't even know the half of it. He couldn't imagine Wei Ming sitting on a plastic chair at the temple with a few small box fans to provide relief from the hot, humid air, listening to music he didn't understand. Ah Hock wanted to enjoy the show, and he didn't want to see Wei Ming's sullen, bored expression if the boy didn't like it as much. But Third Uncle would be there; the boy would make more of an effort for the old man's sake.

Wei Ming came out from the kitchen with a fresh bowl of peeled prawns. Ah Hock braced himself, then spoke to Wei Ming in what he hoped was a kind voice. 'Are you free tonight?'

'Tonight? I guess so. Why?'

'There's a show at Lau Ya Keng. Your mother asked me to invite you,' Ah Hock said.

Wei Ming raised an eyebrow. 'Teochew opera? The last time I went, I was five. Or six.'

Ah Hock was impressed. 'You remember?' That's right, he used to bring the boy when Wei Ming was about four or five, when it was still possible to coax him to follow Ah Hock wherever he went. Back then, Ah Hock would explain to Wei Ming about the stagecraft for Chinese opera. Actors used movement, costumes, face paint and props to convey meaning.

Even if they knew the stories well, the audience came to see good actors perform familiar scenes with finesse. How an actor walked in a circle to show he had gone on a journey, or mimed feeding chickens by scooping up her apron to hold imaginary chicken feed. How a general posed to show his determination and military prowess. Ming's eyes had lit up at the colourful costumes the actors wore and he had even mimicked some of their hand gestures, the swishing of their water sleeves.

'Mostly I remember screechy, high-pitched singing and loud music.'

Ah Hock frowned. Screechy, loud music? How would someone who could not appreciate the fine artistry of Teochew opera understand the essence of cuisine?

'If it sounds that terrible to you, you don't have to go.'

'No, I . . . I want to go.' Wei Ming sounded apprehensive, but before Ah Hock could say more, the boy had gone back to the kitchen. Ah Hock hadn't expected him to accept his invitation. The both of them going out together without Kim Choo! He couldn't remember the last time they had done that. He felt the corners of his mouth lifting, and stopped them in time as new customers came to give him orders. He looked around for Kim Choo to show them an empty table and realised she had been standing at the stairs and had witnessed the exchange between him and Wei Ming. She smiled at him appreciatively, then came down and led the customers to their table.

*

Lau Ya Keng, the Chamber of the Gods, had been spruced up with red paper lanterns. The old temple felt like a second home to Ah Hock, a place in which he sought the occasional refuge, like when he and his father had first arrived in Kuching without a home or family. It was a Teochew temple, and clan members helped each other there.

Ah Hock had been relieved, hearing that familiar language, and seeing Teck Boon thank strangers they had just met, who were happy to see fellow countrymen from the motherland. Ah Hock and his father were allowed to sleep under the stage until they could find suitable lodgings. The floor was cold and hard, the air filled with incense, and his father's snoring next to him woke him up periodically, but it was better than sleeping on the streets. Better than being at the bottom of a ship being swayed back and forth, surrounded by smells of excrement and vomit. Ah Hock shuddered when he recalled the seasickness. He had never been on a boat since.

They arrived early at Lau Ya Keng, around seven in the evening. It was already dark outside, but the temple was lit with powerful fluorescent lights. The hawker stalls were tidied away and the temple was a different world without the sight of steam rising from simmering fish broths and the smells of flash-fried long beans and barbecued pork satay. There were lines of red plastic chairs in front of the theatre. The dark stage was well lit, with a backdrop of cardboard cut-outs of trees and the façade of a house. Red lanterns adorned the ceiling, and above it, the food court's fluorescent lights shone on the sculpture of a pair of dragons that sat on the brown-tiled temple roof with upturned eaves.

There were at least thirty people there, more than usual. Ah Hock saw a few familiar faces but there were many he didn't recognise. They looked young – were his eyes deceiving him? What a surprise! Perhaps there was hope for Teochew opera yet.

The seats were filling up fast, and they managed to take three of the last few available, reserving one for Third Uncle. It wasn't long before they saw him, and Ah Hock motioned him over. 'So glad to see you, Third Uncle! Look at how many people there are here. I wonder why!'

'The goldsmith said tonight's show is a bit different. I think there are some new, young actors. Looks like their friends are here to support them.' Third Uncle took his seat next to Ah Hock. 'You see those young people over there? Normally you won't see any of them around.'

'Yes, I noticed! Better than them watching rubbish on TV or going to the cinema. There's some real culture here they can learn from!' Ah Hock laughed. 'Hey,' he said, nudging Wei Ming. 'Look, people your age watching the show!'

'You're in a good mood,' Wei Ming said. Was that a smile Ah Hock detected on the boy's face? Wei Ming was right, he was in a good mood. He hadn't felt so light in a long time. Having the boy back had given him some hope. And seeing those young people at the theatre lifted his spirits. Perhaps it wasn't all doom and gloom for the new generation, after all. If they could appreciate Teochew opera, they might be more appreciative of other traditions.

'It's good to see you relaxed, Hock.' Third Uncle patted Ah Hock's knee. 'You need a break from work. And from your worries. And great to see Wei Ming here too. You're a good boy, accompanying your father.'

'What's the story about?' Wei Ming asked, looking at the stage.

'It's called *The Tiger's Servant*. I haven't watched it yet,' Ah Hock said. 'Third Uncle knows more about it.'

As Third Uncle chatted with Wei Ming, Ah Hock looked at his son. From this angle, the boy was the spitting image of his mother. Ah Hock's heart was weighed down by the past eight years, spent not knowing if he would ever have his son back. He had not dared to imagine a day when he would be talking to the boy again, let alone watching a Teochew opera with him.

It was Third Uncle who had introduced Ah Hock to the world of Teochew opera many years ago. He had invited Ah Hock and his father to watch *The Tale of Su Liu Niang*. That was the first time Ah Hock had seen Kim Choo on stage. There were rumours of a debuting young actress who was performing the titular role. Su Liu Niang, a beautiful and wealthy maiden, falls in love with her cousin Guo Jichun, while betrothed to someone else by her father to settle his debts. In the end, they elope with the help of her maidservant, Tao Hua, and the boatman. Although the actress who played Taohua was charming and pretty, Ah Hock had eyes only for the forlorn Su Liu Niang pining for her lover.

Every time she threw out her water sleeves on stage, it was to signal she was about to sing. He would look forward to that gesture, which she used to express sorrow or distress. How useful all these gestures and props would be in real life! Even now, after so many years of knowing her, Ah Hock could never tell from Kim Choo's face how she felt inside. And the few times he asked, she would say she was all right.

The next morning, Kim Choo had gone to Teck Boon kopitiam for breakfast with two other cast members. Ah Hock was determined to prepare her bowl of laksa even though his hands were shaking and he almost forgot to add the shredded omelette. Her eyes widened as she took her first sip of the soup, before she turned to smile at him. 'The food of the gods,' she said. It was then that he knew she would be his new beginning in life, a bright spark in his routine of making laksa every day.

When he had to pay for her leaving the troupe, a dowry of sorts, every cent was worth it. She was priceless. He felt privileged she had accepted him and loved him. When they'd had a son, it seemed like their luck had increased threefold.

The strumming of erhu and loud trumpeting interrupted his thoughts. The show was about to begin. Two actors appeared on stage, one with the mask of a tiger and the other the chou, the clown of the show, with the trademark white patch painted around his nose and eyes. He had an over-grown bushy moustache, darkened brows, and carried a spear. The story was that the clown, Er Mao, wanted to be like Wu

Song, the legendary tiger slayer, but ended up being the tiger's servant instead. The tiger demanded to live in Er Mao's house and threatened to eat him if the former's commands were not obeyed.

Ah Hock grinned from ear to ear when Wei Ming howled with laughter at the scene where the tiger took a swipe at Er Mao when the latter refused to cook him rabbit stew. The actors were new but well versed in singing and acrobatics, and Ah Hock was buoyed up by the young people around them chuckling and clapping.

The show ended at midnight to a thunderous round of applause. Wei Ming was wiping tears of laughter from his eyes. 'I never knew Teochew opera could be this funny,' he said. 'Did you see how fast the clown scrambled up the ladder when the tiger was chasing him?'

Ah Hock nodded. 'I didn't think you would enjoy it this much.'

'Maybe because it's a comedy. I didn't understand some parts of the dialogue though.'

'Doesn't matter, the mannerisms of the actors are more important.'

'Yes, I was so impressed. I didn't know Teochew opera had so many acrobatics. The actors were skilled. I'm thinking about that scene where the wife tries to catch the tiger by tempting it with bananas! And I didn't know that character was a doctor until he was attending to Er Mao. What a crazy story!' Wei Ming said, chuckling. 'When's their next show?'

'They don't have many. Only during special occasions. The next one could be during winter solstice. Or Chinese New Year. Will you be here then?' Ah Hock asked in what he hoped was a nonchalant tone.

Wei Ming nodded. 'Sure.'

Ah Hock didn't know what to think. Had the boy decided to stay in Kuching permanently? Had he accepted his inheritance? It was like a birthday wish come true. He looked around the temple and whispered a prayer in his head. He seldom prayed, but gratitude overwhelmed him then. He couldn't wait to tell Kim Choo when they got home.

'You know, your grandfather and I used to sleep under the stage here,' Ah Hock said. 'It's not just the food or opera I like here. It feels like a second home to me. This temple protected us when we first came from China.' He didn't know if he had ever told Wei Ming this. Maybe he had, a long time ago, when the boy had been too young to understand. It felt good telling him again.

Wei Ming gazed at the stage in astonishment. 'But wasn't Ah Kong a famous chef in China? How did you guys end up sleeping in an old temple?'

'We were running away from a war, not having a holiday, you know. I guess he must have just brought whatever gold or money he could fit in his pockets,' Ah Hock said. 'And the broth.'

'Wow. Must've been tough,' Wei Ming said in a sympathetic tone. 'I know what it's like to move to a foreign country. But at least I had a warm room and a job waiting for me.'

Ah Hock scoffed. 'Are you comparing your luxurious plane journey to Hong Kong to my days of vomiting on a ship? But at least when we arrived, we weren't begging on the streets. Thanks to our neighbours here. It was heaven to sleep on a floor that wasn't moving.'

They walked out of Lau Ya Keng with Third Uncle, then bade him goodnight. The kopitiam was dark apart from a flickering flame from a lotus flower candle at the Kuan Yin altar. Kim Choo had gone to bed.

236

'Want some tea, Pa?' Wei Ming reached for the clay zisha pot. Ah Hock smiled. He wasn't sure if Wei Ming could see him in the dim light.

'Not for me. Make some for your Ah Kong.' The joss sticks Kim Choo had put out earlier had burned all the way down. Ah Hock ladled some of the simmering broth to taste. It was time to add more chicken bones and salt.

'Come here,' he called to Wei Ming, who walked over to the pot cautiously. Ah Hock passed him the ladle.

'What? You want me to. . .' Wei Ming said, his words trailing off as he looked confused.

'Try it. See what it needs,' Ah Hock said. He remembered the elation he'd felt the first time he was allowed to ladle the broth, to taste it. It was more magical because he'd been a child. It was as if he had been granted entry into a secret club created by deities.

Wei Ming tasted the broth. Ah Hock watched the boy's eyes to see if he understood. The depth of flavours, their family history. All those generations distilled into one pot.

'Can you tell what's in it?' Ah Hock asked. Now was the time to see if the boy was worth his salt.

'The flavour . . . like the sea and land combined. Dried scallops? Fish bones . . . abalone . . . definitely your dried flatfish. Chicken . . . kampung chicken?'

'And black chicken too,' Ah Hock said. That was okay, it wasn't easy to guess black chicken. 'What else?'

'I can taste the smokiness of roasted pork trotters, just a tinge. Doesn't overwhelm, when it could have.'

Ah Hock felt a tingle in his spine. This was more than he'd expected. The boy was doing well.

Wei Ming tasted it again. 'Peppercorn, but not too much, just for its woodiness not its punch. What blows me away is the balance, like walking a tightrope. A little too much of one thing and the whole thing falls apart. The depth here . . . wow . . .' Wei Ming drank a third spoonful. 'I can taste the sweetness of pork and chicken fat. Did you use them? It's not greasy at all though.'

'Of course. Then I strained the broth.'

'There's something I can't quite put my finger on . . . it's subtle . . . tangy? Salty and sour.'

Not bad at all. Even Kim Choo wouldn't have spotted it. 'Pickled plum. Only one or two. I'm surprised you could taste it.'

'Oh. I didn't know you could put pickled plum in soups. I suppose you do, now that I think about it. In salted mustard duck soup.'

'That's right. One of the few things from my childhood home in Swatow. Our courtyard had this gigantic gingko tree, but also plum trees. Green plums my mother used to pickle in jars. She let me try one, but it was too sour for me then. I don't know why I remember this now,' Ah Hock said in a strangled voice. He blinked back tears, dismayed they had appeared. He was getting old, more emotional. He had to watch himself or he would turn into one of those blubbering old fools.

'Let me guess, you pickle your own plums?' Wei Ming looked around the kitchen as if he expected to see jars of them.

'I wish I did. Plums aren't native here. It's a lot of work. The ones in jars aren't bad.'

'I think . . . it needs more salt though. Is it okay to say that?'

Ah Hock laughed. The boy looked nervous, as if he were unsure what to do or say next. He couldn't blame Wei Ming. He'd surprised himself too. He couldn't remember the last time he had laughed so heartily.

'Yes, it's okay to say that. We can salt it. In fact, it's time to refresh it. That's how we keep the broth fresh for decades. You keep adding ingredients when it's getting thinner. Could do with a couple of pieces of dried flatfish too, I think,' Ah Hock said. 'I'll add them tomorrow. You go on to sleep.'

Wei Ming nodded, then went upstairs. Ah Hock locked the front door, then went back to the altar to light new joss sticks. Teck Boon's portrait stared at him, looking as stern as ever.

'He's ready at last, Father. I'm ready too. You can rest now and stop your journeys into my dreams. Your grandson will take care of the deity's broth from now on. Your legacy will be safe.' Ah Hock clasped the joss sticks in his hands and bowed three times before putting them in the urn. Everything would be all right now. He whistled as he went up the staircase, then stopped and chuckled when he thought how pleased Kim Choo would look when he told her about the good news in the morning.

26

The Wide Sea and the Empty Sky

I didn't know what to pack for a morning at the beach. The last time I'd gone was decades ago, when I was ten? Would we be swimming? I didn't have any trunks. I rummaged through my old wardrobe and eventually found a pair of old shorts I could still wear. I went downstairs, where my parents were busy serving customers. The kopitiam was bustling at eight in the morning.

Ah Hock looked up at me sourly. 'We're so busy and you're going out. Bring this bowl to that old lady before you go.'

He handed me a bowl of laksa. Looked like his good mood hadn't lasted long. At least he had let me taste the broth last night. It felt like a breakthrough somehow.

'Aiyoh. Enough-lah, old man. He's taking one measly day off. Let him explore a bit, he hasn't been home for eight years!' Ma said. Ah Hock grunted and went back to filling bowls with beehoon. 'Going to see Alice and her daughter? That cute little girl, what's her name again?' Ma beamed.

'Misha. Dennis is coming too. What?' I said, trying not to look at her.

'Nothing. Why are you blushing?'

'I'm not blushing,' I said. She rubbed my back.

'Alice is a very nice girl, Ming. You be good to her, okay?'

'I'm not doing anything with her, Ma! We're just all going out to the beach.'

Ma laughed. 'All right, all right, whatever you say.'

'See you later, Pa,' I said. Ah Hock grunted in reply. The tables were all full. I felt bad leaving my parents on a busy day but I'd make it up to them tomorrow. I couldn't wait to have my own restaurant so my parents could finally take a break. I could take care of them and they wouldn't have to work weekends anymore. They could take that trip to China Ah Hock had talked about.

I waited outside the kopitiam, and a few minutes later Dennis arrived. Alice and Misha were in the back seat. Misha waved at me. I waved back then got in the front. Baby powder and citrus-soap shower gel mingled with the mustiness of the car. I turned to say hi to Alice. Her hair was swept back in a ponytail and her face looked bright and fresh. She was wearing a white T-shirt tucked into denim shorts that showed off her shapely, long legs. I wondered if she was going to swim. She looked good and I tried not to stare.

'Hi, Uncle Ming!' Misha chirped. I reached over and ruffled her hair. Such a sweet girl. I'd never been great with kids but Misha had me thinking about schools in Kuching.

'Good morning, Misha! Did you bring any beach toys?'

'Yes! Mummy let me bring all my sand toys. I have a pail, a spade, a wheelbarrow, a cookie cutter, a digger, a schoolbus—'

'She has too many toys!' Alice said.

'What? When I was a boy, I only had a spade. Wait, and a pail? Or was it just a pail?' I put on a sad face. Alice and Misha laughed.

'Yo, man. Ready for a day at the beach?' Dennis said. He was wearing a Hawaiian shirt with a singlet underneath and had a pair of sunglasses on.

'Wow, Ray-Bans, looking cool. Still crazy about *Top Gun*, huh?' Dennis was a huge Tom Cruise fan.

'I'd get the bomber jacket too if they sold it here.'

'Where're we going?'

'Pandan Beach. Gonna be nice and peaceful there.'

'Pandan Beach? That's at least two hours away! I thought we were going to Damai!'

'Damai?' Dennis said with exaggerated scorn. 'Please, it's filled with tourists. I'm taking you to an untouched place.'

'He's so fussy,' Alice said. 'I told him Damai is fine, not too far away, but he insisted.'

'Oh, it's okay, I actually haven't seen much of Kuching.'

Alice laughed. 'What do you mean? You're a Kuching-lang, what.'

'When I was growing up, my parents were always busy with the kopitiam so I mostly hung out in Carpenter Street. Or your parents' house.'

'Yes, you came over often. Well, then Dennis can be your tour guide,' Alice said. Dennis put in a cassette and rewound it until the song 'Smoke on the Water' by Deep Purple played.

'Remember this?'

'Of course,' I said, then turned to Alice. 'He used to play this album all the time when he was in my room. I got so sick of it by the hundredth time!' *Machine Head* was one of Dennis's favourite albums. It brought me back to our secondary school days. Come to think of it, I'd only listened to whatever Dennis recommended then.

The music grounded me, brought me back to simpler times. I looked out the window. The skies were grey and filled with ominous clouds. Before long, tiny droplets covered the windshield.

'Damn it, just when I thought it was going to be a sunny day.' Dennis turned on the wipers. The rain turned heavier and soon the wipers were at top speed.

'Should we turn back?' Alice asked glumly while Misha protested.

'Let's drive on, the rain might stop. Never know,' Dennis said. I looked at the blurry images of trees, shophouses, wooden huts and rural houses we passed. What was it like to live in the middle of nowhere? It felt weird to see so much space after the crowds in Hong Kong.

I lowered the volume of the music so I could hear snippets of Misha's conversation with Alice. She was telling her mother about her new friend George and how she hated Miss Flora, the art teacher. Misha sounded like such a happy child. Her voice radiated sunshine throughout the car. Even if each adult had their own darkness to bear, Misha's voice managed to make us forget about it for a while and listen to her cheeriness. I wouldn't have minded a child like Misha occasionally brightening up the serious mood at Haruto.

*

It took around two hours to reach Lundu, the beach town. Dennis's gamble had worked out for us. The rain had stopped. We drove past more solitary huts and simple brick houses in the vast, empty lands. Dennis stopped the car to buy produce from Iban sellers who were carrying foraged vegetables and corn in their anjats, cylindrical rattan woven backpacks. I was glad the weather wasn't too hot, or the sellers would be walking along the lonely trunk road waiting for buyers to stop their cars in the blazing sun.

We had the whole beach to ourselves. Dennis was right, it was unspoiled. The overcast sky and the foamy waves made the scenery wilder, more dramatic. The sole structure nearby was a small hut that sold canned drinks and fresh coconut water. Dennis and Misha ran towards the waves in their swimsuits while Alice and I laid out a beach mat on the sand.

The sea was the only place my soul could be tranquil. My parents and I had gone on beach holidays in Santubong when I was a young child. Ma would walk with me to the sea so I could feel the waves crash against my knees while Ah Hock sat under a coconut tree, watching us, fidgeting. He was restless outside the kopitiam, like he didn't know what to do with himself. Afterwards, we would eat from the picnic basket Ma had packed, filled with png kueh, a savoury and sticky Teochew glutinous rice cake, as well as fluffy red bean buns and packets of Yeo's chrysanthemum tea. There were fewer such trips as I got older, and they stopped altogether when I turned twelve.

The humid sea air turned Alice's wavy hair curlier, and her skin, glowing from the sun, was smooth and tanned. Her legs were covered in patches of sand. She noticed me staring and smiled. I turned red, then looked away.

'What's it like coming back? You miss Hong Kong yet?' she said.

'Sometimes. At night especially. It's great Lau Ya Keng is still noisy till after dinnertime, but after eleven it's deathly quiet.'

'What, you don't want it quiet? It's bedtime then.'

'I know, but it's too quiet. It's that city buzz I miss. In Hong Kong, I got used to hearing sirens.'

'I know what you mean. It was the same in KL. The sirens were so noisy.'

'What about you? Happy you're back?'

'I wouldn't say happy. But I couldn't stay there.' She looked far into the horizon, as if it would heal her.

'I don't know if I'm being rude, but how are you and Misha handling your husband . . . being gone?' I treaded carefully. It wasn't my place to be so intrusive, but I had to know, even if it meant offending her.

'If there's anything I learned from him . . . it is this. That I must learn to love myself unconditionally. Stop blaming myself for . . . for him leaving us. I'm sad he didn't get a chance to learn that lesson.'

'What do you mean by unconditionally?'

'Like, I don't have to be this or that, you know? A great lawyer? A great mum? The perfect wife, the dutiful daughter? Whatever I am, I should love myself. No matter what. The way I love Misha. If I can be unconditional with her, well, why can't I be the same with myself?'

'I wouldn't find you hard to love at all,' I said.

She blushed. 'Oh, you don't know me. I have a lot of things that are hard to love. I can hide my dark side very well.'

'Like what? I find that hard to believe.'

'We were working such long hours that we were more like roommates than husband and wife. I wanted everything to be . . . I don't know, the way I imagined it, I guess. A nice home. Great jobs. The perfect family. We fought when we were deciding on a school for Misha. Forced him to have holidays in Europe when he had a trial to prepare for. I had . . . have a temper. I said ugly things when I was upset. Vicious things I couldn't take back. I blamed him for every little thing. I never thought about how stressed he was. All I could think about was how stressful it was for me to be a working mum. He wasn't the type who talked about his feelings. Then, when he was gone, I had no one else to blame, so I blamed myself.'

'We all say things we regret. And I know what it's like to work from morning till night in a job that consumes you.' I touched her hand and she didn't pull away. The wind picked up and strands of hair caressed Alice's face. I brushed the strands from her face and she smiled.

'Being a chef must be stressful?' she said.

'I feel funny being called that here. Most of my memories of cooking were in my parents' kopitiam, with my father constantly telling me I wasn't good enough.'

'You're working in Hong Kong as a sushi chef. Still feel like an impostor?'

'My master earned a star for the restaurant. And I lost it when he was in Japan for a year.' As soon as I'd told her, it felt like a boulder had rolled off my chest. I knew she understood the pain of loss better than anyone else.

'It happens. Don't beat yourself up about it. Maybe they only award the stars to the chef who earned them. You're a trained sushi chef! That's all that matters. You should feel proud of yourself for having come this far. Not bad for a Kuching boy.'

'If only my father felt the same way. He still thinks I know nothing.'

'I'm sure he's proud of you. You know, Chinese fathers. Can't let their kids know their feelings, or the world would end as we know it,' she said with a laugh.

'At least Uncle Tan seems like the type who would talk to you and Dennis.'

'Yeah, I guess. He's better than most dads. So, why are you back? Is this really just a holiday? Or are you back for good? You seem comfortable helping your dad out at the kopitiam.'

'I don't know. It's different back here. I'm a kid again. That useless kid.'

'Don't say that.'

'My father said it so often that it's stuck in my head, especially when I'm here. When I'm in Hong Kong, well, I hear it less often, but it's still in my head. Losing the star confirmed it.'

'That's not what I thought at the Heritage Club,' she said. 'What you did for the empurau, highlighting its freshness, it was like you were celebrating its life. That idea alone is what makes you a great chef. And, of course, it tasted amazing.' Alice snuggled up to me and lay in my arms. I let myself sink into her haze of sweet mandarins, and for a moment I wasn't sure if any of it was real. I glanced at where Dennis and Misha were playing, wondering if they could see us. A black hornbill circled in the sky above, its striking yellow bill and casque a contrast against the cloudy sky. It was rare to see the endangered bird in the wild.

I took the mixtape I'd made for Alice out of my pocket and gave it to her. She looked at it and laughed. 'What's this? A mixtape?'

'Believe it or not, I made it for you in secondary school. I've always had a crush on you.'

'I know,' she said.

'But how? I tried my best to pretend you didn't exist.'

'I'm kidding,' she said, punching my arm. 'I was so busy studying, you think I had time to think about boys?'

'True. You were constantly in tuition classes. And look at you now, big-shot lawyer and everything.'

'Yes, look at me now.' She put the mixtape in the pocket of her shorts. 'You know, there's one thing they didn't teach us in school. How to be happy.'

Looking at the horizon made me feel like there was nothing I couldn't do, that everything would work itself out. It was clearer with the expanse before me. This was the only place I could look outward, at the rolling, foaming waves, the infinite sea. Sitting on the sandy beach, watching the sea and my best friend playing with his niece in the distance, I had never felt such contentment before. I could see my life here, running my own place, with the kind of clientele that applauded my creations like they had at the Heritage Club. If Alice and Misha were with me, I wouldn't work all the time anymore. I'd come to the beach with them, like today, and learn to breathe.

As noon approached, the heat crept up on us. Dennis walked towards us, holding Misha's hand. 'They're coming back,' I said. Alice sat up, straightened her T-shirt, and tidied her hair. I let go of her hand and smiled awkwardly. She understood; it was too soon to let them know. The uncle and niece arrived, wet, tanned and smiling.

'Time for lunch! I know this fantastic kolo mee in town. Let's check out the competition!' Dennis said.

'Had fun?' Alice asked. Misha said a resounding yes, then jumped on Alice's lap. 'You're getting me all wet!' The four of us rolled up the beach mat and packed up before walking back to the car.

27

The Emperor's Feast

Ma sharpened the cleaver and took the chickens to the back of the shop. She swiftly cut their throats, then drained their blood into a big bowl. I was amazed at how unflinching she was when slaughtering them. Any hesitation would mean a more painful, drawn-out death.

'Teochew cooking uses very light seasoning, so the ingredients have to be very fresh. *Yuan zhi yuan wei*, the original taste of ingredients. Your Ah Kong told me not to forget this about Teochew cooking,' she said. 'We will make a rich fish maw soup for tonight's party and use the stock as a base for a few of the dishes we're preparing.'

After she plucked the chicken, she washed it thoroughly and removed its innards. I prepared a pot of water for the soup. She put in the chicken and some pork bones she had defrosted earlier. Once the soup came to a boil, she threw away the water, then rinsed the bones and chicken and added them back to a pot of fresh water. She soaked the fish maw and the scallops to soften them before adding them to the soup, which needed at least four to five hours on a slow simmer.

'Before showing me how to cook, your Ah Kong always said the same thing. "The key to good taste is balance. When everything is in harmony, there is balance. Nothing lacking, nothing in excess,"' Ma said. A clean soup was good soup. It was difficult to do with a meat base, but she was trying to keep the soup as clear as she could, skimming away scum and adding water when necessary. Like Ah Hock, she seasoned the broth carefully with salt, tasting before adding more. It reminded me of when Sensei was teaching me how to make suimono, a Japanese clear soup, although there dashi was used as the base of the stock.

'We don't have any seaweed, do we?' I asked, thinking of the dried giant kelp and bonito flakes he used to make dashi.

Ma shook her head. 'It sounds like a good idea though. We'll do that next time.' She tasted the soup. 'Ah, the xian wei is not there yet. I know you don't read or write Chinese, but your grandfather used to say, you could guess at what xian tries to achieve when you look at the Chinese characters. *Xian* is made up of *yu* and *yang*, fish and goat – a balance of meat and fish flavours. *Xian* also means "fresh", so we are looking at something that is fresh and has the perfect balance in flavours. Xian wei is a depth of flavour that is hard to describe. It's almost intuitive.'

'Like Pa wanting depth in his broth?'

'Yes, exactly that. His laksa soup is made of prawns and chicken, a balance of sea and land from the ancestral broth. That's where his xian wei comes from. And xiang wei comes from his spices – the aromatic, fragrant garlic and onions, ginger, the coconut milk. *Xiang* means "fragrant", as you know. But it's a pity most people only taste the five flavours and not the *xiang* or *xian*.'

As the soup simmered, the house was filled with its meaty aroma. Even the ancestral broth was temporarily muted, although after Ma turned off the stove fire, the familiar aroma took its rightful place in the shophouse. She tasted the soup, closing her eyes. It was a few seconds before she spoke, smiling.

'Not bad. It's not the same without your grandfather's broth but it's close enough.'

'Why don't we use it?' I asked. 'Pa let me taste it the other night after the opera. He said I could refresh it if I wanted,' I said shyly, like I was talking to my mother about a new girlfriend.

Ma laughed. 'Finally!'

'I guess the show put him in a good mood.'

She squeezed my shoulder. 'You've always been ready for the broth, Ming. Your father was the one who needed to be ready. Now take two bowls of the broth, and let's add it to our soup.'

We added the broth then let it continue to simmer. I chopped up garlic and shallots while Ma added scallops and dried flatfish to the simmering pot.

'I have a surprise for you,' Ma said. 'I called your boss at the restaurant. I didn't know how else I could reach him. I never called you there before, even though you gave me the number. Luckily, he picked up the phone. I hope he understood my English.'

I nearly dropped the cleaver. I could feel my face burning and hoped Ma didn't notice. I cleared my throat and tried to sound calm, but she could probably hear the tremor in my voice.

'Why did you call him?'

'I invited him to Pa's birthday party. I never expected him to say yes, but he did!'

Shit. No way. How could I face Sensei after everything that had happened? I rubbed my forehead. I wished I had a bottle of Jack Daniel's right now. 'You what?'

'No harm asking. How often will we get to celebrate anything here? I wanted to express my appreciation to your boss. After all, he's been taking care of you in Hong Kong. He's the reason you've had a good life there.'

Had Sensei discovered the shortfall in the till? The missing sake? Why would he agree to come all the way to Kuching after I'd messed everything up? I put down the cleaver and checked on the soup. All these questions swirled in my head while I absent-mindedly stirred the soup too roughly and it splashed onto the fire, making a sizzling sound. 'Be careful!' Ma said and took the ladle from me.

'You shouldn't have called him, Ma,' I said gloomily. I couldn't figure out why Sensei would have accepted Ma's invitation. Maybe he was coming to confront me. But it wasn't like Sensei to have a showdown with anyone. Either way, I couldn't run away anymore.

'Why not? Don't you like him?'

'It's complicated . . . some things happened. When he was in Japan, he left me to run the restaurant. And I lost his star while I was running it.' This was the extent of my confession. I couldn't tell her about the till money or the sake.

'What did he say?'

'He said it wasn't my fault.'

'There, you see? So why are you beating yourself up?'

'There are things in Hong Kong you don't know about. Things that made me come back here.'

'Like what?'

'It's a long story. I gambled. I drank too much. There's a woman. Jiayi. Her boyfriend is a gangster.'

252

'Oh.' Ma wrinkled her brow. 'Why did you get involved with a woman like that, Ming? Gangsters?'

'She's an amazing chef. We used to work together. She's not what you think, Ma.'

'You know your father hates people drinking.'

'I know.'

'And gambling? You should have known better, Ming.' Ma had a look of genuine disappointment in her eyes.

'I'm sorry, Ma. It wasn't easy there and I did want to come back. I couldn't do it without having proven myself. And I still haven't.'

'All the more reason you should stay on in Kuching. There's so much more you can do here. What about Alice?'

'What *about* Alice?'

'Oh, don't be silly with your mother, I can tell you like her. And she likes you too.'

'We're not in secondary school anymore, Ma. And she has a child.'

'So what? I get an instant grandchild.'

I laughed. 'I think you're jumping too far ahead here. Before I can begin to think about Alice, I need to think about what I'll be doing here.' I wanted to tell her about my deal with Towkay Lau. About how everything would work out after I had my own restaurant and made lots of money. Then they wouldn't have to work so hard. If Alice and I got together, they could babysit Misha, retire, have restful days enjoying their grandchild. It all sounded so perfect to me. I couldn't give her false hope though, not until everything was in place. I would tell her when the time was right.

'What's there to think about? Take over the kopitiam. Your father's not getting any younger. Can't you imagine it, son? Let your father retire, you run this shop, with Alice and Misha by your side. The simple life is the best.'

'I can't spend the rest of my life running a laksa shop, Ma. I want more.'

'People always want more. Doesn't mean they'll be happy.'

'I need to do this for myself. I'll never know otherwise, whether I can make it on my own. Without the laksa shop. I don't know who I am, and it's all buried inside, struggling to come out. I need to be myself, and it's terrible when I don't know what that means.' I was trembling. I didn't ask for this hunger, this need that wouldn't go away no matter what I did. I wanted a simple life too, one where I wouldn't always be wondering, *what if?*

'If it's money you need, you have money here. You know the three thousand dollars you sent us every month? I never spent it. Kept it in a fixed deposit account.'

'Ma, you were supposed to spend it on yourself, and Pa. I don't want you both to work so hard.'

'We didn't need it. I saved it for your future wedding. There's almost a hundred thousand ringgit there. Amazing right? Eight years' worth of savings. You can have it for your restaurant.'

'I'm going to need more than that, Ma, but it's really great to know, thank you. Let's cook, we'll discuss this later,' I said, patting my mother's arm. There was no time to argue about this now. I would have to convince Ma first, then gradually ease my father into accepting my plans.

Ma sighed, then placed the seafood we would be cooking that day in the kitchen sink. A medium-sized terubuk she had bought the day before, its white-grey scaly skin glistening, as well as large, feisty mud crabs, tiger prawns, abalone, scallops, and sea cucumbers that had been washed and soaked for days. She gave me a big pail of pork trotters to clean while she worked on the crabs. She slaughtered a crab with a sharp stab to its underside, then expertly removed its abdomen, gills and guts. She steamed the crabs with spring onion, Shaoxing wine and ginger, then put them in the refrigerator after they had cooled down.

I shaved the pork trotters, removing the excess coarse hair, rubbed them with salt to clean them, then cut them up into smaller pieces. The pork had a fresh, comforting scent. My mother had bought them from a butcher she trusted.

'Let me cook the terubuk, Ma. Also chilled?' I asked. After preparing the empurau at the Heritage Club, I couldn't wait to show off my skills to her.

She nodded. 'Your grandfather really liked cold fish. It was the only way he could maximise the full potential of fresh seafood. And it's a way of respecting the fishermen who go out to sea.'

Like the awabi we used at Haruto, which Sensei had often reminded me to prepare with care, as a tribute to the strong, hardy women of Shima who risked their lives to harvest the treasures of the sea. I sprinkled salt all over and inside the terubuk, leaving its scales on, then let it marinate for about ten minutes.

'Don't remove the scales. They protect the fish from drying out during steaming, and keep it moist and sweet,' Ma said.

While the terubuk was being steamed, I blanched the cleaned trotters, then fried garlic, cinnamon, star anise, coriander leaves and galangal in a wok. When the spices released their fragrance, I added light and dark soy sauces, and water, then the trotters. I left them simmering in the braising sauce with hardboiled eggs. The smell of the savoury stew brought me back to my childhood. Ma had cooked it often with pork belly instead of trotters.

Ma deep-fried pieces of flatfish until they were crisp, then drained them and broke them into coarse pieces. She removed the excess oil from the wok then fried old ginger in the remaining oil. As soon as the ginger became fragrant, she added prawns, chicken stock and some Shaoxing wine. She worked as if she were reliving the past, with no need to pause to think about the ingredients to use. I memorised every step she took, the closest thing I had to learning from my grandfather.

After ten minutes, Ma took the terubuk out of the wok, then let it cool down on the counter before putting it into the fridge to chill for an hour. While waiting, she made the tau cheo dip to go with it, salted soybeans, bird's eye chilli, lime and ginger.

'Your grandfather said condiments are important in Teochew cooking. Even his laksa was fashioned that way. You keep adding the sambal until it tastes right. And what tastes right depends on who's eating it. That's why it's different from other shops,' Ma said. She was right – Ah Hock's way of preparing the laksa was in the spirit of Teochew cuisine, even if the laksa itself was the furthest thing from Teochew food.

For dessert, there was none other than orh nee, the Teochew yam pudding my father loved. I helped Ma with the labour-intensive task of mixing the yam paste until it was smooth and creamy. Ma heated up lard and added shallots, frying them until they were golden brown before adding the yam paste. After it was cooked, the pudding was refrigerated so it could be served cold.

'Now for the longevity noodles,' Ma said. Growing up, she used to make them for my birthday celebrations too, but I never really liked them and ate them to humour her. The noodles or the hardboiled eggs dyed red weren't too bad, but I didn't like the concoction of water, ginger, pandan leaves, red dates and rock sugar they were boiled in. It was like eating a noodle dessert, and its indecision whether to be savoury or sweet confused my palate. But it was a tradition Ma never skipped.

By the time we finished cooking, it was almost six in the evening. The guests were supposed to arrive by six-thirty. I took out a large, round folding table from the storeroom, the table we used for Chinese New Year reunion dinners. I hadn't seen that table in eight years. The last reunion dinner we'd had was after Towkay Lau had offered me the job in Hong Kong. Ah Hock had been leaning on that table so heavily that it had tilted when I told him. When it became apparent that nothing would change my decision, Ah Hock had pushed away so roughly from the table that soup had sloshed over its tureen and spilled everywhere. We didn't even have a chance to taste the reunion dinner before Ah Hock stormed upstairs while Ma sobbed her heart out and I sat watching her, my heart broken but not my resolve.

I hadn't known eight years would fly by.

After boiling for four hours, the soup was ready. I tasted a spoonful of it and paused to analyse its flavours. There was no doubt about its depth. I could taste sea and land like a perfect marriage, seamless. It was just soup, yet it felt like we'd taken a journey through time and space to prepare it.

Ma placed the dishes on a table, carefully arranging them. The braised trotters were ladled into a clay pot. The fried prawns, chilled crab and cold terubuk were placed around it. The abalone, scallop and sea cucumber dish took its place next to two ducks that had been braised and chopped into

257

bite-sized pieces, now arranged neatly on serving plates. A big tureen of fish maw soup sat in the centre. Ma and I looked at the dishes like proud parents.

'We did it! The Emperor's Feast! If only your grandfather were here to see it. To see you.' Ma wiped the tears from her eyes. 'You're a filial boy, Ming. I know it wasn't easy for you to come back. But it's the right decision to make. Look at these beautiful dishes we made.'

I put my arm around my mother. These were the sorts of dishes I wanted to serve at my restaurant – dishes that required skill and fresh produce, dishes that brought back memories of home and deep flavour. *Yuan zhi yuan wei*. But most important of all, it was all made with love. I felt a connection to the food I'd never felt before: that it was truly mine, even if it was inherited from my grandfather. The food belonged to me, as much as I belonged to the food.

28

孝 (Xiào)

I was opening the metal folding doors to the kopitiam when a familiar figure alighted from the taxi that stopped in front of Lau Ya Keng. Sensei in T-shirt and jeans, holding a light jacket and his trolley bag. Seeing him made me want to dig a deep hole and bury myself in it. I felt like closing the doors and pretending we weren't home.

When our eyes met, he waved from across the street and walked over to me. As my master stood in front of me, the words wouldn't come out of my mouth so I stared at the pavement, trembling like a little boy who was about to feel the end of a rattan cane.

'Takashi says hello,' Sensei said. I nodded, not knowing what to say in reply. A few seconds passed before I came out of my stupor and invited him into the kopitiam. I took his bag before he could protest.

Inside, I pulled the metal doors shut and gave him a deep bow. 'I don't know what to say, Sensei. I don't even know how to look at you.' I wished I could disappear into thin air. That lightning would strike me and put me out of my misery. I felt his hand on my shoulder and I straightened myself. 'I am truly sorry for everything I've done.'

He closed his eyes and shook his head. 'So am I, Wei Ming. I knew something was wrong . . . but I didn't know what it was. Seeing what has happened, I now understand you were in a very difficult place. You should have talked to me.'

'I didn't know how.' I looked down at my feet. 'I will pay you back everything I took from Haruto. I promise, Sensei.'

'It's not about the money. I always say, it is your restaurant too. You could have asked me. Or told me.'

'I know.'

'Your mother called me just before my father passed. I flew here from Japan.'

'I'm so sorry, Sensei.' I bowed deeply again. Sensei returned the bow. I felt like a bigger shithead now. Sensei had so much on his plate and didn't need me to pile on any more stuff.

'It's all right. I have already said my goodbyes. To both my father and my home. I do not wish to return anytime soon.'

Sensei had a complex relationship with his home country. I understood his sentiments of wanting to be home and away at the same time. He gazed at the tables and chairs around him and traced his fingers along the carved pattern on the armrest of one of the chairs.

'These are made very well,' he said admiringly.

'My grandfather had them made by the carpenters here. There aren't many of these masters left.'

'I have never seen anything like this shop before. You and your family live upstairs?' Sensei asked. I nodded. 'Is the birthday party going to be here?'

'Yes. Thank you for honouring my father, Sensei.'

'It is my pleasure. I have always wanted to see where you grew up.'

260

I couldn't believe my master. After all I'd done to him, I deserved a punch in the face. A slap across my cheek at the very least. I definitely hadn't expected him to fly all the way to Kuching for my father's birthday party.

Sensei took out a brown roll-up leather knife bag from the satchel slung across his chest. 'My father left me his Sakai knives, so I will be using those from now on. These were a gift from my sensei in Tokyo. Now, they are yours.' He handed the bag to me. Not only had he forgiven me, he was giving me his knives too? What the hell was happening here?

'I cannot take your knives, Sensei. I am not worthy of them.' I felt like I was going to cry. He was trying to kill me with kindness. And he was succeeding.

'I have no one else to give them to.' Sensei smiled. 'Grow to be worthy, then. Let them convince you of what you can become.'

I bowed deeply to Sensei, then led my master to an empty table. My heart was heavy, my guilt overflowing. As I was about to fetch a drink for Sensei, I could hear my parents coming down the stairs.

'I told you not to make a fuss and now I have to greet all these fools later.' Ah Hock's voice trailed downstairs. He looked freshly showered and was wearing a short-sleeved shirt and black trousers.

'Shush, don't be rude on your birthday,' Ma said. When she saw Sensei, she hurried down the last few steps to shake his hand.

'Thank you, thank you,' Ma said awkwardly in English before switching back to Mandarin. 'Tell him I'm really happy he's here,' she said, prodding my arm. I translated for Sensei, who then bowed to Ma. He turned to Ah Hock. 'Mr Lim, your son is very talented.'

'Who's this?' Ah Hock looked Sensei up and down.

'Aiyoh, this is Mr Inamura, your son's boss. Be nice!' Ma said.

'Ask your boss if he wants to have laksa,' Ah Hock said. 'I think we have some soup left in the kitchen.'

'The guests are arriving any time now and you want to serve laksa?' Ma said with exasperation. I asked Sensei anyway. I didn't want to pass up the chance to let my master try the delicacy.

'I would be honoured to have this famous laksa I have heard so much about,' Sensei said. As Ah Hock was about to assemble a bowl of laksa, I made him sit at the table with a cup of kopi-o instead and insisted I had to personally prepare the laksa for my boss. Ah Hock tried to protest, but gave up when Ma glared at him and shook her head. Ma sat Sensei down next to Ah Hock, then served him milk tea, which Sensei sniffed at cautiously.

Sensei watched patiently while I squeezed coconut milk from a muslin cloth. I picked up a bowl and assembled the laksa as meticulously as if I were making my masu, taking out imperfect beehoon strands as Ah Hock would have done. I arranged prawns, omelette and beansprouts evenly around the noodles. Then I stood back to look at my work of art before ladling boiling soup into the bowl. I smelled it. Just right.

When I placed the bowl and a small saucer of sambal in front of Sensei, he pressed his palms together in gratitude and said, 'Itadakimasu.'

'This is spicy.' I pointed to the sambal. 'Not too much if you don't like it hot.'

'Don't worry, I can handle it.' Sensei sipped a spoonful of soup. 'It is tasty. Good flavours.'

'You need to add the sambal and adjust it according to what you like,' I said. Sensei took a bit of sambal and mixed it into the laksa soup while I watched him like an anxious mother. Was I turning into Ah Hock? I tried not to hover as Sensei kept tasting while mixing the sambal until he was satisfied that it was exactly how he wanted it. Even Ah Hock was curious and stared at Sensei, who was slurping loudly as if he were eating ramen. After he had finished every drop of the soup, Sensei stood up and bowed deeply to Ah Hock. 'This laksa is unique and full of deep flavours. I feel like it has taught me a lot about Wei Ming's home town. You have taught your son well,' Sensei said. I translated for Ah Hock, and my father, as usual, was fighting back the smile trying to form on his lips.

*

Before long, the guests trickled in. We'd kept the party small. Third Uncle, Ah Lek the fishmonger, Sensei, Dennis, Aunty and Uncle Tan, Alice and Misha. Third Uncle complimented Ah Hock, saying he had never seen him in anything other than singlet and shorts before. Ah Hock greeted everyone warmly and made small talk with the Tans, something he had never done in the past.

Alice had come in a light dewy-green shirt-dress, fresh-faced with curls cascading down her shoulders. She said hello and squeezed my hand as she brushed past me to talk to Ma. Misha bounded up to me with Uncle and Aunty Tan behind her. I gave Misha a hug and greeted the Tans. Dennis slapped me on the back and said, 'Can't wait to taste authentic Teochew dishes!'

'See, I knew this would cheer him up. Imagine if I had listened to him and not had this party!' Ma whispered to me.

It was nice to see my father in high spirits. After the party, I could sit the old man down and persuade him to give up on the dream of passing down the kopitiam. If his good mood lasted, it could soften the blow of the discussion.

I could see it all now. The opening day of my new restaurant, congratulatory flower wreaths at the entrance, my parents looking at me proudly while I served appetisers to friends and family. Alice and Misha, if things worked out, would be there too. We could be one big happy family. I would ask Towkay Lau for the most prime location. Near the five-star hotels? I had to think big. No more settling for less. If I was going to disappoint my father, I had to show him the rewards we would be getting in return.

Everyone sat down to dinner. The chatter subsided as the guests ate. Soon all I could hear were soup spoons clanking against ceramic bowls and the soft slurping of fish maw soup. The sea cucumbers, braised in a thickened scallop sauce, gleamed in a large, elegant porcelain bowl. The prawns were resplendent, shells on, retaining their springy flesh after being flash-fried with dried flatfish and a splash of Shaoxing wine. The aroma of star anise, cinnamon, cloves, and the five-spice powder Ma used for lor ark, the duck braised in sweet, dark soy sauce with boiled eggs, made my mouth water, although I was too nervous to sit and eat. Each dish was more than enough to stand on its own, a sufficient meal paired with rice. When combined, they were certainly nothing less than what an emperor would expect at his banquet.

I hovered around the guests and rushed about serving whoever wanted second or third helpings. Ah Hock was eating quietly, not a sound, not even to comment on the food. It was a good sign. Ma chatted with Mrs Tan and Alice gave me a thumbs up as she spooned a boiled egg and pig trotter gravy onto Misha's mound of rice. I could hear Ah Lek saying to my father, 'Ah, how fresh this fish is! And the crabs! I told you I only sell you the good stuff!' while Dennis called for a second helping of rice.

I stopped next to Sensei to check if he wanted second or third helpings. He had almost finished his rice and was murmuring as he ate the cold crab. As I ladled more rice for him, he looked up at me and rested his hand on my arm briefly.

'Wei Ming, I am very impressed. There is so much umami in all the dishes,' Sensei said. 'They go well with the rice. The grains are small but aromatic.'

My heart leapt in joy at his remarks. Nothing could explain my master's forgiving nature except that I must have racked up some good karma in my past life.

'I learned most of the recipes from my mother, Sensei. She cooked many of the dishes. From my grandfather's recipes.'

Sensei nodded. 'I feel very fortunate tonight,' he said. I tried not to lose my composure as I thanked him. It would take a lifetime to repay the debt I owed to Sensei.

The food was quickly finished and there were no leftovers. I cleared the tables while Ma served everyone the yam pudding and Ah Hock's favourite Tieguanyin. Uncle Tan toasted to my father's good health and goaded everyone to ask him for a speech despite his feeble protests. Ah Hock stood up and cleared his throat.

'For those of you who don't understand Teochew, ask Kim Choo to translate,' he said to ripples of laughter. 'I didn't want this party at first, but my wife persuaded me. She said it is taboo not to celebrate one's sixtieth birthday. I don't know about that. The only taboo I know is to keep my ancestral broth safe. I do not talk much about my past. In fact, the only thing I talk about is the laksa, I know,' he said to more laughter. 'But today is my sixtieth birthday. It is apt that I reminisce about coming to Kuching when I was a small boy. I still dream of being seasick on the ship that brought us, without my mother. My father was a hard man, but he taught me one good thing – that is, how to make his laksa. Whenever I told him I wanted to learn his skills as a chef, he would shake his head and ask me to focus on the laksa. Every day, when I was old enough, he would drill the art of making a perfect bowl of laksa into my head. Know every ingredient, every taste, every spice. Our ancestral broth was the key ingredient and we had to do it justice.'

I listened intently. It was rare my father would open up like this. Then again, one's sixtieth birthday was a big deal. An important milestone.

'I'm not getting any younger. My father constantly said we needed to continue our legacy and pass our ancestral broth down to the next generation. You all know my son, Wei Ming.' Ah Hock pointed at me. I tried to summon a smile, which ended up looking more like a grimace. 'He's finally returned home, after making his mark as a chef in Hong Kong.'

Did I hear right? Ah Hock had never once talked about my work in Hong Kong before, and certainly not in a positive light. If anything, I'd thought Ah Hock looked down on what I did, especially as a sushi chef.

'So, it's fitting I make this announcement, on my birthday, that my son Lim Wei Ming will be taking over this kopitiam, as I did from my father, Lim Teck Boon.' There was a sudden silence, then a resounding 'Good news!' coming from Third Uncle. Everyone clapped and there was happy tittering among the guests.

It took me a few seconds to register what he'd said. My fingers wrapped themselves around the edges of my seat. My face was burning with embarrassment. How could Ah Hock put me on the spot like that? Alice smiled at me. I shook my head at her and frowned. Her smile turned into a look of bewilderment. I couldn't believe what Ah Hock had said. We hadn't had a chance to discuss anything. It was just like the old man to decide things on his own without giving me a choice. It was stupid of me to think anything had changed after eight years.

I excused myself on the pretext of checking something in the kitchen. Right then I wanted to smash all the crockery there. I stared at the pot of broth simmering away in the corner. *It's all your fault he's obsessed*, I wanted to scream. I wanted to kick over the pot, let his treasured broth spill all over the kitchen floor, so we would never have to talk about it again.

I had to wait until the guests left, to keep up pretences, to save my parents' face. Losing face was the worst thing for Ah Hock. Death would be preferable.

Everyone said their goodbyes after finishing their tea. I wasn't sure if anyone had noticed my sombre mood after Ah Hock's speech, but I made no attempts to persuade anyone to stay longer. I eagerly ushered them all out, even Alice who was trying to speak to me. I felt bad about Sensei who had come all that way, but I promised I would meet him at the Holiday Inn, the hotel where he was staying, for a discussion when it was convenient.

When everyone had left, I closed the door and turned to my parents, who were finishing their tea at the table.

'Pa, we need to talk.' I pulled up a chair next to Ah Hock, who was oblivious to my anger. 'Why on earth did you make that announcement when I haven't decided on anything? My boss was there. And you, you decided it was all right to say whatever you wanted,' I said through gritted teeth. Ma looked at me in panic, sensing what was about to happen. She took my hand and squeezed it, shaking her head. I pulled my hand free. I had to say my piece. I couldn't ignore this, not even for Ma.

Ah Hock put down his teacup, looking like a puffer fish about to explode. 'What rubbish are you talking about, boy? You must take over this kopitiam. Who will keep it going after I die?'

'I have other plans, Pa.'

'What do you mean you have other plans?'

'I want to have my own restaurant like Ah Kong did. Towkay Lau says he will give me one,' I said. At this, Ah Hock's face turned as red as the sambal he made. Ma gasped and shook her head.

'Ming! What are you talking about?' she exclaimed.

'You're taking favours from that degenerate! How stupid are you? And what do you have to do in return?' Ah Hock bellowed.

'Nothing,' I said, my face reddening at the thought of the sachet of powder hidden underneath the Kuan Yin statuette.

Ah Hock snorted. 'You really believe that sly fox will give you a restaurant for nothing? All this time, pretending to be a good son, when you've been scheming to escape your responsibilities. Is that what you've learned in Hong Kong? To lie to your parents and abdicate your duty?'

'I never lied to you! I wanted to tell you my plans tonight, but you went ahead and decided without asking me!'

'Ask you? Ask you for what, permission? It's as if you've forgotten who's the father, and who's the son!'

'Ming, we can't lose the bet. We can't give him this kopitiam,' Ma said, tears running down her cheeks. I was dismayed to see her in that state, but in the throes of anger, all I could think about was how selfish Ah Hock was.

'You've been nothing but ungrateful. Always wanting more! You earn your knowledge, you understand? Your grandfather was a master chef in Swatow. Even I could not attain his standards. What's that rubbish in your head about starting a Teochew restaurant?' Ah Hock shouted.

'For once I want to hear that I do enough here. I came back, I help you at the stall. I don't complain. But I'm never good enough, never the son you want. My grandfather was a master chef, my father is a master laksa maker, but I learned nothing here, thanks to you!' Things were escalating but I couldn't stop my runaway train of emotions. All those things I'd been meaning to say to Ah Hock my whole life, I wished I had said it all when I was younger. I couldn't hold back anymore. The dam had burst. Ma kept trying to shush me, but I ignored her.

Ah Hock banged the table with his fists so hard his cup fell over, spilling his tea. 'You learned nothing? If you learned nothing, it's because you chose to learn nothing. Everything here is a lesson. Preparation is the most important step in cooking. When you have prepared well, you save time in cooking. That is vital in a Teochew restaurant, in any restaurant. No job is too small. Learn the hard jobs then work your way to the easier ones. There are no shortcuts. I didn't know I had to talk so much to explain all this basic knowledge. The problem is, you young people just want an easy life. You don't know what it takes to understand cooking!'

'And you do? If you had understood it yourself, you would be the owner of a busy Teochew restaurant, instead of this small, dark kopitiam, where you pretend to be king. The king of laksa! The all-famous laksa where only Third Uncle can appreciate the pains you take to pick the freshest prawns and chicken, the crispiest beansprouts, the way you obsess about how the omelette should be cut, the handmade beehoon. Then charge four fifty per bowl. All that work for four ringgit fifty sen. You know what? Nobody cares about clean beansprouts or handmade noodles! Only you think it's a big deal, while people eat their laksa quickly without analysing the tail of the beansprouts or whether the prawns are fresh enough.'

It felt good getting the right words out, even if it meant enraging Ah Hock, although I was so caught up in my speech I didn't care what happened anymore. 'Do you wonder why Towkay Lau talks to you about business? He's trying to help us but you treat him like dirt, like you're too good for him. He's the one who can afford a big empurau while you quibble over the texture of beehoon. You're embarrassed by me? Ah Kong would have been embarrassed by you.'

It all happened so quickly. Ah Hock jumped to his feet, surprisingly nimble for his age. Then his open palm struck my face. I held my cheek as a searing pain spread across it. Ah Hock stared at me, then at his hand. Ma gave a cry and pulled Ah Hock back.

'Enough! Hock, you've gone too far!' she wailed.

'You good-for-nothing boy!' Ah Hock said, his teeth clenched, his hands in fists.

At that moment I could feel nothing for this man I called my father. I had endured his words and there was no way in hell I would endure a slap.

'Find someone else to take over your precious broth,' I said in the steeliest voice I could muster, and I stormed out of the kopitiam. It was raining but I didn't feel the raindrops pelting my face, didn't hear the thunderclap, didn't see the puddles I was stepping into. All I knew was I had to get away. I could hear Ma calling me but I didn't stop. I ran along Carpenter Street as fast as I could, away from the kopitiam, while her voice crying out my name grew fainter and fainter behind me.

29

The Rice is Cooked

Teck Boon looked different. A younger man, wearing a familiar magua suit. Where had Ah Hock seen it? Ah, the photo on the altar. But he looked so real, it was confusing. Ah Hock felt like a child again, yet he was well aware of his sixty-year-old self. His father standing next to a car, an old Ford. Teck Boon gestured for him to enter the car. Ah Hock felt uneasy, but he couldn't say no to his father.

He got in the front seat and turned to Teck Boon, who started to drive. His father never once looked at him. Ah Hock looked out the window and saw only darkness. He remembered what Kim Choo had said about not following dead loved ones. 'Father,' he called out to Teck Boon, 'I want to get out.'

'You have not treasured the broth,' Teck Boon said, looking straight ahead.

'I have kept it safe,' Ah Hock said unconvincingly. He felt ashamed he could not offer Teck Boon the reassurance that his legacy would continue with Wei Ming.

'You have not heeded my words.'

'I've done my best, Father,' Ah Hock said. 'The boy has a mind of his own. I just need to talk to him more.'

'The luck of the Lims will end with you. The deity will be offended. There will be no end to suffering.' Teck Boon spoke in monotone – not angry, just as if he were simply stating facts. Anger would have been preferable to this indifference. Teck Boon had spoken those words as if he were coldly pronouncing Ah Hock's death. Was his father here to guide him to the underworld?

'I did everything you wanted! Everything! But it was never enough for you,' Ah Hock cried. 'Did you ever ask whether I wanted to cook laksa? What I wanted? What my dreams were? Father!' Ah Hock wiped the tears from his eyes. 'Stop the car!'

When Teck Boon ignored him, Ah Hock frantically unlocked the car door and opened it, tumbling out into a void of darkness as he did so. He woke up in bed, drenched in sweat, with Kim Choo staring at him worriedly.

'What happened?' She touched his shoulder.

'Bad dream,' he muttered, his heart beating wildly.

'I'm worried about you. I think we should bring you to a doctor.'

'Nonsense, I'm fine. A bad dream.'

'At least it was just a dream.' She got up from the bed. 'My nightmare hasn't ended yet.'

'What are you talking about?' He blinked and looked around at the room, glad to be in familiar surroundings.

'What else could I be talking about? Our son! You've driven him away yet again. This time I don't know if he'll come back. You really went too far this time, Hock,' she said, then sat down at her dressing table.

Ah Hock remembered now. He shouldn't have hit Wei Ming, he knew. But the boy's words had been poison-tipped arrows straight through Ah Hock's heart, each word crafted with calculated precision to inflict the greatest possible pain. The power a child had over a parent.

'This filthy temper of yours will destroy happiness,' Kim Choo had often told him. And that Chinese proverb, *if you are patient on one moment of anger, you will escape a hundred days of sorrow*. The last time it had lasted eight years. How long would it be this time?

The audacity of the boy though! Forgetting himself, forgetting his place! If Ah Hock had spoken like that to Teck Boon, it was more than a slap that he would have received. Thrown on the streets, publicly disowned! How else could Ah Hock have reacted? Thanked the boy? Apologised to him? What did she expect? If he wasn't careful, one day he'd have to kowtow to the boy instead of the other way round!

'You're always on his side! When have you ever spared a thought for me?' Ah Hock grumbled.

Kim Choo looked at him incredulously. 'All I've done in my life is think of you or Wei Ming. Does anyone care about *my* feelings? You are both so stubborn! All these years I've kept quiet about your obsessions. When you convinced me to marry you, you said we would have a happy family together. My career was just taking off then. Later, someone from a TV production company approached Master Wong, but that old tyrant didn't tell me about it because you'd paid the huge dowry he demanded. He didn't care, he was getting rid of me one way or another. After all, I was one less mouth to feed. One of the actors from the troupe told me all this before I left. This is why I haven't gone back. It was as if I had been sold from the troupe. You have your pride, Hock, but what about me? I have mine too,' she said, choked with emotion.

'Master Wong didn't say anything to me. He took my money and said you were free to marry. I never knew you were so miserable with me,' Ah Hock said in a small, humble voice.

'I wasn't. I left that life behind. There was a time when you promised me the moon! Saying how devoted you would be to me. I tried hard not to think about what could have been. When Ming was born, I was so happy. I had my own family at last. I forgot my old life because I had a better one. But all my life I've heard nothing but the broth, the laksa, how everything has to be done your way! And now, you've chased our son away again. I don't know if he'll come back this time!' she said, stifling a sob.

'He will,' Ah Hock said sulkily. That hot-headed youngster needed to cool off. Let him stay at his friend's place until he was ready to crawl back home.

Kim Choo threw up her hands and looked at him with tears streaming down her cheeks. 'Why are you like this? Wake up! This is our son, our family. Why won't you listen to me? Is the broth more important than our son? Your legacy? The legacy you keep talking about? Our son is our legacy, yet you have done nothing to nurture him! Please, Hock. Call off the bet. Don't throw away the kopitiam too. Don't make Wei Ming choose between his happiness and us. He's a young man with his own dreams. Let him chase them. Let him have the choices you never had.'

'I never wanted anything. I did my duty, what every son should do!' Ah Hock wanted to reach out to her, but if he touched her, she would break into a thousand pieces. And he wouldn't know how to put her back together.

'You must have something you wanted. Everyone has dreams. You have been a good son for long enough. Now it's time to be a good father.' Kim Choo wiped her cheeks with her sleeves.

Had he been a bad father? Didn't all good fathers want to pass on a legacy to their children, not to mention keep them safe? Didn't Kim Choo realise Wei Ming's refusal would result in misfortune for the whole family? Ah Hock felt stuck in between Teck Boon's warnings and Wei Ming's desires. There had never been room for his own ambitions. All he had known his whole life was what Teck Boon had wanted him to be.

'I can't . . .' Ah Hock felt tears welling up in his eyes as he looked at her. 'I don't know how.'

When she saw his face, she softened. 'It's not too late,' she said. 'You can still try.'

'All I know is how to make good laksa. That's all.' He didn't know what she wanted him to say. He had no time for regrets. He couldn't afford any regrets. He was too old to change his ways, even if he wanted to.

Kim Choo sighed deeply. 'So, this is how things are.' She walked to the windows and opened them. The sky was indigo streaked with orange, on the cusp of dawn. She stood there, staring at the sky. She was still upset, and he wished he could make her feel better. But the deity could not be disobeyed, not even at the cost of a son.

30

A Hundred Days of Sorrow

Queen's 'Bohemian Rhapsody' was blaring loudly from the Denon speakers. It brought me back to when we were teenagers, hanging out in Dennis's room after school. Last night I'd slept on a flimsy spare mattress, and I was still in the pyjamas he'd lent me, even though it was almost noon. We were sitting on the floor in front of the TV, playing *Mortal Kombat II*, a beat-'em-up Dennis was obsessed with. It was funny Dennis still played video games at our age, but I was glad to be distracted from last night.

'Imagine if we had a Super Nintendo during our school days, huh?' Dennis said as he pressed the buttons on the controller rapidly. 'I would've failed all my exams. Probably wouldn't have spent as much time in the kitchen.'

I tried my best to get used to the controls, but Dennis beat me in a matter of minutes and did a fist pump in the air. I threw the controller aside in frustration. Another damn thing I wasn't good at.

'It's just a game, man, don't get angry,' Dennis said.

'I'm not angry at you.' I lay down on the floor and looked at the bedroom ceiling. The redness on my cheek was long gone, but the sting of the slap felt fresh. The weight of Ah

Hock's words last night was still heavy on my heart. All I wanted to do was numb the pain. Pity Dennis didn't have any alcohol lying around the house. If only I had that welcoming relief of the fiery liquid down my throat, the emptiness that came after, the soothed, blanked-out state I got too familiar with.

Dennis's bedroom had transformed into a self-contained entertainment centre, with the TV, the Super Nintendo, a hi-fi set. Next to his bed, there was an amplifier and an electric guitar leaning on it. His Transformers bedsheets were now a dark blue, plain set. The room no longer smelled like used socks; in its place was a whiff of aftershave. No more dirty clothes or wet towels strewn around the floor. The only remnants of Dennis's teenhood were pin-ups of Raquel Welch and Farrah Fawcett in bikinis on his walls, and faded posters of his favourite bands back then – Deep Purple and Queen. The AC/DC 'Highway to Hell' poster stood out from the rest as it looked relatively newer. I pointed at it.

'Nice poster, where did you buy this one?'

'You bought it for me-lah,' Dennis said with a wry smile. 'Can't believe you don't remember. When you arrived in Hong Kong. Believe it or not, there was a time when you bothered to post me stuff from there.'

I blushed. How could I have forgotten? When I had my first month's pay and my first day off from Kowloon Palace, I had gone to a music store and seen the AC/DC poster, knowing Dennis would like it. But later I got caught up in problems at Kowloon Palace, and the last time I'd had any communication with Dennis was a short phone call. I couldn't even remember what we'd talked about.

Dennis took the controller from the floor and switched off the Super Nintendo. Lucky for me, he was the forgiving sort.

'You play guitar now?' I said, trying to change the subject. Dennis grinned and sat on his bed. He switched on the amplifier and picked up his guitar. He played a riff from Nirvana's 'Come As You Are', which I recognised immediately. Takashi played this song over and over at closing time when Sensei had gone home.

'When did you learn this?' I was impressed by how good it sounded.

'When it was released a couple of years ago,' he said, then adjusted his amplifier. 'But I really started learning when you were in Hong Kong and I had nothing better to do. This Skid Row song was one of the earlier ones I learned on my own. "I Remember You".' He played the whole song with a skill I'd never seen before, and belted out the chorus like he was performing at a concert. Seeing him play electric guitar and sing was amazing. Our teenage years had been filled with listening to music, but neither of us had ever attempted to learn any instruments.

I clapped. 'You're really good. I mean you've always loved music, but learning to play on your own, wow. You sing this for the char kueh girl, she's gonna marry you for sure.'

Dennis laughed. 'How many times must I tell you, I'm not into her-lah. Eh, speaking of food, want to make something special in the kitchen or not? Cooking helps me to destress. Might help you too.'

'No mood to cook-lah.' The last thing I wanted to do was enter a kitchen right now. My head was a fog of anger and sadness. There was no way I was calm enough to make anything good.

'Aiyah, cooking doesn't need good mood. I practise even when I'm not hungry. I know, why don't we make orh nee? The one at your father's party was great. I want to try this recipe from my father's Teochew friend, Uncle Teo.'

'My grandfather probably had one. He was the real chef.'

'Aiyoh, if this is how you talk to your father, no wonder he freaked out.'

'I'm just telling the truth.'

'That's your truth, not his. Wanna make it or not? We can send some cold orh nee over as a peace offering to your father. Appease the gods,' Dennis said with a chuckle.

'I'm going through some major problems here and you're acting like it's a joke.'

Dennis's face clouded over. He unplugged his guitar and threw it on the bed. I jumped. 'The world doesn't revolve around you, Lim Wei Ming,' he said in an unexpectedly harsh tone. It was out of character for Dennis to be angry. He seldom showed his frustration, let alone a temper. When we were teenagers, we never had fights.

'Where did that come from?' His words struck the core of my being. This was the first time Dennis had ever said anything remotely hurtful to me. It wasn't in his nature to do so. But here we were now, in our thirties, and years had passed since our carefree youthful days. It was naive of me to think the years had left Dennis unscathed.

'Ever since you've been back, it's been about you, your problems, you wanting to have your own restaurant. Wanting some woman in Hong Kong you can't have and now you're looking at my sister. Get your priorities straight, man.' His look of contempt shrank me to the size of a mouse.

'So this is about Alice? I get it, she's a big-time lawyer, I'm just some uneducated cook—'

'It's not!' Dennis said with a big sigh. 'Look, you're not the only one with problems, okay? It's my dad. He's really sick.'

Uncle Tan looked fine to me. But then Uncle Tan had always been the type to hide any discomfort he felt.

'Why didn't you tell me earlier?' I knew how much Dennis's father meant to him. They were a close-knit family.

'I didn't have a chance, did I?' Dennis sat down on his bed, hunched. 'You come back after eight years, thinking everything's the same, thinking you didn't make a difference when you left. You think I didn't miss you? I lost my friend. I didn't have anyone to tell when my father got diagnosed, and my father told me not to tell Alice yet after what she's been through. When you appeared, I thought I could tell you. But you're so caught up in your own problems, I didn't think I could say anything.'

My face turned tomato-red. What Dennis said about me confirmed what Ah Hock had been saying all these years. That I was selfish, only thinking about my own desires. Dennis had been hanging out with me all this time without saying anything about his father's illness, because there wasn't enough room for both our problems?

'Is it serious?' I asked.

Dennis nodded. 'Cancer.'

My heart sank. I didn't know what to say.

'Doctor gave him a year, at most. He still looks strong, right? My mother knows. Alice can't even guess.'

'I'm sorry. It's horrible.'

'I know you and your father have a lot of problems, but they might seem small when it's his time to go, you know? You can't imagine it now. You'll know the feeling when it happens. My father's made me promise to take over the kolo mee stall.

We don't have a special broth or a legacy or anything. He wants to make sure our customers will always have our kolo mee to eat. Funny, right? Like, who cares about customers when you're about to die. My father does,' Dennis said.

'You're a good son. Unlike me.'

'It's not a competition.' Dennis shrugged.

'My father thinks something bad will happen if I don't take over the kopitiam. Some curse. It's just something he uses to scare me. He said it all the time when I was growing up. At least your father's honest about it. You're a good man, Dennis, for promising him. I don't know if I could do the same.'

'Your father's not on his deathbed yet. How would you know you wouldn't do the same? Like I said, you won't know until it happens, man.'

I wanted to reach over and give Dennis a hug. Instead, I patted his back and squeezed his shoulder.

'I'm here for you, man. Any time.'

Dennis looked at me with reddened eyes. It was the first time I'd ever seen him so filled with anguish. We heard a car pulling up to the front gate.

'They're back.' Dennis wiped his eyes. He went to the bathroom to wash his face while I went downstairs. The Tans said hello to me then brought Misha upstairs for her bath. I helped Alice put her shopping bags on the kitchen table while she unpacked them. We stood so close together I could smell her shampoo, the scent of ripened mangoes.

'You haven't left?' she said, then laughed when she saw my crestfallen face. 'I'm just joking. Stay as long as you like, but eventually you should make up with your parents.'

'I want to, but I'm not sure how.' I hadn't planned anything beyond running to Dennis's house. Last night, all I'd wanted was to get out of there. Away from all the monsters both Ah

Hock and I had unleashed, leaving Ma there to deal with the fallout.

'I'm sure you can work something out.'

'I don't think my father can let go of this idea that I have to take over the kopitiam because of some family curse. It's so stupid.'

'You can't blame him. His father and your ancestors before him all believed it. Look at what they became – artisans, proud of their work. Why shouldn't they continue such a respected profession? I can understand why they would want to leave a legacy behind. But you wouldn't be the first son of a hawker who wants to do more, or something different. I have friends who work in offices because they couldn't stand the life in front of a hot stove, serving people, working from day till night.'

'I can't do what he wants just so he can have a legacy.'

'I know. It's your decision. All I know is, it's been nice having you here.' She squeezed my hand. 'For Misha too. She likes you.' I squeezed her hand back, wanting to do so much more, to sweep her off her feet and kiss her deeply. Go upstairs with her and explore each other's bodies. The image of Jiayi's neck flickered into my mind, her smooth back, the silhouette of her curves, and for a split second I felt guilty. But Jiayi was a red taxi with its light on at three in the morning. Alice was different. A rose growing from a crack in the pavement I wanted to pluck and take home with me. It wouldn't be easy, but nothing worthwhile ever came easy. Maybe I had known all along that things with Jiayi wouldn't last. Maybe that was what had attracted me to her.

'Put these in the fridge?' Alice held out a plastic bag of apples with the smile of a thousand daffodils blooming in a meadow, melting away my anger with Ah Hock. I took the apples then pulled her close to me and kissed her, drinking in all of her, forgetting that Dennis or his parents could walk in on us at any moment.

*

The Tans had dinner late, around seven-thirty. I asked Aunty Tan if I could help her cook while Dennis was watching TV in the living room. It was the least I could do.

'I'm almost done, but you can help me mince some garlic and shallots,' she said. Aunty Tan was about the same age as Ma, but she looked younger; her face was free of lines and her eyes were bright. Her hair did not have a trace of grey and she moved fast in the kitchen. She had the same short curly bouffant as Ma, the only thing about her that hinted at her age. 'I'm cooking simple dishes tonight, omelette with preserved radish, fried spinach, pig intestines with white peppercorn soup. What does your mother cook for dinner?'

'Don't worry, Aunty. I eat anything. She cooks my father's favourite like braised duck, stewed pork trotters and steamed fish, but we eat simple food most of the time.'

Aunty Tan had always treated me like a son when I was growing up. Their house was my second home and I'd experienced nothing but kindness from her whenever I took refuge there. Even as she faced Uncle Tan's prognosis, she was her usual pleasant self. Seeing her put up a brave front made me feel a great sadness for her.

Aunty Tan laughed. 'Your mother must be a great cook to satisfy your father's taste buds.'

'Is it okay if I cook the omelette and fry the spinach, Aunty?' It was the only thing I could do for her.

She smiled. 'Go ahead. Wash the wok first,' she said, then left the kitchen. I oiled the wok then flash-fried the spinach in seconds. It felt liberating cooking without having to worry about Ah Hock refusing to eat slightly wilted spinach or commenting that there was too much oil. I'd told Dennis earlier that I didn't feel like cooking, but I was wrong. Cooking simple food without overthinking anything made me feel free, like a child flying a kite on a windy day, watching it soar.

I fried the tiny pieces of salty preserved radish and poured a bowl of beaten eggs into the wok. It was like the omelette Ma cooked, one of the dishes we had with watery Teochew porridge. Radish omelette, salted eggs, fried mackerel, and salted vegetables fried with thin slices of pork.

After cooking, I helped to set the table as everyone sat down to dinner. The dining room was a small area between the living room and the kitchen, where there was a round marble table with six wooden chairs.

'Come, eat, don't stand on ceremony, Ming,' Uncle Tan said. He took a piece of omelette and ate it with a big spoonful of rice. I served him a portion of spinach and watched him eat with relish. No one would have guessed he had a terminal disease. His appetite was good and his cheery demeanour betrayed nothing. I couldn't imagine how Dennis would cope when the inevitable happened. I had to stick around until then. A chance to redeem myself. To repay the Tans for all they had done for me.

Alice sipped her bowl of soup quietly, then used her chopsticks to take some spinach for Misha, who wrinkled her nose at the sight of the green leaves.

'Take some intestines, Ming,' Aunty Tan said, ladling soup for me. I tried to slurp the soup quietly, not wanting to look like a slob in front of Alice. The white peppercorns Aunty

Tan had used were fragrant and the soup was seasoned with just the right amount of salt. The intestines had been cooked well, not too rubbery, pleasantly flavoured without being too gamey. I finished a bowl of rice, feeling hungrier than I ever had in my life. 'Wei Ming cooked the spinach today, see how crunchy it is! And the omelette is so moist!'

'They're both delicious. Dennis doesn't always help my mum in the kitchen, and he likes to cook!' Alice said.

'Frying vegetables only-mah, so boring,' Dennis said, and refilled his bowl with soup.

'Ya-lah, we know you're an expert chef, only cook complicated dishes,' Aunty Tan said as she served everyone more omelette.

After dinner, we hung out in Dennis's room and talked until he fell asleep. I wasn't sleepy so I tiptoed to the living room down the parquet stairs and checked the VCD collection stacked on top of their VCD player. It was an eclectic selection – *Batman Returns*, *Mrs Doubtfire*, *Basic Instinct*, *Indecent Proposal*, *A Few Good Men*. Probably Dennis's choices. I could tell which ones were Misha's – *Aladdin*, *Beauty and the Beast*.

I'd watched the first five minutes of *The Silence of the Lambs* when I heard footsteps on the stairs and was ready to apologise profusely to Aunty or Uncle Tan. I didn't realise it was midnight until I looked at the wall clock.

It was Alice, in her long, sleeveless nightgown, light blue with faint pink flowers. 'You're not asleep!' she said, surprised.

'Sorry, did I wake you? I put the volume as low as I could. I hope I didn't disturb your parents.'

She shook her head and sat down next to me. Her nightgown brushed my legs. 'Nah, they're so tired after a day's work, thunderstorms wouldn't wake them up. It's drizzling now.' She pointed at the patio. I got up and looked out the patio door, watching the rain trickle down the glass.

'Wanna sit outside? I've got something.' Alice brandished a small joint.

'Is that what I think it is?' Malaysia had strict laws on drugs. A single joint would land you in jail.

She opened the door and beckoned to me. We sat on the living room floor near the open patio, and she lit up the joint.

'Isn't it risky?' I looked around, but no one would be up and about at this hour, and certainly not in the rain.

'Nobody knows if you do it at home.' She took a puff then passed the joint to me. 'Unless our nosy neighbours report us.'

I took a couple of puffs and inhaled, then passed it back to her. 'Why are you up so late?'

'It's time to myself. These days Misha goes to sleep later than she should.'

I moved closer to Alice and stroked her hair. She lay her head on my shoulder.

'Dennis is probably snoring like a pig by now,' Alice said, and I laughed.

'He said he was tired.'

'I envy him,' she said. 'He gets tired, he sleeps. He's a simple guy. When I'm tired, I need to clear my head. At night, like now, after my day ends and before bedtime is when I feel a little human again. A space for me to make peace with myself before I go to sleep.'

'Sorry to invade your space.'

'Oh, you're not. I'm happy to have you in my space.'

'I thought having a sibling meant you would always have someone to talk to. I never did.'

'That's the funny thing. He's my brother but he talks to you more than he ever talks to me. I suppose it's because I'm a girl. Or because we have different interests. I know nothing about cooking.'

'Do you . . . do you think you could ever be with someone like me?' Maybe it was the joint that had relaxed me enough to work up the courage to ask her something like that. But I also felt a sudden urgent need to know, so I could at least have one certain thing in my life.

Alice chuckled softly. 'Are you stoned?'

'A little.' I grinned. 'But I'm serious.'

'Why not?' she said. 'You're a nice guy.'

I'd been hoping for a more definite answer, rather than one that sounded like I was as good a choice as any. At least it wasn't a no.

'You're a hotshot lawyer. I'm just a guy who cooks stuff.'

'You're an artist, like your father. You should believe in yourself, Ming. Most people would kill for your talent.'

'Thanks for trying to cheer me up.'

'I'm not. I'm telling the truth. Have you decided to stay in Kuching?'

'I don't know yet. I think I am.'

'If you're going back to Hong Kong, why are you asking me these questions?'

'I don't know,' I said, feeling like a small boy. 'I wanted to tell you how I feel.'

'We're not teenagers anymore, Ming. I'm not a crush you fantasise about. I'm a widow with a young child. I come with baggage. I *am* baggage.' She took another drag of the joint.

'I'm willing to—'

'Yes, I'm sure you have all the good intentions in the world. But I can't have any hope, until I know it's a sure thing. You're a great guy, and I might even be a little in love with you, but that's not enough.'

'I'll stay for sure then.' I knew I was being impulsive when I didn't know what my plans were, but I felt as if she would slip away if I didn't say it.

'No. Don't decide this for anyone but yourself. I'm going to bed. You should get some sleep too, it's late.' She put out the joint on the ground outside and got up. 'Dennis said the kopitiam bet is tomorrow.'

Was it? I had completely forgotten about the bet! How embarrassing that Dennis remembered and I didn't.

'Go back to your parents, Ming. Help your father win. If you don't, you might regret it for the rest of your life,' Alice said. She walked upstairs, her hair over her shoulders, her nightgown gently swishing against her legs. When I heard her bedroom door close, I lay down on the sofa where she had been, smelling baby powder and listening to the pitter-patter of rain outside.

31

Paper Cannot Wrap Up Fire

I loved early morning walks on Carpenter Street before the clamour of vehicles and people near lunchtime. The other time it was as tranquil was when it rained, when the ancient street turned dark and quiet, reminiscent of the days before cars filled up the road. During the monsoon, raindrops pummelled zinc roofs and sheets of water poured off awnings, before easing into a gentle shower that lasted for minutes, or more often for hours. Time slowed down in these moments, old timers reread their newspapers in the kopitiams, and people ordered a second or third teh si or kopi-o, waiting for the rain to stop.

I decided to drop by Third Uncle's place before seeing my parents. If anyone could get through to my father, it would be him. Even if I admired Ah Kong, Third Uncle was like a grandfather to me – often the mediator between me and Ah Hock, dispensing pieces of advice to me even if I didn't always heed them.

Third Uncle lived in a shophouse a few blocks away from the kopitiam. It was only a couple of minutes' walk, but I took my time, looking at the various shops and buildings along the way.

Wedged between the shophouses was the Hiang Tiang

Siang Ti temple, which had been around since the nineteenth century, built by Teochew immigrants. It was small but nevertheless a grand presence, with its entrance decorated with bright red pillars and door frames, paintings of a tiger and a dragon on the walls, and a sweeping emerald-green tiled roof with upturned eaves, adorned with carved dragons. Ma used to bring me there when I was a child. I would cough at the odour of burning incense and she would insist on me offering joss sticks and kneeling before altars. I didn't remember the last time I'd set foot in the temple. What Ah Hock had said about sleeping under the stage at Lau Ya Keng, I wondered if the people who had shown kindness to Teck Boon and Ah Hock when they arrived in Borneo all those years ago were the children of the same immigrants who had built this temple.

Beside the temple was a bookshop where a cat lay napping on piles of books, oblivious to the sounds of a carpenter sanding a table next door. I watched the carpenter for a while as he smoothed the edges of the table, imagining the finished product with shellac or whatever he used to glaze furniture. He looked up as I stared and we exchanged brief nods. He was one of the remaining carpenters there, a relic of history. I prayed he would be around for a while longer.

I turned the corner into China Street, or pak ti kay, as Ah Hock called it. The sounds of hammer and tongs hitting metal, the tinsmiths making the many broth pots and woks that worked hard for decades and seldom needed to be replaced. It was an honour to live among these artisans.

Third Uncle's shop was a nondescript shophouse that could be easily missed if not for the metal folding doors that were half open. It was ironic that a sign-maker did not have a signboard for his own shop.

I knocked on the door and called for the old man. Before long, Third Uncle shuffled to the door, and waved me into the shophouse as if he'd been expecting my visit. Inside was dark, with two windows open. Blocks of wood were strewn around the floor. A rectangular wooden table was in the middle of the shop, covered with calligraphy paper and carving tools.

'Come, help me to mix this ink,' Third Uncle said in Teochew, gesturing for me to come to the table. There was a black round ink stone, and beside it a well-used ink stick with intricate gold characters carved into it. Third Uncle used a wet calligraphy brush to dampen the ink stone. 'Now gently grind the ink stick on the stone.'

I rubbed the ink stick in a circular motion on the stone, enjoying the meditative process. I hadn't been working on my masu much. Perhaps I could pick up calligraphy, another art form that cultivated a peaceful state of mind.

'It's nice, isn't it?' Third Uncle said. 'The quiet that allows you to think. It allows me to meditate on the sign I'll be painting after I'm done.' After five minutes, Third Uncle told me it was ready. I put the ink stick back in its case carefully.

'Where did you buy this?' I asked in Mandarin, admiring the ink stick. Luckily, Third Uncle understood the language, although he would reply in Teochew.

'I used to buy my ink sticks from one of the Shanghainese sellers here on attap kay.' Third Uncle called Carpenter Street by its old name, Attap Street, referring back to the time when roofs were made of palm fronds. 'He's dead now. I think when this one runs out, I'll have to ask around to see if anyone can get me some more from China. But I don't need many these days. At my age, there's no need to make so many signboards.'

'Why did you start making signboards?'

'I needed work when I first arrived from China all those years ago. A young man with no money, no prospects.' He laughed. 'Came here, lots of carpenters needed apprentices. I liked the look of the signboards. Making them calmed me. I treat each one like a child. I create it, nurture it, then release it into the world.'

'My master in Hong Kong taught me Japanese carpentry. I like it but I'm not very good at it.'

'Everything needs practice. I'm sure your master told you.' After a pause, he added, 'You're a good boy. Your father is worried about you.'

'You mean disappointed. Angry. It's not my fault I'm not the son he wants.'

'You're the only one he has.' He put down the carving knife. 'Did your father ever tell you how he and your grandfather came to Kuching?'

'He seldom talks about Ah Kong. My mother told me not to ask him either.'

'I'll make you a cup of tea.' Third Uncle shuffled to the kitchen. Moments later, he came back with a tea set much like the one my parents had. He poured the steeped tea leaves over the two cups, then refilled the teapot with hot water. When Third Uncle was about to pour tea for me, I protested and took the teapot from him. I wasn't about to let my elder pour tea for me.

'Your grandfather was a unique character. A real story-teller, but only to those he trusted. He was a talented man, very intelligent. Could be good at anything he did. I suppose that's why he could suddenly cook laksa in another country, a dish totally unfamiliar to him. Created his own recipe too.'

'The only thing I know is that he was a great chef in Swatow.'

Third Uncle nodded. 'Yes, everybody knows that. There were other things we heard about too. Folks from Swatow who came over, knew a bit more about what went on.'

'What do you mean?'

'Do not tell your parents what I am about to tell you,' Third Uncle said. I nodded before the old man continued. 'He got too famous too young, some people said. He had a good life, he was making lots of money from his restaurant, government officials frequented his place, he had lots of female admirers. Your grandmother was from a good family, but she wasn't enough to stop his roving eye. It's not easy for a man, those women were throwing themselves at him, the great master.'

'My Ah Kong was a womaniser?' That revelation cast a shadow over my idea of Teck Boon. All this time I'd pictured him immersed in his craft, caring only about the texture of tofu or the flavours of freshly caught mullet. I'd never imagined he would be embroiled in love affairs.

I thought about the women who had sat on my lap at the Jade Pavilion countless times. I was the last person to judge anyone, especially my own grandfather.

Third Uncle wagged his finger at me. 'Don't be disrespectful. He was weak when it came to women. Like a man presented with too many dishes in front of him. He didn't know how to choose, or whether to stick to what he knew best. Your grandfather was too young to wield the power he possessed. He didn't know how to handle it.'

'What happened to him?'

'He had an affair with a married woman. Her husband found out and went to his restaurant kitchen with a gun. Your grandfather was in the middle of making Emperor's Soup with shredded tofu, something that requires much precision and skill. When the jealous husband stormed into the kitchen and startled your grandfather, he dropped the tofu on the floor. The kitchen staff cleared out of the kitchen, leaving the two men alone. Your grandfather was in a rage, because the man had stormed into his kitchen with a gun, but also because his tofu was ruined. He tried to wrestle the gun from the husband, and in the end, the man was shot and killed.'

I gasped. Teck Boon had killed a man! Goosebumps prickled my arms. Never, never in my wildest dreams would I have imagined Teck Boon embroiled in a love triangle that resulted in the death of someone. Did Ah Hock know this?

'My father has never mentioned this. Neither has my mother.'

'He might have heard rumours, I don't know. Of course, Teck Boon would never have told Ah Hock this. It would have made Ah Hock hate him.'

'I guess my grandfather never paid for his crime?'

'He ran. He took your father, and he ran. He took the first ship out of the harbour, which went to Singapore, then here.'

'What about my grandmother?' I had never heard my grandmother mentioned before. Whenever I asked Ah Hock about her, he would simply shrug and ignore me, or change the subject. Even Ma didn't know anything about her. I'd just assumed she had died in China and that I shouldn't probe further into the painful subject.

'All I know is there wasn't much love between your grandfather and his wife. It had been an arranged marriage. A general Teck Boon couldn't offend if he valued his life. Heads rolled freely in those days. This same general who bought your grandfather his restaurant in Swatow as a wedding gift.'

'My father says they ran from Swatow because of the Japanese invasion.'

'The invasion happened only after they left. After that, Teck Boon and Ah Hock never heard from your grandmother or the rest of their family again. Your grandfather arrived here with Ah Hock, with some jewellery and gold in his pockets, some of which had already been used to pay their passage. Ah, of course, and his beloved broth. Almost as precious as his son.'

'More precious, probably,' I said bitterly. If Teck Boon had treasured the broth over Ah Hock, it was no surprise Ah Hock had become the man he was today.

'He still needed an heir to pass it on. One cannot be without the other.'

'Just to avoid the big, scary curse, huh?' I couldn't help sneering. I felt cursed already, forced to live a life designed to avoid the one thing that terrified Ah Hock.

Third Uncle shook his head. 'I'm not one to believe in any old superstition, but I wouldn't dismiss it that lightly. Your father is so worried about it that he's making himself ill.'

'He looks fine to me. Strong enough to shout at me.'

'He had his heart checked in the hospital. He needs to see a specialist. Don't worry your mother about this, okay?'

So Towkay Lau wasn't lying. It was just like Ah Hock not to tell Ma. 'How bad is it?' I asked, preparing myself for the worst.

'All the doctor said was Ah Hock should see a heart specialist. No harm getting a proper check-up.'

Okay. Third Uncle didn't say we had to rush Ah Hock to the hospital just yet. *Don't sweat it. One step at a time.* We needed to get through the bet first, then I'd take him to see the best cardiologist in town.

'He should've said something.'

'He keeps a lot of things inside. That man, too much pride, like your grandfather. The pride is what destroys them.'

'Pride? The famous Lim Teck Boon was an adulterer and a murderer,' I declared with some disgust. I couldn't help feeling disappointed. So much for being my idol. I'd been shaping my whole life around the god-like spectre of my grandfather, the greatest chef in Swatow. Any admiration for him had dissolved into that abysmal broth.

When I was younger, whenever I passed by the broth, I would look at it, thinking I was the heir to some greatness in the blood. That the talent bestowed upon my grandfather would pass down to me in some way, if I were persistent enough, if I wanted it enough, unlike Ah Hock. Instead, my grandfather had been a fugitive, a coward who had run from the consequences of his actions and left his wife behind to face the humiliation. But was I any different? I had agreed to betray my own father so Towkay Lau could give me a restaurant. Maybe it wasn't greatness that ran in the blood after all.

Third Uncle shook his head. 'Things are never as simple as they appear. Your grandmother's family was a powerful one in China. They had dinner at the restaurant your grandfather worked in one night and were enamoured by the food. The general, your grandmother's father, insisted he had to pay his compliments to the chef in person. Your grandfather came to the table and bowed as he received his compliments, but when the general saw this handsome young chef before him, he immediately saw marriage potential for his youngest daughter. Marriage was the last thing on Teck Boon's mind, but he could not refuse the demands of a powerful general. Do you understand now? Where your grandfather's unhappiness came from?'

'Is that an excuse for his behaviour?'

'It's easy to say that when you have more freedom these days. I'm not defending your grandfather or the choices he made, Ming. I'm simply telling you what he told me. He didn't speak much to anyone else. I don't know why he chose to confide in me. Maybe he knew I wouldn't judge him.'

'So the name Lim Teck Boon is sullied in Swatow,' I said glumly.

Third Uncle chuckled. 'Don't worry, it was probably not his real name. In those days, people sometimes had to change their names to get on the ship. Ah, this life is one big opera performance. *Nang zo hi, hi zo nang*. Truth can be stranger than fiction. I suppose he coped the best way he could, with his greatest love, cooking. Making food was his one passion and he threw himself into it.'

'You mean obsession. Everything became secondary to cooking, or the broth. It sounds like he cared more about the broth than my father.'

'The truth is, the broth may not have lasted the journey. But it was important for Teck Boon to believe he wasn't breaking the ancient promise when he ran away. Speaking of names, let me test this ink.'

Third Uncle took a calligraphy brush and wet it with the ink I had ground. He wrote a character, 铭, on a piece of square paper with swift strokes. The character looked familiar but I didn't know what it meant.

'For you,' Third Uncle said, then gave me the piece of paper. 'Be careful, let it dry properly.'

'What word is this, Third Uncle?'

Third Uncle roared with laughter while I blushed. 'You don't know your own name? I always forget you didn't go to Chinese school. It's "Ming". The name your parents chose for you. It means "to engrave, or make a mark". Make your mark in this world, Wei Ming. As deeply as I engrave these signboards.'

The old man got up, walked to a nearby shelf and took a tin of tea from it. 'Come, I have some good Pu'er for your father. Give it to him as a peace offering. Don't forget, you must give him a ladder to come down from his high horse,' Third Uncle said. 'Teochew men cannot live without their pride.'

I thanked him for the tea and the calligraphy. Third Uncle sat back down at his workstation to continue carving his signboard, and I left the shophouse still in a daze from his revelations and almost tripped over the threshold. My heart softened for Ah Hock, but that didn't make it any easier anticipating what he would say to me after the fight. That I had dishonoured him and the family name. That I was the most unfilial child in the world. Even if that were true, all Ah Hock's obsession had done was drive father and son further apart. All this talking about continuing the generations, but what was the use of generations of fathers and sons who couldn't be honest with each other? Sons who continued to resent their fathers for forced obligations, canings, and stern words instead of love? I had put my grandfather, Lim Teck Boon, on a pedestal for far too long. He was no deity. None of us were. Deep inside we were still little boys who never got our father's love when we needed it. Just like any other mortal.

The first thing I would do when I got to the kopitiam would be to throw away the sachet underneath the Kuan Yin statuette. It was time to face my fears. I wouldn't run away, like Teck Boon did. And I knew I would never look at my grandfather's altar the same way again.

32

Feast At Swan Goose Gate

At eight o'clock, a white van and Towkay Lau's Mercedes pulled up in front of the kopitiam. Towkay Lau and an attractive woman in her late twenties alighted from the car. She was in a white chef's jacket and black trousers. Her glossy black hair was in a bun, and she wore small, elegant diamond stud earrings. Although young, her face looked hardened. Her demeanour was guarded and she kept looking around as if she were expecting an ambush.

The day of the bet had finally arrived. Ah Hock tried to ignore his dry mouth and shaky hands. What awful timing it was, after the fiasco with Wei Ming! It had all gone wrong. Wei Ming was supposed to be the happy heir of the kopitiam, and they were supposed to win the bet together. How quickly the blue skies had turned into a thunderstorm!

He maintained his composure, so Towkay Lau suspected nothing. The businessman waved at Ah Hock as if they were best friends.

'Ah Hock! Today's the day, I hope you're prepared! This is Ms Chong Jiayi, an award-winning chef from Hong Kong. Her restaurant Malaysian Kitchen is famous in Kowloon! She's the first Malaysian chef to have won a star from the Global Restaurants

Guild! How impressive is that, eh?' Towkay Lau said. The young woman greeted Ah Hock and Kim Choo, but she looked uncomfortable, as if she wanted to be anywhere else but there. Hadn't Towkay Lau said he was bringing some white man from New York? Ah Hock wondered if he had heard wrongly.

'What happened to the angmoh you wanted to bring over?' Ah Hock asked.

'Ah, he had a family emergency. Luckily for us, Chef Chong was available. Knowing you, Ah Hock, you must be thinking how can this little girl judge your cooking, right? But you'd be wrong. This lady earned her star through serving the highest-quality food in Kowloon.' Towkay Lau said. Ah Hock wondered if this would play out in his favour. After all, she was Malaysian too. She would be better poised to decide which laksa was the genuine article.

'Whatever. Let's get this over with,' Ah Hock said. Kim Choo touched his shoulder.

'Don't worry, yours is the best. It has always been the best,' she said, but he could see the fear in her eyes, and doubt flooded his mind.

'As a mark of respect, we will come to your shop first, Ah Hock. I'm sure you're more than ready for today. Please, prepare a bowl of your laksa for Chef Chong.' Towkay Lau sat down at one of the tables with the chef.

Ah Hock's stomach churned, but he didn't let any of his uneasiness show. He took a small sip of the laksa broth and shook his head. Something was missing again. Damn this inconsistency! Today of all days! No, he was just nervous, it was probably all right. The spices were balanced, the depth of flavour was there. Okay, it was slightly bland, which a pinch of salt would fix.

He could feel his heart fluttering, and had to grip the edge of the steel counter to steady himself. This was no time to worry. He tried not to think about Teck Boon's ominous warnings in the dream. Hadn't Third Uncle said the laksa soup's been good? *You're getting insecure in your old age*, he chided himself. But what if the dream was an omen? Is that what Teck Boon had meant? That he would lose the kopitiam today?

A handful of beehoon fell from his jittery hand and Kim Choo picked it up from the floor. Towkay Lau smiled. Ah Hock wanted to smack the tycoon's face. It was too late to turn back now. He would just have to soldier on and do his best.

As Ah Hock was about to start assembling the bowl of laksa, Wei Ming appeared at the door like an apparition. The deity wasn't punishing him after all. Ah Hock's heart sang, but he refused to make eye contact with Wei Ming. The boy wasn't going to get away with his unforgivable behaviour that easily. In the old days, the only recompense had been for the son to kneel in front of the father and beg for forgiveness. Fat chance getting that from the boy!

He noticed Wei Ming's expression change when he saw the chef. Something was wrong. She had a similar expression when she saw Wei Ming, a look of remorse and fear. Ah Hock noticed them exchange meaningful glances. Did they know each other? But neither acknowledged this.

'Wei Ming! It looks like you've broken our deal. I didn't think you were the type who'd break promises.' Towkay Lau stared daggers at Wei Ming and it chilled Ah Hock's bones.

'I'm sorry, Mr Lau. Forget what we discussed. I don't need anything from you,' Wei Ming said, staring straight back at Towkay Lau. Ah Hock exhaled. The boy could hold his own, but Ah Hock couldn't shake off the uneasy feeling he had when he saw Towkay Lau's demeanour towards Wei Ming.

'Oh, you think it's so easy to change your mind whenever you like? Oral agreements are binding, you know. I'd like to see your team of lawyers helping you get out of this deal.'

So there was an agreement between them. Surely the boy hadn't been so foolish as to promise . . . No, there was no time to think about that now. Wei Ming was here, with him, and that was all that mattered. 'Don't talk to my son that way,' Ah Hock shouted as Wei Ming nudged him away from Towkay Lau.

'Pa, I'll . . . I'll handle it, don't worry,' Wei Ming said in a tone that didn't reassure Ah Hock. Never mind, there was no time to think about that now! They had to win the bet no matter what happened. With Wei Ming by his side, there was nothing they couldn't do!

'Really? Everyone needs something from me. They just don't know what it is until I tell them.' Towkay Lau smirked at the chef. She was staring at the table, her hand fiddling with her earring, not looking at anyone, although she would steal glances at Wei Ming. If earlier she had looked uncomfortable, now she looked ready to fly out of the place at any moment. Wei Ming ignored Towkay Lau and joined Ah Hock at the laksa stall. He took a sip of the laksa broth and looked at Ah Hock.

'It's missing something,' Wei Ming whispered, then went into the kitchen without explaining further.

He knew it! Not so old and feeble, after all. But that meant the soup needed improving. What could the boy be getting? Flatfish? More broth?

Wei Ming came back, holding a container.

'What's that?' Ah Hock asked him.

'The salted terubuk from Dennis.'

'Are you crazy? I've never put this in the soup before!'

Ah Hock said, his voice getting louder. Wei Ming shushed him.

'Trust me. It has lots of umami.'

'Lots of what?'

'Xian wei. Deep flavours. It'll work,' Wei Ming said. Before Ah Hock could stop him, Wei Ming took out two big pieces of the salted herring and crumbled the pieces into the simmering laksa broth. They stood, waiting, while Kim Choo offered the chef and Towkay Lau iced milk tea. The chef took a sip, then thanked Kim Choo.

'Don't keep Chef Chong waiting too long.' Towkay Lau's eyes narrowed. He tapped his foot on the floor impatiently. Ah Hock was about to reach for another bowl when Wei Ming stopped him.

'Don't worry, Pa. I can manage,' Wei Ming said. Ah Hock nodded. Wei Ming looked surprised, perhaps thinking he would put up more of a fight.

But Ah Hock was tired. He stood by and watched his son pick the freshest, juiciest prawns and lay them on the pristine white bed of beehoon. As Wei Ming assembled the bowl of laksa, Ah Hock took a sip of its soup. The boy was right. It was full of flavour now. If he hadn't known what it lacked before, the salted herring had completed it. He didn't know how it worked but it did.

He nodded at Wei Ming, who ladled soup into the bowl, then served it to the chef himself. 'Please enjoy, Chef,' Wei Ming said, with an emphasis on the last word as he placed the bowl in front of her. The chef winced, as if she had been scalded by the soup. She started to eat the laksa only at Towkay Lau's urging. She sipped the broth, then made notes in a notebook she had brought along.

She ate spoonfuls of beehoon, prawn, omelette and broth. Wei Ming and Ah Hock waited for a reaction but she said nothing. There were times when she paused after a spoonful of soup, but she did not comment and simply scribbled a bit more in her notebook. Where was that awe he'd been hoping for? That look of contentment? Ah Hock had a bad feeling. First-timers could never help themselves from expressing their delight at the first taste of the laksa soup. He felt sweat trickle down the back of his neck, and he reached for a white Good Morning towel to wipe it off.

When the chef had finished tasting the laksa, she stood and thanked Ah Hock. He noticed she hadn't finished the soup. A bad sign. Ah Hock stared at the sambal on the table, completely untouched. Why hadn't she added that, and the calamansi lime too? Some chef!

Wei Ming noticed Ah Hock's despondent face and patted his shoulder. 'Don't worry, Pa. Let's go there now and see what Billy's prepared. We've done our best.'

They were about to go next door to the Good Luck Café for Billy's turn, when Dennis and Alice arrived, huffing and puffing as though they had been running.

'Sorry, man, it was hard to find parking! Are we too late? Is the competition over?' Dennis said, panting.

'We're going next door now for the judging of Towkay Lau's laksa,' Wei Ming said. Alice threw her arms around him. Ah Hock noticed the chef staring at them, then looking away as if the sight hurt her eyes. That's it, the boy must know her. They could even be lovers! But what about this new girl, that Dennis boy's sister? No time to figure it all out now. Time to see what rubbish that Bobby or whatever his name was could serve up next door.

'You go ahead,' Kim Choo said. 'I can't watch. I'll wait here with Dennis and Alice.' Before Ah Hock could persuade Kim Choo to follow them, Wei Ming urged him to hurry, so he left her standing there, watching them like they were going off to war and might not return.

*

It was Ah Hock's first time at the Good Luck Café. The blast of cold air that hit him as he entered the place chilled his bones. He had never seen a place like this selling laksa. Wouldn't the air conditioning cool down the soup faster? Was this really what people wanted these days? Air conditioning, fancy decor? Soft music in the background? What about the food? He took a whiff of the scent of laksa that hovered in the air, familiar yet different. He didn't have to taste it to know there was too much turmeric, too much cumin.

'Billy! I hope you're ready to impress Chef Chong!' Towkay Lau called loudly to his cook. As they were led to the stall, the snot-nosed boy was in chef's whites and looked like he was glowing. He was wearing a chef's hat, what a clown! His skin was so white and smooth . . . was he wearing make-up? Wouldn't put it past him, that sorry excuse for a cook!

The chef took her seat at a table while Billy began assembling a bowl of laksa for her. Ah Hock gave the many bowls of ingredients furtive glances. Fish balls? Tofu, lobster, crayfish, clams. The chicken pieces looked grey, overcooked. The omelette wasn't shredded properly and didn't have the same bright yellow sheen of the fresh eggs Ah Hock used. Ah Hock could hardly bring himself to look at the toppings. A sacrilege, that's what it was! Billy was heaping piles of lobster and crayfish on the beehoon. Figured they weren't bothering with the quality of their simpler ingredients. The expensive seafood would overshadow them. At least, for the pedestrian customer.

After ladling the laksa soup into the bowl, Billy brought the laksa over to the chef and set it in front of her. 'I made this omelette with a touch of shrimp paste, not too salty, and it adds that unique flavour no other laksa has!' Billy beamed. The chef ate a spoonful of soup with lobster and scribbled in her notebook. If she were a chef worth her salt, she wouldn't be impressed by lobster. So what if there was lobster? Were they cooking laksa or a seafood medley?

From what Ah Hock could see, the chef had a small bite of the omelette Billy was raving about and had even less of the soup. Billy hadn't given her sambal or limes! Hah! Which sane chef would be impressed by such an exhibition of mediocrity? Perhaps there was hope after all. When this madness was over, things could get back to the way they were. No more talk of branches or franchises from that frivolous Towkay Lau. He'd had to put up with the businessman's nagging for more than thirty years now.

The persistence of that man! You had to give him some credit for it. Still, the thought of never hearing him mention the word 'branches' again almost made Ah Hock grin. He closed his eyes and prayed fervently to any deity who would listen.

The chef put down her chopsticks, and thanked Billy. She wrote a bit more in her notebook and looked up. She didn't smile or look like she had enjoyed the laksa either. Ah Hock exhaled. Probably her lack of enthusiasm didn't mean anything. Some people were poker-faced like that. He didn't like how he was being kept in suspense. The butterflies in his stomach continued to flutter as he waited for her to announce the winner.

Towkay Lau spoke to her in English, on purpose probably. Ah Hock tugged at Wei Ming's elbow, asking him to translate. 'He's asking her to announce the winner and to explain the reasons,' Wei Ming replied, trying to hear the rest of the conversation. The chef approached Ah Hock. She faced him but could not bear to look him in the eye. She wasn't wearing any make-up, but that wasn't why her face was ashen. Even before the words tumbled out of her mouth, he knew it was over.

'I'm sorry, Uncle,' she said in Mandarin, in a voice one reserved for the bereaved. She touched his arm in a gesture of apology and he recoiled.

It couldn't be. Was he in a dream? A nightmare. Something, something was not right. His fate could not be decided like this, on a whim, by some young woman who clearly didn't know what she was doing. How could anyone eat the rubbish Billy had prepared? A good chef knew how good ingredients were even without tasting them.

'It was the sambal, we forgot to give you the sambal. Please, taste it again with the sambal. You have to add the sambal until the taste suits you, it's different for everybody and . . .' He choked back tears. Foolish old man! Losing his pride in front of this young woman! For the first time in his life, he was begging someone to eat his laksa. All was lost. And worst of all, that scoundrel was watching every moment of Ah Hock's humiliation with his arms folded and the smile of a fox in a hen house.

'No.' The chef looked at the floor. 'It was not the sambal. You make a good laksa, Uncle. I could taste the depth of the soup even without the sambal.'

308

'Then why?' The words came out of Ah Hock like a howl. He wasn't sure what was happening. She shook her head and apologised again before turning to Towkay Lau and saying something in English.

It was as if everything was happening in slow motion. Towkay Lau was clapping, and Billy bowing, thanking the chef. Wei Ming stood frozen, staring at them.

'What is she saying?' Ah Hock asked Wei Ming, whose face had turned grim.

'She said Billy's laksa won because the fresh seafood was impressive. The soup was full of flavour and the uniqueness of the omelette gave it an edge. That it is a creative take on the idea of laksa.'

A creative take? The *idea* of laksa? What about taste? Freshness? Authenticity? What nonsense were they talking about? The room was spinning. Ah Hock's knees buckled and Wei Ming held his arms to steady him.

'It's rigged, Pa. I . . . I know the chef. She's one of the best chefs I know. Her palate is impeccable. She must have been forced to do this. It's Towkay Lau—' Wei Ming said. Ah Hock pushed Wei Ming aside and approached the chef.

'How could you sell your dignity like this! A cheap chef! You might as well call yourself a prostitute!' Ah Hock continued to berate her until Wei Ming pulled him away. The chef's face turned bright red. Ah Hock shook free of Wei Ming's hold and stormed back to their kopitiam.

Kim Choo had been standing at the entrance, waiting for them, as if she had guessed what the outcome would be. She said nothing but touched Ah Hock's arm. Dennis comforted Wei Ming as Alice held his hands, her eyes brimming with tears.

The chef came back to the kopitiam carrying something, pausing as she observed Alice with Wei Ming. What the hell did she want now? He should've known Towkay Lau would rig the game. Ah Hock was about to chase her away when Wei Ming stopped him.

The chef held out a canvas bag. 'I brought your knife back,' she said. Ah Hock couldn't believe his eyes. Not only had she betrayed them, now she was giving a knife as a present to Wei Ming? Was she doing it on purpose? She was Chinese, she should know what a taboo it was, giving a knife to someone!

Wei Ming made no attempt to take it from her. 'You should have kept it,' he said quietly.

'He threatened me,' the chef said. Her eyes were red and she spoke in almost a whisper, but loud enough for Ah Hock to hear. 'The money Man Kor used to buy Malaysian Kitchen . . . it was from Towkay Lau. He said he could take it all back. I can't let him do that, Wei Ming. It's my blood, sweat and tears. I'm sorry.'

'You have no idea what you've done here,' Wei Ming said, in the iciest voice Ah Hock had ever heard.

'It doesn't matter what you say to me anymore. Take care of yourself, Wei Ming. Stay here. It's safer.' She left the bag on a table before leaving the kopitiam. Wei Ming touched the bag without opening it. He looked ashamed, and Ah Hock didn't know why.

Before Ah Hock had a chance to process what had happened, Towkay Lau entered the kopitiam, a triumphant smile on his face.

'Get out,' Ah Hock growled, but Towkay Lau ignored him and sat down at his usual table. He was unfazed, smiling coldly. He was a different person, no longer the family friend, and in his place was the heartless businessman who made his fortune through any means necessary.

'I'll be taking over the Teck Boon kopitiam branding. Now I own Teck Boon's name,' Towkay Lau said. 'And you are to vacate the premises in one week.'

Ah Hock felt the words float by as if he were in a dream. 'Why are you doing this? What have I ever done to you?'

'All these years I have asked you to work with me. Offered you a chance. And what did you do? Dismissed me as if I were a beggar. Me, a big-time businessman, with businesses all over the world. Who do you think you are? I didn't need to beg you like I did. You're an arrogant bastard. Just like your father.'

'How dare you mention my father! You soil his good name by allowing it to pass through your filthy lips. You get out! Get out now!'

'His good name?' Towkay Lau laughed. 'You'll want to ask the people of Swatow about his good name. Listen, I know you're stubborn, but don't tell me you want to dishonour our bet? Isn't it bad enough he didn't take responsibility for his crime in Swatow, you want to do the same here too? Like father, like son.' He turned to Wei Ming. 'Like grandson too. What kind of man doesn't keep his word? A dishonourable family, indeed!'

'Dishonourable? What a joke! Who's dishonourable here? Choosing a judge who would decide in your favour! Knowing who Jiayi is to me,' Wei Ming shouted, standing between Towkay Lau and Ah Hock.

Ah Hock's head was spinning. All these words flying around like crows circling above him. What was the boy saying? That Towkay Lau had cheated? And why the hell was he going on about some crime in Swatow?

'What are you talking about? What happened in Swatow?' Ah Hock asked. His gut tightened at the sinister look on Towkay Lau's face.

'Ah, I guess your father never told you. He ran away because he killed a man in Swatow. I have people there who still talk about the famous chef who was talented but loved screwing around. One day he killed some cheap woman's husband, can you imagine? Took his son and abandoned the mother of his child, then escaped to Borneo,' Towkay Lau said. 'What a story, eh? Like a film! A better ending would have been if the villain had paid for his crime!'

'My grandfather did what he had to do to protect his family.' Wei Ming spoke in a cryptic manner, as if he were hiding something. Ah Hock didn't understand. And how did he know anything about what had happened? What was there to be ashamed of? Should Teck Boon be blamed for protecting his son, the ancestral broth? He'd had no choice!

'No, no, we were escaping the Japanese,' Ah Hock said. That wily fox was twisting stories again. 'You stop your slander now!'

'That's what he wanted you to think. What do you think of your father now, eh, Ah Hock? Spent your whole life trying to please him, when he was nothing but an adulterer, a coward. And now you've shown yourself to be exactly like him. A bet's a bet. Don't run away like your father did.'

Towkay Lau couldn't be telling the truth, could he? A flash of Ah Hock's mother's anguished face resurfaced from the depths of his memory. Calling out to Teck Boon. Begging him not to take their son away. Not because of the war. He'd been running from his troubles. From her.

Ah Hock blinked back his tears. 'Get the hell out!' He lunged at Towkay Lau but Wei Ming stood between them.

'Do you remember how your father treated me like dirt?' Towkay Lau said. Just then, Ah Hock saw the hatred in his eyes.

312

'What nonsense are you talking about?'

'Forty years ago. It was right here, in this kopitiam. I came here, without a cent. Pleading with your father to let me be his apprentice. I was willing to work for food. He waved me away at first, as if I were a fly disturbing his meal. Then he took me on, after realising how he could work me to the bone for next to nothing.' Towkay Lau scowled at the memory. Gone were the years of complimenting the laksa, the words of encouragement and his smiles, which Ah Hock now knew had hidden a plan for revenge.

'I don't remember that. And what has it got to do with me?' Ah Hock said.

'You never appreciated what you had, Hock. A father who taught you to cook his laksa. You've forgotten, and yet I only lived a few shops away. My aunt's shop sold coffins. The neighbourhood kids used to call me the coffin boy. They teased and bullied me about it.'

'But I don't know anything about you,' Ah Hock said. 'I didn't even know you until you started coming every morning.'

'I was an orphan. My aunt never treated me like a son, let alone a nephew. Always let her children eat before me. And when I turned eighteen, she pushed me out the door, let me fend for myself. I have her to thank for my success today.' Towkay Lau looked around the kopitiam, as if he was seeing it for the first time, or perhaps the last.

He walked over to Teck Boon's altar and stared at his portrait. 'And I have your father to thank, too. All those months of being his slave, doing menial chores for free, only to have him tell me eventually that I wasn't destined for the kitchen. He dared to mention destiny, after all that free labour he got. But if he hadn't disposed of me like rubbish, I wouldn't have resolved to be the success I am today. When a tiger dies, he leaves behind his skin. When a man dies, he leaves behind his name. If only Lim Teck Boon were alive to see me today, taking his signboard, taking his name.'

'You've waited forty years to do this? To take revenge on my father?'

'You don't know how patient I can be. That's why I would've been a good apprentice. I know how to make good soup. Oh, yes. That image of your father waving me away. Simmering for forty years.'

Towkay Lau went outside the kopitiam and called some workers over. Kim Choo and Wei Ming held Ah Hock back as two workers climbed up a stepladder to remove the wooden signboard, then left it on the floor. Towkay Lau picked it up and looked at it. 'Third Uncle must have made this. It's a good signboard,' he said. He carried it under his arm, then dumped it into a green wheelie bin near the drains before walking towards his parked Mercedes, where his driver was waiting for him.

33

Sai Weng Lost His Horse

Nobody felt like eating after what Towkay Lau had done, but Ma insisted we should have dinner at Lau Ya Keng to cheer Ah Hock up. As expected, my father barely touched his food even though we ordered all his favourites – hot and sour fish head soup, fried salted mustard leaves with slices of braised duck, midin stir-fried with sweet red wine. For Ma's sake, I tried to eat as much as I could and almost choked on a clump of salted vegetables I had forgotten to chew.

'Eat more rice, Hock.' Ma spooned some fish soup for him, but he didn't say anything. She sighed, then passed me some midin with her chopsticks. Ma ate more than either of us, but she seemed distracted. Every time Ah Hock grunted and said he wanted to go home, she would persuade him to just take another bite.

When Ah Hock couldn't wait anymore, he pushed away from the table and stood up to leave. Ma quickly paid the bill, then ran after Ah Hock who was walking briskly back to the kopitiam. She called out to him, asking him to visit Third Uncle's shop. He ignored her and continued walking.

'Please, Ming, go after your father.' Ma seemed worried, and I didn't know why she was so anxious for Ah Hock to see Third Uncle. I tried asking Ah Hock, but he merely shook his head and gestured for me to unlock the kopitiam doors. Ma looked desperately at me but I shrugged and unlocked the doors. When I pulled them open, I could smell something in the air. Smoke. Ah Hock had already entered the kopitiam ahead of me, while Ma tried to pull him back out.

'Leave the kopitiam, I think there's a fire.' I'd said the words calmly but Ah Hock's eyes turned wild. Thick smoke was already filling up the kopitiam and I could feel heat.

'I need to save the broth!' Ah Hock shouted as he shook his arm free from Ma and ran towards the kitchen.

I turned to Ma and yelled for her to go back to the food court. 'Leave now, I'll take him!'

Ma hesitated, then ran to the food court. The smoke was getting thicker, and I knew there wasn't much time before both of us succumbed to it. I managed to grab Ah Hock before he entered the kitchen. Despite his age, Ah Hock seemed to have superhuman strength as he struggled to free himself. I had to put him in a bear hug from behind to restrain him. 'Come on, Pa! We need to leave!' I said, coughing.

'Not before I get the broth! Let go of me!'

'You'll die! We'll both die if we don't leave now!'

'Your grandfather would never forgive me!' Ah Hock coughed as he inhaled more smoke.

'He's dead! We are alive! Your family is Ma, and me!' I screamed. Damn it to hell! I felt like leaving him behind. What was the difference? The old man didn't appreciate us. He was blind to everything except his bloody broth, and it looked as if he was ready to die with it. I almost loosened my grip on Ah Hock, but Ma was waiting at Lau Ya Keng for the both of us to return.

Summoning all my strength, I managed to drag Ah Hock out of the burning kopitiam. Once we were outside, a few of the neighbours helped me get him to safety at Lau Ya Keng, where Ma was sitting with Third Uncle at a nearby table, in shock. She'd already made the emergency call to 999 from the telephone booth nearby.

Ah Hock sat in a stupor and occasionally stood up, repeating, 'I need to get the broth!' I had to restrain him again and again. The kuay chap seller from Lau Ya Keng came and tried to console him. Ah Hock sat back down only when I shouted 'I'll go, you stay!' I got a wet dishcloth from the kuay chap seller and ran to the kopitiam before Ma could stop me.

Inside, the kitchen was ablaze. I tried going round the back to see if I could access it from there, but the fire was fiercer, its monstrous flames hungrily licking the walls of the kitchen. No way could I get to the pot of broth. As I was about to leave, I heard a feeble cry for help from the back of the Good Luck Café. I looked over and saw Towkay Lau on the floor, coughing, his eyes closed.

What the hell was he doing there alone? Wasn't Billy around to help? I didn't see signs of anyone else in the area. Seeing that evil man lying helpless on the ground gave me a surge of satisfaction. Karma was indeed real. Towkay Lau's face was blackened with soot and I could see the business-man mouthing words. It wouldn't take much longer for him to die from the smoke inhalation. In fact, I was surprised he had lasted this long. No one would blame me if I left him. I'd say I never saw or heard him. Good riddance to bad rubbish.

For some reason I thought about what Sensei might do and I sighed deeply. I put the dishcloth over my mouth and nose, grabbed Towkay Lau's arms and dragged him out to the street, where I called other people to help him. I had already done too much by saving him from the fire.

I went back to join my parents, where the tenants of Carpenter Street watched the horrifying scene in silence, some dabbing their eyes. An angry orange hue lit up the night sky as the flames licked hungrily at the walls of Teck Boon kopitiam and the Good Luck Café. Ma was staring at the blaze serenely, as if she had made peace with the fire, while Ah Hock sobbed.

The great Lim Ah Hock, proud and angry laksa master, now reduced to a weeping old man. Seeing Ah Hock like this shattered my heart into a million pieces. I understood now the pain he had been carrying beneath his hard exterior. He was broken, his anguish apparent to me, and I wished I didn't have to see the pieces.

Then the rain came, as if the gods had decided to show mercy on us. The downpour was sudden and heavy, pelting the zinc roofs of the shophouses, taming the flames. For the first time, I welcomed the heavy rains, relief washing over me. Minutes later, the fire engine arrived but the rain had done most of the work of saving the buildings. Shortly after, an ambulance arrived as well. The firefighters hosed the shophouses and dispersed the small crowd that had gathered, making sure people weren't near the fire.

'Ming, there's something wrong,' Ma cried. Ah Hock was clutching his chest and left arm. 'Hock! What's happening?' Ah Hock gasped for breath, as if the gods were squeezing the air out of him, until the world went black.

*

I looked at Ah Hock sleeping, the only time his face was tranquil. His chest rose and fell with the steady rhythm of his breathing. I squeezed his hand. It had been years since our hands touched. There had been a time when my father would hold my hand everywhere we went, until I turned seven and Ah Hock decided I was too old for it. Who made the rules, anyway? The warmth of Ah Hock's hands, his fingers intertwined with mine, as we crossed Carpenter Street and strolled to the sundry shops, where I would ask for sweets and fluffy butter buns. I couldn't remember the last time we'd held hands like that. How does a father decide when will be the last time he will hold his young son's hand?

I could hear a muffled conversation between the doctor and Ma outside the room before the door opened and they came in. I released Ah Hock's hand, then ushered Ma to the chair next to the bed.

'How is he, Doctor?' I asked.

'He's stabilised. It was a mild heart attack. The stress of the fire might have triggered it, but one of his arteries was blocked in any event. He's fine now after the angioplasty. We've put a stent in.' The doctor said she would be back to check on him later that day.

'I thought he was a goner for sure, like his father. Your Ah Kong had a heart attack at this age too, but he couldn't be saved,' Ma said with tears in her eyes. 'We are lucky.'

'It's okay, Ma, there's been a lot of advancement in medical treatments for heart problems. Pa needs to learn to take it easy. Well, easier,' I said. There was a knock at the door, and Third Uncle came into the room.

'How is he?' Third Uncle asked, patting my back.

'He's okay. He had a mild heart attack.'

Our conversation woke Ah Hock up, and he opened his eyes weakly to look at Ma.

'We are finished, Ah Choo. I have nothing left, nothing,' Ah Hock whimpered, a tear rolling down his cheek. Ma bent over him and stroked his face tenderly.

'We are not finished, Hock. I have fire insurance for the kopitiam. We'll use the money to rebuild it. It'll look better than before.'

I was relieved to hear about the insurance, but Ah Hock didn't look consoled.

'The curse. We've offended the gods and now they've destroyed the kopitiam. The broth is gone.' He broke into a sob. 'I deserved this punishment. I didn't train my son to pass it on.'

Third Uncle shook his head. 'You didn't offend anyone, Hock. The broth your father brought over here, it didn't survive the journey. He had to make a new broth. Of course, he couldn't tell anyone. One night, after too much whisky, he accidentally mentioned it to me.'

Third Uncle's remarks surprised me. Earlier he'd said he wasn't sure whether the broth was real or not? Then Third Uncle smiled at me, and I understood this was the story that could help Ah Hock move on.

Ah Hock widened his eyes. 'Why didn't you tell me this before?'

'There was no reason to. I'm saying this now so you know you can start over. Like your father did when he crossed the seas. You're alive, and your family is with you. That's what's important,' Third Uncle said.

There was another knock at the door, and I opened it to see Sensei standing outside the room.

'I hope I'm not intruding, Wei Ming,' he said. I stepped out of the room and closed the door behind me, reassuring Sensei he wasn't. 'How's your father?'

'He's all right. Resting. Of course, he's upset about the shop.'

Sensei nodded. 'Yes, it is understandable and most unfortunate. I would be devastated if the same thing happened to Haruto. I had gone back to your father's shop to look for you today, and I was shocked to see what happened. Your neighbours at Carpenter Street are helpful and friendly. They told me where to find you.'

'How . . . how did the shophouse look?' I asked, afraid of the answer. In the commotion, I hadn't thought about going back to see what I could salvage.

'Most of it is still standing. We could go there now, to see if there's anything you can take back,' Sensei suggested. Just then, a nurse pushing a wheelchair towards us caught my eye. Towkay Lau in a hospital gown, slightly hunched. His skin looked grey and there were bags under his dulled eyes. He looked like he had aged ten years, and in that wheelchair, he was small and unknown.

'Wei Ming,' he said, reaching his hand out to me. 'I wanted to thank you. For saving my life.'

I didn't take his hand. 'Don't thank me. I wanted to leave you there. You deserved it for rigging the bet. My father had a heart attack because of the stress.'

Towkay Lau looked taken aback at first, but then grinned. 'Looks like I've woken up the tiger in the cub.'

'Mock me, if you want. And just so you know, we're not leaving the kopitiam. I won't let you take it. Go ahead and sue me, my friend's sister is a lawyer. I don't need a team. She's enough.' I sounded confident, even if I didn't have anything planned. All I knew was, I had to save my family. If that meant taking on Towkay Lau, so be it.

Towkay Lau gave a small laugh, then coughed and held his chest. The nurse was about to wheel him away when he motioned for her to wait. 'You're right, Ming. It was rigged. Like life was rigged for me, until I learned to play the game.'

'A game? The only games you play are the ones you create, then use innocent people like my family as pawns. You should be ashamed of yourself. People think you're a great business-man, towkay of Kuching town, but in the end you're just a cheat.' I had never been this harsh with Towkay Lau before but the man deserved every brutal word. I stared at him, hoping to see him in pain, and that my words struck him like a whet-stone. But in typical Towkay Lau fashion, he simply smiled.

'You think I'm a cheat but I'm just playing to survive. I won't bother you or your family anymore. This is payment for my life. We're even now, Lim Wei Ming.'

All those years, I'd never even known the Lim family owed him a debt. Still, it was a relief to hear Towkay Lau say he would leave our family alone. Something in the way he'd said it made me believe him.

After the nurse wheeled him off, Sensei asked who he was.

The man who sent me to Hong Kong. The man who broke my father. A foe, an ally. The lesson I had to learn.

'A family friend,' I said. The room door opened and Third Uncle came out.

'Leaving already, Third Uncle?' I asked.

The old man nodded. 'Better let your father rest. He's had enough excitement for a while.'

'Is it true? About the broth? It's not the same one?' I asked, although what difference did it make? Even if it wasn't the original broth, it was still Teck Boon's broth. A broth that was almost sixty years old.

Third Uncle smiled and shook his head. 'Your grandfather told many stories. I don't know which ones are true or not. I merely listened. He was a good storyteller. Whatever helps your father, let him believe that version. Take care of your father, Ming.' Third Uncle rested his hand on my shoulder before heading for the lifts. All those years of believing they were tending to a broth that was centuries old. Did it matter, after all? But now I knew what I had to do.

34

Manzoku

The hospital was only twenty minutes away, but the journey to Carpenter Street felt like hours. I parked the car in one of the back lanes, then trudged on to the charred shophouse with Sensei. Yellow tapes with the words 'Fire Line' and 'Do Not Cross' sealed the entrance. I went under them, then stepped into the kopitiam with Sensei.

The walls were blackened, and the chairs and tables were half-burnt. I was careful not to trip over the debris. The interior of the dining area was intact, but the kitchen looked completely destroyed. I walked to the corner where the pot used to simmer and breathed a sigh of relief when I saw it there, lying on the floor.

I crouched down and took a closer look at it. The brass was blackened but not much more than it had been before. I exhaled. At least it had survived the fire. I was glad I could bring it back to Ah Hock.

'The pot, is it valuable?' Sensei asked, looking at it.

'Yes. It belonged to my grandfather. My father inherited it, and he has been boiling our ancestral broth since before I was born,' I said. 'Had,' I added, touching the pot lightly. I knew it was empty, but I looked inside to check anyway. Nothing but burnt, crusty residue at the bottom.

'I'm so sorry, Wei Ming,' Sensei said. I picked up the pot and shook my head.

'It's for the best. My mother says they have insurance so we can rebuild this place. But Sensei, this means I have to help my family here. I don't know if I can go back to Haruto any time soon,' I said apologetically. 'I promise to pay you back. You have my word.'

Sensei nodded. 'I have expected this. I have some news too. After my father's death, I have been doing some thinking. I think fifteen years in Hong Kong may be enough for me. It is time for a change of scenery. This is what my father used to grumble about – my restlessness,' he said with a light laugh. 'But it is simply because I cannot stay in a place when I have outgrown it. I will keep Haruto open for a few more months before making the announcement. I saw a diner in Sai Kung that needs some renovation, but it is suitable. I'm going to make an offer on it.'

A thought struck me. It was a long shot, but I had to try. 'What if . . . would you consider having a shokudo here, Sensei?'

Sensei raised his eyebrows. 'You mean, here in Kuching?'

'Here, on Carpenter Street . . .' I let my words trail off after realising how ridiculous they sounded. Why would Sensei come all the way here? I hadn't even made amends for what I'd done to Haruto. 'Sorry, Sensei, forget what I said, it's stupid. I guess I'm in shock. I . . . I want to help you. But Takashi is there, he can help you set up in Sai Kung.'

'Takashi wants to go back to Tokyo. He has decided he will finish his university studies. He is grateful for his work experience, but says the culinary world is not for him.' Sensei looked out to Carpenter Street contemplatively. 'Your proposal is not such a crazy one, Wei Ming. Something pulls me to this place.

325

Something ancient, many voices speak to me here. I cannot explain it,' he said. 'If I decide to open a restaurant here, Wei Ming, I would like you to help me, if you can.'

I gave an enthusiastic nod. 'Of course, Sensei.'

We stepped into the street, which was swathed in light from the late morning sun. The smell of pork soup and satay on charcoal filled the air. Cars were bumper to bumper on the road. Despite the previous day's events, the daily bustle on Carpenter Street remained the same, the stark omission being the smell of laksa wafting from Teck Boon kopitiam.

*

Ah Hock was discharged after a few days, when the doctor was sure he had fully stabilised. She warned him to watch his temper and Ah Hock nodded like an obedient child, to our amusement, and promised to take his medication.

Dennis had offered to house us but Ah Hock wanted to stay at Third Uncle's shophouse. Ma said I could go to Dennis's but I didn't want to leave my parents alone in case Ma needed help with Ah Hock. Third Uncle only had one small spare room, so I insisted my parents stay there while I slept downstairs near the signboards, calligraphy paper and ink, on a foldable mattress Dennis lent me. I couldn't sleep well, so I often woke up early and went to the market to buy produce to make the broth I'd promised Ah Hock.

Kampung chicken, carrots, turnip, winter melon, lotus root, celery, anything I bought had to be the freshest even if it meant I took hours to find them. For seafood, I went to my father's supplier, Ah Lek, at Pending and bought abalone, oysters, fish, clams. Like Ah Hock, I bought flatfish and dried them myself at the back of Third Uncle's shophouse while Ma stared and shook her head.

'You're turning flatfish-mad like your father,' she said reproachfully.

'Don't worry, I won't always have time to do this.' I chuckled. 'But this first bowl of broth has to be perfect. At least, for Pa.'

It took a few days to dry the flatfish but I waited. I picked a day to make the broth, telling Ma to make sure Ah Hock wouldn't be in the kitchen to interfere. She bought him his favourite kuay chap that day, making sure he was well fed in bed upstairs while Third Uncle kept him busy with old stories.

I went to the market and bought live chickens, which were slaughtered before I came straight back to Third Uncle's shophouse. After I had plucked and cleaned the chickens, rinsed and cut the vegetables, gutted and washed the seafood, I put all of these ingredients into the blackened brass pot filled with water. I put it on a new charcoal stove I had bought from a sundry shop nearby, then waited for it to boil.

The years of learning to make suimono from Sensei, boiling Japanese soup that demanded broth as clear as water while retaining depth of flavour, had strengthened my skills for preparing the broth. And from Ah Hock I had learned the art of standing before the pot, tending to it patiently as if it were a child not yet ready to behave, salting it until, at last, when I tasted it, my reaction was a sigh of contentment. Manzoku.

Ma arranged for Ah Hock to come downstairs for dinner, where I had already cooked a simple meal of rice porridge with preserved radish omelette, white tofu and stir-fried midin. Ah Hock sat down at the table and looked at the glistening white tofu, garnished with a splash of soy sauce and fried garlic. He ate a spoonful of the tofu and murmured his approval.

'Where did you buy this? It's really smooth. I've never tasted such a well-made tofu before,' he said.

I stifled a laugh. 'I made it.'

Ah Hock stared at me in disbelief. 'Really?' he said. He savoured his meal while Third Uncle, Ma and I stood around him. As Ah Hock finished the last of the omelette, I went to the kitchen where the broth was simmering in the brass pot on the charcoal stove. I tasted it again before ladling the broth into the best soup bowl Third Uncle had, a blue porcelain rice grain dragon bowl.

'What's this?' Ah Hock asked as the soup was set down before him.

'Our broth. Try it,' I said. Ah Hock looked nervous before he drank the first spoonful, then closed his eyes. As if he wasn't sure, he took a second spoonful, then another, before speaking.

'Was there any of the broth left? I mean, Ah Kong's broth,' he asked.

'No, Pa. Not a drop.'

'You made this from scratch?'

'Yes.'

Ah Hock put down his soup spoon and stared at the bowl of broth. Then he took the bowl in both hands and held it to his lips. He drank deeply, as if he hadn't had a drink of water in days. When every drop of the broth was finished, he put the bowl down and wiped his mouth with the back of his hand as a child would. His eyes were moist. I saw but pretended I didn't.

'I think I need to salt it more,' I said, looking at the bowl instead of Ah Hock. He would be sure to say it lacked something.

Ah Hock shook his head. 'No. It's enough.' He stood up, then rested his hand on my shoulder for a second, before trudging back upstairs.

*

When everyone had gone to bed, I sat down at Third Uncle's table and thought about my future. I could see myself in Kuching, helping my father but also making my own plans. I felt like a chef in my own right, no longer hanging on to the coat-tails of Sensei or standing in Ah Kong's shadow.

I now had approval from one of the best cooks in town, my own father. That should count for something.

'Not asleep yet?' Ma's voice in the dark startled me.

'Soon, Ma. What about you?' I switched on the lights. Ma shuffled to the table and sat down next to me.

'Couldn't sleep,' she said, then touched my hand. 'Something on your mind?'

'Just wondering what my plan is in Kuching.'

'You know, with the insurance money, we could renovate the kopitiam the way you want. Remember, we have your savings too. You can have your restaurant right here on Carpenter Street. There's enough space for you and your father,' she said with a smile. 'For all three of us.'

'I don't know if I'm ready.'

'You've always been ready, Ming. You just needed to know you could do it.'

I squeezed her hand. I was so lucky to have a mother who had believed in me all these years, and forgave me for being away for so long. 'We're lucky you bought insurance. Can't imagine Pa buying fire insurance, let alone remembering to make the payments.'

'Did you see the place? After . . .?'

'Yeah, the furniture's ruined. At least we have the brass pot,' I said. 'It's a good thing it rained when it did. Otherwise, there would be nothing left.'

'I guess it didn't take long for the wood to go up in flames.' She stared into the distance. 'I hope your grandfather will forgive me.'

What? I looked at her. 'What do you mean, Ma?'

'He'll understand. He knows difficult decisions must be made for the sake of family. Of all people, he should understand,' she said dreamily, then leaned over and cupped my face in her hands. 'Sometimes, we have to destroy everything so we can rebuild, you know? Sometimes, that is the only way to start anew.'

I was baffled by what she'd said. Maybe she was overtired. We'd gone through a traumatic event, after all. 'You need to rest, Ma. Stop thinking about weird things.'

'All I ever feared in this world was losing you and your father. I just wanted a family. That's all I ever wanted, Ming. I didn't have it until I met your father and had you.'

I'd never seen Ma like this before. It was if she had turned into another person. Or a younger version of herself. I moved her hands from my face and held them. 'Go to sleep, Ma. Everything will be okay tomorrow. You need rest.'

Ma nodded. As she walked upstairs, she said, 'Make sure nothing's boiling on the stove, okay? Goodnight, my precious son.'

35

Furusato

One Year Later

Sensei had built Furusato almost entirely by his own hand. Towkay Lau was only too happy to sell what remained of the fire-damaged Good Luck Café to him at a bargain price. He was grateful I'd saved his life, but he was still a businessman. I doubt it was gratitude alone that sealed the deal.

With the help of some local carpenters, Sensei managed to source ironwood and meranti bunga, a light hardwood with a pinkish hue like hinoki. The signboard, handmade by Third Uncle, said 'Furusato' in kanji and English, and hung above the entrance to the shokudo. Latticed shoji doors slid open to a bright space with large windows, letting in ample natural light. Sensei finally had a place with enough space to make the kumiko shoji he had always wanted.

The sushi counter was made of hinoki, as were Sensei's lanterns that hung at the entrance just before the noren, and his intricately carved andons near the sushi counter. The decor was reminiscent of Haruto, with a dash of local flavour in the tea bowls with Bornean designs that Sensei had incorporated into his pottery making.

I found Sensei in the kitchen rummaging through the boxes of seafood that had come in from Tsukiji. 'Good morning, Sensei. How's the fish today?'

'Ohayo, Wei Ming. Yes, Ito-san sent us some fresh tuna. Expensive, but very good. I'm planning to make wappa meshi again. Does your father want some?' Sensei asked. I smiled. He was considerate, as usual.

'Of course. It's his favourite. May I pay my respects, Sensei?' I gestured towards the altar Sensei had set up for his parents. He bowed his thanks. I knelt before his parents' memorial tablets and offered incense, praying for Sensei's well-being and his new business. I got up, then walked back to Sensei and handed him a wooden box. 'Sensei, I have brought a present for you.'

'Arigato, Wei Ming. What's the celebration?' Sensei opened the box to reveal two wooden masu cups. 'Ah, you have completed them.' He took the cups and turned them this way and that, feeling the edges of the joined pieces. 'Nice work. Thank you. Come, let's have some tuak,' he said, taking the cups with him out to the sushi counter.

He opened a bottle of the local rice wine and poured it into the cups. My master had truly taken to the local culture, even developing a taste for the bootlegged wine. As Sensei poured the tuak into the cups, I looked at them nervously, hoping there would be no liquid seeping from the edges.

'Do not worry, Wei Ming. They are fine,' Sensei said, reading my thoughts. 'You have done well. Oh, I have something for you.' He took out a small square box from one of the drawers behind the sushi counter. It was a plain hinoki box with a ribbon tied around it. I carefully undid the ribbon then opened the box, revealing the sky-blue tea bowl I had broken in Haruto. Now there were streaks of gold keeping the broken pieces together. I had forgotten about it, and blushed in recollection.

'I'm sorry about this, Sensei, I never got a chance to tell you about it.'

'Takashi had it repaired well. It is more beautiful than before.' He took the cup and traced his finger over the patterned gold that sealed the cracks. Sensei was right, the cup was improved by the gold that held it together. I blinked my tears away before giving Sensei another deep bow. 'I am forever grateful to you, Sensei, for all that you've done for me. And for your forgiveness.'

Sensei shook his head. 'No apology needed,' he said. 'Come, try out the cup.' I put the cup on the counter while Sensei poured tuak into it. The wine tasted even sweeter from the repaired cup. I told myself I would call Takashi in Tokyo and thank him for finding such a skilled kintsugi master.

I wondered what I had done in my life to deserve such a good mentor. If I were as selfless as him, I would willingly dedicate my life to the art of making laksa simply to continue Ah Hock's legacy. But it was a promise I couldn't make. At least, not yet. Who knew what I would agree to at Ah Hock's deathbed. Like Dennis said, you didn't know until it happened.

After the lunch rush, I went back to Lim Family Kitchen to prepare for the evening's sittings. There were two bookings, one from my regulars, a family of gourmets who loved whatever I created for them. The other booking was a corporate group from an international bank, new clients, and I was nervous about that, not knowing what they liked. They would have to trust the chef's choice. My choice. Like I'd had to trust myself when I opened this restaurant.

The broth was used as a base for most of my stews and sauces. Sensei had generously given me some eel which I was going to marinate in rice wine and grill. Prawn umai, a Sarawakian ceviche dish made with lime juice, bird's eye chillies, shallots, garlic and ginger, would be a palette cleanser. Then there was fried terubuk roe with midin. White cold tofu with scallop sauce, my grandfather's recipe. To conclude the medley, pork belly braised in dark sweet soy sauce, a home-made comfort dish, so the last thing they tasted would remind them of home.

Figuring out the menus was a joy. I worked with whatever I could find at farmers' markets, or the neighbourhood morning markets. Occasionally, Sensei went to Muara Tebas, a fishing village forty minutes from Kuching city, and brought back threadfin or stingray. Or we might find some unique wild forest fern sold by roadside traders, or wherever people chose to hawk their produce. I had Dennis to thank for igniting the excitement of the unknown in the kitchen. All those years of experimenting together in Dennis's family kitchen had given me the courage to find myself and to show it to friends, family and strangers alike.

Ma offered to help with the preparations for the evening sittings, but I encouraged her to either rest with Ah Hock upstairs or visit Third Uncle and have evening tea at his place. This was the compromise we had reached to share the same workspace. At night, the Lim Family Kitchen was mine alone.

I took out my *Kind of Blue* album and played 'Blue in Green' on the CD player I had behind the counter. It brought me back to Hong Kong nights at Haruto's closing time. The melancholic trumpet transported me to the lonely sushi counter after the day's bustle, when I would fight the urge to take the ferry to Tsim Sha Tsui to see Jiayi. The neon lights of girlie bars and roast meat shops beckoning. The crowds on Nathan Road, the hustlers in the Temple Street

Market. I knew it hadn't been good for me – that destructive, romantic feeling, that chasing emptiness I had mistaken for dreams – but I missed it anyway. In another life, Jiayi and I might have had a future together, working in sync, tasting each other's dishes, chasing culinary stars. I wondered if she was still running Malaysian Kitchen on Nathan Road. I hoped she was far away from the likes of Man Kor or Towkay Lau, working in a new restaurant in London or New York. She was a survivor, no doubt about it. She would land on her feet no matter where life tossed her. I hoped she was happy, wherever she was. And free.

'You did it, Wei Ming. It's wonderful.' A woman's voice shook me from my reverie. Alice, in the doorway, ravishing even in jeans and a plain white blouse. Her casual clothes accentuated her natural elegance. I turned down the volume on the CD player. She walked over and took a seat at the counter. Up close, I could see dark circles under her eyes and her pallor made her look drawn, although it did nothing to diminish her beauty.

She noticed me staring. 'I know, I look tired. The late nights at the office. I didn't wear concealer today.'

Not long after the fire, while we were busy planning the renovations, Alice took up a job offer in KL. They made her partner at a large, thriving law firm. We sometimes spoke on the phone, but most of the time both of us were too busy with work. Seeing her again was like finding a final piece of the puzzle, only I wasn't sure if it would fit.

I shook my head, my face reddening. 'No, no, you look great. I guess you're back to see your mum. How's she doing?' Uncle Tan had succumbed to cancer two months ago.

'She's all right. Better than expected. Dennis has good and bad moments. He tells me you check in on him whenever you're free.' She touched my arm lightly. 'He's lucky you're here during this time.'

'What about you?' I asked, searching her face. She smiled.

'I'm all right. I'm just focused on Misha most of the time. I'm taking my mum to New York. Distract her a bit. My firm's transferring me there actually.'

Did I hear right? New York? The other end of the world. I'd never thought she might move anywhere else. KL was far enough, but at least we were always a phone call or a short flight away. New York wasn't even in the same time zone.

'Wow, that's far. Sounds exciting,' I said, with a forced smile.

'I know. It's always been my dream to go there. Before I leave, I have to eat all my favourite food in Kuching. That includes your father's laksa, of course,' Alice said. 'I can't wait to visit all the museums. The Met, Broadway, the Empire State Building, Central Park, Times Square. All those places I've seen in movies,' she gushed, her eyes twinkling and distant as if she was already there.

'Will you be coming back often?'

'I don't know. It's far. Maybe once a year.'

'Dennis is going to miss you.' I cleared my throat. 'I'm going to miss you.'

She smiled and shook her head. I could see a faint blush on her cheeks. 'You'll be too busy to miss me.'

'I mean it. I always thought, maybe one day, you'd move back here with Misha. Instead you're moving even further away.'

She tilted her head at me in her familiar way, but I knew we would always be unfamiliar with each other. She was the daughter of the Jade Emperor, the Weaver Girl who charmed a humble cowherd with her beauty. But I wasn't the cowherd, and there was no bridge of magpies to close the distance between us.

'You can always come visit us. I'll bring you to a jazz club in Greenwich Village. Or SoHo.' She sounded like she had it all planned out in her head, like I'd already booked my flight. But maybe one day Lim Family Kitchen would expand to New York. Have branches everywhere! Make big money! I chuckled at the echo of Towkay Lau's voice in my head. Although, as promised, he hadn't cast his shadow on Carpenter Street for a whole year now.

'What's so funny?' Alice asked. I shook my head and smiled.

'Nothing. Sure, I'll visit you guys. Especially if it's all expenses paid.'

She laughed heartily. 'I'll let you stay with us but that's about it. You'll have to buy your own flight ticket to New York. Shouldn't be a problem for a hotshot chef at the Lim Family Kitchen.'

'Where's Misha? She must be excited.'

'With my mum and Dennis. I just came by to see your place. All those positive reviews I read in the newspapers. I'm happy for you.'

'Thanks. Dennis helps when I need ideas. I've asked him to join me, but I know he promised your father to keep the stall open. Says he can't let the customers down.'

Alice nodded. 'I hope they appreciate him.'

'He's selling ayam pansoh alongside his kolo mee. Have you tried it?'

She laughed. 'Yes, it's delicious. I remember when you guys experimented with it last year. I'm glad Dennis is making something of his own at the stall.'

'It's a big change, moving to New York. I hope you'll be happy there. Come back if you're not.' I tried to make it sound like a joke, but I couldn't hide the melancholy in my voice.

Alice reached out and held my hand, looked as if she were about to say something, then thought better of it. As she got up to leave, I blurted out, 'Do you have time for a snack?' There was half an hour before the first sitting. 'I'll make tamagoyaki for you. Since you never made it to our sushiya in Hong Kong.'

She smiled, then sat back down at the counter. I went to the kitchen and took out my rectangular omelette pan and whisked a bowl of eggs with a pair of chopsticks. My nights at Haruto came back to me again, mixing dashi stock, sweet mirin and soy sauce, then adding the mixture to a bowl of whisked eggs.

But now, instead of dashi, I ladled a small bowl of the simmering broth – the hallmark of all my dishes at the Lim Family Kitchen – and mixed it into the eggs. I would make that omelette I'd made a thousand times before and would make a thousand times again. When the tamagoyaki was ready, I would place it on a hinoki tsuke-dai and present it to her like a work of art. She would gaze at it and delay eating it for a while to preserve its beauty. And that alone would be enough, for now.

36

The Lim Family Kitchen

Ah Hock couldn't believe a year had already passed since the fire. The renovated kopitiam looked like an elegant vintage restaurant now, a place he could imagine Teck Boon owning back in Swatow in the 1930s.

He didn't know how, but the boy had managed to find reasonably priced ironwood to make solid tables and chairs, all carved by their talented neighbours. The kopitiam was no longer open-air, but even walled up it had many windows letting in natural light, with bamboo blinds to shield customers from the glare of the sun. There was an auspicious painting of eight horses on the wall, and a framed photo of Teck Boon with a short write-up next to it, explaining the history of the Lim Family Kitchen. The air conditioning was turned on at night, and during the day, large electric wooden ceiling fans ensured a pleasant breeze throughout the kopitiam.

The newspaper reporter sat at a table near the kitchen while interviewing Wei Ming. Ah Hock muttered irritably as he assembled a bowl of laksa.

'What is it, old man?' Kim Choo asked.

'I don't know why she didn't order the special.'

'The reporter? She's here to interview Ming, maybe she's

not fussy about the food,' Kim Choo said, then looked as if she regretted the words as soon as they had left her lips.

'Not fussy about the food?' Ah Hock growled, staring at the reporter. How could she not be particular about laksa if she were here writing a story on it?

'I mean, I'm sure she's on a tight schedule. Calm down, remember what your doctor said?'

Ah Hock shrugged. 'Then she won't notice if I put in just two small prawns.'

Kim Choo laughed. 'Sixty-one years old, behaving like a child. You rest, let me make you kopi-o and I'll take over.' Ah Hock poured the laksa soup into the bowl he had assembled then passed it to Kim Choo.

'Come, have a drink, it'll settle you,' she said, putting a cup of kopi-o on a table. He sat down and took a sip, letting the hot, earthy liquid fill his insides. He couldn't believe that one year on he found himself here with Wei Ming, sharing the same cooking space, when all that time he'd thought there had been no room for the two of them to co-exist. He could take it easier now, and Kim Choo was as strong as ever, rejuvenated by Wei Ming's return.

The boy shared this space to cook Teochew cuisine at night. His dishes weren't half bad either, despite being fusion. Some strange dishes, but palatable. Wei Ming had done well. And who would've thought the Japanese sushi master would open his restaurant right next door where the tinsmith had been? It wasn't just sushi he served, there were stews, soups, and one warm rice dish with fish that Ah Hock loved. He didn't know its name, only that he was amazed something so foreign could taste so familiar to him.

Ah Hock was surprised at how well he could get along with Inamura despite the language barrier. It was the language of taste they shared, that same look of satisfaction and understanding when they had achieved the sense of balance in their cooking, the thing that balanced their worlds. He had gone as far as to use Inamura's Japanese fish sauce, ishiri, in the laksa. At Inamura's suggestion, he had added katsuobushi made from skipjack tuna and good-quality kombu to the broth. It was a different creature now, the broth, no longer staying the same, always changing, evolving to complement whatever dish Wei Ming wanted to make for his dinner guests.

Wei Ming got up and led the reporter over to Ah Hock's table. 'Pa, this is Janice Chan from *Hornbill Daily*. She wants you to comment on the new revamped kopitiam.'

The reporter held out her hand, and Ah Hock grudgingly shook it. 'Hello, Master Lim, congratulations on opening the Lim Family Kitchen! Thank you for keeping your legacy alive for Kuching people. We are proud to recommend your laksa to visitors,' the reporter said in Hokkien. Ah Hock nodded unsmilingly. 'Wei Ming has already answered most of my questions, so I won't bother you much. I just need you to tell our readers, what is the secret to good cooking?' When she asked, Wei Ming stifled a chuckle and looked at Ah Hock.

'No secret. Taste your food, and don't use shortcuts. Like some of those people out there using chicken cubes. Our ingredients are fresh,' Ah Hock muttered.

'Wei Ming mentions an ancestral broth that you use. Do you think that's the secret?' the reporter continued.

Ah Hock turned to glare at her. The cheek of this young girl! 'Are you saying I can't cook without the broth?' he demanded.

The reporter gave a nervous laugh and looked at Wei Ming. 'Oh, I'm not saying that at all. I'm sorry, Mr Lim, I didn't mean to offend you, I'm just trying to write an interesting story.'

'The broth is definitely something we use and honour,' Wei Ming said, coming to her rescue. 'But cooking skill can only come with practice and dedication. Doing the same thing every day no matter how monotonous it is. There's nothing glamorous about striving for perfection, only hard work.'

She scribbled furiously as he spoke, then thanked him and took her leave hastily.

'She forgot to eat her laksa. What a waste,' Ah Hock said with disgust. Wei Ming took the bowl and sat down next to him.

'I'll eat it, Pa. Drink your kopi-o. I've got to go help Inamura soon, it's almost lunchtime,' Wei Ming said. Ah Hock finished his kopi-o then watched Wei Ming as he ate. What a privilege it was, to watch his son devour the laksa they were both proud of. That look of contentment, though subtle, was apparent on the boy's face as he mixed the sambal into the soup until it tasted right.

Ah Hock put his cup in the sink and walked to the pot of broth. The broth had been consistently good for a year now, and he felt grateful for every day of it. Still simmering on a charcoal stove in a corner of the kitchen, this golden broth Wei Ming helped to maintain. No more days of being unsure, or feeling something was missing. No more ominous dreams waking him up in the twilight hours. The last dream he'd had of Teck Boon was of him in chef's whites, as if he were back in his Swatow kitchen. The old man was smiling, a rare occurrence, which was how Ah Hock knew it had been a dream when he woke up.

Would the broth simmer for another sixty years, or a hundred years? But how? He glanced at Wei Ming slurping the laksa soup loudly. Where were the descendants who were going to ensure the pot continued simmering? The boy didn't even have a girlfriend! Unless you counted that kolo mee seller's daughter, what was her name again? Kim Choo liked her. But why would a classy girl like her take any notice of him? Only the gods would know.

Ah Hock took a deep breath. Let Kim Choo be the one to nag Wei Ming to get a wife, although he had no idea when the boy would have time for dates when he juggled three eateries in one day.

'I'm off!' Wei Ming put his empty bowl in the kitchen sink.

'Wait! Offer incense to your Ah Ma and Ah Kong first.' It felt both strange and familiar to say those words. They had two altars now, thanks to Wei Ming who'd gone to a lot of trouble to enquire about his grandmother's family in Swatow. Apparently, Ah Hock still had cousins there. There was no photograph for her altar, only an ancestral tablet. There were no details of her birth date or death, but at least they had her name: Chen Liyen. Beautiful Swallow.

The day Wei Ming had brought the tablet home for the new altar, Ah Hock could have sworn he smelled sweet peonies and the perfume of his mother's favourite Tieguanyin.

Wei Ming offered joss sticks at his grandparents' altars, then waved at Ah Hock as he ran next door to help his master. Ah Hock stood before the pot, looking at the simmering golden liquid, inhaling its rich aroma. He took a spoonful and tasted it. Today it had a tinge of charcoal-roasted pork trotters and salty sweet flatfish. It tasted right. Wei Ming made sure of it. Ah Hock ladled two bowls of soup for his parents' altars, and prayed for peace instead of forgiveness, while the broth simmered quietly in its usual corner of the kitchen, its undying embers gleaming red, continuing to listen to the conversations of the generations to come.

Acknowledgements

My memories of the food I loved growing up in Kuching are rooted in the many hawker stalls that served mouthwatering dishes – be it laksa, chicken rice, noodles in bowls of soul-nourishing soup or noodles fried in a wok blackened from decades of use. As the years have passed, some of these stalls have been handed down through generations, but when they have not, it was the end of an era for the simple yet artisanal meals that they served and that now can only be imagined.

One such kopitiam on Carpenter Street, which has since shuttered its business, inspired this novel. For many years, it served the best laksa I had ever tasted in Kuching. I can only hope that my love letter to Malaysian food will do its memory justice.

Through this debut novel, I have not only learnt a great deal about the craft of writing, but also about myself. This is a lifelong dream made possible by the support and belief of the people in my life.

To my husband, who has been my pillar of support through the ups and downs of our life adventures together, as well as the writing and publishing journey. Thank you for your love, strength and divine patience.

To my son, for your endless creativity from which I always draw inspiration. Thank you for the joy and laughter you bring into my world.

Many thanks to my family who have patiently waited for the publication of this book. To my parents, who taught me how to be a discerning eater, and that great food is often found in the humblest and simplest of places. To my sisters, who have always believed in me, and provided ample humour and support for me during the challenges in my life. Thank you for putting up with the idiosyncrasies of this middle child.

To D. K. Furutani, who helped me see the angel in my marble and set it free. I am in awe of your talent. Thank you for being an insightful critique partner and providing valuable feedback, sharing knowledge on the writing craft and, most of all, your encouragement.

To Samuel Burr, my selfless mentor who is one of the most brilliant writers I know. Your storytelling skills are matched only by your kindness and generosity. Thank you for having me as your mentee, which was the start of other wonderful things to come.

My heartfelt thanks to Elinor Davies – you made my dreams come true when you reached out to me with that fateful email. I am eternally grateful for your vision for my novel and for starting me on the path to publication.

To Jessica Leeke, thank you for your enthusiasm and for answering all my questions patiently as I navigate this publishing world. Many thanks to Valentina Paulmichl for her brilliant work on foreign rights.

I am deeply grateful to my agent, Safae El-Ouahabi, for her unwavering support and belief in my work. Thank you for your expertise and positive vibes, which ease my publishing journey.

A million thanks to my editor, Ellie Steel, for changing my life when you took a chance on this novel and brought it out into the world. Your understanding of the characters and the pulse of the story has brought it to new heights.

To my copyeditor, Gemma Wain, for your eagle-eyed precision and care in improving my story. Thank you for your hard work and professionalism. Many thanks to Lucy Chaudhuri, Managing Editor at Vintage, for coordinating the publication process so smoothly. To Kris Potter in the Vintage design team, for your creativity and hard work on my cover design. Thank you also to Betty Qui for the delightful illustrations that grace my book cover. To everyone in the teams at Harvill and Vintage, thank you for publicising and championing my book, and for making my debut publication journey so enjoyable.

I would be remiss if I did not mention the 2023 Tin House Winter Online Workshop, a treasured experience that taught me the importance of community in a solitary occupation. Little did I know it would mark the beginning of many exciting opportunities. Much appreciation goes out to Ru Freeman, our instructor, and the accomplished writers in our cohort – Qian Cheng, D. K. Furutani, Anthony Garrett, Andrea Malin, Giovannai Rosa, Virginia Lee Wood and LiAnne Yu – for reading my sample chapter and providing astute comments that opened my eyes to a world of possibilities. Thank you to Jeanne Thornton, my mentor at Tin House, for your careful reading of my early draft and for sharing your knowledge of writing and publishing.

I am grateful to all the editors who gave me the opportunity to publish short stories in literary journals and publications early in my writing journey.

To Chor Shy Miin – lifelong friend, meditation teacher and fellow artist. Thank you for your wisdom, your appreciation of beauty and for teaching me how to find peace in everything I do.

Many thanks to Tan Twan Eng, for letting me pick your brains about craft and publishing, and for your friendship.

To all my friends, thank you for lending your ears whenever I needed them, and for your support and patience in waiting for this book. I am glad this was a promise I could keep.

To my readers, thank you for picking up this book. I hope you will share the same comfort I had in writing about how simple but delicious food can bring us back home.